Luca Di Fulvio, born in 1957, lives and works in Rome. His self-avowed schizophrenic nature leads him to write, with equal passion, gruesome thrillers and delicate fairytales for children, which he publishes under a pseudonym. He wrote *Zelter* (1996), *The Mannequin Man* (originally published as *L'impagliatore* in 2000 and the basis for the film *Eyes of Crystal*, launched at the Venice Film Festival in 2004) and *Dover Beach* (2002), of which a film is currently in production.

The Mannequin Man was chosen as one of the ten best European crime novels of 2003 by the French magazine *Le Point*.

D0027675

THE MANNEQUIN MAN

Luca Di Fulvio

Translated from the Italian by
Patrick McKeown

BITTER LEMON PRESS
LONDON

BITTER LEMON PRESS

First published in the United Kingdom in 2005 by
Bitter Lemon Press, 37 Arundel Gardens, London W11 2LW

www.bitterlemonpress.com

First published in Italian as *L'impagliatore* by
Gruppo Ugo Mursia Editore S.p.A., Milano, 2000

Bitter Lemon Press graterfully acknowledges the financial
assistance of the Arts Council of England

Published with the financial assistance of the
Italian Ministry of Foreign Affairs

© Gruppo Ugo Mursia Editore S.p.A., Milano, 2000
© Giulio Einaudi editore s.p.a., Torino, 2004
English translation © Patrick McKeown, 2005

All rights reserved. No part of this publication may be
reproduced in any form or by any means without written
permission of the publisher

The moral rights of Luca Di Fulvio and Patrick McKeown have been
asserted in accordance with the Copyright, Designs, and Patents
Act 1988

A CIP record for this book is available from the British Library

ISBN 1-904738-13-3

Typeset by RefineCatch Limited, Broad Street, Bungay, Suffolk
Printed and bound in Great Britain by
Bookmarque Ltd, Croydon, Surrey

To Sam,
who taught me how absurd it would be
not to accept the angels and demons
as we invented them ourselves . . .

to Anna . . .

and to my father.

Death, lie thou there, by
a dead man interred.

William Shakespeare, *Romeo and Juliet*, V iii 87

Acknowledgements

This book would not exist without the support and daily help of Carla Vangelista, who believed and believes in me with a constancy and strength that I would never have dared imagine even in my most optimistic dreams.

I owe particular thanks to Professor Paola Franchetti, my guardian angel, to Dr Roberto Fornara, psychiatrist, and to Dr Antonio del Greco, Senior Medical Officer with the Police Force, whose valuable suggestions and affectionate rereading made the writing of this book possible.

I am very grateful to Carlo Macchitella and to Riccardo Tozzi, to Francesco Longardi and to Carlo Brancaleoni who have brought the book to life a second time through the cinema. And finally, my heartfelt thanks to my two friends and agents, Kylee Doust and Leonardo Coletti, who look after my work with a generosity and enthusiasm that goes beyond the call of duty.

Patrick McKeown would like to express his heartfelt thanks to Julia Silk for her care and attention in editing the English edition.

I

The country lane he knew so well, that he had walked along with his load of traps every Sunday for years, was slippery. The frosty morning air had seeped into the straggly line of grass that struggled to survive along the middle of the path, and had soaked the two narrow earthy channels either side that were forever under attack from the overgrown border. Here and there, a few insects had clambered to the top of some of the taller stems or sprigs in the hope that the faint morning sun would dry out their wings. As the man passed by, a few of them made clumsy attempts at escape; others simply huddled within their wings. But heavy, heedless boots marched on and the more careless, if they sprang the wrong way, were crushed into the ground or swept into the mud.

The world was stirring then, still not awake, and the man took advantage of this state of slumber to practise deceit upon sparrows, rabbits, hedgehogs, and other little creatures.

He also had the shotgun with him that morning. The hunting season had officially opened ten days earlier. Although his vocation was to keep his victims as intact as possible, he simply could not resist the allure of a spray of shot. The sight of the blood fortified him. A bird's flight abruptly arrested, the frozen silence that followed the gunshot, then the animal's graceless plunge, all lightness gone, the few yards of bolting inertia from a rabbit, or the headlong tumbling of a

1

fox (he sometimes got one), and the yelps that reached his ears, more startled than pained. All of this filled him with a morbid frenzy. He would close his eyes, and wait for the dull thud upon the grass, or the ringing splash; he would part his lips and suck in death's breath, a mouthful of death. And think, "There. Now it's happened."

His passion for taxidermy had come to him when he was already grown up, but he had known it immediately as the bedrock of his own being. Perhaps subdued, perhaps still uncovered, but his own nature, nonetheless. The two stages of his work, first the capture of his prey and then its successive preparation, fused his sadistic nature with the pleasure of atonement.

As he walked on, his head lowered, the jars and traps clattered together, beating out a broken, rhythmic rattle that would have resonated in his victims' ears like a warning they would understand too late. Understanding would dawn just as the sound itself, an ever distant vibration, dwindled away into the blackness of the approaching end. It would pour out of fatal wounds, draining away the searing image of the hunter, impressed upon desperate retina, until that too had disappeared. Not one of those animals managed to warn its fellows. He didn't give them the time. There and then, he killed them. There was a time, when he had first set out on his adventure, when he used to bring his victims home, just the way he had trapped them. But killing them somewhere else, different from where he caught them, didn't give him the same pleasure. To tighten his hand around a nightingale stuck fast by the quick-setting resin he used to the branch on which it had so witlessly settled, to hold that trembling warmth and then to give its neck a brisk, effortless, twist, to savour the stiffening of its legs, then their limpness, to feel the struggle in those feeble wings that soon began to droop, more defenceless in death than it had been in life, galvanized him. And just as the animal began to grow cold, he was suffused by a sudden burst of love. It was only then that he came into contact with what they were, or had been. He would cosset them, give them a name, start talking to them. Perhaps that was why he had become so good at the techniques that preceded the stuffing itself: it was his way of showing respect, of communicating with them, of loving them. He beheld himself in their grey, veiled eyes; he and he alone saw the messages, the thoughts that lay within. The world itself conformed to his way of seeing and understanding existence. He made his peace with life. He chatted with death.

And how languid, how sensual was his remorse.

On that day, after walking for a good half hour, accompanied by the swish of his steps and the clang of the junk he carried with him like some priceless treasure to keep him company, he spotted a bush that looked perfect. He cut across the meadow and stopped in front of the thorn tree, examined it closely, decided which branches were the most suitable, and set his equipment on the ground, the shotgun last of all. From a grey canvas army bag he took a clear glass jar with a hermetic seal. He turned it over in his hands, and the thick amber liquid inside sluggishly submitted to the laws of gravity, as slow and irrevocable as his own will. He placed it on an ash tree stump riddled with fungus and rummaged in his bag again. From a side pocket he took a bristle brush, flat and encrusted, wrapped in plastic. He placed that beside the jar. Then he checked the branches once more, tested their toughness, examined the matted thorns to make sure no nests were present, and sat down on the ground.

3

The damp soon breached the fabric of his trousers and reached his buttocks. When he felt he was soaked enough in that morning fluid he breathed in deeply and began his hunt. Even as he rose from the ground his expression changed and became radiant.

"It's about to happen," he said.

His excitement was thickening, becoming tangible. His imagination was racing, and as he savoured the holocaust to come, his salivary glands pumped his mouth full with an almost unpleasant, almost painful flood of spittle.

Once the brush was unwrapped, he took up the jar and began to cover the chosen branches with the resin. He was careful not to brush on too much, or too little. When he had finished with the branches he turned his attention to the stump, which glistened brightly for a few minutes. Then the resin began to dry and gradually lose its sheen, until it formed an invisible, treacherous layer. Although the man had become quite proficient in the preparation of his glues, which were always odourless, he took some little bottles of essential oils from the pocket of his parka. He checked the labels on each and chose two. The others he put back in his pocket. He unscrewed the tops and shook some drops of rosehip oil over the bush and some musk over the tree stump. He did not really know if these little details made any difference, but they were part of the hunting ritual, and the preparations were as exciting as the hunt itself.

From another bag, more colourful than the first, almost a shopping bag, he took a creaking tin, battered and rusty, which contained earthworms. He glued a few, by one end, to the stump, where their thrashing about would make them all the more visible, and stuck a few others onto the thorn branches. He put the lid

4

back on and ran the index finger of his left hand round the metal rim to clean it. He rubbed his thumb and index together and sniffed his sticky fingertip. He rubbed his finger down his jacket and brought it closer to his nose. It smelled of saliva, nothing else. He put the tin back in the bag and took out a piece of dry bread. He crumbled it up and scattered it on the ground. He looked round in satisfaction, gathered up the rat and hare traps, shifted them onto his shoulder along with the two bags and his shotgun, and headed for some thick scrub some fifty feet away. That was where he would disappear among the foliage. It was a good spot to watch from.

From a hunter's point of view it would have made more sense to set more traps, to cover the area in collection points, but that would have prevented him from observing panic seize the imprisoned animal. His joy was distilled in being there, in being present, and thinking, There, it's about to happen. It's going to happen now. And I'm here. So he preferred to return home with less bounty and take care of his victims personally, one by one, so he would know and remember with morbid precision just what each one had done. How they had reacted, if they had tried to flee, what had flashed by in their eyes as he approached them. Like an expert playwright, he sketched out the background for their common story that closer acquaintance later would help him fill out. Some of them, the smaller birds, for instance, simply died of fright. He never grew fond of them, because they deprived him of the pleasure and the power of giving death.

When he had reached the edge of the scrub he turned round. The distance was just right. With the sharp knife he kept in his pocket he cut some twigs and stuck them in the ground, in a semicircle, between two poplars. He arranged his traps and bags, leaned his shotgun against one of the smooth trunks, made sure that the first rays of morning sunlight didn't strike the shiny surfaces of the jars, as the glare would have frightened his prey, or drawn their attention and made them suspicious. He took off his parka and folded it a number of times until it formed a soft and comfortable cushion and then he sat down to wait.

A drop of resin had stuck to the knee of his right trouser leg. He picked up a twig and played with it. Each time he touched it to the resin the glue sucked at the twig and held it. The man pulled upwards and the fabric of his trousers followed the movement and formed a peak. Then he pushed a little harder and, with an almost imperceptible sound, the twig broke away from the trouser leg, which dropped back onto his knee. He did the same thing over and over until the resin was too dry to be any fun. Then he massaged the little finger of his left hand. What was left of it. Ever since they had amputated the last two phalanges he had had to manipulate the stump a lot, especially in the cold and damp. If he didn't he developed terrible pins and needles. He rubbed his eyes and looked curiously through the twigs.

He had known that spot for years. Since childhood. A rustling noise behind him distracted him from his memories. He turned round.

A thin hunting dog stretched its nose towards him, nostrils twitching. Its front paw was raised. He had once taken one. It was called Homer now, because the glass eyes hadn't worked out properly and its gaze was blank. But one dog was quite enough for his collection. They were big animals and took up too much space. He made an aggressive, abrupt gesture and the animal whimpered and turned tail. Shortly after he heard the muffled steps of the dog's master. They were probably headed for the river, along the canal. Huge colonies of hares lived in those untended fields, and one often came across pheasant strolling in the shade of the willow trees snatched from the river banks, searching for an easy meal of worms among the exposed tree roots. In their unchecked spread, the twisted roots had encompassed the smooth white stones of the river banks and seemed to be petrified in the act of devouring them, mouths open and stones almost completely digested. The river banks had been his domain when he was a boy. He handled with expert ease the flat round stones from the river bank that he sent skipping over the water many times before they disappeared. He was equally expert with the nearby gravel pebbles which were deadly against the lizards he managed to strike. As a lonely spectator he applauded the struggles between stag beetles in the mating season, as they agitated their fearsome pointed mandibles and hurled themselves against one another in lethal flight colliding terribly. Hoping vainly that his solitary child's shadow would be joined by another, he loomed over the carcass of the loser, which was immediately assailed by ants that emptied it with great precision until nothing was left but the chitinous shell. He would then pick up the dead, take them home, display them proudly on his window sill or on his desk and give them a name, contenting himself with their silent company.

An imperious movement in the air drew his attention towards the trap. A magnificent example of *Egret alba*, the white heron, flapped in the air and then landed. Its long neck described an S. It was very rare to see one at that time of year because, even though they weren't edible, hunters frustrated by a poor day's catch would often vent their anger on the birds. The herons usually stayed in their nests at the top of the poplars and flew down at night to feast on frogs.

That particular heron must have been very hungry, because it carefully snatched up all the bread crumbs in its long yellow beak. Then it spotted the two worms on the log. Its dark, thin legs moved cautiously towards the rotten trunk. The bird looked about it then pecked at one of the worms. The worm stretched unnaturally, pulled at one end by the heron and stuck firm at the other by the resin. When the heron released it the worm seemed to shrivel up like a worn elastic band. The heron's expression revealed a certain surprise. Warily it closed its beak on the other worm and pulled listlessly at first, looking around, then yanked on the worm, which split. The heron stood still, a piece of worm dangling from its beak, its round eyes ever vigilant. It swallowed the worm and attacked the other half. The resin held firm. The heron spread its wings.

The man studied the long, straight flight feathers, which were easy to keep intact but so very heavy that it was difficult to maintain the bird in the position designated by the taxidermist.

The bird bounced forward onto the log, where it thought it could finish off the job with greater ease. The resin stuck to its feet as soon as the bird touched the log. The frightened heron cawed and beat its wings.

"Now," said the hunter, ordering himself into motion. He slipped from his hiding place and rushed towards his prey. He knew he had only a few seconds to hand.

The graceless bird was terrified and kept its balance using its wings. It lifted first one leg then the other. But one limb always remained stuck. Strident notes gurgled from the base of the long neck that had lost all its elegance, and caught in the animal's throat.

The taxidermist was just three feet away when in a supreme effort the heron's mighty wings managed to free the bird from the log and carry it to safety. A few seconds later it had disappeared among the treetops.

The man looked at the remaining half of the worm and squashed it under the sole of his boot. The resin showed the tread of his boot.

Three feet, just three feet. He had seen the bird's sphincter open in fear; he had caught the stench on the wind. Now all that was left was half a worm and a grey-and-white splat of excrement. The excitement of the hunt gave way to a blind rage. He tried to calm down, to control his breathing. He lay down on the still damp ground. He buried his face in the grass and spread his arms. The smell of musk and mushrooms filled his lungs. He sank his fingers into the earth and felt the wet grains of soil burrow under his fingernails. He stayed that way until he thought he had regained control. Then he got up, went over to his hiding place, folded his parka, took another worm from the metal box and glued it to the log. The prints left by the heron and his boot were slowly fading. To the touch the resin seemed to be working still. The other worm was barely moving. He tickled it and it began twisting again. He shivered. His sweater was soaking wet. Once back at his lookout he pulled on his jacket but that too was wet, and he resigned himself to feeling the cold.

He wasn't afraid to wait. He had never returned home empty handed before. Sooner or later something would die in his hands that morning.

But he still felt frustrated at the heron's escape. And his frustration kindled his anger. His hiding place became oppressive. The muscles in his legs were beginning to cramp. He punched his own thighs in an effort to control them. Then he bolted to his feet, beaten. He needed to move. He left his arsenal where it was and began walking. He had taken a few steps when he thought it might be better to have at least the shotgun with him and went back to get it. A veiled sun spread its listless light over the damp countryside.

He reached the man-made canal that supplied water to the rice fields and the power station. He inspected the concrete embankment. On a cracked kerb a rat was sniffing the air. The man pointed the gun at it, aimed and prepared to fire. It was an easy target but the animal would have fallen in the water. He returned the gun to his shoulder. Only then did the rat notice the danger. It bolted along the kerb, lost its balance and splashed into the canal. It swam for a bit with its nose held high, slicing through the water and leaving behind it two little double waves that forked before fading away into the canal's muddy calm. The hunter hurled a stone at the rat, which disappeared under the water.

His boots swished along the path again. In the distance he saw the path widen and turn right towards a small pond, a smear of stagnant water surrounded by reeds. Only then did he notice car tracks in the mud. It must have been the usual lazy hunter. It was not uncommon to find cars parked in the clearing by the pond. It wasn't possible to go any further as the trail faded away to a thin grassless line that went down to the river. He began walking more quickly and in a few minutes his suspicions were confirmed: a blue runabout was parked in the middle of the field. Its mudguards were rusty and there was a very visible dent in the driver's door. His curiosity piqued, he decided to examine it. There was something unusual about the car. There was no mud on the floor mats, nor boxes of cartridges, nor the old blanket covered in hairs in the back, for the all important dog. And, even stranger, he could see a woman's handbag sticking out from under one of the seats. He cupped his hands to his temples, leant against the window and peered beyond his reflection to see inside. The black bag in punched leather had a brass buckle and a short handle. It was the kind of bag women used when they went walking in town, where there is little risk of getting themselves dirty. The kind of bag that had just enough room for a purse and some make-up. Hardly suited to the countryside. And women didn't like hunting. It was very rare to see any women about, especially at that hour. The driver's seat was set back from the wheel, so unless the car was driven by a giantess, it probably belonged to a man. And a young man judging by the stereo that had been imprudently left in its slot and the piles of cassettes in the glove compartment. The original knob on the gear stick had been changed to a garish gadget that reflected a fervent devotion to sport. On looking more closely, the man noticed a little box in a corner of the back seat. The box was hard, open, lined with velvet and had a slot to hold and display a ring. He couldn't make out the upper part of the box completely but from the few gold letters he could see he concluded that it came from a jeweller's in a nearby town. Beside the box there lay a printed note and a heart cut roughly from card. He could just make out a date. It was that Sunday. He walked round the car and changed his viewpoint. In a side pocket he recognized a box of condoms. One of the back windows was slightly open and he breathed in the smell of tobacco and woman's perfume that came from inside. The tobacco smell struck him as being from a cigar and the ashtray confirmed his supposition, because, although there were no butts in the tray, the ash was thicker, heavier than cigarette ash. He didn't recognize the perfume. It was fruity, sweet. He caught hints of vanilla and tuberose. The other elements were smothered by the thick smell of nicotine. His eye was drawn to something that glittered beside the hand brake. A little golden cylinder, ridged on the surface, reflected the sunlight. A lipstick.

And the man lost himself in that lipstick, or, rather, in what it evoked. He slipped into a fantasy full of women's lips; shiny, scarlet, perfectly outlined by the compact smoothness of the make-up. He pictured them kissed by other lips. Upon contact, the lipstick smeared, melted, blended into the man's saliva . . . Yes, there was a male as well, a male he didn't want to recognize . . . and one woman. Two familiar lips. The initial composure disintegrated . . . the woman's passionate, yielding look . . . her chin unnaturally red . . . The male unlaced himself from the embrace and brushed his finger over the woman's lips. Domination. Contempt. Attraction. He smeared the lipstick around that victim's mouth. The woman's eyes closed, like a doll tilted back. The mouth, like an ulcer, became deformed. It opened wide to reveal its depths.

The man bolted upright. He clenched his jaw. His wide eyes filled with tears. He ground his teeth.

"No," he whispered. "No."

He gave a savage kick to the dented car door. He couldn't bear the metallic retort and fled into the reeds around the pond. He was holding the gun and gripped it spasmodically. The woman's provocative panting still rang in his ears, torturing him. He dropped the gun. He clamped his hands over his ears, even though he knew it was pointless, because that obscene panting came from inside him, where he was dirtiest.

To his great surprise the panting did stop.

His mind cleared and reason took command. The hunter's senses began to tingle. Wary now, he tried to make as little noise as possible. He strained his ears. He caught the hissed breathing again. At times it became a kind of high-pitched moan that spread unexpectedly through the air and faded away gently in a smothered sigh. He strained to hear again, and caught a different sound, a kind of low grunt, slimy, that covered the first noise. The man drew himself further into his hiding place and tried to pinpoint the source of the noises. They were coming from his right, it seemed. He would have to turn round. He did so carefully, pushing aside the reeds. He saw some planks of wood buried under the vegetation: a little jetty spanned the marshiest part of the pond. He craned his neck and made out the far end of the jetty, anchored to two thick poles stuck firmly into the water. Rotten ropes swayed in the air. He had never noticed the landing point before. He continued to push aside the reeds with caution, in an attempt to widen his field of vision, and caught sight of a patch of colour. A corner of a blanket. He could see nothing else from where he was; just a patch of tartan blanket. Green. The breathing sounds were coming from there. If he wanted to see more he would have to move closer and further to the right. He picked up the gun. Driven by an implacable curiosity, and trying to make as little noise as possible, he pushed on through the bulrushes. Hairy pennants swayed down as he went past. Every inch gained made him more nervous and more courageous.

A rather reckless couple, he thought. They hadn't stopped their obscene practice when he had kicked their car door. The shore finished abruptly and the man fell face first into the marshy waters. He pulled himself up, covered in mud and frightened.

The two lovers stared at him in amazement.

The hunter may well have run away at that point if

he had not seen a third man, his sparse white hair plastered against his forehead, crouching behind a bush. The third man had a firm grip on his trouser zip. He was holding something. The hunter saw himself reflected in that filthy old brute. He heard a voice spiral out of his past, imperious and terrifying.

Loading the shotgun he started to walk through the stagnant waters and pulled himself easily onto the jetty. In his path, a few steps away, the pair of lovers.

The young man sprang to his feet at the hunter's approach. His trousers were round his ankles and his shirt and sweater were rolled up to just under his arms. That defenceless flap of white flesh shrank before the intruder. The woman was naked and huddled beside her lover, covering her pubis.

He was just a step away, now. He opened fire.

The spray of pellets, spreading like a rose, hit the woman side on, mutilating her right breast and carrying on past her into the young man's stomach, lifting him off the jetty and throwing him backwards into the water. The woman howled and clutched at a dangling scrap of flesh.

The hunter walked past her without so much as a glance.

The old man, petrified with terror, understood that the other was coming for him. By the time he made up his mind to flee it was too late. The shot caught him in the side, knocking him to the ground. He hadn't even attempted to get up before the hunter snapped open the smoking gun, took two new cartridges from his pocket and loaded.

The woman on the jetty screamed, and tried desperately to attach her breast, paying no heed to anything else, turning round and round, as if chasing herself.

The hunter stood over the old man, who dragged

14

himself along the grass. He kicked him over onto his back. The old man's hand, still clamped on his zip, was wizened like a leech. The hunter leaned the barrel of his shotgun against the old man's hand and squeezed the trigger. The recoil almost toppled him. Mute, the old man raised his stump of a hand. Blood spurted into his face, blinding him. There was no more zip. In its place, an oozing hole.

The second shot exploded his heart.

The hunter turned towards the woman, who was still screaming.

The jetty was awash with blood. He set the gun down and took out his knife. He cut off a strip of the tartan blanket, staunched the wound, and then lifted the dangling breast, so soft and big, but almost empty. He put the mangled scrap of flesh back in place, cut off another strip of blanket, wrapped it round the woman's chest and tied a firm knot behind her back. She wasn't a woman, but a girl, no more than eighteen years old. She had full lips. Her chin was stained with lipstick. Blood spurted from her wound, following the heart's own rhythm, and flowed down her stomach. It ran like a stream and pooled in her groin and drained off into her pubic hair, the same blond colour as the hair on her head. He hugged her to him and gradually she stopped screaming. An unnatural silence fell around them.

When he had calmed the girl down he smashed her skull in with the butt of his gun.

On his way home, as he brushed the mud off himself, he forgot to gather up his tools, otherwise he would have seen a magnificent swallowtail that had unwisely landed on the resin-coated ash tree stump. A curious hunting dog looked on as the butterfly madly beat its black-veined yellow wings. Every time the insect opened and closed its wings it revealed the red eye on the underside. The dog cocked its head and whined. It pawed the stump, inviting the butterfly to play.

A high-pitched whistle from the dog's master called it away.

The dog hesitated for a moment and then gambolled off. The butterfly also managed to pull free.

It was the second time that day that the hunter's traps had failed.

II

At exactly a quarter to six the coffee pot began to gurgle. Giacomo Amaldi lowered the flame and let the dense, dark liquid climb slowly up the metal spout, filling the kitchen with its aroma. The coffee stopped spluttering. Amaldi turned off the gas and poured his breakfast into a large mug and added milk and sugar. Then he went to the window and pushed aside the faded, greying nylon curtains. He took the first sip with his eyes closed. His throat welcomed the warm trickle with pleasure. He opened his eyes again to reveal their indefinable colour that shifted from bright yellow to a warm shade of toasted tea. Eyes that were almost almond shaped, as if he always kept them half closed. Sensitive to light, and unafraid of the dark. Cat's eyes.

Outside the city was still hidden from view, but he could already sense that vague, fractious Monday-morning nervousness in the air. A few passers-by, constantly checking their watches, headed up the white steps flanked by narrow flower beds. When they reached the equestrian statue they looked around them, unfolded the rolled up newspaper from their pockets, scanned the headlines, huffed and then started walking again. He would soon hear the blare of car horns, the noise of engines revving and people yelling at one another. But for now the world was still.

What he would not hear that morning was the familiar sound of the refuse-collection lorries. It was the first day of the rubbish-collectors' strike and the contactors had declared war on the mayor and his councillors.

Giacomo Amaldi wasn't particularly interested in the strike, just as he wasn't particularly interested in his new apartment in the city's more desirable area. An apartment he was paying for with a mortgage at a very attractive rate reserved for state employees. He had chosen and bought it through sheer inertia. Or perhaps, as had become increasingly clear to him in those last few months since he had started living there, perhaps he had bought it to honour a promise. An old and, by now, pointless promise. It was a fine apartment: the high ceilings had beautiful stucco moulding, the big windows, despite the recent refurbishment, were still generously draughty, thick walls separated him from the neighbours and the noises of the outside world. There were stout oak doors with inlaid jambs. It was far too big for a man living alone. Apart from the bedroom, the apartment had a dining room, a spacious kitchen, a living room, a study and two bathrooms. He had set foot in the visitor's bathroom, bigger and more comfortable than the tiny space in the apartment in which he had grown up, just once, when he had seen the apartment for the first time before buying it.

He had chosen it for the light. Because many years ago, when he was just a boy, he had promised someone the light.

It had taken him weeks to start living there, as if he couldn't manage to let go of the drab one-room place that for the past fifteen years had borne witness to his stubborn solitude. Then an acquaintance who worked in interior design, a thirty-something architect with red hair and ample breasts, had offered to help him do it up. Free of charge, she had explained. They had ended up in bed together before the paint on the living room

18

walls had had a chance to dry. Another of his many brief, lazy affairs, no fuss, no drama. Amaldi dropped his trousers and absent-mindedly ploughed his penis into her vagina, her mouth, between her buttocks that were damp and sticky from the summer's cloying heat, and lost himself in the past while stroking her abundant breasts. They could smell him out, he had always told himself. They didn't expect any more or less from him than he was able to give. And then, just as it had started, the relationship had come to an end, without pain, without regrets. In the meantime the living room had been finished. The walls had been painted a delicate orange colour that gave the impression of a never-ending sunset, no matter what time of day it was; the two tasteful sofas with their three cushions had been upholstered in green, a warm, beckoning colour that spoke of rest; an old hatch from a hay barn had been turned into a rather original coffee table; the floor had been impeccably polished and decorated with a Chinese carpet that, in the words of his consultant, was not only a bargain but also a great investment; the walls had been covered in pictures, engravings and walnut shelves heavy with glossy art books, novels and trinkets, real antiques, not the usual glass rubbish. There was the bust of a Negro dressed in a waiter's outfit. The smiling figure held out his hand into which, once upon a time, right-thinking folk used to drop a coin or two that the slave, when you moved the right lever, swallowed, still smiling, and stored away for the good of whatever dark-skinned community he ideally represented. There was a battered old brass intercom, once part of the fittings on some transatlantic liner. There were fossils of fish, and strange creatures with shells that resembled enormous woodlice, as well as aquatic plants that were probably the forerunners of anemones and cuttlefish. There were two horse heads, carved in wood, which had once held up and embellished a lintel or mantelpiece in some far-flung colonial residence. There were old apothecary vases and a lot of other knick-knacks that Amaldi couldn't even be bothered to look at. The rest of the apartment was desolate. More or less as it had been when he had bought the place. The end of the affair had meant the end of the interior decorating. In the bedroom Amaldi had his bed, a small table he kept the alarm clock on, and a chair onto which he tossed his clothes. In the study there was a wardrobe which he messily piled full of vests, socks, ties, threadbare clothes, and shoes. There was nothing in the dining room, except for a few unopened boxes gathering dust. The kitchen contained two chairs and a table, where he ate and worked. Apart from the living room, with its imposing crystal and wrought-iron chandelier and the strategically placed little spotlights in the four corners, the apartment was lit by a few bare bulbs. The painters had put a single layer of undercoat on the other walls, while they waited for the owner to make up his mind about the final colour. Amaldi rarely went into the living room and when he did it wasn't to relax on those restful green sofas. The double frosted-glass doors that gave onto the room were almost always closed.

The only thing that Amaldi had done of his own accord was to hang those horrible frayed nylon curtains at the kitchen window. He had kept them with him since his parents died, and they were the last relic of his childhood. He still remembered the day his father had brought them home and hung them at his mother's window to stop the neighbours spying on her. And he clearly recalled that feeling of amazement when his father, with a conjurer's air, had brushed his forearm against the bottom half of the curtain and his black hairs had stood up with an electric crackle, under the spell of the miraculous synthetic fibre.

"If you listen closely," his father had explained, "it sounds like a badly tuned radio, coming from somewhere outside."

Amaldi smoothed down the curtains.

After his coffee, he had a hasty shower, got dressed and went out. He nodded to the doorkeeper and headed down the white granite steps that seemed to fade away into the little round forecourt with its fountain caked in limescale. He glanced briefly at the new municipal theatre and turned right. The huge tunnel before him was not yet crammed with cars, but Amaldi needed open space. He took the long way round, as usual, going past the venerable café that had welcomed kings and then presidents. He walked on past the remains of the opera house, which had been bombed in the war and somehow never rebuilt by the local authorities. He walked up the street that was home to the hotel where actors and musicians liked to stay and turned onto the avenue that made its way gently to the sea. On his left, steep, slippery slopes and narrow steps led down to the poverty of the old town. His lips pursed in a kind of smile. Perhaps the old town's only really enduring habit, he said to himself, was hardship. Like a flag. In his memory the cats and dogs, men and women were always active, always asleep. It was the same for the waves in the harbour, crushed and frothy with rage, exhausting themselves against the grey concrete breakwaters. Amaldi had been brought up in a poor home, down in the old town, near the port. The smell of fish rotting in the rubbish bins, the stink of cat's urine, the petrol and diesel fumes that came gusting off the ships, all fought with the smell of the sea

21

without ever completely overwhelming it. His father would have that smell on him when he came home in the afternoon. And that stink. The odours were in the very fabric of his shapeless clothes, engrained in the wrinkles etched by sweat, in the indelible patch between the strong wings of his shoulders.

A passing patrol car hailed him with a burst of its siren.

"Can we give you a lift, sir?" asked one of the two young officers.

He raised his hand in a negative motion.

"Well, it's time for us to get some sleep," said the other policeman.

His head bowed, Amaldi continued walking through the old town. He walked as if he were carrying with him everything he knew, everything he had seen, everything he had ever felt, clutching it to himself with fierce parsimony, without losing or sharing with his fellow men a single crumb.

He was thirty-seven years old. He was a chief inspector whose career was certainly not going to stop there. Quite a few politicians already had their eye on him, and some had tried to ingratiate themselves, savouring the favours they thought they would win from him later. But Amaldi was incorruptible, a man who kept his distance and knew how to step lightly through the minefield of bureaucracy and politics. He kept on good terms with everyone, and made sure things never went any further than that.

He looked at his watch: half past six. It would take him no more than ten minutes to finish the journey that separated him from his office and the kind of stately desk that befitted a chief inspector. He had always persuaded himself that he would avoid the plague of habit because he had a mission to fulfil.

Because when something became just another routine it looked less and less like the truth, and more and more like the quagmire of hopelessness. But avoiding that slime was just a kid's daydream, he thought, the slime covered the pavements and footpaths, homes and offices, even the sea itself. And now at thirty-seven years old he suddenly felt very tired. His legs were limp, as if he spent all his time sprinting, chasing something that was always there, within reach, but which he could never quite grab hold of. Just like the elusive smell of the sea, which seemed to struggle against the ambient stench only to dupe rather than reward the poor wretches of the old town with its acrid, salty taste. It was as if the filth and slime were in charge, sadistically preserving just a hint of the salt, in order to make its absence all the more bitter. Like a memory that refused to be washed away. And now when he was finally tired of running and had turned around to look for the very first time, he had found himself in an unfamiliar place. He was lost, and was no longer able to put together the pieces of his past. There was just the promise. His mission. As uncertain as the fickle smell of the sea.

He had grown up in the dirty, crooked streets of the old town, home to bag-snatchers and prostitutes, dockers and good women, where more often than not good and evil, right and wrong, lived together in the same bare rooms, which watched on impassively, mutely observing the conflicting natures of their occupants, offering them impartial shelter from the cold and rain, from creditors and police. It was in this oppressive greyness, which the sun managed to reach and dry out only at midday, wedging its way through the choked thickets of buildings, that Amaldi saw and immediately fell in love with the girl with the flaxen hair, the dazzling girl with the beautiful skin. When she had grown up in every sense, her beauty grew even more potent. From the perfect, natural oval of her face, with the dark mole behind her right ear, to her blue, slightly shadowed eyes, the only sign of that sensuality that so enflamed him, to the tiny waist, so unsuitable for childbearing, but which allowed her to flow gracefully through crowds, unlike the more fleshy matrons whose abundant hips forced them to change gear and turn sideways when they met someone else on the narrow streets around the port. And her breasts, her best feature. Big but not too big, firm but not hard, soft but not flaccid, pert but not pulled taut by some invisible wire. Breasts that resisted the laws of gravity, especially when she would give a little joyful leap at a surprise, any surprise, or when she heard good news, or was served a hearty meal. When he was very young Amaldi had already decided that he would run away with her to a house full of light, that he would win the right to wide, tree-lined streets full of fresh air. Just for her, he had promised.

There was a crack in the pavement that Amaldi knew all too well: it meant that several feet later he would turn right, cut across the avenue and head up a short dead-end street. That was where his lair was, his office, his window on the world. It would have made more sense to walk on the right-hand pavement, to avoid having to cross the road twice, unnecessarily, but Amaldi felt that the road, like a moat, cut him off from the imaginary line that marked the edge of the old town. So he preferred to keep to the left-hand side and walk along the boundary. It was not only the style of the buildings or the abrupt shift in social class that made the boundary a reality; its existence was also evidenced by people's behaviour. Amaldi had remarked that everyone who came up from the old town paused for a moment, instinctively, as soon as

their feet touched the pavement, often dusting themselves off, perhaps with no more than a flick at their
trouser hem with the back of their hand, and then they
would gulp the air, as if they had just surfaced from too
long a time underwater. And it made no difference
whether they belonged to the old town or not, whether
they were rich or poor.

Amaldi pressed the buzzer. Inside a sleepy cop
peered absently at the familiar face displayed on the
closed circuit monitor, awash with the green light of
the lamp that came on automatically. He buzzed the
inspector through the outer door and waited until it
had closed behind him before opening the armour-
plated inner door. Amaldi briefly raised his hand as he
went by without looking at him. The man at the desk
didn't bother to return the greeting, thinking that it
was pointless to greet someone who didn't see you.

As the lift doors groaned on runners that were never
oiled and a bell rang to let him know the cabin was
about to start moving, the inspector regarded himself
in the mirror. His brow was furrowed, his fair eyebrows
almost joined up just above his thin nose, and his
nostrils seemed permanently flared. His sharp, high
cheekbones stood out on his slightly sunken face. The
corners of his wide mouth dipped a little. He attempted
a smile; he tried smoothing out the wrinkles, and his
eyebrows. He looked like a doll with clear glass eyes.
He turned his back on his reflection. It was a mask he
was all too familiar with, a tough grimace he had always
worn, even when he was a kid, strutting cockily about
the alleys of the old town. That serious, determined
look was his guarantee that he would get on in life, the
dockers used to tell him whenever he went down to the
wharf to take lunch to his father. And he had got on in
life, and would doubtless go even further.

The bell rang again: fifth floor. The lift came to a halt with a slight shudder, the doors opened and Amaldi was immediately assaulted by the reek of stale smoke left by the night shift. He caught sight of something glossy in the waste bin just to his left. He reached into the bin and pulled out a pornographic magazine. He opened it. A young woman with cellulite on her thighs, pert breasts, dressed in just a kitchen apron, was coquettishly slicing a cucumber while the postman handed her a letter. On the next page the cucumber was in her vagina, the postman's trousers were round his ankles, and the woman was busily sucking his erection. There were two photos on the next page. In the first, another man, probably the woman's husband, watched the postman ejaculate onto the woman's hair as she rubbed the perfumed cucumber between her breasts; in the second, the husband was being sodomized by the once more tumescent postman, while the visibly satisfied wife looked on as she finished off a plate of pasta left over by her occasional lover.

"Boning up, I see."

Amaldi didn't jump or give a start, as anyone else might have done in the circumstances. He wasn't gripped by that sense of guilt that all men feel when they are caught out in public spying on something forbidden. Nor did he feel the slightest urge to hide the magazine behind his back.

"Morning, Nicola," he replied calmly. "Fancy some salad?" He held up the cucumber photo.

The other man snickered.

Nicola Frese was forty-nine years old and Amaldi's closest colleague. He was short and stocky, and because of the first of those defects he rarely spent more than a few seconds talking to someone as tall as his superior if he had nowhere to sit down. If there was no chair available he usually cut short the conversation and disappeared. For the same reason he hardly ever showed up for official ceremonies during which those in authority had to stand in a line in front of photographers and journalists.

"I've got work to do," he said, already on his way up the corridor. "If you need me, I'll be over at Records, with Peschiera. Are the two of us really the only ones who know how to do our jobs properly around here?"

Amaldi watched him move off with dignified steps, his chest thrust out, almost on tiptoe. It was comical, a man this squat moving about like a ballerina. Yet the overall effect wasn't so ridiculous. Amaldi turned the magazine over in his hand, rolled it up and put it back in the waste bin.

His office was open and the cigarette stench had invaded the room. He closed the door and opened one of the windows wide. The cold damp air kneaded its way through the smoke, and slowly the odours of the port and the smell of car exhausts supplanted the nicotine. Small consolation, thought Amaldi. But that was what he always did: make do and get on with things.

In plain view on his desk, surrounded by what he imagined were useless complaints from angry citizens calling upon him to resolve the rubbish-collectors' strike, there was a fax, with a handwritten note in red marker declaring it URGENT. The first line of the communication, in bold type, read REQUEST FOR COOPERATION. The microscopically tiny print of the second line cited the regulation that authorized the request. It came from a nearby provincial town outside his jurisdiction.

There was a Post-it note beside the fax and he recognized his own writing. He had noted the name of a girl who had come in a few days earlier. A girl with big tits.

And long, slim legs, and delicate hands that trembled slightly as she signed the complaint she was filing. Her grey eyes had looked right into him, but without scraping his soul. He had caught sight of something in those eyes, something that pressed him to want to open up to her, to let her compassion find its way into him. It had only lasted a moment. And then he'd gone back to being the Amaldi he always was.

"Three bodies found near . . ." he began to read out loud, holding the fax in his hand. "Two men shot to death . . . and a woman . . ." He lowered his voice. ". . . her breast . . ." Amaldi felt suddenly winded, ". . . mutilated and . . ." He put down the sheet of paper and closed his eyes. He knew that feeling, halfway between fear and excitement. He started to read again. The report sketched the scene of the triple murder that had taken place the day before, Sunday, gave a few details about the weapon, or weapons, used and the approximate time of death. The victims were a couple of young lovers from some place in the countryside, and an old ex-con, known to the police, with previous arrests and convictions for lewd acts. At the bottom of the report there was a handwritten note, couched in diplomatic terms, from the investigating officer, asking all districts within a thirty-mile radius to cooperate. A bureaucratic formality, nothing more. In the early stages of an investigation they tried everything, they knocked on every door. Amaldi made a quick calculation. Ten other detectives in ten other districts were probably reading the same fax, which in all likelihood would end up in ten waste bins. And the officer conducting the investigation doubtless expected no more.

Amaldi mechanically dusted off the lapel of his jacket. He folded the fax and placed it on his desk. He wasn't going to throw it away. He picked up the phone and dialled an internal extension. He waited. No one answered. Then he remembered that Frese was over in Records. He dialled another number and waited again.

"Can you come over for a minute?" he said into the receiver.

A few seconds later, announced by a hasty rap on the door, Frese came in. He didn't wait for a sign from Amaldi and threw himself into the swivel chair in front of the inspector's desk.

"Have you read this?" Amaldi held up the fax.

"Yes, I have," Frese replied, recognizing the fax. "You know what a tedious turd Iafisco can be. He gave me my very own photocopy. I've already binned it. You know, maybe we should find a few other words for rubbish and refuse and trash and bins for the time being. What do you think?"

"Right," sighed Amaldi. "Look at this." He gestured at the pile of protest letters.

Frese sniggered.

"What's so funny?"

"The zealous citizenry calling upon the cavalry, right?"

"Of course. And it's just the beginning."

"This bloody strike is going to be hell," said Frese.

"Let's hope not."

"Yeah, let's hope not." Frese was clearly unconvinced. "It's still going to be hell, though."

"Well, let's not make things worse before we need to, then."

"You're right. Anything else?" Frese got up, took the fax and shoved it in the waste bin. Then he pushed down on the contents with his foot.

"Any thoughts on the fax?" Amaldi asked him.

"No thoughts. No, I do think something. I think it's none of our business. It's not our patch. We have enough shit of our own to take care of. Come on, Giacomo, don't get started on your —" He broke off, red in the face. It didn't take much to make him flare up.

"Obsession?" Amaldi finished for him.

"Shit, Giacomo. I know . . . but I don't think you should —"

"Not another word. Stop right there."

Amaldi never lost control, never broke his frosty demeanour. But nor did he have to say something twice to make himself understood.

Frese returned to his chair.

Amaldi sat in silence. Frese wasn't his friend. Their banter never went beyond work. They never went out in the evening together, never talked about their private lives, but Amaldi knew all there was to know about Frese's private life. The man carried it around with him. All there was to know was in the smell that had already filled up Amaldi's office. It was more the smell of the man's soul than his body, the outward sign of that plodding, inner shabbiness that was never quite overcome by the endless round of dinners and nights on the town. Through constant, obsessive repetition, these too had become just another aspect of Frese's stagnation. The smell of stale sweat, the lingering odour of grease and smoke, tiny stains and traces of dirt that individually were invisible but together, layer upon layer, made up his characteristic grubbiness.

"Look," began Frese, steering the conversation onto other ground. "You're from the city, right. What do you know about the fire in the orphanage?"

"What orphanage?" asked Amaldi and squeezed his eyes half-closed. Distracted by his jumble of thoughts, he was finding it very hard to focus that morning. He did know, however, exactly what he had thought

30

of when he came across the girl in the fax. He remembered. A body like a sack.

He shook himself. "What orphanage?"

"The city orphanage. The one that burned down all those years ago. You must remember. There's only ever been one orphanage."

"Yes, of course." He nodded. "The city orphanage. The one that burned down."

"The very same."

"Yes, of course I remember."

But if Frese wasn't his friend, then who was? Who were his friends? And while he told Frese that though he couldn't possibly remember the orphanage fire because he had been a baby at the time, he did know that it had gone up in smoke because that's all anyone had talked about for years, the blackened bodies, the burned orphans, the nun in flames who had shot like a canon ball out of a second-storey window and even though she was already dead had continued thrashing and writhing on the road, like a witch or saint burned at the stake. Amaldi thought about his friends. He thought of the old dockers he went to see at the port. Colleagues of his father who would never carry anything else on their bent backs and shaky legs. But they weren't his friends either. He felt just as oppressed after meeting up with them as he did before.

". . . it was just a thought," Frese was saying. "I only asked you on the off chance you might remember something out of the ordinary . . ."

"No."

"Well, if something comes up, I'll let you know, okay?"

"Fine."

"I need your signature to file the insurance claim."

"What insurance claim?"

"Giacomo, where have you been?"

"Nowhere. What insurance claim?"

Frese looked at him for a moment, tried to look beyond Amaldi's icy expression. He knew about the inspector's mission. They called him "the Crusader" when he wasn't around to hear. But he couldn't see what troubled him. No one knew what went on in the head of the brilliant Inspector Amaldi. No one managed to get close enough to find out. Some people said it was the man's coldness that made him such a good cop. Frese had always thought that one day Amaldi would crack.

"The insurance company that covered the orphanage went bankrupt," he began again. "The new one, I mean. Two copies of the bankruptcy papers have to be attached to the orphanage file. And because the orphanage went up in smoke and people died, well, the matter was handed over to us, not to City Hall. I'm talking thirty-five years ago here. Everything clear so far?"

Amaldi nodded.

"That's why I need your signature, because the case —"

"What case?"

"All right, don't you start as well. I meant the file. The file has been passed over to you."

"Why?"

"How the hell should I know? Someone had to get it. Bureaucracy, right. It could have been someone else, it just happened to be you."

"Okay, go on."

"End of story. You need to sign so we can shelve the file."

"What's it got to do with you? Why didn't the archivist come straight to me to sign?"

"He did come straight to you to sign but you weren't around so he came straight to me and bored the arse off me. But if you want to take care of it yourself, be my guest. You know where Records is, right?"

"Nicola, get to the point because I can't take any more of your pussyfooting around. Do you just want my autograph or is there something else?"

"I don't know if there is anything else," began Frese, who never liked to get straight to the point.

It's all just theatre to him, thought Amaldi. He has to follow the script right up to the final grand revelation. The digressions and non sequiturs that broke up the thread of what he was saying served to heighten the tension. Strategies and wordplay that were more like marketplace haggling than an ordinary conversation between two people. And Amaldi, who didn't like digressions, who always preferred to nail down the facts of the matter as soon as possible to make sure things wouldn't get lost in an uncontrolled gush of words, had to admit he found Frese's way of doing things quite fascinating. There was something of the hustler about the man, at times he was patently bogus, but nevertheless he was an absolute original. And Amaldi was a connoisseur, a collector of personalities. It was thanks to his own strength of character and intelligence, the two features he appreciated most in his fellows, that Amaldi had managed to drag himself out of the ghetto that was the old town. He had got on in life because of those gifts, although he had got off to a much more disadvantaged start than many of his colleagues and subordinates.

"So . . .?" he asked.

Frese twiddled a tuft of dark hairs that sprouted from one of his nostrils. "They more you cut them, the harder they become," he remarked.

Amaldi bowed his head in resignation.

"And if you pull them out . . . Have you ever tried?"

"No, can't say that I have."

"Try it and see. You'll squeal like a pig."

"So . . .?"

"So, it looks like there are some documents missing. There's a list on the front of the file. Document one, document two and so on. For example, document six is missing. They didn't bother to put what it was, mind you. Don't know if it was somebody's statement, or a 'report closed' note or a death certificate. See what I mean? Documents one, five, six, twelve and thirteen. Five documents and not a sign of them."

"Is that all?" Amaldi asked impatiently.

"I did tell you maybe there was nothing in it. If something comes up I'll let you know."

"What could come up?"

"How should I know?" Frese spread his arms, revealing an old sweat stain on his jacket, just under the armpit. "I only thought that these documents shouldn't be missing, that's all."

"Thirty-five-year-old documents?"

Silence fell between the two men. There was nothing left to say. And, Amaldi reflected, he hadn't even listened to what little had been said.

"Yeah," said Frese.

"Yeah," repeated Amaldi and considered his subordinate with some envy. Frese's easygoing humanity, somewhere between the slob and the rogue, his behaviour that was often just a whisker away from being illegal, ensured that he was widely appreciated among the troops, as he liked to call them. A favour here, a favour there, a few strings pulled, courtesy visits to well-connected shopkeepers and businessmen, as well as to a few shady intermediaries. Nothing that was

34

concretely illegal. Yet all of this kept Frese in dinner invitations and nights out, earned him smiles in the corridor and shared jokes on the two-way. The kind of thing that never happened to Amaldi.

Frese was about to get up when he said, "Oh, I almost forgot . . ."

"What?"

"You know Ajaccio?"

"Who?"

"Ajaccio. He's one of ours."

"One of the new boys?"

"No, Giacomo, one of the old boys."

"Don't know him. Maybe by sight. What about him?"

"He's in hospital. Cancer. One of those nasty tumours you get when you're fifty-two years old." Frese stopped and stared at his superior, waiting for Amaldi to work it out for himself. When the inspector remained silent, Frese continued. "The chief should really go to see him, but he doesn't feel like it, so he told me to let you know that he is passing the job on to you."

"Me!" snapped Amaldi, suddenly standing.

"You, yes, you . . . A courtesy visit. Official, you know, to show him we're all part of one big happy family. To console him, I suppose. Well, I've told you, now it's up to you." As soon as he had finished, Frese was out the door.

Left alone, Amaldi went over to the window. The air was frosty. He was not going to visit a dying man he didn't know. They couldn't ask him to do that. He let his eyes wander over the outside world. The shop shutters were up by now, and customers were going in and out of stores. A police van was parked in front of the main entrance, next to a modern sentry-box, a polygonal affair in brick and bullet-proof plate glass. Two cops wearing regulation protective jackets were chatting together. It wasn't possible to see beyond the buildings opposite. But Amaldi knew what was there: the port. The heart of the city. He turned back to his desk and picked up the Post-it note on which he had written down the name of the girl with the big breasts. He had found her address on the form she had filled in when she had made her complaint against a person or persons unknown. He knew that side street in the old town very well indeed. It wasn't hard for him to picture the decrepit entrance with the door gnawed by mice and rising damp that the girl probably opened and closed every day, pushing it with both hands because it refused to turn on its rusty hinges. Those slim, nervous hands that trembled slightly when she signed her complaint, hands that he had so wanted to take in his, to reassure her. To warm himself.

He was about to roll the note into a pellet and toss it into the waste bin but he held back, without asking himself why. He stuck it at the back of a drawer, under a pile of paper, convinced that he would soon forget it. The note and the girl.

Then he got down to work. His mission. He picked up the phone and dialled a number in another district. He had had to peer at the faded fax in order to make out the figures.

There was something about that triple murder that concerned him directly. Something to do with the reason he had joined the Force.

III

The pale, imposing bulk of the building, with its huge slabs of granite that were more grey than white by now, with the regular shapes of the windows that brought to mind hospital wards more than university lecture rooms, appeared before him, as it did every Tuesday. It was only then that Professor Avildsen stopped thinking about the rubbish strike, a train of thought that had kept him company on the long and somewhat tortuous journey into town from his villa on the coast. The huge green bins suffocated by parked cars were already packed full. The gaping, dislocated maws could no longer be closed. It was an intolerable act of abandonment, this giving the city over to itself, a wanton confession of filthiness. There was something profoundly immoral in that gangrene, he had thought obsessively, without finding a way out of his labyrinthine reasoning. Indeed, he simply took up the same refrain every time his line of thinking came to a halt.

As he went up the stone steps, through flocks of students leaning against each other, chattering like birds, smoking, exchanging telephone numbers, clearly anxious to get lost in the mass, to confirm themselves in the hive, Professor Avildsen began to revive.

He made his way through the warren of dusty corridors and caught snatches of voices from his class, which grew louder the closer he came to the double mahogany doors scored with messages, savouring in advance the moment when he would close those doors behind him and shut the world out from his realm. Of what possible importance to him was the refuse-collectors' strike at that moment? The university lecture hall freed him of a much heavier burden: the room freed him from himself. Before taking the last turn in the corridor, he breathed in deeply and bared his white teeth. Then he made his entrance. The mass of students slowly settled down into silence.

A fat youth with snub nose, bleary little eyes and teeth like a beaver held his breath. A few minutes earlier, when the lecture hall had still been empty, he had written a number of obscene words on the no longer black blackboards. The words weren't directed at the teacher. Their intended victim was in the front row. The fat youth had watched the girl's reaction closely, had seen her embarrassment and had avoided her look of enquiry. While he sat imagining what was going through the girl's head, he had even felt a brief stirring in his underpants.

The students watched the professor slyly as he went up to the podium and put his leather satchel on the desk. The obscene words were clearly visible behind his back. An amused buzz spread its way around the room. The professor turned round, looked about and picked a stub of chalk up off the floor. With a conscientious air he then wrote in large, childish letters, four more words, two on each blackboard, which if anything were even more offensive than the words already there. When he had finished writing, he stepped back, to take a good look at his handiwork, then turned to face the packed room with a triumphant smile on his face. The chalk seemed to slip out of his fingers but when he crushed it under foot he did so with firm and fierce intention. His smile disappeared as he scraped the chalk under the sole of his shoe.

"Fine," he said in a cold, metallic voice that was not in the least reassuring. "Have I passed your little exam? Do I know how to speak your language?"

After a moment of embarrassed silence a few students began to laugh, half-heartedly, soon followed by others, and their staggered laughter sounded strangely like a sputtering engine that had trouble starting. And that was just what they were, thought Professor Avildsen: a sputtering engine. A single, incoherent entity. A village full of fog.

The girl in the front row, however, kept a straight face.

"What it behoves us now to understand," continued Avildsen, "is whether *you* are capable of assimilating and speaking *my* language."

This was the first lesson in the anthropology course: the simplest and the most gratifying. A foretaste of what they would have to endure in order to connect with the subject he taught. Not to connect with him, of course. He would never allow any of them to get too close. He detested such familiarity. He abhorred the idea of taking someone out of the herd, of acknowledging something individual about that person, or remembering names and birthdays. He could not stand the thought that one of his students might register as a discrete, tangible presence in his memory. His teaching rested on one tenet: leave the village, abandon it. But certainly not with the aim of creating another one. No, everyone was to go off on his own path. Alone.

Nonetheless, he couldn't help noticing the myopic gaze of a girl in the front row who squeezed her eyes to see things better. He knew her. Professor Avildsen never forgot a face. She was a little over twenty, her ash-coloured hair fell straight onto her bony shoulders. She was tall, slim, with long legs, perhaps too long, because

39

she couldn't keep them still, constantly crossing and uncrossing them, forming ripples at odds with her otherwise rigid pose. Her arms and hands, like her legs, were long and slender and lithe, but more docile, not so restless. Her hands were resting on the white Formica bench top, and every so often one would enclose the other in a half caress, following the straight line of a finger or lingering on the palm, which spread open so willingly at the soft touch of those fingertips, as if the two hands did not belong to the same person; one was the girl's and the other was her lover's. Avildsen observed her for a moment more. The girl stretched her back in a languid little movement and Avildsen caught sight of her bust, which had been hidden by her large coat. It struck him as being unreasonably large. Then he remembered where he had seen her before. In one of the city's hospitals, dressed as a nurse. Over a month ago.

He cast his eye over the thronged lecture hall. It was time to begin.

For her part, the girl in the front row felt a flush creep into her cheeks when she realized the teacher was holding up the lesson because he was looking at her. Did he know that those foul words were directed at her? Was that why he had challenged the students? To show her how to fight? That liquid, penetrating glance shook her from her thoughts and brought her back to earth. She pressed a button on her portable recorder and the little tape began to soak up the anthropologist's voice. She settled her glasses on her straight nose and squinted, all the better to funnel more light into her grey irises, to make up for her defective vision. Many girls in the faculty were secretly in love with Dr Avildsen, with his bright, green eyes, like two shiny scarabs, with his full mouth with those fleshy, almost adolescent lips that were always slightly parted, with that sharp, aquiline nose, with his closely trimmed beard that shifted from the brown of his hair to a dark, flinty red on his chin and throat. And she could understand why. The man had the same effect on her. He was very charismatic; he stood out from the crowd. He was up there on a pedestal; so unreachable and so different from the other teachers at the university. But unlike her fellow students she realized that she was enthralled by the personality and not the person.

She gave a further, annoyed glance at the fat boy sitting not far from her, who continued to ogle her out of the corner of his eye, convinced she didn't realize what he was doing. The girl thought about the five letters and the dozen or so obscene phone calls she had received recently. The very same words that were up there on the blackboards. That was why she knew those words were meant for her. Exasperated and angry, she had gone to the police to file a complaint. Against a person or persons unknown, although she was certain that the "person unknown" was the revolting fat boy who constantly darted looks at her and kept licking his big teeth every time he did so. She had felt soiled, and not in the usual, everyday way she might have felt on the street when she was whistled at or made the butt of some lewd remark. Somehow, perhaps because she was used to them by now, that kind of act seemed almost harmless, impersonal. The catcalls and rude jokes were directed at a category, not at one person in particular; at all women, not just her. The fact that she, and not some other woman, was on the receiving end was just a coincidence. But those letters with her name and her address, with a number that clearly identified her door on that street, and those foul things whispered in that foul voice on her telephone, a telephone that had a number which had been looked for and found, a number that could only be hers, that showed clearly that someone had made a very deliberate choice. That was premeditation. This maniac wasn't directing his attention at women in general; he was stalking her in particular. And that was why Giuditta Luzzatto felt so furious, so soiled. She pulled her coat around her to hide the big bust that had blossomed on her before its time, and which she had always hated, which men stared at without reserve, as if her breasts belonged to all of them because they were so obvious.

"Sickness," the teacher was saying, "is the fulcrum of anthropology. Of my anthropology. Of the anthropology that you will strive to comprehend. Sickness, grand and dignified, which at times we may also call Fear. Fear and Sickness, two synonyms for our new vocabulary. As is the word Unknown, for that matter. Our Destiny is Unknown. Destiny and the Unknown are two other synonyms for anthropologists. Sickness . . . Fear . . . Unknown . . . Destiny. Try to separate them. You will never succeed. Our only certain destination is Death. Everything else is Sickness, Fear, Destiny and Unknown. Synonyms. Death is the opposite of all that. It is the end of consciousness. It is the end of Sickness. The end of the line for a long agony we persist in calling Life. If you manage to tune in to this message, then anthropology will unfold before you like a red velvet trail, which you will follow with firm steps, never faltering, never stumbling. This is the path we will follow, without digressions, without abandoning it even for an instant . . . And why? Because, as Goethe says, only when 'the world of visible forms becomes allegory does it acquire value and meaning for men'. Is this not what you are looking for, what you have always been looking for? Be you hunter gatherers or industrialized workers. Sense and meaning?"

While Professor Avildsen became increasingly agitated, holding the whole of the class spellbound, Giuditta could not shake off a feeling of unease. Not only because the fat boy continued to spy on her, but because of the teacher's words. Or perhaps, she told herself, what lay behind the words. Avildsen's vision of the world. It was as though awareness, knowledge of life depended on and coincided with the immanent sickness the lecturer was so taken with. But perhaps that wasn't why, either. It was probably something within Professor Avildsen himself. Something that permeated the man and spread through the room. The dull snap of the tape recorder stopping interrupted her thoughts. She took out the cassette and turned it over, pressing the record button again. She scolded herself; the letters and phone calls had put her unnecessarily on the defensive and on the alert. She felt reflexively guilty for what she had just thought about Professor Avildsen and turned her attention back to the lesson. The anthropology exam would be the crowning glory of her university career if, as she hoped, she managed to get top marks. The course was famous not only for the instructor's fascinating theories, but also for the swathes of hopeful young students who were mown down at every exam session. Avildsen was inflexible, demanding and pitiless. He insisted on an original rendering of the course material and countless students, after any number of failed attempts, gratefully accepted a paltry grade that would ruin their final degree result. Giuditta knew she couldn't allow that to happen. To rise above her own condition she needed to excel.

"Sickness has profound roots in man," declared the professor. "As profound as the roots of Death. It is a trumpet blast before the final battle, or if you prefer something a little more prosaic it is the chime of the front doorbell. On the other side of the door, so long as the lock and hinges hold, stands Death. To study man is thus to study his Death. What I expect you to do is lower yourselves down into that dark hole. Only when you no longer know how to get out, only then will you be able to partake of the banquet of the peoples."

Avildsen left the podium and walked up the central aisle. He went silently up every step, looking straight ahead at the wall lacquered with the prints of thousands of sweaty hands. As he passed each row of students, heads turned in unison to follow him, elbows landed on the bench behind, scattering books and provoking apologies. This was control. Twenty-seven steps. One step per second. Twenty-seven seconds. This was power. When he reached the top of the steps he propped himself against the wall on ramrod arms and lowered his head, theatrically.

"Just as the material world is but the stage on which the dance of primordial images takes shape and thus becomes allegory," began Avildsen, his voice cavernous, his back to the students, "by analogy the material body is but the stage where the images of consciousness express themselves."

The professor turned round.

"Physical sickness is no more than the external manifestation of the forced and relentless celebration of the Ego in opposition to the Id. A way to remember not Death . . . but *my* death. After me, transformation goes on, life goes on . . . but it is the life of Creation, not my life! And upon this assumption are founded many anthropological theories that I contest. They take a village and go through their list: the archetypes, the ancestral themes ... No! Do you know just where mankind's alleged and much-vaunted impulse to socialize is focused? In Sickness. Sickness is the glue. Flock together, herd together, become but one, turn ourselves into a village so that my fear becomes your fear and his fear and so on. But this is self-deception. The fear remains my fear, for all that. The sickness continues to be my sickness and I continue to celebrate it, invoke it, banish it. The sick man," he articulated every word as he walked back down the steps and withdrew behind the podium, "the sick man is not the innocent victim of the imperfections of nature ... He is the very agent of that Sickness."

He stabbed his finger at a blond youth in the third row.

"This is what I want from you ..." he pointed at another student, "... and you," at a girl, "... and you ..." He pointed at ten others. "And you, and you, and you ..."

He walked back to the students. He took a girl by the arm and made her stand up. The girl laughed in embarrassment. Avildsen stood in silence until the girl's fit of nerves had passed.

"And this is what I want from you."

He displayed the girl to the lecture hall. The students' eyes reflected the same cruelty as their teacher's. The prey did not have the strength to defend herself.

"This is what I want from you," he said, staring into the girl's eyes. "Leave the pack. You carry within you the saint and the assassin, the fool and the sage. Be exceptional ... burn the village to the ground and live alone in the world."

When he released his grip, the girl collapsed, pale faced, back into her seat.

"What use is it to you to know about the customs of the Toradja of Central Celebes, or the Indian tribes of Ottawa, of the Sakalava or of a Turik from the River Baram in Borneo? What possible use is it –" and a pained tremor affected his voice – "if you continue to live in the village, making the sicknesses of others your own. You are not here to memorize sterile information . . . Our task is that of a megalomaniac psychoanalyst who has millions upon millions of patients, so many in the past and so few in the present, some are alive, but most are already dead. A psychoanalyst whose aim is not to save his patients, but to cure himself through their sickness."

Professor Avildsen went back to the podium and picked up his leather satchel. He opened it and showed the contents to his students.

"Nothing," he declared and shook out the emptiness it contained. "Nothing. That is what you will get from me if you are unable to follow me."

A confused murmur followed this last assertion. Avildsen looked at his watch. Exactly forty-two minutes had passed.

"I have nothing more to say."

He closed the satchel, ran his hand through his hair and opened the double doors. Before him stretched the dark corridors. That day he couldn't go straight home, as he liked to do. The vice-chancellor had summoned him for one of the many little consultations he was obliged to give free of charge on the man's private collection. Masks, ritual objects, everyday things, floor mats, clothing, aboriginal paintings. A load of rubbish without value, history or real purpose, which, Avildsen suspected, the vice-chancellor bought with university funds.

46

"Professor . . ." came a timid female voice behind him.

Deep in his own thoughts, Avildsen didn't hear.

Giuditta stopped herself. She waited until the teacher was swallowed up by the shadows in the corridor. She had followed him to ask for some other references she could use for study, but he hadn't turned round. She decided to let the matter drop and headed back to the lecture theatre. She gathered up her pencils, rubber and sharpener. Then she noticed that her recorder was still on. She was sure she had turned it off.

"Well? What did you think of the lesson?" the fat boy asked her quite casually, as her passed her by. "Will you start drooling over Avildsen like all the others?"

Giuditta glared at him and turned on her heel.

The fat youth smiled and stuck his hand in a jacket pocket. He pulled out a lump of greasy paper that smelled strongly of onions. He unwrapped the contents and set about attacking his *pannino* with determination. He finally managed to swallow the lump of food in his mouth. A trickle of saliva broke through his lips and got ready to leap into the void. He rubbed his florid mouth with the back of his hand and on his way out his elbow brushed against the breast of a brown-haired girl he had seen earlier. Then he headed for the toilets. The hand in his pocket was beginning to fidget already.

Outside, the sun, a bright point the size of a pinhead, cut through dark clouds heavy with rain and unease, and struck the plate glass of the main university entrance. Giuditta was dazzled by the reflected glare for a moment as she turned round to make sure the fat boy wasn't following her. She shielded her eyes with one hand while with the other she pulled a milk carton, a tinfoil container and a baby's bottle from her

47

multi-coloured bag with the horizontal stripes. She headed off at a brisk pace towards the far corner of the university building, reached down over the parapet separating the steps from the lawn, which was always littered with cigarette butts and scraps of paper, and re-emerged smiling and holding a ginger kitten by the scruff of the neck. The kitten was only a few weeks old. Stroking and cuddling it, she sat down, took it in her arms, filled the bottle with milk and brought the rubber teat to the animal's mouth. The kitten seemed to turn up its nose at first. It curled its pink lips and bared its tiny, sharp white teeth before latching firmly onto the maternal substitute, closing its furry eyes in contentment. Giuditta looked on, stroking the kitten between its little pointed ears smiling up at the students who stopped to look at the touching scene.

Giuditta knew how to take care of animals, and of people. It was a gift she had. That was why she did volunteer work three afternoons a week at the city hospital. She helped the nurses with menial tasks and jobs that required no particular skill. She entertained the patients, especially the older ones. It wasn't burdensome, and she didn't do it for social reasons. And she didn't feel shy with the sick. She had told herself more than once that perhaps that was why she visited them.

Once over the initial burst of guzzling, the kitten started to drink more slowly and to purr. Giuditta heard something rustle behind her and a thin, mangy ginger-and-black cat brushed against her legs. She filled the tinfoil container with what was left of the milk and held it out to the mother cat, which began to lap the milk up gratefully, from time to time throwing a wary glance at its only offspring.

A few minutes later Professor Avildsen had finished his little chat with the vice-chancellor, having dissuaded the man from acquiring an aboriginal fetish that was clearly a fake, and was on his way out of the faculty building. While on his way in to lectures his routine called for him to walk serenely up the middle of the steps, when he left the building he always preferred to turn right as soon as he was out of the door and to follow the wall, denuding himself of his famous charisma, in an effort to pass unnoticed. He could not abide the idle chatter of students who would try to work their way into his favour.

"Goodbye, Dr Avildsen."

That was why he turned around in annoyance at the sound of his name.

"Yes, goodbye," he muttered in Giuditta's direction and returned her greeting with a brief nod, thrown by that unsolicited contact. He saw the cat, smeared with milk, fluffy, toying with a brown rubber teat from where it was ensconced on the girl's chest. And then nausea gripped him. Avildsen turned abruptly on his heel and bolted down the steps. He crossed the road and leaned against his car, panting, his chest heaving.

Giuditta watched him go. The kitten struggled in her grasp and tried to free itself. She put it back in its lair behind the parapet, stroked the mother cat, which blithely ignored her, and, deciding it was time for her to go home, she gathered up her things.

Professor Avildsen, leaning heavily against his car while he tried to fight back the growing urge to vomit, caught sight of the girl as she came down the steps, her thoughts clearly elsewhere. Her coat had opened. Every step she took corresponded to a dip in her breasts followed by her flesh springing up again before settling, ready for the next dip. The professor took a deep breath, then another and another. He felt light-headed, unwell. A revolting smell had invaded his nostrils. He doubled up. Then, his vision clouded by tears and his breathing lacerated, he yanked open the door of his car and turned the key in the ignition.

Giuditta had reached the bottom of the steps and looked across the road. A man was leaning heavily against the top of a car. Then he seemed to fold up and disappear. He rose again, clutching his head, and then sank once more. He lurched. It was Professor Avildsen. Driven by her nurse's instincts she hastened across the road towards him. Then she saw him pull away in his car. Among the bags of rubbish that no one had bothered collecting that day she noticed a frothy patch of bile that was slowly spreading out on the pavement.

"Fresh vomit," remarked the fat boy knowingly from behind her back, and laughed.

IV

Augusto Ajaccio's mouth was dry. He reached across to his bedside table and drank some water. For a brief moment he experienced a feeling of relief and then his saliva became thick and gummy once again. He wiped the corners of his mouth with the thumb and forefinger of his left hand and lay back. The rough sheets reminded him of his childhood and he felt ill at ease. It was not a time of his life that he liked to think about.

The bottom half of the walls of his hospital room were painted to a height of six and a half feet in green gloss. Above that line the walls were a matte white. A strip of protective clear plastic had been placed along the wall behind the backs of the two chairs meant for visitors. On his right, through the window that looked out onto a slice of the city reaching all the way to the port, where he could see mounds of rubbish bags that no one was collecting, the red light of dawn that had found him awake had given way to a bleary glare that was forcing its way through the slats of the venetian blind, also green. To his left there was a tall aluminium stand at the top of which perched the saline solution feeding his drip. Also to his left was the bedside cabinet, the first drawer of which was empty. The larger, second drawer contained his bedpan and slippers. Then there was the door that opened onto the corridor that nurses clattered along in hospital clogs and patients shuffled along in their slippers.

"The angiographic tests show, especially for the lateral projections, that the carotid siphon, the intra-cranial section of the inner carotid, that is, appears unravelled, less contorted . . . and the medium cere-bral artery is slightly raised and curved . . . The various branches of the Sylvian system appear to be closer together than usual . . ." the senior consultant's assist-ant had explained to him a few days before, as if the man were reciting something he had learned by heart. When the doctor had come into the room, he had been fanning himself with a file that Ajaccio immediately understood to be his. There was a note of reproach in that waving motion, as if there were something repre-hensible about the file's contents. There had been the same reproachful tone in the doctor's voice when he had asked Ajaccio if it were indeed true, as seemed to be the case, that he had no relatives. When the police-man had confirmed the information, the consultant's assistant had spread his arms, sighed heavily, pulled one of the chairs over to Ajaccio's bedside and, after a pause during which his head had twitched from side to side, underlining his disapproval, had declared that he was in a deeply embarrassing position.

"You do understand that you are putting us in a very awkward position. We usually give patients all the infor-mation they are entitled to know, but as a rule we deal directly with family members when it comes to taking the necessary, erm, decisions. I'm sure you understand our position . . ." And the man had stumbled on with a thousand "You do understand"s and "it's quite a prob-lem, you know"s and "we really didn't need this extra issue"s and explained that as it was their duty to inform someone of all the facts, and as Ajaccio had no one to look after him, he would have to bear the brunt of everything that needed to be said, warts and all. It was a question of ethics, and there was simply no other solution. At which point the man had then stood up, reinvigorated, wearing the expression of someone who has just generously forgiven a tiresome patient who didn't have the decency to avoid obliging the whole hospital to talk openly about death with the future corpse. He had put the chair back in its place against the wall and then remained standing for the rest of his speech.

"Mr . . ." he glanced down at the name on the file. "Mr Ajaccio . . . you have a tumour in your temporal lobe. A glioblastoma multiforme, to be precise. Quite widespread . . . and quite serious. Surgery is not an option: it would be impossible to remove the tumour definitively."

Ajaccio had listened attentively to what had increasingly seemed to him to be delirious rambling, nodding and trying to be cooperative, as they had asked him to be, as his role required. At the same time, the fog was slowly lifting; the fog that he had been shrouded in for the last two weeks, since he had learned of his illness during the annual check-up to which all members of the Force had to submit. He remembered the face of the embarrassed army doctor who had first examined him, and who had constantly licked his lips as if searching the air for words he couldn't say. He remembered the various check-ups and examinations and tests that had preceded his hospitalization. It was as though he had been living in a state of unawareness. The shapes of things and people were blurred, colourless. Life was suspended. Then suddenly, while the consultant's assistant had been discoursing on IV injections and glucose and magnesium sulphate and radiotherapy, Ajaccio had realized for the first time that the man was talking about him. He had craned his neck, brought his ear as close as possible to his chest, as though he were seeking confirmation of that fear in his own heartbeat. But everything seemed calm. Even his breathing.

Now he was alone. The dazzling sunlight that stabbed through the slats of the blind sliced long shadows onto the wall opposite him. Ajaccio's expression was vacant, pained.

"Why?" he asked aloud.

He recognized in that question an intonation that he had heard many times before. Every time he had had to break the news of a death, of a son to his mother, or a husband to his wife. It was always the same, tragic note. A sense of despair that could be expressed in no other way.

His eyelids were heavy, dragging him towards rest, in a crescendo of tiredness that somehow seemed alien to him. He closed his eyes and willed himself asleep. Sleep had always been a great help. When he wasn't on duty, he usually managed to doze, if not to sleep deeply, for the whole day. But for some time now sleep had stopped being that silent hiding place and had become a tiring and populous arena, full of rowdy, demanding people. Once upon a time his thoughts didn't stop to chat; they were harmless passers-by that vanished into thin air as soon as he had conceived them. Now, however, and he lowered his ear once more to his heart, now all the images of his past and present, and, incredibly, of his future, were no longer ruled by weakness and indolence, but stopped to gaze upon themselves in the mirror of consciousness, pirouetting in front of it like little girls admiring themselves in a new dress. A strange uncontrollable feeling that there was some grand design hovered about him, flattering him, wooing him. The world appeared different, and the fog was lifting.

"Why?"

Augusto Ajaccio, at the age of fifty-two and already on the verge of retirement, was still a beat cop, and his highly mediocre career could be explained by his limited intellect. He was well aware of this and often told himself as much. Not with a torturer's wilful cruelty, but with the singsong innocence of a humble soul. It hadn't pained him to acknowledge the fact and all that was left was a faded bruise, a youthful memory of the time when he had first understood. For almost thirty years he had lived in the same furnished bedsit on the second floor of a crumbling building that overlooked the harbour. He had aged along with his room and his landlady, a mean and petty widow. In all those years they had never once had dinner together. Ajaccio would usually find two dishes, sometimes one, waiting for him in the oven. His landlady would have dolloped something onto the plates and the tepid meal would be accompanied by an aluminium knife and fork, a spoon if she had prepared soup, and a glass half full of vinegary red wine. He would carry everything slowly into his room, avoiding turning on the dim lights in the corridor, and often didn't even bother to open the window to let the noises from the street keep him company. He had tiptoed through this wasteland almost without noticing, as though the life he lived wasn't his, or indeed anyone's, just something he couldn't get away from and submitted to through sheer laziness. If a corner of the brown wallpaper unfurled he would quietly, in the course of a week, stick it back in place in the sure knowledge that his repair work wouldn't last and that soon enough another hole would open in the fragile fabric of his one-roomed world and that he would repair that too, but not for his own sake, simply because it was something that needed doing, something anyone would have done. And that, patch by patch, was how he had spent the last thirty years.

"Why?" he said again and threw back the bed covers, which had begun to smother him.

Ajaccio wasn't a vagrant, indeed, he looked quite the opposite, but there was something rootless about him. And to such a degree that not only would he never be able to lay claim to the city, there was not a street or a bar he could say was his. Not even his own room belonged to him. Meeting him in the street, people would have found it difficult to say that he possessed anything or that he came from somewhere in particular. The world wasn't his and he wasn't part of the world. He had lived on the edges, feeding on whatever he managed to find going through the bins. But he had never felt any of that, before now.

There was a slight tremor in the air as the door opened and closed.

Ajaccio turned and saw a face which for a moment struck him as familiar and comforting. He felt a smile form on his lips. Without speaking the man came over to the bed and looked down at him with cold, penetrating eyes.

"Does it hurt?" he asked at length, in a hushed voice and pointed at Ajaccio's temple.

The policeman nodded, feeling uncomfortable.

"I'm Professor Civita," said the man, suddenly affable. "I'm the head of this department."

Ajaccio looked at him closely. All of the doctors should dress like that, he thought, no white lab coat, just a jacket. Dr Civita could have been any visitor, a friend maybe. Once again he felt he knew the man from somewhere. He smiled.

Then Dr Civita, still in hushed tones, but increasingly agitated, began to speak, gesturing in order to outline notions that Ajaccio found extraordinarily vivid and vibrant. He used what he claimed was an interesting metaphor. He compared the human body to a country, and explained that just as the State expected individual citizens to act in such a way as to preserve the whole, the individual required his organs to function in such a way as to keep him alive. And thus each organ expected its cells to do their duty, for the same reason. In this hierarchical logic, each individual was caught up in a clash between personal existence and subordination to the interests of the superior entity. "Every complex structure," the doctor went on, quite impassioned, "men, like countries . . . work to ensure that all the elements accept the common good and serve it. And if the body can accept a lack of productivity on the part of the few, it absolutely cannot allow itself the luxury of tolerating open revolution. For every revolution, in refusing to acknowledge shared ideals, sooner or later will provoke the collapse of the established whole. Your disease is just such a revolution. Subversive elements that not only refuse to cooperate, but that also set about corrupting the other elements with which they come into contact. And it is a revolution with no other goal than to exhaust the soil in which it grows. These are terrorist cells, fanatics, which after years of peaceful cooperation have suddenly changed allegiance and abandoned the common identity. From that moment on they pursue their own goals, without concerning themselves with the rest. The comparison with revolutionary movements is most appropriate from the point of view of strategy because as they multiply they proceed along two paths. Infiltration, disregarding all morphological boundaries, and the creation of their own camps, or metastasis. The only recourse available to the State is to suppress the rebels before they begin . . ." A pause during which Ajaccio thought Professor Civita was going to smile. "Alas, in your case, we have arrived too late."

He seemed to reflect upon some deep matter for a moment. Then he looked Ajaccio squarely in the eye. The policeman's feeling of familiarity gave way to a sense of profound unease.

"You must be prepared for that fact that perhaps . . . in the final stages of your disease . . . you might have trouble remembering who you are. This type of tumour is often accompanied by convulsions that resemble epileptic attacks or by personality disorders. You will find yourself having to deal with moments of sensorial instability, waves of sensation when you experience unpleasant odours, tastes, and perhaps even sounds and sights. Concomitantly, you may be affected by a particular disturbance in your consciousness, a sense of unreality, a persistent feeling that you are seeing things from the past, your waking moments will be informed by a strong oneiric sensation, what we call the 'dream state'. It can be very painful . . ." The doctor paused briefly, as though he wanted to appraise the effect of the word "painful" on his patient. "You may even experience hallucinations," he continued. "The strangest things can happen. On one occasion I found one of my patients, a man I was treating in his own home, where he had lived for more than forty years, I found him crying like a baby in a corner of the living room. He was terrified. Just like a baby. And do you know why?" A smile. "Because he couldn't remember the way back to his bedroom. His own bedroom, in his own house." He looked at Ajaccio again. "You do understand what you are going to have to face?"

"Of course."

"Good. *Very* good indeed," the other man said after a

long and embarrassing silence. Then, without another word, he went to the door, pulled it ajar, looked out into the corridor, first right then left, and disappeared as silently as he had come.

Ajaccio turned his back on the door. He was alone once again.

"You should get some sleep," he forced himself to say out loud.

But he knew he wouldn't manage. He was alert, watchful. As if he had scented danger. He sat down, took the glass of water from the bedside cabinet, drank and put the glass down again. Then he noticed his glasses and put them in the drawer. In the drawer he also found a sheet of paper. His own name and surname had been written on the sheet, dozens of times. He didn't remember doing that. The initial A of his name and surname were lower case. Some of the other letters had been written in block capitals and scored into the paper to make them stand out. The paper was nearly worn through in places.

Ajaccio felt an immense pressure in his head, as though his skull was about to split open. The thing that was invading him, or his brain itself, or both, wanted out.

V

The young doctor went over to a valuable old cherry-wood tallboy, opened one of the drawers and took out a butterfly needle, a rubber tube, a nozzle, a jar full of a dense, reddish liquid and a plastic harness. In silence she positioned the harness at the top of the back of the chair where the old woman was sitting, then inserted the pointed tip of the nozzle into one end of the rubber tube and the butterfly needle into the other. Then she inserted the nozzle into the top of the bottle and placed the bottle upside down in the harness. Without ceremony she jabbed the needle into the old woman's arm, piercing a tumescent violet vein. The doctor made sure the contents of the bottle were dripping normally and, satisfied, turned to face the master of the house.

"Well, lunch is served," she remarked, jokingly, and pushed back a lock of hair that kept falling in front of her almost almond-shaped eyes. "You don't mind clearing up, after, do you, sir?"

"No, of course not."

"You might just massage the vein a little, after you take out the needle. It helps the tissues . . . They are under a lot of stress, of course.

"Of course."

The doctor took a little pad of receipts from her bag and handed it to the man.

"Could you sign, please."

The man scribbled something on the receipt printed with the hospital crest and returned the pad to the

60

young woman. "Let me show you out," he said, already heading across the shadowy bedroom towards the dark, heavy door.

The woman followed him but not at her usual brisk pace. She watched the man. She looked like someone who had to broach a delicate subject and was putting off the moment by making a short journey longer.

The bedroom, the adjacent bathroom, another bedroom, the living room and a kitchen, on the first of the eighteenth-century villa's two upper storeys, were heated well enough; south facing and exposed to the winds off the gulf. The rest of the house, starting with the long corridor with the cast-iron balustrade that led to the hallway with the sumptuous yellow marble floor, was ruled by the cold and the damp. The shutters, almost always closed, kept out most of the light. All of the rooms on the second and ground floors were kept locked. The villa's outward appearance did not reflect the devastation inside. Forty years earlier the original layout had been thrown into disarray by the requirements of the new orphanage. The construction work had been carried out with an eye to saving as much money as possible, with the result that the load-bearing walls had been undermined. As a stopgap, now that the villa was no longer an orphanage, huge iron rods crossed the rooms at different heights where support was necessary. These dark, rusty lines blocked the way and made it necessary to undertake long, circuitous journeys round the house just to travel between two spots that were actually next to each other.

The miasma of formalin, tanning acids and wasted flesh gusted under the cracks in the door and hung in the air.

On her way out, the doctor twitched her nose and breathed out two or three times, aware of the stench.

She then gave the master of the house what she thought was a meaningful look. The man didn't return her look. He moved briskly ahead to throw open the front door, a door that at one time had been kept closed only at night. The white veins in the yellow marble floor glinted as light flooded into the entrance hall. They both shielded their eyes. Outside, on the four steps whose rounded edges melded into the wall, as though they were not related to each other but were distinct offspring of the villa, the doctor stopped, just as the man, on the verge of closing the door, was thinking he had made a mistake.

"Look," the doctor said, clearing her throat. "I don't want to give you any false hopes over an improvement in your mother's condition, but I do think it would be better if she were transferred to a private clinic. You see—"

"Thank you for your opinion, Doctor," he said, cutting her off.

"The problem is . . ." she pushed on, undaunted though a little uneasy, with the unstoppable force of someone who has procrastinated for too long. "It isn't just my opinion, you see. We have discussed this in the hospital with the head of department and a psychologist. Your mother requires constant care and qualified assistance . . ."

"Thank you. I will think about it."

"Just a moment, no, don't close the door just yet," said the woman going back up the steps a mild threat in the tense muscles of the hand she stretched out to stop the door from closing. She was determined to make him listen, politely of course.

The man noticed a slight smear of red lipstick at the corner of the woman's mouth.

"There is a wonderful opportunity," the doctor

62

insisted. "A room will be available in a few days. It's fully equipped, television, telephone, air-conditioning . . ."

"I don't believe the matter interests me."

"Well, I must tell you, and these aren't my words, the head of department told me that in certain situations we have to . . . we have to act firmly. I'm sorry, but your house . . . this villa . . . this villa is not exactly the ideal place for a woman in your mother's condition. A health inspector . . . if someone were to make a complaint . . . well, an inspector might decide to oblige you to hospitalize your mother, given the state of . . . I mean, the extent of the decay . . . with all due respect."

When she was nervous, the doctor's tongue tended to dart to the side of her mouth and the man understood how the smear of lipstick had got there.

"Think of your mother's needs," she began again, chidingly. "Even if you hired a full-time nurse, day and night, there are situations even the most experienced nurse couldn't handle on her own. Moreover, the patient's mental health is vital for good recovery. Please don't let this opportunity pass. It's a wonderful room, I promise you. And you could visit your mother at any time . . . What do you say?"

The man absorbed the threat of a visit from the health inspector without batting an eyelid. His heart beat a little faster for a moment, nothing that an observer would have noticed. The month before, alone in the big cold house, without his mother, rushed to hospital with a stroke, he had felt free at first, a sensation of lightness. But then a feeling of imminent danger wound its way through the rooms along with the smell of his stuffed animals. He had listened to this feeling at night, in the dark, huddled up in bed like a child. He had felt it come into his bedroom and snake its way under the blankets, work itself between his legs and coil up, poisonous and relaxed, on his soft stomach. It was a pleasant feeling of danger, so pleasant that he had reached out his hand, not thinking about what it brought with it, to caress that sensation, which had lashed out and bitten him and then kissed him. He had rushed to the hospital, signed the papers and taken his mother home. That same night his mother's grey eyes, the eyes he had not inherited, eyes that everyone found cold but that were simply inscrutable, alive, harsh and noble, like the harsh and noble lines of her face, that same night those severe, immobile eyes had watched over and protected him. They had kept the fear and the danger and the pleasure at bay.

"And when would it be free?" he asked.

"From Saturday. We could take your mother in on Sunday morning," replied the doctor. "I'm glad you are giving the matter proper attention. It's for the good of your mother."

"Of course."

"Well, I'll be back again this evening."

"Yes. Until this evening."

"You will remember to massage that vein, won't you? Goodbye."

The woman rattled a bunch of keys free from her bag. Her car was parked on the gravel in front of the main entrance. The patch had once been bordered by a laurel hedge. Left to their own devices, the plants had thrust untidily towards the heavens, trying to outgrow each other, long since losing the graceful lines bestowed on them by careful gardening.

The man closed the door and darkness reclaimed the hall. He observed the doctor through a small, shutterless window, covered by an intricate wrought-iron grate. After she had started the engine, the woman

64

checked herself in the rear-view mirror, noticed the lipstick smear, wiped it away with the corner of a paper tissue, took a shiny metal cylinder from her bag, pushed up the lipstick and filled the gap left by her cleaning. Then she drove off. The man shuddered.

He went back up the stairs to the wing of the villa that he and his mother had chosen for their private apartment when their home had been turned into an orphanage. His ancestors stared down from their mildewed portraits. The lacklustre arabesque handrail uncurled half-heartedly under his fingers. The peeling varnish had puckered in places, forming blisters that exploded at the slightest touch.

His mother was waiting for him in her usual place, the drip needle stuck in her arm, sitting in her satin-covered chair, the one she had always liked best. But she wouldn't always be there to wait for him, according to that doctor. She would have to go back into a bright hospital room, where she would be surrounded by nurses and doctors who would look after her better than he. The old woman's eyes would have accused him of being useless, as they had always done. And inadequate, as he had always felt. Her gaze would have reminded him of his weakness and his weakness would have shouted for joy, because no one would have been there to hold it in check.

He went into the room. His mother looked younger in the dim light. The way he remembered her. Her bony face, the skin stretched taut on sharp cheekbones, the thin limbs, like a boy's, although nothing about the woman would allow one to think that youth had lingered any longer than nature required on that bony, angular form, and perhaps even less. He thought he caught a slight tremor in her pupils when he coughed to announce his presence. Nothing else. She was as still as a doll. And as cold and smooth to the touch as a doll. He leaned on the armchair, standing behind her, and hugged the satin and the inlaid cherrywood as if he were hugging his mother. There had never been that kind of intimacy between them. She had always found physical contact to be vulgar, as it reminded her of her husband. The armchair tipped back slightly. As the old woman's eyelids closed, the thin lashes that he never forgot to put mascara on fluttered. He unentwined himself from this strange embrace and let the chair return to its upright position. Her eyes opened, with difficulty, like a doll's.

Then he took a seat and a small writing desk and sat down in front of his mother. He covered the desk with sheets of paper and books and began to study under the old woman's vitreous, impassive gaze.

"Mother," he said, looking up from his books. "I think you'll have to go back into hospital."

Once again an almost imperceptible, but this time threatening, movement of her pupils. He perceived it as a ripple in the air because he simply didn't have the courage to sustain his mother's gaze. His own eyes travelled the length of the rubber tube that linked the purple vein to the bottle above the armchair. Up and down. Up and down. The blurred image of his mother receded, without losing any of the terror it exercised on the man's mind. It became as big as a plaster doll that they both remembered perfectly well, even if the doll had stubby, fragile fingers, frizzy blond hair that fell about its plump, expressionless oval face, and velvet clothes under which fluttered delicate lace petticoats. The plaster doll that had once sat in his mother's chair, as though it were saving her place for her while she scurried after the administration and the organization of the orphanage. The same doll that, come evening, after dinner, would sit in the exhausted woman's arms, as though it were her only source of comfort. The cruel doll that watched over him while he studied, or when he was punished, isolated within his own isolation, because he had been a wicked child, or had thought wicked thoughts, or had spied on the orphans as they played in the garden and yearned to be with them. "Serves you right," the doll would say to him, silently, with her blue glass eyes. "Mother prefers a plaster doll to you, made from flesh and blood." His mother had so much to do, she couldn't keep her eye on him all the time. "I see you through her eyes. You watch out or she'll come and tell me," his mother had threatened, putting the doll down beside him on his desk. Upright, rigid, its splayed legs revealing the lace undergarments, the lids that would close, hiding its eyes, each time it was tipped back or forward. He was so deeply intimidated by that doll that for the longest time he had been afraid to touch it, even though he ardently desired to throw it out the window, torture it, smash it into a thousand pieces. But as soon as such a thought dawned in his ever alert brain he convinced himself that the doll knew what he was thinking, could read his mind, would spy on him and denounce his wicked intentions. So he tried as hard as he could to banish the thoughts that would have led his mother to love him even less. Indecent thoughts that should never have crossed his mind. The doll's eyelids, those thought thieves, opened and closed, opened and closed, opened and closed.

And she did tell you everything, he thought to himself. Then, responding to an old reflex, he massaged what remained of the little finger on his left hand, even though at that moment he hadn't felt the familiar prickling sensation that he had been living with for years. In his heart of hearts he had always known that the doll would betray him. Dolls were evil.

"I have to leave you on your own for a little while," he said to the old woman as he got up.

He could no longer bear her gaze, constantly upon him no matter where he was. And he was afraid that she could read his thoughts even more clearly now that she had become as immobile as the doll, as severe yet just as violable as the doll, her inert legs spreading to reveal her underwear when he put her to bed, the eyelids that rolled up and down, the cold skin slippery as chalk, the age-hardened nipples that puckered the fold of her nightdress, and that he might have been attached to forty years ago.

"I'll be back soon," he told her.

The drip bottle was still half full.

"I'll be back soon."

Weak, from a weakness he could not overcome and that soiled him, he left the room and headed down the cold corridor. The dormitory was on the second floor. Now that the villa was no longer used as an orphanage, each of those rusting berths was occupied by one or two of the stuffed animals, to which the man had given names, and with which, trying to remain undiscovered by his mother, he spent long hours talking, hidden. Those animals spoke the same language as the orphans, and like the orphans they had a pathetic little story to tell, and each and every one of them adored him and waited impatiently for that time of day when he would come up to play. He took a bunch of keys out from behind a grandfather clock and made his way upstairs. His stuffed friends were waiting to comfort him, to give him what no one else had ever given him.

In the past few days they had told him a new story,

they had shown him a new path. The light. A thin red line. They didn't judge him; they didn't think he was wicked. The thin red line outlined a marvellous design. His salvation.

Already grateful, he opened the door.

VI

Chief Inspector Giacomo Amaldi turned into a dark alley in the old town, after switching off his pager. He needed to be on his own. To think.

"I'm tired," he had told Frese that morning, and was astounded to realize just how true the words rang.

The street surface was wet and slippery, uneven, covered in litter. But not because of the rubbish strike. The old town had always been that dirty. The walls of the houses he leaned against to keep himself steady on his way downhill were just as damp as the street, the plaster crumbled into dust and stuck to his palms. Poor man's talc, they called it down at the port. In that gloom in the middle of the day Amaldi stopped in front of a green door with a brass knocker that hung painfully crooked, frozen in the act of snapping off. He leaned his forehead against the door, looking for something he feared he had lost. Frightened by the tiredness that cast shadows on his mission. He heard someone shuffling behind the door and then it opened. Amaldi tensed, as if he expected to see a ghost.

"Looking for me, love?" asked the smiling woman who might have been around fifty years old. A prostitute.

The client who was on his way out looked down guiltily at the ground, mumbled goodbye and vanished.

"No, I . . ." began Amaldi.

"Shy, are you? Come inside and I'll get you a coffee

". . . and maybe something else . . ." The woman winked.

The inspector went inside the apartment, darker than the street.

"You'll have to wait a bit, love," said the woman, pulling her nylon negligée about her. "I need a coffee. Do you mind?"

"No, no . . ." managed Amaldi.

"Good. Sit yourself down there, then." And she pointed at a tiny, windowless room.

Amaldi sank into a worn ribbed green velvet armchair. He rubbed his plaster-covered palm on the arm of the chair. The room was like a burial cell, low and narrow and, apart from the armchair, there was only room for another rickety chair. The darkness smelled of impatient men. Underfoot, on the sticky, wrinkled linoleum, he could feel a rolled up magazine. He didn't bend down to pick it up. He breathed in that air heavy with the smell of condoms and stimulating creams. The scent of love, he thought. He didn't know the prostitute, but he did know the little apartment. And the smell, the one and only time he had set foot there, had been exactly the same. Nothing had changed in twenty years.

"Here I am," announced the prostitute, appearing.

Amaldi stood up.

"I'm sorry, there's been a misunderstanding," he said.

"And what might that be?" asked the woman, immediately on the defensive.

"Many years ago I knew someone who lived here."

"A pro?" said the woman, opening her negligée with an expert flourish to reveal a red bra with holes around her nipples. The openings were edged with lace. She smiled, placed her teaspoon in her mouth and sucked on it, winking. Then she rubbed the spoon between her legs. Her knickers were also red and there was a split for easy access.

"I just wanted to see the apartment," said Amaldi.

"Can't get it up?" The prostitute was becoming aggressive.

"I have to go. I'm sorry. I didn't mean to waste your time."

"Are you queer?" The woman called after him, following him out of the door.

Amaldi sped up, without answering her as if he were trying to outdistance the feeling of pain that had suddenly begun to smother him. The more the pain grew, the stronger he felt. He was finding his path again. A path he believed he had lost some time ago. He broke into a run. He ran as he had done until a few months earlier when that question had begun to buzz around in his head. A question he hadn't wanted to answer. But now he knew he had done it. He knew he had resurrected a body that had never been buried. Once again. That was why he had gone into the old town. To find out something he already knew. Certainly not to screw some prostitute. The pain he couldn't shake off, the pain he had been feeling for twenty years, made him feel safe again. Protected. No, he wouldn't forget. He had promised. He would never forget. He didn't care if his colleagues called him "the Crusader". He wasn't like them. Being a policeman wasn't a job to him. It was a mission.

He came to a halt when he reached the boundary between the old town and the rest of the city. Two people coming out of the shop where he had stopped bumped into him. Amaldi paid no heed. He heard them apologize. He didn't respond. He started walking again.

"Just what are they going to do? It's blackmail, pure and simple," one of the pair was saying.

"I don't care what they do, as long as they call off their shitty strike," said the other, and kicked a bag of rubbish out of the way.

Amaldi turned to look at them. He could no longer hear their words. He saw them gesticulating, absorbed in their invective against the strike. The bag flew into the road and was reduced to shreds under the wheels of a car. Inside the vehicle, the driver also started gesticulating, all by himself.

Head down, Amaldi ploughed on through the space before him. His mind had started working again. When he raised his eyes he noticed he had wandered into the new part of town. Huge tower blocks with no past, no smell, no rancour or wealth or poverty. On the drawing board the white of the limestone blocks had been intended to dominate. Now, just a few decades after the apartments had been built, white had proved to be an uninspired visual investment and over the years had been replaced by grey. Not a brooding grey full of character; just a bland, flat, modest grey, apparently rather shy, more a faded non-colour than anything else. It didn't rob your breathe but nor did it leave enough air. A featureless grey that filtered light, without ever reflecting it, in a state of listless confusion, without will or desire. And that was how the world appeared to Inspector Giacomo Amaldi. Just like the people in it. Everything surviving without dying. Everything vegetating without a heart beating inside the breast of the phoney city. The days of every human being were controlled by an inertial impulse. Everyone rolled forward together. Sometimes in an orderly way.

A few hundred yards further on the hospital rose up. In one of those rooms a cop lay dying of cancer. To go and comfort him, make him feel he was part of one big happy family, that the chiefs knew about and were very saddened by his grave situation: that was what they wanted from Giacomo Amaldi. Even though he couldn't remember what the policeman looked like. Even though he couldn't even remember the man's name.

The hospital stood out amongst the tower blocks. It was made of the same limestone as the tower blocks, cracked, grey and porous, and from its enormous, vulgar outline the entrance canopy thrust out into the road. Above the entrance huge letters lit up in neon at night spelled out the hospital's name. Tired, Amaldi started moving off in the opposite direction. He hadn't joined the Force to comfort the terminally ill. His talent was tracking down homicidal maniacs. That was his mission. That was all he had done for the last twenty years, even while he pretended to be busy chasing bag-snatchers and car thieves. He was especially interested in men who killed women. That was why he hadn't thrown away the fax that referred to what the papers were already calling the "Rice Fields Massacre". He had caught the scent of a maniac, and was sure he was on the right track.

The local police had a theory that it was just someone settling scores with the old peeping Tom, who had previous convictions and most definitely a very dubious circle of friends. A punishment killing, in other words. The other hypothesis was a jealous ex-boyfriend in the throes of some generic homicidal fit. They were on the wrong track. Amaldi knew it. He had known it immediately. He couldn't absolutely rule out premeditation, or that it was someone who knew the victims. But jealousy and settling old scores had nothing to do with it. He hadn't been to the crime scene but the reports he had obtained from the investigating officer on the flimsy pretext of comparing the case with a crime he had invented on the spot were very detailed. The weapon lent support to a premeditated act: it wasn't an ordinary hunting gun. The pellets were heavier than usual. Hunters shot their prey with a view to displaying the animals later. Those pellets would have reduced any animal, bird or rabbit, to pulp. Just a shapeless, bloody mess. Thus, technically, the killer wasn't a hunter. Amaldi, following his instinct, was convinced that the incident had been some kind of general rehearsal. This killer liked killing. The first shot had been for the young man. Dead on the spot. They had found the cartridge in the water and it was clear to Amaldi that the killer couldn't have cared less about the boy. Which was why he ruled out jealousy. Then he must have set to work on the old man. The body had four gunshot wounds. The fatal shot to the heart was presumably the last one fired. Amaldi agreed with the police reconstruction. The first shot had hit him in the side, while his back was turned. There was a trail of blood that showed he had tried to save himself, dragging himself along the grass, after he had been hit. But he hadn't been killed because he had been a witness to the other crime, to the youth's murder. Otherwise the killer would have just shot him through the heart and had done with it. He must have come closer because he was attracted by something and he was thinking about that something as he reloaded. And that was the second shot. The fact that the killer had shot the man in the groin, at close range according to Ballistics, showed vicious intent. The intent to wipe out a part of the man's anatomy. Probably because it was indecent. This was the basis of the score-settling theory and it was reasonably convincing, upon first analysis. The old man was missing much of one hand. According to the local police, the old man had lost his hand by chance because he had instinctively covered his groin when the killer had fired. But the more Amaldi thought about it, the more convinced he became that things had gone differently. The killer may well have ordered the old man to cover his penis with his hand and then shot him. That might be it. The man was clearly a sadist. But however the scene had played out, the score-settling theory still held up. Amaldi was certain the old man had been the first to attract the killer's attention. He had directed all his rage at the peeping Tom. The inspector just didn't know why, yet.

He had tried talking to Frese about the case again that morning. But the deputy inspector didn't hold with being called upon in that way. Everyone should mind their own business, take care of their own affairs. That was his philosophy. Amaldi had half an idea that Frese was simply trying to dissuade him from carrying on because he was concerned about him. They weren't friends, but Frese knew him better than anyone else. That was why he could get away with pronouncing the word "obsession". Amaldi wouldn't have let anyone else do that. But Amaldi had a vocation, not an obsession. Mission, promise, character. Not obsession. Even though, with his degree in psychology, if he had had a personal file on someone like himself in front of him, Amaldi would probably have assessed the man as an obsessive. And for that matter he would probably have recommended suspending the officer from duty. But he might have been wrong. What did an assessment file say anyway? What could you learn from a few hasty interviews? According to official criteria, it was an obsessive way to behave, but normality is an abstract notion, the ephemeral result of calculations based on statistics. The only thing of any real value was the individual, beyond any terms of comparison. Assessed in all his inalienable wholeness, the sum of experiences that were irreproducible because the possible combinations were infinite. Of course, it was a dangerous line of reasoning, he knew that. It could be extended to include the maniacs he hunted. But the difference was blatantly obvious: he had never deliberately sought to hurt anyone. Apart from that youth who used to rape women in hallways. Amaldi had shot him. In the knee. While he was assaulting his seventh victim. And not in the head, as he would have wanted. The youth was crippled. Amaldi had not carried a gun since that day. But none of them had gone through what he had. None of them knew what it was to see a girl like a sack.

He shook himself out of his maudlin wallowing and walked towards his office. He remembered to switch his pager back on and his mind returned to the Rice Fields Massacre. He was convinced that something about the old man had set the killer off. The way the man had been so savagely shot showed a desire to wipe him out. Maybe it was something from the man's past, or maybe not. The killer might even have been some religious fanatic. He could have been anyone and have done it for any reason. But Amaldi was certain that it wasn't just a matter of score-settling, because of what, in all likelihood, had happened next. The killer had noticed the girl with the wounded breast. The coroner's report referred to significant mutilation. The girl's blood was found in only one spot on the jetty, which meant she hadn't moved. She hadn't fled. Why? Perhaps she had fainted. Unlikely, given the amount of adrenaline in her veins. But she could have fainted. Or maybe she was scared stiff from shock. In either case she had let the killer approach her. Did she know him? It was possible. She hadn't run away, because she knew the man. Amaldi's instinct told him that things had not happened that way, but he didn't reject anything on principle. That wasn't the point. His policeman's senses hadn't been alerted by the slaughter in and of itself. There were dozens of deaths every day. But this madman – and Amaldi didn't know how else to describe him – had bandaged the girl's wound. And before that he had cleaned it and staunched the blood. They had found a piece of blanket that was caked in blood and breast tissue. He had put her breast *back in place*. That was what he had done, just before smashing her skull with a blunt object. Why hadn't he shot her like the other two? Much quicker, more practical. Run out of ammunition? Unlikely. Not enough time? Impossible; he had taken all the time he needed. Time for that man, for the whole world, had come to a standstill until he had put the girl's breast *back in place*. And in Amaldi's view that proved the man was completely unbalanced. It meant that the man had chanced upon his true nature, had plumbed his own depths. The majority of people believed that madness was concentrated in one brutal act. It was more often the contrary. Fits of homicidal mania actually occurred quite often, and rather easily. Man's psyche had not been designed to disregard his animal instincts, to resist his aggressive impulses, for ever. Anyone could commit a crime. Or slaughter. It was, after all, the same instinct that might drive a different person to throw himself out a window. But to tidy things up, sort them out, now there was a signal that should have made any policeman's skin crawl. The killer had put the girl's breast *back in place*. The countdown had started. It was like the first germ in a sickness. The body had been infected and there was no antidote to fend off the disease. Years might pass, and he might forget the dead people, but the man would put all the pieces back together. He would remember only that act, a kindness really, the fact that he had put the girl's breast back together again. And who knew where it would go from there?

"Are you sure he's going to come?" he heard a female voice asking as he went through the armour-plated door into district headquarters, his head down as usual. "It's just that I've got a lesson at the university soon . . . Oh, hello, Inspector."

Amaldi squinted and turned to look at a dim corner where members of the public were made to wait. He recognized her at once, even before the cold fluorescent light hanging overhead in the hall had revealed her face, before she had got up from the hard seat in the dark corner that was laid out deliberately to be oppressive and uncomfortable in order to deter time-wasters. Her name sprang into his mind from the Post-it note on which he had written it a few days earlier. Giuditta held out her hand at the very moment that Amaldi was picturing the many prints the killer had left on the girl's body. Fingertips soaked in blood. Dark red, sticky prints. He couldn't bring himself to shake Giuditta's hand. He was displeased to see the girl's expression become serious as her smile wilted. But he just couldn't touch her at that moment. He would have contaminated her if he had. He couldn't have touched another human being after what he had been thinking.

Giuditta had already been there for over an hour, ignoring the polite but persistent suggestions from the policeman on the other side of the bullet-proof glass, who had tried to dissuade her from waiting for Amaldi, while she fidgeted in that uncomfortable chair, trying to hide the long legs that the same cop hadn't stopped stealing glances at. Rather than calming her down, the long wait had only served to increase her anxious rage. She had twisted her hands until they hurt, tried to read a book and then a magazine in an effort to pass the time, but the place where they had told her to sit was dark. Finally, she had gone through her bag, looking for heaven knew what, she didn't even know herself, and her hand had chanced upon the rough rectangle of her tape recorder. She had snatched her hand back out of the bag with such exaggeration that the policeman on the other side of the glass had actually stopped his embarrassing contemplation of her legs. She had smiled at him while she seethed, feeling soiled once more.

The day before, back home and seated at her desk, she had turned on the recording of the anthropology lesson in order to write up some notes. But towards the end, at the point she remembered having turned off the recording, the cassette had carried on. A whisper, obscene words, the meticulous description of even more obscene acts, which, the voice promised, would soon become reality. Giuditta had sat completely still, incapable of interrupting the flow of noise. Powerless. And that had made her feel all the worse, once the tape had come to a halt. She couldn't even push a button, she had said to herself, furiously. The voice carried on buzzing in her head and did not stop even after she had gone to bed, huddled up on the sofa-bed that she could open out only after her father had finished watching television. And then, as sleep finally rolled over her, and the noise of the drunks in the streets of the old town got louder and louder, as they shouted their solitude, Giuditta had thought again about the detective she had met a few days earlier, when she had gone to file a complaint for harassment against persons unknown. Without saying anything in particular, the man had comforted her. His expression had struck her. Hard and resolute. But also sullen, on closer examination. Despite the first signs of grey creeping into his temples, barely visible in his proud head of thick fair hair, Giuditta had sensed a childlike purity in the man. A serious child one could rely on. Giuditta had even had the curious feeling that the man had wanted to take her hands in his. And she would have let him. She would have entrusted herself to him without a moment's hesitation, without fear of being dirtied.

"I filed a complaint for harassment a few days ago . . ." she said.

And now he didn't even shake her hand.

"I remember you. Giuditta Luzzatto," Amaldi interrupted her, trying to smile in as friendly a way as possible. "You must forgive me, I was lost in thought . . . What can we do for you?" he asked. "What can I do for you?"

Giuditta rather liked the sound of that *I*. It seemed to go beyond his role, beyond his work, it was something personal. She took a good look at him and remembered thinking that the inspector was quite attractive. The strong, square jaw, the fair eyebrows, the sharp nose, like the sharp cheekbones under taut, tanned skin. His eyes were of some indefinable colour, with dark shadows below and slightly drooping lids above that gave him the appearance of a boxer, tired and sore. All you had to do was get behind that aloof air he affected. She realized she was blushing. Yes, she did find him attractive. She continued to think the same thing as he gently guided her towards the lift, obviously taking pains not to touch her. He had the grace of a cat. Even though he was tall and muscular, he gave

81

the impression that, just like a cat, he would be able to make himself thin so he could get into narrow spaces, spurred by the need to hide or to track down his prey. His movements were delicate but there was the feeling that beneath the apparent indolence muscles, nerves and tendons would contract with the speed of lightning, ready to leap over impossible obstacles or to lash out. Giuditta observed the man more closely and became convinced that he had a cat's knack for smoothing out the world's rough edges, for transforming even the most impractical of surfaces into a springboard from which to leap, or solid ground upon which to land. His leather shoes didn't squeak. With each padded footfall, Amaldi's shoes seemed to produce a cushion of air that made his velvet steps all the softer. He glided. He dominated without ostentation. His senses were alert, while he pretended to be distracted.

She studied him, looking for a wedding ring, and for a moment she was mesmerized by those slim, sensitive fingers, on hands that were delicate without being feminine, full of a strength that didn't disturb her. She examined him while following a hint that told her something about the private life of Inspector Giacomo Amaldi, quite forgetting that she didn't like lifts, especially if they were the modern kind, small and suffocating like the one she was in at the moment.

"Please, take a seat," said Amaldi and pointed to the swivel chair in his office. Then he went round to the other side of his desk and sat down.

The girl was red in the face. She must have been quite shy. A pretty girl. Amaldi liked her. He had been attracted to her immediately, which didn't happen very often. But now, before him, in the cold intimacy of his office, he put it down to his tiredness. He didn't really like the girl, he told himself, he was simply attracted to the idea of dropping everything, of ceasing to run after his pain and his promise. The girl was just a distraction he had invented to bring himself to a halt.

"Now, tell me everything from the beginning," he said, in a detached tone.

While Giuditta told him what had happened she saw something she didn't like. The inspector was no longer the warm, protective figure she had sensed during their first, chance, encounter. Nor was he the kind man who had accompanied her into his office. All of a sudden he had become cold. She hurried to the end of her story and stood up.

"I'm sorry to bother you with this nonsense . . ."

Amaldi sprang up.

"Sit down, please."

As she took her place in the swivel chair Giuditta found him again. Behind the icy glaze she caught sight again of that warm, childlike expression that had first attracted her. Amaldi sat down too. Giuditta propped her elbows on his desk and leaned forward, invading the space that separated her from the policeman, casually stretching her arms towards his side of the desk.

Amaldi pulled his chair closer and just as casually leaned on the desk. Their hands were quite close together. They were quite close to one another. Their hands remained still, separated by a few inches.

"You are sure it couldn't have happened somewhere else?" the inspector asked her.

"No, in the background you can hear the voices of other students talking about the lecture."

"Ah, yes . . ."

"Yes . . ."

"Yes, that must be what happened . . ."

Giuditta believed she knew how to appraise people

and was convinced she could understand what they felt. Her instinct said clearly that Inspector Amaldi was not the type of person who forgot things, details such as the voices of other students in the background, for instance. Maybe it was a police technique. They pretended to be distracted, their minds elsewhere, in order to encourage witnesses to remember, to make them talk. It could be anything, but she knew they were both talking about her harasser just to stay together. As though she didn't want to go, and he didn't want to let her leave.

"So it is possible to suppose that one of the other students might have seen whoever it was who recorded that message," said Amaldi.

"Yes . . ." replied Giuditta, suddenly realizing that she could have identified her stalker and put an end to the torture. "Maybe, but there's always so much going on in class . . ."

"It's worth trying," insisted Amaldi.

Giuditta had a fleshy mouth. Naturally full, thought Amaldi. A mouth that smiled often. And big white teeth, the kind he had always liked. The upper lip had tiny lines that would become deeper with age. Amaldi imagined caressing those lips. In his imagination Giuditta laughed in amusement while she squeezed her myopic grey eyes with their unusual shape, elongated, with the lids pulled slightly downwards in the middle, towards her nose, which gave her a rather melancholy air even when she wasn't. Surprised at these thoughts he imagined he caught the girl moving her hand ever so slightly towards his. He suddenly straightened up.

At the same instant there was a knock and Frese, without waiting for permission, put his head round the door. "Ah, you're here."

84

Giuditta also stiffened on the swivel chair.

"Interrupting anything?" asked Frese, taking a long look at Giuditta.

"No," said the girl.

"No" said Amaldi, getting to his feet.

"I'm sorry," stammered Giuditta, realizing that the question had been directed at the inspector. She stood up.

Frese came up to her shoulder. He instinctively took a step back.

"Well," Amaldi said to Giuditta. "I'll make those inquiries and then I'll get back to you . . ."

"Let me give you my home number . . . if you want."

"I'm sure we have it in the file. But it might be a good idea . . ."

"Do you have a pen?"

Frese handed her a pen, keeping his eye on Amaldi. The inspector avoided his gaze.

"Where would you like me to write it?"

Amaldi passed her a little yellow pad.

After she had written down her number Giuditta did not hold out her hand.

"Goodbye," she said to Frese, without shaking his hand either, and left.

"Wait here," Amaldi said to his deputy as he scribbled something on another Post-it before rushing out of the office. He reached the lift but didn't see Giuditta. Then he heard noises in the stairwell. He leaned over the balustrade and caught sight of the long legs.

"Miss Luzzatto," he called.

Her head appeared in the stairwell, her straight hair falling into empty space. Amaldi caught up with her.

"If you need anything you can reach me here . . . just in case . . . This is my direct line, this is my pager, and this is my home number. I mean, I usually forget to turn on the pager, so . . ."

"Thank you," she said, and Amaldi had the impression that the girl caressed the note.

"Goodbye."

"Goodbye."

Amaldi reached out his hand.

Giuditta took it in hers with a grateful look on her face. She didn't know why she thought it, but she had the distinct impression that he had just made some enormous effort.

Her skin was soft and warm, thought Amaldi. Then he turned and disappeared up the stairs.

Giuditta left, too, smiling.

"Since when do senior detectives from Serious Crime take care of that kind of trivial crap?" Frese asked Amaldi as soon as he returned to his office. "You know what I would do with a girl with tits like that?" he carried on.

"Did you have something urgent to tell me?" Amaldi interrupted his deputy.

Frese shook his head, spread his arms and dropped heavily into the swivel chair. He gave a little bleat of pleasure.

"Marvellous. I can still feel her warm arse just here," he joked.

Amaldi turned an icy gaze on him.

"Well?"

"I've found one of the documents missing from the orphanage file. And do you know where? In Augusto Ajaccio's personal file."

"Who?" Amaldi asked, only half listening. He couldn't believe what he had just done. He had given his home phone number to a girl he didn't know. She was probably some hysteric who would torture him with phone calls to tell him about the mystery wanker's latest exploits.

"Ajaccio. The poor guy who's dying of cancer. Have you been to see him, by the way?"

"Yes," lied Amaldi.

VII

"He hasn't been?" Frese asked Augusto Ajaccio. "You're sure?"

"Yes."

"Yesterday?"

"No."

Frese scratched his head then mechanically brushed off his shoulders and cleaned his nails.

"Suffer from dandruff?" he asked Ajaccio.

"No, not from that."

"Oh shit, Ajaccio," grunted Frese. "I'm sorry."

"It doesn't matter . . ."

"No, really, I'm sorry. What a dickhead." He thumped himself on one of his squat thighs and got up from the Formica and metal chair.

"It doesn't matter, Detective."

"Frese, call me Frese."

"Yes . . ."

"Nice view you've got from here," said Frese, standing by the window and trying to change the subject.

"Ah yes. I can give very accurate bulletins on the state of the mounting heap of rubbish . . ."

"The sea, Ajaccio. I can see the sea."

"It's not the sea. It's just the harbour. That's filthy too."

"They don't carry it up in a bucket from the sewers, you know. The harbour water comes from the sea, too."

"You know how inviting a nice roast chicken can be in a delicatessen's window? The aroma of the roast meat, that crispy, shiny skin, the rosemary, those lovely crunchy potatoes. Can you picture it, Detective?"

"Call me Frese, Ajaccio."

"The next day it's in some rubbish bag. Cartilage, pale skin, a few bones with a bit of black gristle still attached to them ... a foul smell ... You wouldn't touch it for anything in the world, right? Is it the same chicken, Detective?"

"For Christ's sake, call me Frese."

Augusto Ajaccio rolled over, turning his back on the window that overlooked a world he had never understood, which he had never been part of. Silence filled the room. Frese had gone to see him to find out if he had the slightest idea why the missing document about the orphanage fire had found its way into his file. He didn't expect any answers. It was certainly strange, though, finding that document in an orphan's file. The only orphan cop on the Force, as far as Frese knew. An orphan who had grown up in that orphanage and survived that fire. But what would Ajaccio know about it anyway? Frese looked at the strong back of a man condemned to die at fifty-two years of age. He was only three years older than Frese himself. "Shit happens," he had said when he had first heard. But things were different now he was there in that room. And perhaps he hadn't come about that document after all, Frese thought, perhaps he was there to see just what the death he feared so much looked like. Yes, being there certainly made things different. And Ajaccio was different from what he remembered, too. Different from the man depicted in his personal file. This wasn't the same Ajaccio he had come across in the corridors back at the station, not the listless cop with the puffy, lifeless eyes he sometimes bumped into at the bar at lunch time.

"I'm tired," said Ajaccio. "I'm tired and I'm cold."

"Pull the covers up. Want me to do it for you?" And without waiting for an answer, he went over to the bed and covered him. He noticed that a pale purple mark curled out from under the collar of Ajaccio's pyjama top and licked up the length of his neck. Like a tongue. It was a burn mark, an old and striking burn mark

Ajaccio closed his eyes. He was thinking about what had happened to him that morning. Lying in bed, he had caught himself emerging from a sickening vortex caused by the massive doses of medication they gave him. He had had the distinct impression that his tongue was thicker. There had been a bitter taste in his mouth. He had shaken his head to clear the fog from his dazed brain. The muscles in his neck hurt. How long had he been asleep? He had sat up. He had stretched out his arms, opened and closed his hands a number of times, then he had stopped, his breathing laboured, looking around himself, without recognizing anything, with the same feeling of being outside things, being cut off, as a traveller in a speeding train leaning against the window to look at the world on the other side of the glass. There, he had thought, I'm looking outside myself. But he still didn't know who he was or where he was. Then he had noticed that his head was expanding, that his thoughts were multiplying and increasing the size of his brain, that the bones in his skull were straining, and he had recognized his disease for what it was. Then everything had gone back to the way it had been and he had understood beyond a shadow of doubt that he was sick with cancer and that he was in the hospital.

He opened his eyes and noticed that Frese was staring at him as the tears welled up, unbidden, liberating. They streaked his cheeks and made his lips salty. The strong smell of incense filled his nostrils. He strained his ear to catch the mumble of some religious litany: maybe they were blessing the hospital.

Just at that moment the nurse came into the room. Ajaccio saw her as the air became thicker with the smoke and the scent of incense.

"Is everything all right, Mr Ajaccio?" asked the blonde nurse from the door, after she had smiled at Frese.

"What's this incense I can smell?" Ajaccio asked.

The nurse sniffed the air and then a thought flickered across her face. She looked at Frese. Just the briefest of glances that Ajaccio caught. The incense vanished. The air was clear and translucent. Frese and the nursed stared at each other, embarrassed. "Olfactory hallucinations," Ajaccio remembered.

Oh good God, he thought.

And the thing that was hurting him really hurt him for the first time.

"I was just joking," he said to the blonde nurse. She was pretty, her uniform tight across her bust.

The nurse smiled.

"I'm fine."

She studied him for a few seconds, hiding behind her pitying smile, then, throwing a last glance at Frese, she began to pull the door shut.

"I was only joking ..." Ajaccio whispered once again.

He remained still, pinned down by pain and shame.

He had been eighteen years old the first time he had smelled incense and twenty when he had smelled if for the last. He had never set foot in a church again. Maybe he had forgotten churches existed. And incense. If only he had known how to pray. But that was why he had left the seminary in the first place. Because he was neither stupid nor enlightened enough to trust his life to God. He simply didn't understand God, that was all.

His past, illuminated by this new intelligence that seemed to draw its force from the same disease that was going to destroy him, was unfolding before him. He slid effortlessly over it, without fatigue, without gasping for breath, on a wave of detached melancholy. His thoughts were shimmering wakes, streaking freely towards a future that was becoming ever darker. Those useless thoughts that all his life he had been incapable of thinking. Soon, they would be the only things left, as his body disintegrated.

"I've got to go now," said Frese, looking at his watch and returning the chair to its place against the wall. "Take care of yourself. I'll be back soon."

Ajaccio nodded, listlessly, and watched Frese leave. He saw the door open and close. He was alone. He continued to stare at the door. In the half-light he thought he could make out a tiny black spot. He felt drawn to it. He looked for his glasses in the drawer of the bedside cabinet. As he reached out his hand he realized the spot was a fly. It was thirteen feet away. It wasn't physically possible for him to see it so clearly at that distance, yet he could. The insect was rubbing its front limbs over its large eyes. Then it vibrated its transparent wings. Ajaccio sprang up. With unsteady steps he went towards the door and the fly buzzed away.

"It really was a fly," he said in amazement. "A fly cleaning itself thirteen feet away from me."

He leaned his shoulders against the door in an effort to regain the equilibrium that the surprise and the medication had taken from him. He checked the distance. Four shaky paces back to the bed. Unconvinced, he measured out four steps back to the door. The smell of incense returned and Ajaccio felt uneasy. He looked at the bed again, without focusing on anything in particular. As his nostrils flared the better to suck in the imaginary smell of incense, he noticed that his pillow case was puckered with wrinkles and that he could make out the edges of every one, every crest and trough and the shadow they threw onto the wall opposite the window. It wasn't logical. His vision just wasn't that acute. Even as a child. He rubbed his eyes and pinched his cheeks. Was he asleep? Was he dreaming? No. Four more steps and he slid under the covers. Warily, alert to the danger that wafted through the incense. An unknown danger that may well have been emanating from him.

Or perhaps he himself was transmuting into that danger.

Resting his head on the pillow he felt the folds of the fabric against his neck and scalp. The folds were hard, or seemed so to him. He closed his eyes for a moment and saw them: nine. Three of which branched off into just as many fading pleats. White dominated the image, but all the hues of grey were also there, and he could even distinguish on the far edges of the pillow a greenish reflection cast by the wall. If he pushed his vision further he could pick out the weave of the cotton.

He opened his eyes in fear. His heart was thumping and he felt as if he was suffocating. He panted, scrambling for his glass of water. What was happening to him? Had they drugged him? The back of his hand collided with the smooth surface of the glass, which began to topple over. But it fell in slow motion, clearly, because when he realized what was happening he had time to turn on his side, bend down and stop the glass's fall a few inches from the floor. His grip was firm. The water bounced on the marble floor and splintered into smooth, minuscule droplets that splashed his face. He remained in that position until his back muscles stiffened and began to hurt. He pulled himself up, drank what was left in the glass and placed it on top of the bedside cabinet. The sound of the glass against the white-flecked green Formica filled the room. He heard the walls absorb the vibrations and transmit them into the corridor.

He was assailed by a new wave of terror, he felt weak and was certain he was going to faint. He lay down and looked at the ceiling, making sure he didn't focus on anything in particular. He didn't feel like making any other discoveries.

"Help," he murmured.

Slowly, a vast tiredness forced him to relax his limbs, stretched tight with stupor. He believed he was falling asleep. He had the impression that the door opened again, but he couldn't care any more. His head was throbbing and transported him far away. Everything he perceived was now pale and indistinct, just as everything had been sharp and vivid a few moments before. There was a strange taste in his mouth. The taste of water. Sweet and unnatural. He also thought he heard a noise coming towards him. Like a shadow joining the other shadows. He tried to open his eyes but his lids were heavy, as if they were glued together. The darkness into which he was plunged became thick and almost palpable. And he was swimming in that darkness. No, he was floating, carried along on a slow current that made no waves. Then the colours exploded. Lights and dazzling flares. They passed by without touching him. He felt cold, as if he were naked. Weak. And a voice, which he could see in black and red ripples of sound in the darkness, began talking to him, first gently, then harshly, then gently again. But it was so far away that he couldn't make out individual words. It was nothing more than a familiar buzz, as though he were listening to the voice of his own thoughts. Another self, who talked to him without managing to communicate. It grew colder. His muscles didn't react. He didn't even shiver. Then he felt ants swarming over his chest. No, not ants. It was something bigger. Sometimes heavy, sometimes light. They left behind a wet, cold streak. And a smell that irritated his nostrils. Maybe they were snails. Fast snails. And the voice went on murmuring.

An hour later the nurse who came to check up on him found Ajaccio lying in bed. The covers were on the floor and his pyjama jacket was open.

Across his sallow chest there was an inscription in red: aUguSTo aJaCcIo.

The patient, quite unconscious, was clutching a red marker in his hand.

VIII

The man walked up the main avenue for the seventh time, following the flow of Sunday strollers as they walked under the porticos. It was late afternoon. The increasingly oblique sunlight cast long, thin shadows, barely warmed by the lilac hints of approaching evening.

It would soon be night. A blossoming of the darkness made all the more special because the man had an appointment. And a plan.

That morning he had signed his mother into a brightly lit room in the city hospital. He had stood observing the coming and going of the doctors and nurses, and had caught the sickly sweet aroma of medicines and the penetrating smell of disinfectants. And with feverish impatience he had sought out the suffering and the fear of dying in the eyes of the patients. But he couldn't leave immediately, he couldn't draw attention by acting strangely. The knowledge that he had a grand plan gave him an extraordinary gift. Before him, as his mother had always wanted, there unfurled a dazzling future. His solitude would be filled. The only price he had to pay was that of becoming anonymous. He had to learn to be invisible. Anyman. Even though he was exceptional. So, huddled in a corner of the room, he had recited his part, asking the doctors concerned questions and tolerating their ill-mannered condescension, their professional aloofness. But in a way he was grateful to that rotten tribe of medical workers because they had unwittingly and obtusely helped him feel small and invisible, insignificant and useless. That was the grandeur of his design: the whole world seemed to bend to his purpose. After no more than an hour he had felt ready. He had confidently crossed corridors and departments, following the map in his head, without drawing anyone's attention, without attracting a single glance. He had hugged the walls like a shadow. He had reached the first floor, gone into an operating theatre that had been carelessly left open, had gone through the drawers with easy efficiency and found what he needed. The scalpel, the surgical saw, the thick pencils surgeons sometimes used. He had stowed everything in his canvas bag, along with the curved suture needle, the quick-acting glue, the fish hooks, the tough twist thread, the nylon wire, and the green velvet ribbon. Then he had hidden the bag under his heavy herringbone grey coat that was neither too elegant nor too worn. In his pocket, preserved intact inside a rigid card envelope, three dry leaves.

He had felt invincible behind his new mask as Anyman. He had walked calmly towards the exit, like any other visitor, with his shoulders slightly bowed, as he pretended to carry with him the painful burden of a hospitalized friend or relative. At the door he had turned back, attracted by the squalor of the entrance. He had studied it as if he were seeing it for the first time. On either side, to the left and right, there was a little waiting room. The armchairs and sofas were in imitation tan leather that puckered round a huge button on the arms. The low tables were in a dull black plastic, their tops littered with tattered old magazines. Some had nothing more than their covers left. In the right-hand waiting room, a rug continued to fight the good fight, although it was curling up at the corners. The man sank into one of the armchairs. The stolen surgical instruments collided, producing a faint tinkle.

In front of him rose the imposing dark green marble counter, with black and ochre veins. A nurse emerged from behind it. The man looked at her. She was about fifty. Her straw-coloured hair, thin and greasy, with dark roots, was held back by a rather twee sky-blue ribbon that matched the colour of her clear, vacant eyes. Her hands fidgeted mechanically with a pen, with all the ease of someone used to repeating the gesture over and over again. Her nails were long, sharp and varnished silver. While she was busy answering the phone the woman studied her nails out of the corner of her eye. He was convinced that somewhere nearby, carefully hidden from public view, the nurse kept a full array of nail files, clippers, acetone and varnish. The man sucked in the profoundly human atmosphere that filled the air in the entrance to that vale of tears. Everything he had refused until then, everything his mother had forced him to reject, from that morning onwards would become his second nature. He closed his eyes and pretended to doze off. He concentrated on the sounds; on the odours the suffering hospital community trailed in its wake, as it went back and forth; on the snatches of conversation, most of which were about the rubbish-collectors' strike. From the moment he reopened his eyes, his imitation of Anyman was perfect.

Then he left.

He took a shapeless parcel from the boot of his car. It was about a foot wide and three feet long. The brown wrapping paper crunched faintly when he jammed the pack under his right arm. Then he walked off into the city.

Now that his metamorphosis was underway, like some great event, now that he was finally invisible and, growing, could savour his freedom, now that no one could point him out and hold him up to shame, he was not afraid to let himself be carried along and jostled by the river of people that it seemed would never reach the sea. Now he could do that. Waiting for the darkness that his deed would illuminate. Not one of the people walking a few feet from him had the remotest idea of what was happening, none of them saw the sickness as he did, hurtling through the city streets, crouching down by the overflowing litter bins, dancing in the ruins of the old opera house, skulking in dark alleys. And they didn't notice anything, because the sickness was sly, it knew how to hide itself from the eyes of men by showing itself to them, walking side by side with them, just like one of them, as visible and commonplace. But all the time acting, contaminating, spreading. And without worrying about good or evil, because in either case sickness had only one aim: to ensure that it fulfilled its destiny.

His life was now a design that already existed in the pencil and hand of the painter. His life was simple and straight like a long corridor. All he had to do was follow it to the end. It was just a question of time. And time, which he had to keep track of for practical reasons, was something that seemed to concern others more than him. Those, or she, who time was going to condemn. As for him, time flowed both slowly and quickly in step with the lengthening darkness that presaged the next step. Slowly because once decided the thing itself was already accomplished, or at least the most important part, the decision to do it, was already accomplished. Accepting the implicit grandeur of the plan. And that was why he wasn't in a hurry. Quickly, because a tiny part of him still resisted the decision and this resistance brought him closer to the moment of truth and of willingness in which he would have to consecrate himself in action, resolve himself in the moment of performing the deed. And as speed and slowness came together in a single feeling, all that he had left was a sensation of immobility in which it wasn't really he who was walking but, more likely, it was the city that rolled under his feet.

Thus, sliding by, the city had presented him with the store and destiny had handed him the antique-dealer.

He had seen her for the first time thirty-two years earlier, when she was a young storekeeper who enjoyed the trust of many of the city's patrician families, and he was an adolescent of twelve. His mother had received the woman in one of the rooms on the first floor. He had heard them exchange amiable banter, but there was a tense undertone to their convivial chatter. This had made him anxious and persuaded him to spy on them. The woman had examined some jewels with a rapacious eye and then she had gone round the room, touching and examining the furniture. The lady of the house wanted discreetly to get rid of some. He followed them from the shadows. He could only see them intermittently, to make sure he wasn't discovered, but he could clearly make out their footsteps. His mother's nervous tick-tack and the dealer's feigned bored shuffle. Once the inspection was finished the two women had gone back to the first-floor room, far from the prying ears of the nuns. The dealer had established a price for every item, without referring to the list the lady of the house had provided. From his observation point halfway up the stairs that led to the second floor, hidden behind a wrought-iron grill decorated with a gilded bronze Cupid, he had seen his mother's face harden, her eye's narrow to slits. She had said nothing to the antique-dealer, had not disputed the estimates. As an adult, the adolescent who had spied upon them had understood that that miserable offer was the price of discretion. Every stamp, every mark connected with the family, every heraldic sign would be erased. Every trace of the transaction would disappear, as if it had never happened, the dealer had assured his mother. The price of silence. When they said goodbye the two women looked transfigured. His mother was withered. The young antique-dealer spread radiant smiles around her, delighted by the deal she had just closed. Apart from two vulgar commas that curled from her ears down to her cheeks, her platinum-blond hair was bouffant. As she had stood up she had straightened her tight, pale green skirt that stopped just above the knee. She had quickly popped her index finger into her mouth, rubbed it against her thumb and leaned down to halt a run that was starting in her tights. As she had bent down, her soft white breast had pushed against the square neckline of her pink, sleeveless blouse. Then she had pulled on a short tight-waisted jacket, pale green like her skirt. She had opened her small, stiff light-coloured bag with a scarf tied to the handle, and had pulled out her cheque book and she had written out the figure she was going to pay the lady of the house. In an ill-controlled burst of euphoria, the antique-dealer had moved closer to Mrs Cascarino, as though to kiss her on the cheek. He had seen his mother pull back hastily and move to show the other woman out. She may have been young, but the antique-dealer had a flabby bottom that sagged against the material and zip of her skirt. As he watched her swing her hips, the adolescent had felt a sudden stabbing pain in the stump of the little finger of his left hand.

The recently sewn stitches were still encrusted with blood and the swollen, yellow stump pulsed painfully. But at least the infection was under control.

Thirty-two years later, as if he were really invisible, the man slipped into the antique-dealer's shop. The city was emptying. Stores were closing. People were heading home. He hid inside a nineteenth-century pantry cupboard that smelled of beeswax and placed his parcel on the ground without making the slightest noise. He waited, completely still, for at least ten minutes, reducing his breathing to the merest whisper that did not travel beyond the rough wooden sides of the cupboard. His heart boomed in his ears, slowly, calmly, marking out the slow seconds that passed by slowly and inexorably.

That afternoon he had spied on her for the last time through her shop window crowded with dusty items. He had watched her from behind a pillar blackened by the fumes of cars and distant factories, concentrating on the round arms, the plump hands that had enveloped his mother's and had signed the cheque given to Mrs Cascarino thirty-two years ago. He had stared at the sausage fingers pulled tight by the many old, gold-alloy rings that had once belonged to some family in distress. She was fifty-five years old now, hair still platinum blond, like before, with big curls. Her skin was fair, almost transparent. Her stupid eyes seemed made of glass. She was alone and wandered busily around the long, narrow store. The man had deduced that she was really more concerned about her advancing years and declining looks and she continually checked her appearance in the many mirrors on dressing tables and wardrobes. He surmised that she was the kind of woman who deliberately got a bit plumper with age, in order to smooth out her skin and keep wrinkles at bay. Her backside was flabbier than ever.

He had spied on her for a long time without knowing why. Finally he had understood the role the woman who had touched his mother was to have in the glorious plan he had to fulfil. A week had passed since his trip to the countryside, since his revelation. Since he had reached the certainty that chance played no part in his destiny. Every event was linked with the preceding event and the following event, by the precise will that he accomplish what it had been decided he accomplish, not a few days or months before, but since he had been born, because it was written that in the end a part of his blood would carry him finally to the path that had been reserved for him. The path that would have raised him out of the dark, malodorous hole into which he had been cast so that he might arise from it once more, cleaner than before. Stronger. More alone.

He heard the antique-dealer pull down the metal shutter, puffing as she bent down to the lock, and he imagined her white breast straining against her neckline, like all before. He waited until she turned off the lights and then came out of his hiding place.

Perhaps the woman saw in that shadow the face of a customer who had purchased a very special object from her years before, perhaps not. But when he was nearly upon her she certainly understood the glint in his eye. She understood at once what was going to happen and she stumbled backwards, her fat hands and varnished nails held up against her killer. She tried to escape but couldn't run, she didn't have the strength to run, and the man was upon her in an instant. He didn't run, either, because he knew he could have if it had been necessary. He took hold of her and turned her round. For a moment the two were clasped together, one pulling the other pushing, thrashing about in an unseemly and heavy-footed dance. They crushed each other's feet. And then her feet, anchored to the floor by her desire not to be snatched from life, were lifted up with the rest of her and the woman found herself seated upon an old chest of drawers.

"Hold still," snapped the man, giving orders to the staring eyes, the silent, gaping mouth, the muscles clamped rigid in fear.

Then he very calmly took down from the wall a seventeenth-century halberd with a rusty blade that looked like a lily.

IX

"What we will endeavour to investigate today," began Professor Avildsen, addressing no one in particular, but speaking to the packed lecture theatre in general, "is the enormous analogy that exists between the sweet scent of sanctity and the stench of corruption."

Giuditta Luzzatto had already turned on her recorder. From her usual place in the front row she had already noticed that the teacher's bag was swollen. It wasn't empty, as in the previous lecture. She saw him bend down and undo the clasp. But he didn't take anything out of it. It was as though, she thought, he wanted to air whatever was inside. As the professor cleared his throat, she glanced round instinctively to check on the fat boy. He too was in his usual place, darting looks at her. But Giuditta was determined not to be intimidated. Chief Inspector Giacomo Amaldi had assured her. The police would do something about the matter. And if the police didn't, she would. She wasn't going to be passive any more. She wasn't going to just sit there and submit. She didn't want her private life to be dictated by that disgusting fat boy. She was certain he was the one tormenting her, but the police had advised her to file a complaint against persons unknown. Slander was a criminal offence, after all. One needed concrete proof to accuse someone. Out of caution she hadn't pointed the finger at him. Even though she was sure it was him. In those pig-like eyes, that thick tongue that was forever licking his big front teeth like a rodent's, Giuditta thought she could make out the satisfaction of someone who drank up other people's misery. And he wanted her to know. To be afraid. But she had had enough. The time had come to say stop. She gave him a harsh, contemptuous glare.

"The uneven road that we are going to set out on today, the trajectory the covers the gamut of sanctity and corruption," Avildsen was intoning in his priestly voice, "or rather, everything that is bound by Absolute Good and Absolute Evil, will lead us to discover, or at least look for, the soul. You will not find a Christian, Buddhist or Islamic soul. The soul I am speaking of is something you can grasp, kill, love, hold, suck, eat, pull up, plant, steal or give. It is the soul of the people, of all peoples. It is life." Just as his life was there in that lecture room, perforce populated by spectators for whom he did not nurture the slightest interest. He was revolted by the sentimental claptrap he heard from certain colleagues in the staff room who remembered fondly, after many years, the names and faces of their more brilliant students, some of whose careers they had followed, some of whom had even become their assistants. Avildsen felt no such affection for his students, always ensuring he forgot, indeed, never even memorized, their names and details. He concentrated on himself, on his superior intellect, on his astounding ability to hypnotize a room full of young people. Their emotions, their admiration, were food for his soul. He fed on them avidly, but without taking part in their human affairs. They were really the answering echo of his knowledge, his science, which kept it alive and vital, which helped it to flourish and to feel pride exclusively in its own achievements.

"There are three seats of the soul which correspond, for us Westerners, to the three initiates, or philosophers if you prefer, who have revolutionized man's path through life. The heart, or Christ, that is, love. The head, or Marx, that is, reason. The genitals, or Freud, that is, sexuality in relation to our past . . . A past that psychology identifies in our parents." There was the slightest tremor of annoyance in his voice. "But this marvellous journey, which it has taken us centuries to uncover, exists independently of our ability to understand it. The peoples of the Earth have carried it within them, like a gift or a curse, since time immemorial. They observe it, they build rites and customs around this triple truth."

Giuditta watched him closely. She felt attracted and at the same time repelled by the charismatic figure who held the most intimate part of the world's peoples in the palm of his hand with such nonchalance. As though he were master of their lives, while Inspector Amaldi was but the guardian. Giuditta found herself smiling as she thought of him.

"We shall begin with the head. Why? The reason is that the heart, especially for us Westerners, is a rather distant memory. Our civilization has worked most diligently to forget it, to bury it. The genitals, on the other hand, are a recent conquest, and we still tend to confuse them with the heart, for which we apparently feel a certain nostalgia. Whence the cult of sex, which is a surrogate."

Giuditta didn't consider herself to be tormented, like the majority of her contemporaries, she was just a little bewildered sometimes; frightened, yet cocksure, too. This dichotomy led her on the one hand not to want to get involved in other people's lives, and on the other to push herself forward, to take care of other people's problems. She couldn't alleviate pain, but she did have the gift of insight into other people's problems, although she couldn't manage to apply the same clarity to her own situation. There was a description of Shakespeare by Anthony Burgess that suited her perfectly. The first time she had read it she had recognized herself in those words and had copied the quote into her diary, into her notebook and had even turned it into a screensaver. The description read: "He sees the minutiae of the natural world, as well as the writing on the human face, with the excessive clarity of one who peers, rather than looks." And even her way of seeing things changed: at times they became bigger, at times they shrank. When she came into close contact with something, with someone, it was as though she were looking through a magnifying glass; things left in the distance, on the other hand, remained foggy. Blurred outlines, washed-out colours, minimal, stylized forms. Giuditta only grasped details. Her broader vision was somewhat lacking. But as soon as things or people crossed the imaginary chalk line etched out by her myopia, shapes became vital, and the substance began to emerge from the husk. And then she was seized by such enthusiasm that she couldn't help wanting to get to the bottom of things, to find out what that other world contained. Her life was one long process of deduction, and never induction. With each encounter she added another tile to the mosaic that had been forbidden to her; each new personal experience helped her build the larger picture. As a result she had developed two traits: imagination, which had to compensate for her inability to gain a 360-degree purchase on the world, and intuition, which had taught her how not to be duped by appearances. In studying the world so acutely, she had learned how to *feel*.

And it was for that reason, although she knew she was just as fascinated by Professor Avildsen as the other girls, she *felt* she shouldn't yield to the temptation to get closer to him.

"So we shall postpone our analysis of heart and genitals. What we have left is the head: the great blasphemy, the realm of science and progress, the most comfortable nest for our demi-godhood."

Avildsen leaned down behind the podium and took a squat cylinder out of his bag. It was about a foot high and just as broad. It was made of white porcelain and should probably have reminded them of an upturned chamber-pot, but Giuditta couldn't help thinking it looked rather like a peculiar cover for keeping meals warm, perhaps because of the galvanized handle attached to the top. Or maybe it was the plate it rested on, wider than the base of the cylinder, and attached to it by two clasps.

The class was curious, but Avildsen showed no sign that he was going to reveal what lay under the cylinder.

"But the head," and before him Professor Avildsen saw dozens of different heads, all with their eyes riveted on him, "the head is also the receptacle par excellence of the soul. Think of Descartes, who located the soul in the centre of the brain, in the pituitary, protected and inaccessible. Or Plato, who compared it to the universe because of its spherical form. A microcosm. As if it represented all the burning ardour of the active principle, or the spirit of its own manifestation. And let us think of the Maori, for whom the head of a chief was so sacred that should the chief himself touch his own head he must place the offending fingers on his nose and breathe in the sanctity the digits had absorbed from that contact so as to restore it to whence it had come."

With infinite slowness Professor Avildsen raised a hand and plunged it into his hair, ruffled it, then

109

brought his fingers to his nose and breathed in deeply. The little scene, played out dozens of times in years past, always hit the mark. The students began laughing. Many of them followed their professor's example and the lecture hall was soon filled with the sound of nostrils sniffing blessed fingertips. No one paid any more attention to the squat cylinder. When the students had settled down, the professor began speaking again.

"And in West Africa, when the Alake, or king, of Abeokuta dies, the leading villager decapitates him and offers the head on a plate to the new ruler."

With two quick flicks of his fingers, the professor opened the cylinder and lifted it up. There were muffled screams from some of the girls. The boys stopped playing with their fingertips. On the plate, stuck on a square, red base, was a mummified head. It was minuscule, shrunken, with skin like tobacco, long, sparse hair, fleshless lips, teeth bared in a grimace, the eyes two terrifyingly expressive black balls.

"The head becomes a fetish," continued the professor, enjoying the sudden shift in gear brought about by his second theatrical flourish, savouring the tense silence that grew in the room after the initial reactions had passed. "The personal fetish of the new ruler, who must perforce bestow all honours upon it, live in function of it, organize his existence around this dead man's head."

As he said this, holding the plate in one outstretched hand, the shrunken head wobbling dangerously, his own head bowed like a priest, he stepped down from the podium and moved about the room. Many of the girls turned away as he passed; the young men tried to appear unaffected, but none of them lasted very long under the blind gaze of the mummified head.

110

When he walked past her, Giuditta studied him carefully and thought she saw a look of satisfaction in his eyes. The man and the head left in their wake the smell of mould and some aromatic oil that Giuditta couldn't place.

When he had finished his lap of the lecture hall, Avildsen returned to the podium and put the plate down on the desk. The hair of the mummified head stirred slightly. The strands must have been like stiff gristle. Then the professor placed the fetish in the cylinder and closed the clasps with exaggerated slowness. The head had disappeared. But Avildsen knew that in that way it became all the more frightening. If he had left it in plain view, his students would have become used to the cracked and wrinkled skin, to the eyelids that looked as though they were made from papier mâché. Hidden, the head would take on monstrous characteristics that it did not, in fact, possess. It would loom large and terrifying in each student's imagination. They would all of them have created an image that burrowed into their most fragile, sensitive depths.

"Moreover," he continued, "following the death of a family member, for instance, or in the wake of some grave misfortune, even the lowliest members of the village could fall under a taboo. They are not permitted to touch their heads, they cannot even bring their hands to their mouths to feed themselves. They are forced to kneel down like dogs in front of a bowl that is left for them at the edge of the village. Why? My colleagues put forward any number of theories and usually come to blows at conferences in order to promote their own views. However, the truth, the truth that you must make your own, is that the wisdom of primitive man is absolute. It is the thoughts, remember this,

111

the thoughts that are banished from the village. The thoughts of a disturbed man? Ghosts? Ideas? It doesn't matter what we call them. These are thoughts that can travel down from the head and through the hand, if we are eating, can enter the body. They can contaminate it. The savage, as we like to call him, is much more honest than we are. He knows that certain thoughts must not be thought . . ." Avildsen looked at the lecture theatre and in a pained voice repeated, ". . . certain thoughts must not be thought."

Giuditta listened closely. Beyond the words. Inside the words. For a moment it was as if the professor had spoken to someone in particular, someone he knew well. She turned round, looking for the person the teacher was talking to, but the students' faces were a uniform mass.

"But why is the same kind of treatment meted out to a king? Why is he also forbidden from touching his head? Why is he not allowed to feed himself, but must be fed by another? What is the difference? No one can be above his head . . . Why? Why does a king suffer the same fate, isolation and marginalization as an outcast? The difference between king and subject, the difference between a saint and a sinner, the difference between a cripple and a healthy man, the difference between an outcast and a village-dweller is bridged in the same ritual practice. Why? Sanctity and corruption . . . One of them is born of the light's own light. That is why he is king. The other is obscure and dwells in darkness. Why?" He looked at a student. "Why?" He looked at another student and raised his voice. "Why?" He looked at another one and in dramatic, thundering tones demanded "Why?". Then he slumped in his chair for the first time, his elbows resting on the podium and his head in his hands.

112

The room was silent. The girls quivered.

"Man was born a million years ago," Avildsen began again, without changing position. His voice was no more than a deep murmur, as if he were about to tell an unpleasant fable. "How? Just how was man born? Have you ever asked yourselves that? What was it that made him different from the other animals? Certainly not the fact of walking upright on two legs . . . nor the point of a spear . . . nor fire . . . nor some drawing on the cave wall where he lived. What then?" He lifted his face, slowly, and brought his hands together in an attitude of prayer, under his chin. "I know. And so do you." A hypnotic singsong. "You have experienced the very same sensation as your ancestor, the primate who was *forced* to stop being an animal. Remember?" The voice became a thin, distant vibration. "Do you remember a dark, noiseless night, a night suspended that found you awake, alone in your bed, more alone than you could ever have imagined possible, your limbs stiff and paralysed by fear? Do you remember the Voices?" He paused, his gaze vacant. "The Voices . . ." Another pause. "At that moment, in that darkness, you were *forced* to become different from the other animals. By the Voices that whispered in the night." He was silent for a long time, his eyes fixed on the darkness he had called into being, before he started speaking again. "That ape . . . your mother . . . a million years ago was but a defenceless baby . . . like you. It lay in a bed so very different and so very similar to your own. The darkness, her darkness, filled up with the Voices, the same, obsessive, repetitive Voices. Voices that told of the passing of Time. Without those Voices, the past would be no more than a comforting daub, bereft of colour and untouched by the rules of perspective. It would be just the same past as that of its ape parents,

113

who had assimilated only the most empirical of teachings. Fire burns, so I won't put my paw in the flames again. But that night, in the darkness, the baby ape discovered Time, and Time invented the baby's nightmare: tomorrow. Thus the baby ape, already no longer a member of its own species, understands that every tomorrow of every today will be populated by the same terrifying Voices. Tomorrow had yet to come, but it was already known, an anticipation of fear. Time, measurable yet unknown. The Voices showed much, but not all. Conscience without Control. The Uncontrollable made flesh. Flesh and the thoughts of the flesh. Life became a hateful, uncontrollable river whose source the ape remembered and whose mouth it imagined, but whose current it could not subdue. All the baby ape wanted was to buy some of his desires. But the ghosts of the sins and of the pleasures, the empty-eyed ghosts that were not deceased but rather had never been born into the pack of apes to which it used to belong before the night the Voices came, those spirits opposed to nature and instinct, that up until that moment had loitered, harmless, in darkness, that had remained in silent contemplation of their faces that had never seen the light, still and tired, exhausted, worn out not by effort but by the eternal and eternally unfulfilled hope of being, suddenly, in the very instant in which the baby ape set himself apart from the beasts . . . the ghosts appeared and tore him to pieces. He was born. From an aberration. From a sickness. From the Voices that whispered in the night. The Monkey King was born."

A perplexed murmur eddied across the room.

"He was the Other. And when he had finished contaminating the whole tribe, making them all like him, making them sick with his sickness, the village was born. But the Voices were never satiated. They revealed another abomination to the baby ape. This time in daylight. That way it would come to light from light itself. The King of Men."

The professor picked up a book. He turned the pages until he came to the place he wanted.

"One of the founding texts of Zen reads thus: 'Light and darkness clash. Nevertheless, the one depends on the other, as the step of the right leg depends on that of the left.' Because the Voices that buzzed in the head of the man cub decided it was so. Because it is not the King who commands, and it is not the outcast who is persecuted."

Professor Avildsen snapped the book shut, put it back in his bag, and with his left hand raised the squat porcelain cylinder a few inches, just enough to refresh the students' memories about its contents. Then he put his ear to the cylinder and listened carefully. "Because there are only the Voices," he said.

Some of the students shivered.

"The lesson is over. Next time we will speak about peoples such as the Windessi, or those who live in the Waningela delta in Papua New Guinea, the Tolalaki of Celebes, the natives of Bontoc in the interior of Luzon, in the Philippines, the peoples of Borneo, of the islands of Timor and Pelew." In silence he placed the index finger of his right hand on a point on the nape of his neck and described a circle around his throat. "Head-hunters."

He then put the cylinder back in his bag and disappeared through the double doors.

Like all the other students, Giuditta had drunk in the professor's words in a kind of trance. When Avildsen left the room she had the feeling she was shaking herself awake from an unpleasant but compelling

115

dream. And like all the other students she sat stunned for a few moments then, while the others broke into conversation and exchanged forced jokes in an attempt to convince themselves they were still living the same life as always, she gathered up her things and went outside. In her hand she carried the baby's bottle and the milk carton. She heard the kitten mew and looked up. The animal was in the arms of the fat boy, who was smiling his toothy, rodent's smile.

"Leave it alone, don't touch it," said Giuditta.

The fat boy, still smiling, reached out as if to give her the kitten, placed the animal onto Giuditta's chest, and in so doing gave her breast a long and slimy caress. Blind with rage, Giuditta kicked him hard in the shin. The boy yelled and staggered back. The frightened kitten planted its claws into Giuditta's flesh. A few passing students turned to see what was happening.

"Cunt," snarled the fat boy and limped off down the stairs.

Giuditta slumped against the low wall, stroking the kitten, which twitched its thin tail nervously. She wanted to cry but she held herself in check, biting back her tears and feeling the briny taste in her mouth. She got out her organizer and ran her finger down to Amaldi's name, which she had written in clear handwriting, along with his numbers, on a clean page, just for him. She felt like a silly little girl.

X

The stench was unbearable when Chief Inspector
Giacomo Amaldi entered the shop through the back
door. An officer offered him a perfumed tissue to
anaesthetize his nostrils, but Amaldi waved him away.
Smells were part of the crime scene. Wax, mould, sea-
soned wood, dust, oil for zips and rusty old locks. Blood.
Out of the corner of his eye he noticed Frese holding
back the young pathologist who was trying to approach
him. The man obviously didn't know that absolutely
no one was allowed to speak to the inspector while he
formed his first, fundamental impressions.

The store was long and narrow, a jumble of furniture
squeezed haphazardly into an intestinally tight passage. It looked more like a junk shop than an antique-
dealer's. Some of the objects on display struck him as
quite valuable, others seemed completely worthless.
The floor was a dull colour. His attention was drawn to
a collection of ancient weapons in a wooden display
case. He went closer. The weapons were covered in
dust. The case contained a flintlock, a launcher, an
ironclad mace and a crossbow. Only the halberd was
free of dust. The dark wooden handle glistened and
the blade, although rusty, was clean. You needed a
special licence to sell weapons, even antiques. His men
would check it out. There were mirrors everywhere:
bevelled, mercury-spotted, flaking, dimmed with time.
When Amaldi caught sight of his own reflection, he
recognized the image he always projected: serious

and certain. The shop's artificial light accentuated his wrinkles and shadows. His cheekbones seemed sharper and his hair fairer.

As he was about to step inside the shop he had felt his heart in his throat, and as usual he was seized by the urge to turn and run. The same thing happened every time. A while back he had gone out to dinner with an actress. They hadn't ended up in bed together, because the woman had talked incessantly about herself all evening and Amaldi had lost interest. But he remembered the evening because the actress had told him that each and every time she had to go on, she was seized by a terrible panic, afraid she might forget her lines. Then she would make her entrance, stepping over the flimsy line between reality and fiction marked out by the theatre wings, and the spotlights would blind her and she would simply forget her worries. The same thing happened to Amaldi, every time he stepped over the line between reality and the crime scene that was marked out by the red and white police cordon. He became a block of ice. It was as if he no longer had a heart, it seemed, and played his part to perfection. They were two separate worlds. The rules that governed in one were unknown in the other.

He had finished walking round the store. He stopped in front of the metal shutter that was still closed. He planted the index finger of his right hand between his eyebrows, looking firmly at the floor. He emptied himself even further, and walked to the middle of the store. He breathed in. That was where the smell of blood was coming from. Then he looked.

The woman was smiling and her eyes were wide open. Staring at nothing. She was sitting in an orderly manner on an old writing desk covered in worn leather. Her legs dangled inertly around sixteen inches above the floor and the flesh-coloured tights had been carefully rolled down about her ankles. Her brown woollen dress was lacerated at the stomach and the deep wound had been stuffed with dust cloths. On the floor, the puddle formed by the blood that had flowed down from the desk had stopped spreading some hours ago and a thin, dull film had begun to form on the menacing patch, wrinkled and lumpy at one end. Amaldi noticed the shoe print immediately, but did not turn to look at Frese. He hadn't finished yet. The sleeves from her woollen dress were in the woman's lap. They hadn't been torn off during the assault, they had been carefully unstitched. But there was more. Much more. Her hands were shiny and smelled of shellac. Her arms were shiny and smelled of shellac. Wrists and elbows were made from burnished metal. At first glance the joints seemed well oiled.

The limbs were made of wood. Light-coloured wood with barely visible veins.

The corpse held its arms out to Amaldi, as though it wanted to embrace him. They were held taut by two nylon wires attached to the edge of a country-style cupboard positioned in front of the desk. Amaldi had never seen anything like it.

When he turned around Frese was already standing behind him. They looked at one another as little as possible, to avoid seeing their fear reflected in the other's eyes. They broke into conversation immediately, in an effort to smother their horror. They made an effort to speak in detached tones.

"Know why she's smiling?" asked Frese, pointing a small torch at the corpse. "Fish hooks. Two fish hooks at the corners of her mouth, a bit of nylon, pull it round the back of the head and tie a knot. Pretty straightforward, right?"

119

Amaldi noticed the metallic glint at the corners of the taut mouth.

"He used rubber glue to keep the eyelids open. They're glued back. Probably some quick-acting stuff, but we'll know better after the tests."

Amaldi stared down at the print in the puddle of blood. He threw a questioning look at Frese who was already shaking his head.

"New guy. I don't know why they can't give us real professionals for jobs like this. You should talk to the chief about it. Anyway, fortunately we'd already finished with the photos before that idiot put his foot in it. I sent him home before he could screw up again."

Amaldi nodded in silence.

"And then there's this," said Frese, pointing to a length of green velvet ribbon, about two inches wide, that was wrapped around the woman's throat. He used a pen to lift the ribbon, revealing a brown line, made with a thick pencil. "He drew a perfect circle, look, right round the neck. See here . . .?" In an attempt to give his superior a better view, Frese leaned forward and lost his balance. Ink from the pen in his hand smeared the woman's skin. "Ah fuck!" he swore. Still holding the ribbon away from the skin, he put the index finger of his free hand into his mouth, moistened it and rubbed the pencil line until he had removed the ink smear. The woman's skin did not redden under the pressure, as it would have done if she had been alive.

"Professionals on the job, right?" remarked Amaldi.

"Well, okay," said Frese, unfazed. He wiped his finger on his coat. "Nothing major. No problem."

"Of course. You've got everything under control."

"Don't tell anyone, right."

"Like the grave. Even if they decide to arrest you

120

because of the saliva traces you've just left on the victim's body and there's no one else to prosecute."

"Thanks."

"No problem."

"And then, of course, there are these." Frese lightly twanged the two nylon wires attached to the cupboard. The corpse waved its arms. Pieces of a heavy, light-coloured cloth had been nailed to the tops of the two wooden limbs. "Real craftsmanship," remarked Frese, lifting the dress at the shoulders. The fabric had been stitched to the skin with thick, dark thread. Neither of the men mentioned the dead woman's real arms.

"Let's go," said Amaldi firmly and turned his back on the antique-dealer, who had not once stopped smiling or inviting him to embrace her. "I've seen enough."

The team that was going to check for prints, the one that was going to itemize the contents of the shop, and the one with the evidence vacuums, who looked like an ordinary squad of cleaners, were all waiting at the back of the store. Nobody was talking. Everyone was looking at the ground. The young pathologist was pale and shaken. When he saw Amaldi, he advanced towards the inspector with a finger raised.

"Later," Amaldi said brusquely and walked past the man.

The pathologist stood there for a moment, his finger still raised like a flagless pole, and then, although he was still outside, covered his nose with his perfumed handkerchief. The officers going in shoved him aside without looking at him.

"Got your car?" asked Frese.

"No."

"You walked here?"

"Yes, I walked here."

"Mine's over there," said Frese, and headed off.

Amaldi glanced at the knot of people that had gathered at the mouth of the blind alley. A uniformed officer, his arms outstretched above the red and white police cordon that was attached to either side of the narrow street, struggled to keep back curious onlookers who were bombarding him with questions, craning their necks trying to see beyond the fragile police barrier. Amaldi looked up. The windows of the tower blocks were crammed with faces.

"What a show," remarked Frese, who had reached his car.

Amaldi caught up with him and opened the right-hand door. The alleyway ended in a low wall, about three feet high, and beyond the wall there was another street, at a lower level, so that the alley looked like a bridge that had never been finished but seemed to jut out towards the balcony of the building opposite.

"They can't even be bothered to carry it downstairs now," he heard Frese say. Then he saw his deputy through the windscreen as he leaned over and picked a bag of rubbish off the front of the car. "They just throw it out the window, and it lands where it lands," his deputy yelled, face blazing, rubbish bag in hand. He stared up at the windows crowded with curious faces and then hurled the bag to the ground. It burst open with a squelch that was cut through by the sound of broken glass and crumpled cans.

"You lot can't even stop a rubbish strike. What chance have you got to catch a killer?!" yelled someone in the crowd.

"You lot are the rubbish around here," snarled Frese, waving a clenched fist.

Amaldi opened the driver's door and leaned out to Frese.

"Shut up and get in. Now," he snapped.

122

Furious, Frese got into the car and turned the key in the ignition. He put the car in reverse and blared his horn to alert the cop on the line. The officer unhooked the cordon and motioned at the crowd to let the car pass. But the onlookers refused to budge. The officer managed to push some of them away to one side, but when he moved on they simply squeezed back into the spot they had vacated, elbowing to move forward a few inches.

"Will you just look at them? Those animals," grunted Frese, completely losing his patience. "They got here before me. Look at them. Look at those faces. The smug bastards. At last, something to talk about. Doesn't matter if some poor bugger gets stiffed. The first one on the scene phoned his mother and then his aunt, and then his friends and his cousins and look at them all here now. How many of the buggers are there? Seventy, eighty dickheads all in a row to see the corpse. Shift your arses!" Frese yelled, his head out the window, putting his foot on the accelerator.

The crowd parted in a loud wave of protests and curses. The car wheels brushed against legs. A camera flash exploded in the grey morning light.

"Fancy a trip to the seaside?" Frese asked.

Amaldi nodded in silence.

The two men said nothing as they left behind the older part of town and passed through the anonymous suburbs. As soon as the houses became less and less frequent, and the road more tortuous, Frese rolled down the window and breathed in deeply. The frosty air saturated his lungs. Amaldi pulled his coat around him.

"Are you cold?"

Amaldi didn't reply.

"Well, where would you like to go? Anywhere in particular?" asked Frese.

Below them lay the grey rocks, the foaming waves, trees clutching the cliff face and buffeted by the wind, just like the handful of straggling cottages that clung onto the craggy slopes.

Amaldi was looking straight ahead, his gaze lost in time, lost in space. He remembered what a struggle it was to pedal up that road with the girl, who was very serious because of the decision they had taken. From time to time she wiped away the sweat from his forehead with a paper tissue. And he remembered her big breasts that would soon be abandoned to his caresses and the sea air, and her firm backside ridged by the bike crossbar.

"I'll stop here," said Frese, slowing down.

"No, go on. A few more bends and there's a dirt path on the left. There's a big pine tree . . . or there was twenty years ago, anyway."

Feelings, emotions, a quivering that had never been allowed to grow up, to grow old.

"You're destroying my car," muttered Frese, navigating rocks and potholes.

"Just a bit further. You see that clearing down there?"

The car gave one last shudder and came to a halt. The sea before them was dark and restless. When Frese turned off the engine they could hear the hissing of the wind.

"Penny for them," said Frese.

Amaldi turned to his colleague. His smile was wan. All those years ago the sun had been shining. It had been warm.

"When you think of a woman," Frese asked Amaldi, a newspaper in his hand, "what do you think about first, tits or fanny?"

"What?"

"Nothing, I was just reading this test here in the

124

paper." As he said this, Frese tossed the paper onto the back seat. "According to these geniuses, guys like me, I always imagine her tits first, guys like me are immature adolescents with a mother fixation."

"I haven't got a mother fixation," said Amaldi, absently.

"But you think of tits first, right?"

"Yes."

"I knew that these tests were all a load of bullshit," remarked Frese, getting out of the car.

Amaldi followed him, mechanically. They both stood on the cliff edge. Frese stretched upwards and then stepped away from his superior. Amaldi was just too tall. He walked around in a circle a few times and then pointed towards an eighteenth-century building.

"Isn't that Villa Cascarino?" he asked.

"Yes," replied Amaldi, without turning to look.

He was thinking. That day he and the girl had put a blanket on the ground that had been taken furtively from home. For quite a few minutes they hadn't even been able to kiss. They hadn't looked each other in the face, nor had they spoken. They had suddenly become complete strangers. Then she had put a hand on his face and pulled him towards her.

". . . it's strange, isn't it?" Frese was saying, and waved both his hands in the direction of the villa.

"Yes," replied Amaldi.

"Have you been listening to a word I've said?"

"Yes."

"Well, it is strange, isn't it? It's strange that a whole file on a serious incident like that . . . with all those kids and nuns dead in that fire . . . should be scattered around the whole of Records. The one I found isn't much, okay, just blueprints and plans. But the date written by the architect predates the fire by nearly three months. It wasn't just a little bit of redecorating, they were going to move walls around, heavy work. One of the sheets was marked 'Refectory'. Who the hell keeps a refectory at home?"

"Hospices have refectories."

"All right, I thought the same thing. How about 'Dormitory One' and 'Dormitory Two'? Do they bring to mind a hospice? You can just see all those old guys snoring and farting together come night time."

"Have you ever been to a hospice? To one of those places for poor people?"

"Wait a minute . . . You mean, you've got a bloody listed building here, a historical building, I mean, a villa like that and you need to make some money. . . You know Mrs Cascarino was practically destitute before she turned the villa into an orphanage? Well, you'd take in old folk with money, not penniless vagrants, right? You wouldn't build 'Dormitory One' and 'Dormitory Two', would you? You'd build lots of nice little rooms with their own bathroom . . . Unless . . ."

"Unless what?"

"Unless you knew that the city orphanage was going to go up in smoke and the mayor would give you a shitload of money rather than build a new one. It would suit you both that way."

Amaldi turned round slowly to look at Villa Cascarino. The building's pink and graceful shape stood out against the livid sky. He kicked at a stone.

"You've nothing to go on."

"I don't need anyone to tell me that." A pause. "I know it's a bit tasteless, but listen, I smell something rotten here." He took a deep breath and continued in hushed tones. "The detective who oversaw the investigation is none other than our present mayor." Another

126

pause. "He's a good man, the mayor, or so I've always thought, anyway."

Amaldi didn't know what to say. Surely, he thought, Frese had known all along who had been in charge of the investigation. He hadn't wanted to name names until he had something concrete to go on. And now they both knew.

"Until you have something certain, or, better, absolutely solid, to go on, you are not officially covered, and I will deny everything."

"Fine," said Frese. So he could carry on digging, then.

Amaldi turned back to lose himself in the gulf that stretched out before him. He breathed in the smell of the sea, then lowered his gaze and let his eyes travel down the cliff face. A 650-foot drop studded with shrubs and rocks, battered by the waves. The railway track sliced across his view halfway down. A grand structure. The tracks clung precariously to a thin strip of land, rolled flat by man's sheer stubbornness.

That day they had thrown stones down the cliff, that day. Like kids. Because at sixteen they had still just been kids.

"Let's come back to the present," he said to his deputy.

"The present?" echoed Frese, talking almost to himself. He knew his superior better than anyone else. "I see you're still looking into the Rice Fields Massacre."

"What about it?" There was a note of irritation in Amaldi's voice.

"Nothing, it's just that the word present from you has a strange sound about it, that's all."

"What's that got to do with the Rice Fields Massacre?"

"I know why you've taken an interest. You don't believe in any of those stupid theories about ex-boyfriends or revenge killings. You read about that poor girl and decided it was the work of some maniac."

"And what if it was?" Amaldi already had his annoyance under control.

"And if it was . . . It would have nothing to do with the present, would it? It would have nothing to do with that girl. If it was, it wouldn't be just any maniac, would it, it would be the same one as always, right?"

Amaldi remained impassive.

"That happened in the past, not the present," exploded Frese. "For Christ's sake, we all know what happened to you in the past!"

Amaldi seemed to deflate, suddenly, as if he had just been forced to hold his breath for too long. But it was a barely noticeable reaction, at gut level.

"No. You don't know."

He turned his back on Frese and walked with stiff, measured steps to the front of the car, and sat on the bonnet. He patted the space beside him, inviting Frese to join him.

"Come over here," he said.

His back was ramrod straight, as though no weight burdened his shoulders, and his face was unnaturally relaxed. His eyes were fixed on some point out on the horizon. When Frese had sat down beside him, Amaldi began his story, in flat, impersonal tones. The rhythm of his speech, thought Frese, was just like an ordinary conversation; his voice was cordial enough. But Amaldi spoke without emphasis, without pitch, without speeding up or slowing down or pausing. His voice flowed on like a placid river, free of rapids and currents, without bends or foam. Detached from the atrocity he was describing, untouched by the violent passions the story should have awoken, deaf to the echoes of the past. It was an emotionless voice, telling someone else's story with the kind of indifference one might feel towards a perfect stranger. Just like a tape recording, thought Frese. And Amaldi was the tape recorder, just a machine. Unmoving, absolutely still, Amaldi did not once look towards Frese. His hands lay lifeless on his thighs, his chest moved with the regular rhythm of his breathing. Frese was convinced that even Amaldi's heartbeat had not altered in the slightest.

When he had finished his story Amaldi stopped talking, as simply as he had started.

"There, that's the story," he said, turning to look at Frese for the first time, a friendly but vacant smile on his lips. He raised his head and stared at the horizon again.

Frese said nothing. They both remained still. The cold breeze rustled the dry twigs and drove dust through the air, bending the grasses. Then the wind died and the silence was absolute. The absence of noise was so unnatural that Frese couldn't even imagine the sound of the waves breaking on the rocks below. It was as if the whole world had gone mute.

Into that calm without oblivion broke a sudden uncontained sound. It was like a restrained lowing. The car shook. Frese did not look at Amaldi. Then after a few moments the sound came again. It was no longer a lowing noise, it sounded like someone almost retching. Frese looked at Amaldi out of the corner of his eye. His superior was haggard. Amaldi's face struck Frese as grotesque, repulsive. It was like watching a mask dissolving in flames, crumpling in the heat, losing its shape. Amaldi was racked by another sob, a kind of inner upheaval that he tried to resist with all his strength, but without succeeding. He began to shudder rhythmically, as if he were in the throes of labour. With each heaving jolt Amaldi's breathing was choked, pained. Frese had no idea what to do. He watched Amaldi struggle, suffer. Lose.

Amaldi yielded, the dam yielded, the walls yielded, the foundations yielded. His rigid body folded. His drawn lips twitched until ripped open by the sound welling in his throat. Amaldi clamped his hands over his mouth, in a desperate effort to block the scream, to smother it. But the scream pushed its way out first through his eyes, through his stomach, through the hands that fought to hold it back. Amaldi bent in two and cried out in a mangled voice that suffocated him. He screamed when he exhaled and screamed when he breathed in. An endless, hissing, wrenching sound that was barely audible. As if he was screaming in a whisper.

Only then did Frese realize that Amaldi was trying to cry.

It was dusk when, numbed by the cold, they got back into the car and turned on the heating.

"What was her name?" asked Amaldi in his new voice.

"Viviana Justic, fifty-five, unmarried, shop-owner and sole licence-holder, trusted antique-dealer to the noble families of our fair city, because she knew how to keep a secret. She had a good business going there."

Amaldi listened and nodded. His eyes were red and there was dried spittle on his chin.

"Thank you," he said.

XI

That same night, with the case file under his arm, Chief Inspector Giacomo Amaldi returned to the antiques shop, alone. Every investigator knew he had to pursue the trail while it was still hot, the first hours were often essential in capturing the killer. Instead he had spent those first hours telling Frese a distant story, the story of a spirit that could not find peace. He had never talked about it with anyone. Not even with the psychologists during training at the Academy. A story that had led him to join the police and get a degree in psychology. His degree dissertation had been entitled: "Aberrational behaviour and sexually motivated homicides. Analysis of deviant personalities through examination of crime scene findings: investigative deductions." And since then, nothing. Not one word. And then that river of emotion, that reckless sobbing. Hot tears on cheeks cold from the northern wind. Now, a few hours later, it seemed to him that he had finally given the funeral oration that he had selfishly held within him. Perhaps he had buried that ruined corpse, perhaps he had handed it over to the peace of abandonment. But now was not the time to think about what he was going to do. There was no time to ask if he would be free, or if he would become a ghost without a destination. There was no time to weigh things up, to take stock of his past life, to speculate about his future. He would just have to put those thoughts off to another time.

It was time to bring all his attention to bear on Viviana Justic. He owed her that.

He spread his folder open on a low ottoman, the folder that would get thicker and thicker as the days passed, and sat down, torch in hand. They still hadn't found the last person to see the antique-dealer alive. Probably a customer. Someone who had come into the shop during their Sunday afternoon stroll. An absented-minded person who had browsed through the knick-knacks and antiques and who wouldn't have remembered the woman's face if they hadn't seen it on the front page of the newspaper at breakfast or in the office the following day. Looking at the photo or reading the report they would have transformed the incident into something personal, as if they had been brushed by the hand of death. They would probably have found it all very exciting and turned the story into the high point of their repertoire of anecdotes. They would certainly come forward to talk with the police. No doubt about it.

The report that had led the police to find the body had been made by one Joaquim Boca, a foreigner known to the police for previous convictions on minor charges: working as a prostitute and transvestite. In certain sexual aberrations, envy of women, especially women who were, according to their statistics, shapely, could lead to violence and even murder. But Joaquim Boca was just a hustler, not a pervert. He probably had a violent childhood, a background of poverty. But on first analysis he didn't seem to be a psychotic. Amaldi had interrogated the man himself, and had heard in Boca's insecure, singsong voice just what had been in the report. Sunday evening the man had buzzed the woman at her apartment. They had a date. She had taken him off the street, according to Boca. In other words she was keeping him and he had become her lover. Boca was not a true homosexual: he liked women but earned his living having sex with men. That afternoon he had been with a client, just to make a bit of extra cash, and on Sunday evening, when the victim didn't answer the intercom, Boca supposed she had discovered what he had been up to. He had felt guilty and had gone off to get drunk in a bar frequented for the most part by homosexuals. A number of witnesses had confirmed as much. He had spent Monday morning at home, trying to get over his hangover, but he had telephoned Justic, whose shop was closed on Monday mornings, repeatedly without an answer. In the afternoon, ready to eat humble pie, he had gone to the shop. The sight of the still shuttered store had made him suspicious. His lover was very involved with her work. When she had to leave the shop to make important evaluations she always had a trusted friend stand in for her. When questioned, the friend said she hadn't seen Viviana Justic since the previous Friday. Boca had waited until evening then had gone round to the antique-dealer's home again and buzzed her intercom insistently. Still no answer. At which point he had phoned the police for the first time to report her missing, but he hadn't left his name. They police didn't follow up the matter; they never did for that kind of anonymous call. The shop was still closed on Tuesday morning and Boca had gone to a local station to make a full report. Just by chance a cop who knew the victim overheard Boca making his declaration; otherwise Viviana Justic's corpse would have been found much later. The officer had extended his usual beat and gone to look at the alley behind the shop. When he had seen the key broken off in the shutter lock and the red writing on the door he had phoned for back-up immediately. A few neighbours had declared that they had noticed the writing, but they had just imagined it was the usual vandals' graffiti. Amaldi looked at the photo of the door and the blow-up of what was written on it, and shook his head. People really did see only what it suited them to see.

The words "viSitA intEriOra teRRae reCtificandO iNvEnies OcCuLtUm lapIdEm" had been written on the door.

A first attempt had produced the translation: "Descend into the bowels of the earth, rectifying you will find the occult stone."

Above the words there was a stylized drawing of an angel holding a bow in its right hand and in its left an arrow pointing upwards. There was a little circle above the arrow. At the beginning and the end of the phrase there were the prints of a rather small hand. The writing, the drawing and the prints were almost black by the time the police had found them. But it was immediately clear that blood had been used as ink. The lab tests to establish if it was the victim's blood were still under way, but no one had any doubts about it. It was unlikely that the killer, in the very likely event that he had been the one to leave that message, had brought the blood with him, given that he had so much to hand. And it was also obvious that the crime was premeditated. It hadn't been the product of coincidence or some sort of homicidal fit.

The neighbours hadn't seen anyone smear the door, nor leave by it.

What did strike Amaldi was the degree of risk the killer had taken. Writing that phrase couldn't have been a quick and easy thing to do, nor drawing the angel and leaving the handprints. The whole thing had a clearly pre-established geometry and order. It was an integral part of the horrible ritual that had been carried out inside the shop. But while the killer had been alone and protected inside the store, he had been out in the open in the alley. Even if he had waited for nightfall, which was more than likely what he had done, it was still a big risk. A first analysis showed that he had used his fingers, suitably protected, to write and draw. But how had he managed it? Had he gone back and forth to the pool of blood that was forming on the floor under Viviana Justic every time he needed more of his sticky red ink? Or had he collected some in a container while it was flowing? Amaldi shivered, thinking of that improvised inkpot. The handprints were among the most macabre things he could think of. He had already told his men to check every single print inside the shop and at the antique-dealer's home. Was it possible that the killer, after writing and drawing with gloves on, would leave such a signature? Unlikely. Was it possible that the killer had such small hands, a woman's hands, when everything pointed to his being a man? Unlikely. The logical conclusion was that the hands, dipped in their own blood, belonged to Viviana Justic. They belonged to the arms the killer had ampu-tated and taken away with him, like a trophy, and replaced with life-size puppet's limbs.

Amaldi went out into the alley and studied the door. The locksmith had done a clean job, but the door and lock had been scratched by his tools. He imagined what it must have been like to manipulate the arms and to leave the palm prints. Another dangerous oper-ation and plainly visible at a distance, which would surely have alarmed anyone who noticed it. But there had been no insomniac having a late-night smoke at their bedroom window in the building opposite that night. The murderer's daring had paid off. Luck had made him invisible. Amaldi wasn't ready to know what he might have done with the arms. A team had orders to go through all the bins in the area. If they didn't find anything they would go through every bin in the city. And that would take time. No one from the municipal refuse collection company would lift a finger to help, however. The strike was still on. Amaldi had asked the chief to phone the contractors and request the road-sweepers' and bin men's help. But the unions were determined not to move even the smallest scrap of rubbish as long as the strike lasted. Their demands were more important than the arms of some dead woman. Fine, Amaldi told himself, they would find the arms themselves, if the killer had dumped them somewhere.

But Amaldi's instinct told him that the killer wouldn't have got rid of the arms. He had spent a lot of time getting them, had done too good a job not to keep them for himself. According to the coroner, he had sectioned the skin with a scalpel, after marking out the line to follow with a thick pencil. He had removed the flesh from the shoulder, exposed the head of the bone, cut the tendons, and undone the joint without leaving more than very superficial scratches on the cartilage. Then he had taken needle and thread and stitched the artificial limbs in place, with a great deal of care, as the new arms were stiff and heavy. He had checked that the stitches held. He couldn't have known when the corpse would be found. He couldn't run the risk that time would ruin his masterpiece. He had paid attention to the sleeves of the dress. A good surgeon, a good tailor. An excellent butcher.

Amaldi went back inside. Had the killer decided to dismember the woman? To cut her into pieces? And then run out of time? No, that was unlikely. All he wanted from that woman were her arms. For reasons that Amaldi could not yet discern. Did he know her? When had he entered the shop? By the back door after the antique-dealer had lowered the shutter? It was the most credible theory. He knew her, he had knocked at the door and she had let him in. If he had ambushed her instead, he had waited for her to leave by the back door and then had forced her inside. There weren't any signs of a tussle, but he might have put everything back in place afterwards. The halberd was the murder weapon. Amaldi supposed that the killer had cleaned it not to hide his tracks, but out of some need for order. According to the first reconstruction, the woman had been killed on the spot where they had found her. But how had he immobilized her? The corpse showed no signs of ligatures; her skull was intact, apart from a tiny bruise on her scalp, which wouldn't have been enough to make her faint.

Amaldi wandered about the store, without really looking for anything in particular, trying to develop an impression of Viviana Justic. She had been a very particular kind of antique-dealer. Somehow, years before, she had gained the trust of the city's patrician families, who turned to her whenever they needed to part with some valuable item, or jewellery. Justic made sure she removed every identifying trace of the item, including the transaction itself. The objects never showed up in her books, either going in or going out. It was, strictly speaking, illegal. But it was also one debt that the law would not be able to make her repay. She had not been married at her death, or earlier. She had a young man to take care of her other needs. A transvestite. They must have been very particular needs. Not necessarily from the point of view of sex. Perhaps Justic liked the idea of exercising some kind of power, of milking her young man's gratitude for having saved him. Perhaps that was all a fat, unattractive fifty-five-year-old could get.

He bent down beneath the writing desk on which they had found the dead woman. The blood had been cleaned up but had left a dark stain on the floor. The desk had a leather top and two compartments, one on either side, which went down to the floor. Each contained three drawers. He rummaged under the drawer on the right. A splinter of wood jabbed him. He sucked his finger. Then he tried the compartment on the left. As soon as he put his hand to the wood he felt them. They rustled under his touch. He got up, moved the desk away from the wall and turned it over. He shone his torch beam on the underside. Three torn, dry leaves were stuck to the wood with drawing pins.

He went over to the shop phone and Frese answered on the seventh ring.

"You weren't asleep, were you?"

"Well, you know, every once in a while . . ."

Amaldi heard a sleepy, woman's voice in the background.

"I'm sorry . . ."

"Yeah, fine."

"I've found something. I haven't got anything here to do it myself. I need a team here."

"Where?"

"At the shop."

"I'll send someone."

"Yes."

"They did a shit job, right?"

"I would say yes to that."

"Great."

Twenty minutes later the same team arrived that had checked out the store earlier. The two young

138

officers, clearly the worse for a dressing down from Frese, entered the store with stooped shoulders and mortified faces. Frese wasn't with them. He was in a warm bed with a woman with a sleepy voice. Amaldi didn't say a word. He merely pointed at his discovery. The two officers took photos of the bottom of the desk and then collected the leaves and the drawing pins in numbered containers.

"Check everything, all over again," was the first and only thing Amaldi said to them as he went out, his icy tone full of contempt.

When he got home he saw there were two messages on his answering machine. The first was silent. The second had been left a few minutes later. "This is Giuditta Luzzatto, Inspector Amaldi." The girl's distorted voice echoed around the desolate apartment. "I just wanted to . . . say thank you. No, there's nothing wrong, don't worry. I just wanted . . . Well, it was very kind of you, the other day, thank you. I haven't received any other phone calls or letters, but it was a pleasure to meet you. I feel much safer. Well, that's everything, then. I hope I haven't bothered you. This is Giuditta Luzzatto, did I say that already?"

Amaldi felt tired. He might have buried his ghost, but he certainly wasn't ready for life's other little games. He still didn't know who he was or who he wanted to become. He didn't know if he had a new life ahead of him, or darkness. The void. He was just tired. He had a very hot shower and looked at himself in the mirror after he had wiped away the steam with the palm of his hand. He didn't see anything. Just a steam-reddened body. Before going to bed he switched on the answering machine again. The first, silent, message. And then the girl's voice. "This is Giuditta Luzzatto, Inspector Amaldi. I just wanted to . . . say

139

thank you. No, there's nothing wrong, don't worry. I just wanted . . . Well, it was very kind of you, the other day, thank you. I haven't received any other phone calls or letters, but it was a pleasure to meet you. I feel much safer. Well, that's everything, then. I hope I haven't bothered you. This is Giuditta Luzzatto, did I say that already?"

Amaldi rewound the tape and listened to Giuditta's first, silent, message. He turned off the machine. Then slowly, in the stillness that followed, he fell asleep.

XII

Once again the man found himself on the edge of the precipice that led down to the old town. The route he took with mechanical determination every Wednesday brought him to a little street that could be considered the main artery for access downtown. It was a street, neither wide, nor narrow, nor slippery, that began in the same main square from where the principal avenue started. It followed a gentle incline at first, and on either side, for a 165-foot stretch the pavements were lined with decent shops, clean bars and well-supplied newsagents. Then the street wilted into a small square that was always choked with cars. From here on, it would have been impossible, for anyone wanting to go on, to find the ideal continuation of the street on the other side of the square. The appearance of the city changed radically and many people instinctively turned back, just to make sure they hadn't wandered into another world. Three streets led off from the little square. They were already infected with the putrid stench of rot and damp that permeated the streets of the old town. Just like in the scribbled drawing of a child, none of the three streets described anything approaching a straight line that might have given the impression that they, albeit strangulated, still carried on. Without any discernable logic, the three little roads went into a frenzy. The shops showed signs of undergoing the same metamorphosis: their windows were neglected without actually being dirty or bare, obedient to the pragmatism and poverty of pragmatic and poor economic signals. The clothes on display seemed almost washed out, as though they had been designed to have the same shapes and garish colours as the more expensive clothes in the chic stores on the main avenue but then the atmosphere, or something that floated in the air, had caused them to fade and become threadbare.

The man turned down one of the three streets. He began to walk more slowly, as though he wanted to savour fully that spell of immersion, and breathed in deeply. The old fishermen said they could still smell the perfume of the sea. The youngest children didn't even know it existed. The odour the man picked up most clearly was the latex smell of condoms. He would come across dozens of them on his reconnaissance expeditions, sometimes so many together that they saturated the air with their unique blend of human and synthetic stench. Every time he saw one on the ground, he crushed it under his shoe, waiting for the wet squelching noise it would make that reminded him of spitting saliva through his teeth.

He arrived at the bar where he stopped for a while at the same time every Wednesday afternoon. As soon as the owner saw him he took out a folding chair and set it beside a little table covered in a plasticized sheet decorated with red and white squares, wiped the wretched thing with a damp cloth and while the man settled down he went to the bar and filled a glass full of milk. Then he put the glass on the table, smiled and disappeared.

The man let his gaze come to rest on a narrow shop at the corner of two streets. The shop was about sixty-five feet away and had big windows that overlooked both side streets. The place had no secrets for the man and he could have pictured it in every detail in his imagination, which he often did. The wallpaper was pink with wide red stripes; there were two prints on the walls, crinkled with damp; a spotlight with a red lamp hung limply from the low ceiling; a single bedside cabinet in some sort of light-coloured wood had been placed beside the double bed with the dirty headrest; during winter the bed was covered in a kind of quilt made from flowery satin, and under the bed there were mounds of magazines, some gossip rags, some pornographic.

This shop had one product for sale which, with the passage of time, was beginning to wear out. The name of the prostitute, in her fifties, both shopkeeper and goods at the same time, was Clara.

The man had seen her for the first time some years before. By chance he had read an article on prostitution in a magazine. According to the report, the vast majority of professional sex workers had chosen their job for psychological, rather than economic, reasons. The two researchers who had compiled the article claimed that somewhere in the childhood of that type of woman there had been some form of sexual violence, real or perceived, within the family. What months of assiduous interviewing had revealed was the common desire on the part of these traders in flesh to exert some form of control over their adult sex lives, a desire so strong, so compelling that it became a need. The psyche of all of these women, whether they were young or more mature, floundered in confusion between sexual pleasure and the guilt they felt for what had happened in childhood. Pleasure and shame merged in their everyday lives to such a perfect degree that it was no longer possible to separate the two. The result was a quite unique blend of equal parts of tenderness and violence, security and risk. Their craft allowed them to combine the contradictory impulses. It was as though they were reliving the hell of their past while ensuring a degree of control that they never had as children.

This assessment had fascinated the man. He had felt attuned to the prostitutes' need to harmonize pain and pleasure, to their contradictory need to relive horrible experiences in voluptuous delight; as if by such repetition, and only by such repetition, of the original pattern was their identity confirmed and consecrated. From that day on he had taken to coming down to the old town to spy on prostitutes and sometimes he even "interviewed" them, as he explained to the women, in order to learn if indeed there had been that kind of violence in their childhood. Initially, he had been pushed by something that might have been called affection, if only he had been capable of feeling such an emotion.

But all that had taken place in times of darkness, when he was still a long way from being enlightened. Now that he had discovered his path, his destiny, now that he had taken the first step and had been shown the proof that he would be able to carry out his grand design that had been prepared for him since birth, he no longer felt the slightest interest for the prostitutes. He could have looked at them for hours, without experiencing that intense and lacerating burning sensation that beaded his forehead with sweat and took root in his mind for days on end, tormenting him, pushing him to ecstasy. Now they meant nothing to him. Just like all the others. They were inferior beings. And he was beginning to hate them for their arrogance, for their presumption in raising themselves to his level.

But among all these women, Clara was different. The same, certainly, because she was a whore, but different, nonetheless. He acknowledged her role in his grand design. A marginal role. She was only a messenger. But she had a role to play, nonetheless. He had appreciated a sensitivity in Clara that was superior to her colleagues, she was less vulgar than them, she crossed her legs in a chaste, almost virginal way, without making crude allusions to the mashed fruit that lay between those legs, on sale for a few pence. When Clara received a client, she looked at him with a warm and comforting expression on her face, unlike her colleagues; she didn't pry or pass judgement; there was never a trace of contempt in her eyes. Indeed, she always seemed ready to comprehend, to accept and caress the sickness she had before her. She was a real whore, the man had thought, because she knew exactly what men wanted. Men who passed down from generation to generation the same burden of being men, all of them afflicted with the same disease, the same hunger. That was why men went to her. To show her their deformities without restraint. To have her caress them. To shed their disguises and reveal their hunched back, their forked penis, their cloven hooves, the goat's fur thick on their chest, their eyes like serpent slits and their curled tail. And they wanted to hurt, to kill, to mortify. Always blessed, and sheltered. They weren't looking for a fleshy vagina, but a lake into which they could pour the briny crocodile tears that no other lake would ever have accepted. Tears that would have polluted any water. Killing it.

He, on the other hand, was there for a different reason. And he respected Clara for another reason again. She was neither vagina nor lake. If anything, she was a river. An unwitting river chosen by his shining destiny

145

to carry someone precious and dangerous that he had forgotten to look for.

That someone held the key to the man's terrible secret.

"Is it to your liking, sir?" asked the bar owner, popping up behind him.

The man pulled his gaze from the little store where Clara offered herself for sale.

"Yes, thank you," he replied.

"Have you heard about this rubbish strike, then?" asked the barman, still standing, the greying, damp cloth draped over his forearm.

"Yes, I've heard about it."

"And what have they been saying, then?"

"That it's a mess, I suppose."

"Indeed. I suppose anyone with a bit of sense would say it was a mess, right?"

"Right. I would say that we could call it a mess."

"Mess is the right word."

"Yes, mess."

"Mess. But for that matter, isn't the whole world a bit of a mess?"

"Yes, I suppose it is."

"But that doesn't mean we have to turn it into a bigger mess than it is already."

"No, we needn't do that."

"Well . . ." sighed the bar owner. "What can you do, eh?"

"What indeed?"

"You're quite right, sir," said the other man, shaking his head. He looked around him then said, "Well, I have to get back to work. If you'll excuse me?"

"Of course," said the man

The bar owner turned on his heel and went over to the till.

146

"Good man, that guy," he heard the bar owner remark to the acne-faced youth behind the counter. "Educated."

The boy gave a distracted nod of agreement.

A quiver of pleasure travelled up the man's spine as he turned to observe Clara. The barman hadn't recognized him. His disguise as Anyman was working. That useless little grunt hadn't noticed the new light that was emanating from him. And the light had taught him how to talk like one of them, in the rough speech of the old town that was hardly even a dialect. The man felt invisible. He smiled in Clara's direction. If he had only wanted to, he could have taken her. As he had done with the antique-dealer. No one had seen him. Not even while he was writing the notice. His new vocation made him invisible and protected him. No one had noticed as he returned home with his two bloody gifts. Yes, if he had only wanted to, he could have taken Clara. But the notice wasn't meant for her. Clara was an unknowing accessory to his design. He would let her live. In token of his gratitude for what she had done.

It had happened one evening four years ago, towards dusk, before his mother's accident, which had left her paralysed. As he had sat sipping his milk, that pure, sensual milk that held within it all information, both sex and nourishment, he had watched Clara. He watched her receive her clients and move gracefully about as she pulled down the metal shutters on both sides; he imagined and timed the pleasures the prostitute dispensed without prejudice. That evening, however, he had caught sight of a grimace on Clara's face, perhaps of fear, as if all the security offered by control had evaporated at the sight of a client he had never noticed before. He hadn't been able to place the man

147

at first. There had been something vaguely familiar about him, the way someone one instinctively finds attractive or repulsive might be familiar. Then, as the shutters were lowered, the man's face had been caught in the light from the street lamp on the corner. A face he knew. Many years had passed, a lifetime now, but when their eyes had met for a fraction of a second, the man had been sucked back into the past, and he had seen the boy pointing up at him. When he had recognized that face, and remembered the name of that orphan who had survived the fire with the sole aim of tormenting him, he had felt his eyes sting and swell with the tears he had never once shed in all those years. When the enemy had gone, the man had seen Clara sitting in a corner of her store, huddled in her satin negligée, her hands crossed over her breasts, her legs stiff, her long pointed nose twitching in search of air, and he had understood that she was also a victim of the orphan. Sitting at the bar, physically unreachable, he had thought that there was no way out, now that his enemy had been resurrected from the past to persecute him again and again. Because he and Clara were the orphan's victims.

"I'm sorry, sir," said the bar owner, elbowing his way into the man's thoughts and making him start. "I'm afraid I have to close early today . . ."

"What? Oh, yes . . . close early . . ."

"If you don't mind?"

"No, of course not," he said, and got up, dropping a banknote onto the table and walking away, slowly, with heavy steps.

"Aren't you going to drink your milk, sir?" the bar owner asked after him.

The man didn't hear him. He put one foot in front of the other and headed back up the alley that was as steep as a cliff face and as corroded as a river bed. When he reached the top he turned back to look. The lights from Clara's boutique gradually disappeared. Everything was under control, now. The streets flowed out before him, buildings bowed to him as he passed by, the sky darkened so his own light could shine forth all the brighter.

When he got to the hospital he had already reviewed the old story. He went into his mother's room without being noticed and sat down beside the bed where the old woman lay, still, her glass eyes stared at the ceiling. With the stump of his little finger he stroked a corner of the sheet that covered his mother. There was a stabbing sensation in the amputated member. Not violent and not painful. But violently and painfully pleasurable.

"I'm not going to touch you, Mother, don't worry," thought the man to himself in a child's voice.

Then he took a sheet of paper and began writing obsessively the orphan's name he had memorized thirty-five years earlier. He wrote it so many times that there was no white left on the sheet.

"Good evening," said a woman's voice.

The man turned.

"Have you seen how well your mother is doing here?" asked the young doctor, smiling.

He had never seen her in her hospital whites. When she came to their house to check up on his mother she was always dressed in everyday clothes. Now, in all that white, she struck him as prettier. As the doctor bent over the old woman with her stethoscope and concentrated on listening to her breathing, he looked at her carefully. She had well-turned legs. Strong bone structure. Her skin did not seem delicate underneath her tights. Perhaps she was hairy. Hairy women often had thicker skin.

149

The doctor straightened up, draped her stethoscope about her neck, put a hand on her side and arched her back. She was tired. He could see that in her face.

"Do you spend a lot of time on your feet?" he asked her.

"Sorry?"

"I imagine your legs must hurt a bit, come the end of the day."

"Yes, they do. You know, we hospital doctors suffer from the same ailments as waiters," she said, laughing.

"I'm sorry you suffer."

"Oh . . . thank you," she replied, embarrassed.

"You ought to lie down and put your feet up, to encourage freer blood flow."

"Yes . . . well, I do that, often, actually."

"At home?"

"Yes . . . in the evenings."

"That's good. You should take good care of your legs."

The doctor couldn't think of an answer.

"You have good legs," the man added

The woman realized her cheeks were blazing. She darted her tongue nervously darted to the side of her mouth.

He had already noticed that she didn't wear lipstick in the hospital.

The doctor smiled again, more shyly this time, bowing her head slightly.

"Thank you . . ." she murmured.

She had always thought he was good looking, even if he did intimidate her a bit. He seemed to be different, though, recently. Less distant. More approachable. And now that remark about her legs.

"And does someone put a cushion under your ankles?"

"Sorry?"

"Who lifts your legs for you onto a nice soft cushion, when you're home in the evenings?"

The woman felt her cheeks burn. The way he looked at you was so intense, almost feverish. Did he want to know if she was free? If she was available?

"No one . . ." she managed, her heart pounding.

"Now there's a pity."

XIII

Giuditta watched her mother shuffle towards the kitchen with a bowl of hot soup in her hand. She heard her mother put the bowl back in the oven.

"Your father said he won't be home for dinner." The woman's voice was resigned and plaintive. "Just for a change."

"Well, Mum, it's like he's on holiday at the moment." Giuditta made an effort to defuse the situation. She stroked the upholstered armchair where her father always sat in their sad, drab living room. Her father worked on the bins and since the beginning of the strike he had rarely come home for dinner. He stayed behind at the bar or in some café with his friends. "You don't mind, do you, love?" he had asked his daughter and not his wife. Giuditta had given him her blessing.

"If only he wouldn't always wait until the last minute before telling me," her mother continued to grumble in the greasy kitchen. It was saturated with the smell of cheap fish from the harbour. The floor was laid with chipped, brown octagonal tiles. There was a strip of worn lino near the sink, and electric wires, blackened and joined together with duct tape, ran haphazardly along the walls. The kitchen was a dim place, weakly illuminated by the light filtering through a wall of dull glass bricks held up by some sort of metal grid. And on the other side, suspended over the drop down into the courtyard, was the bathroom, with a ceramic bowl without a seat, a chrome tube with a peeling

152

pommel that served as the shower, and, under the sink, a plastic bidet that no one ever used. It was a cold, draughty bathroom that afforded no privacy and harboured no secrets.

"I just wish he wouldn't treat me like a servant." Giuditta's mother began again, in her defeated voice, as Giuditta passed through the kitchen to have a shower. "He phones me at seven when everything's ready ... You watch out, my girl, don't throw your life away because men ..."

Giuditta didn't hear the rest. Shower water crashed down on her noisily, and formed a pool on the pockmarked floor. She was familiar with her mother's speech, anyway. Her father had many faults as a husband, Giuditta could see that perfectly well. She had always known it. That was why she understood her mother's rancorous monologue, her constant warnings, her lack of faith in the future and her general disgust with life. For all that, the man had always been an affectionate and attentive father to her. He had always made her feel safe and strong. He was proud of his daughter. When he came across Giuditta bent over a pile of books he would smile proudly and say, "I'm a very lucky man. With a daughter like you, I've got nothing to worry about." Then he would stroke Giuditta's hair and add, "Live life, Giuditta, and if ever you need anything, you come to me." Her father had always been her safe haven. He had always been there for her. In high school, if one of her teachers complained about her progress, her father would roll up his sleeves and, although he was a rough man with little education, he would defend her on every score. At night, unnoticed, she had seen him more than once take her books and turn them over, incredulous, in his hardened hands. Giuditta knew how much it meant to him for her to graduate. He had never once tried to make her feel guilty about the things he went without, or about the money he put away, just for her. Giuditta turned off the water and pulled on her bathrobe.

". . . and watch out for their hands. They all think the same thing, that women are easy. Even your own father thought I was that kind of girl, at the start. But I didn't give in. Not that I got much out of marrying him, mind you. Just look at how I live. I spend all bloody day turning up hems and taking in waistlines to make ends meet . . . But at least I got married. If you knew how many ruined girls I've seen . . . good girls that lost their way because they didn't know how to make a man keep his hands to himself . . ."

The rush of the hairdryer drowned out her mother's voice. When she had finished Giuditta went into her parents' bedroom and took a plain outfit from the wardrobe, dabbed a trace of make-up on her eyes and put an almost invisible film of lipstick on her lips. When she went back into the living room her mother was shaking her head in front of the television. The images on the screen were reflected in the thick glasses she wore for her short-sightedness. Giuditta's father had sent her to an optician to get contact lenses so she wouldn't have to wear glasses all day long. Her mother had said that she didn't understand how anybody could put bits of glass in their eyes, but Giuditta had seen her mother rub the bridge of her nose, notched by her own glasses, probably thinking that her husband had never shown the same concern for her. Sometimes it was hard to be the daughter of both of them.

"Did you get me the things I asked for?" said her mother without looking away from the television.

"I'm just going there now, Mum."

"Dinner's ready."

"It's still early, Mum. I'll just go to the fabric shop and come back. But if you're hungry start without me."

"Always on my own, lunch and dinner. You're just like your father . . ."

Giuditta was nettled by that remark as she made her way to the door, then she felt guilty and returned to the little dining room that had a smear of sea for a view and planted a kiss on her mother's head.

Her mother didn't react.

In the street two children were running after each other through the rubbish bags and filth. The strike had brought nothing new to the old town, nothing that the residents weren't already used to, at any rate. Giuditta rummaged in her pocket and checked the list of things she had to get for her mother while she headed down to the port. Needles, bobbins, ribbons, synthetic fabric for lining, shoulder pads, She was very happy her father had given her the opportunity to go to university, and she had no intention of letting him, or herself, down. She wasn't going to end up as a seamstress in some clothes shop, her fingertips forever swollen and raw from needle pricks, ruining her eyes on hems and petticoats.

Next to the haberdasher's where her mother had an account that she paid off at the beginning of every month there was a bar that smelled of bad wine. From inside came the heated voices of old dockers who couldn't tear themselves away from the port, not even after their backs had finally buckled under the years of carrying heavy weights. Giuditta saw a familiar face leave the bar. A familiar face that was also out of place.

"Inspector," she called out cheerfully.

Giacomo Amaldi turned round wearily. He smiled when he saw her.

"Giuditta . . ."

"What brings you down here?"

"Oh, I was saying hello to some friends," he replied. Then, seeing the perplexed look on the girl's face, he added, "I was born and bred just round the corner." He pointed towards the houses of the old town, the poor ghetto, the swarming warren, the dingy cafés, the crowded washing lines, the smell of fish and rising damp, the tall, narrow buildings down whose stained façades the rivulets of water had left their traces, the peeling ochre exposing the stone underneath.

"Do you miss it?" she asked.

"Do you think you'll miss it when you get away?"

"No . . . I don't think I will."

"I don't think you will, either. But there's no time to lose," he said and turned to look at an old man who held a wineglass in his huge hands. The man's eyes were bright but inexpressive, a hapless smile on lips that were etched between the deep lines of his cheeks. "Otherwise you'll end up like that." He gave Giuditta a melancholy smile. "Either you escape right away, or you never get away. I knew an old docker once who won a fortune on the lottery. He said he would buy himself a fine house out in the suburbs and then live it up on the rest of the money. He spent his days here in this bar, buying drinks for everyone. For years."

"What happened?"

"He died of liver cirrhosis. All that money and he still couldn't buy decent wine."

"That's a sad story."

"That's the story of the old town, Giuditta. That's why you need to get away as soon as you can."

"Well, I'm trying."

"Good . . . And what brings you here, if I can ask?"

"Just getting a few things for my mother."

156

"Oh, well, I won't keep you, then," said Amaldi in embarrassment, and put his hands in his pockets.

Equally ill at ease, Giuditta, head lowered, described a figure of eight with the toe of her shoe on the ground, but didn't say goodbye. Amaldi didn't speak.

"Well, goodbye, then," Giuditta said at last. She gave him a wan smile and headed for the haberdasher's.

"Goodbye," murmured Amaldi.

He remained standing where he was and watched Giuditta go into the store without turning round. He took a few steps towards the window. Giuditta was talking to the shopkeeper. Her straight hair shone under the shop's fluorescent lights, and she moved her hands gracefully. Amaldi felt an urge to go into the store just to listen to her voice. He stiffened. He was about to leave when Giuditta saw him through the shop window. She smiled at him in surprise. A pleasantly surprised smile. She appeared in the doorway.

"Do you need a ribbon for your hair, Inspector?" she asked him and laughed.

"What colour do you recommend?" he replied, thinking how pretty she was when she laughed.

"Oh, blue of course. Blue is for boys."

The shopkeeper called out to Giuditta, a piece of material in her hand. Giuditta didn't budge.

"Would you keep me company at dinner?" asked Amaldi, his heart in his mouth.

"When?"

"Now."

Giuditta smiled.

"Yes," she said and went back inside the haberdasher's.

Amaldi saw her make a phone call, hand a note over to the shop-owner and leave the shop.

"What about your errand?" he asked her.

"Oh, no hurry. Tomorrow will do. Right now my mother is probably getting her fix."

"Pardon me?"

"Television."

Amaldi laughed. They walked on slowly, without a particular destination in mind, side by side but without touching. They exchanged a few convivial remarks, but they were both embarrassed. They fell silent and carried on walking, past one little restaurant, and then another. They skirted a drunk and smiled at each other once more.

"We had a little table with metal legs," began Amaldi, in a voice that was too loud. "Whenever I was sick and the doctor would come to our home, my mother used to get out a tray she had won in some competition, or raffle, and she would put two croissants and a tea cup on it. I don't know why but at any time of the year the paper napkins in our house always had mistletoe on them ... complete with red berries and the words 'Merry Christmas'.".

Giuditta laughed.

For the first time in his life, and with a feeling of desperate relief, Amaldi admitted to himself that he loathed the old town with every fibre of his being. And then he laughed aloud with Giuditta. He took her by the hand and asked, "Where would you like to eat then?"

"In a place where I can be just Giuditta and you can be Giacomo," Giuditta replied impulsively

Amaldi looked about him. From around the corner came excited voices and the sound of plates.

"Then we need a greasy spoon café," he said and pulled Giuditta towards the noise.

They sat at a corner table covered in a paper tablecloth. A scrawny old waiter, with two enormous bags under his vacant eyes, slowly laid the table, one place at a time. Occasionally a voice from the kitchen screamed "Amedeo!" and the waiter would spread his arms sorrowfully, and mumble "Coming" in such a low voice that he probably had trouble hearing it himself. When he had finished he wandered off at the same shambling speed with which he had laid the table. After a long interval he returned with a notepad. Amaldi and Giuditta ordered with admirable despatch and while the waiter shuffled away they burst out laughing again.

"I heard your message the other evening," Amaldi said. "I'm sorry I didn't get back to you."

"Well, I imagined you had a lot to take care of . . . I saw the papers . . ."

"Ah, yes."

"Why?"

"It's my job."

"No, I mean, why do they do it?"

"Why? Well, the sacred texts . . ." he paused for a moment and slapped the bottom of the salt cellar against the palm of his hand. It was an instinctive gesture, while he played for time. He could only really justify a short pause, however. He couldn't manage to think coherently; he produced a partial thought, the distillate of a flash of unease. But when he started talking again, his voice was different. "The sacred texts of criminal psychology inform us that the problem with this kind of person is their inability to feel. As if their soul was missing something. As if their eyes and mind were able to perceive only one side of the human condition. And they see that side in microscopic close-up, every single little detail. And the other side, the one they don't know, they one they can't focus on but feel must exist, that side becomes something frightening,

159

fearful. The dark side they hate. And they hate the people who possess it." And suddenly grim, Amaldi carried on with his thought in his own head: then that sort of man destroys and ravages and learns to love violence because only brutality and ferocity manage to stimulate a sentiment that resembles love. "But there is no real why . . . Nothing we can really understand."

"I'm sorry I brought up the subject," said Giuditta. She was mortified by the change she had noticed in Amaldi's mood.

"Don't worry, it doesn't matter. At least you didn't ask me if I've killed anyone."

"That was next on my list," said Giuditta and smiled.

The look in Amaldi's eye was remote, as if he hadn't heard her. He was thinking that he wasn't ready, that maybe he would never be ready for the little games people played. It had been stupid to invite the girl out to dinner. He was just setting her up. He had nothing to give. Nothing. Unseen by Giuditta he made his pager bleep. His face showed disappointment, he looked at the pager, stood up and went in search of a telephone with an expression of annoyance on his face.

The waiter had brought their meals.

"I'm sorry, Giuditta. A problem at the office. Well that's my life for you. We'll have to do it again another time. Let's go. I'll walk you home."

They walked briskly back the way they had come, so unlike their earlier journey, and Amaldi took his leave coolly and hastily. The girl pretended not to be upset but Amaldi could picture her going up the stairs that would take her back to her prison cell of an apartment. Maybe she would start crying. And her face would become ugly. Amaldi remembered his mother. When the doctor asked where the bathroom was, at the end of his visit, Amaldi's mother became uglier too. Because of her sense of shame. And Amaldi had hated that doctor, because his mother could tidy herself up and put on a bit of make-up and get the best tea service out of the cupboard and cover the table with a clean table-cloth, but she couldn't change the bathroom or the kitchen and she couldn't hide the smell of meat sauce and toilet bowl. And so Amaldi hated his father too, because he forced them all to live in that apartment. He saw the make-up dissolve on his mother's face, and the best dress in tatters, the teacups shattered into a thousand pieces, and the whole picture cracked. If he could have ordered a huge avalanche of mud to roll over and bury the old town, he would have done it. He felt himself racked by an ancient fury.

He looked up at the second floor of the building. He saw a light come on. Maybe it was Giuditta's room. But Giuditta was not his mother, Amaldi told himself. That wasn't why he was furious. And it wasn't because some doctor had wanted to wash his hands; the man had probably seen hundreds of poor homes like theirs, day in day out, all of them desperately alike. It wasn't the poverty, or the drab toilets, or the persistent smell of sauce. It was him. A mediocre little detective who ran away from everything and everyone. Someone who lived in terror but couldn't remember why or who he was fleeing.

He felt an urge to start running, to run away, but he was afraid Giuditta, at her window, might hear the old town laughing at him.

XIV

"Well, to cut a long story short, at the meeting with the mayor that you were supposed to be at too . . . by the way the chief would have set fire to you if he had been able to get his hands on you . . ." Frese had already launched into his speech.

"What's this doing on my desk?" Amaldi interrupted brusquely, fanning himself with a folder that was some indefinable shade of pink. It was well-thumbed, dog-eared and bore the words AUGUSTO AJACCIO.

"I told you the chief dumped Ajaccio on you. You have to sign a clearance form for the insurance people, for Ajaccio's hospital expenses. It's inside . . . the top sheet."

Amaldi opened the folder and initialled the form.

"You can read the personal file if you like. Isn't that much to read, mind you. A blank sheet would do just as well. Poor bugger. He's a good man, really he is. He never did anything incredibly amazing, but he didn't screw up, either. He isn't a shirker, and wouldn't want to be one, either, but . . ."

But, thought Amaldi, he was a useless human being, incapable of incarnating either good or evil. A creature so totally empty that he had no purpose in life either way. Amaldi knew dozens of men like that, men who were nothing, and at the same time a bit of everything, a sketch by a painter trying out shapes and colours.

". . . But . . . he's a good man," said Frese, finally settling for his first definition.

162

While Amaldi skimmed the officer's notes, his deputy took an envelope out of the inside pocket of his jacket and put in on the desk. It was marked "For A. Ajaccio".

"Anyway, the meeting was almost over, the usual non-conclusion you get when you talk with the unions," Frese was saying, "and we were all sitting about waffling and saying the usual rubbish just so we could say we were all working together, when someone . . . Who was it? I can't remember now . . . But anyway, someone mentioned out loud this guy's name and as it was a name I'd read only recently I recognized it right away . . . You can it read it for yourself in the file, it's there under 'Father'. There's the orphanage details and a name, the same name I heard at the meeting, the name of the bin man who found Ajaccio when he was just a few hours old, lying beside a pile of rubbish. So I turned round and realized it couldn't have been him because the guy I saw must have been about fifty . . . But I went over to him anyway and asked if he was a relative and he told me he's the guy's son. A piece of shit, between us, a real union dickhead who wouldn't dare get his hands dirty on rubbish. And he spoke really badly of his father, as if he was rubbish, too . . . Anyway, I tell him about Ajaccio, about the state he's in and that I would really appreciate being able to talk to his father . . . Not that I thought anything would come of it, what could he tell me? I just thought, well, I don't know what I thought. Don't know why I can't keep my nose out of other people's business . . . more like a hairdresser than a cop. Anyway, I asked him where I could find his father. So the union shithead tells me his father died last year in a home I wouldn't even leave my dog in, and the bugger didn't look like he couldn't have afforded a better place. With a little help from the union ... Okay, he's not rolling in gold, but still ... What do you think? We're talking about the man's father, here."

Amaldi put the folder to one side and focused on a photocopy of the writing that had been left on the wall of the antiques shop. There had to be an answer in those block capitals and lower-case letters. It wasn't a coincidence. This killer did nothing by chance.

Frese was still talking.

"I've learned a few things that aren't in the file. The union man has never set eyes on Ajaccio. Doesn't know if he's fat or thin. But he told me that Ajaccio was all his father talked about, especially towards the end, you know how old people get, they fixate on something and everything they talk about comes round to the same thing, a bit like crazy people, know what I mean? You're talking about bread and sausages, and the next thing they say is 'Oh, talking about bread and sausages, I remember when ...' and then they rabbit on about something that has nothing to do with bread and sausages, and you sit there like a cretin all the way to the end of the story, boiling your brain away trying to work out what the connection is, and then you discover that there is no connection, at least not with bread and sausages ..."

"viSitA intEriOra teRRae reCtificandO iNvEnies OcCuLtUm lapIdEm."

S, A, E, O, R, R, C, O, N, E, O, C, L, U, I, E.

Sixteen block capitals, and forty lower-case letters.

"Where was I? Oh yes. What isn't on the file is the real story of Augusto Ajaccio, you might say. It's a really sad story, pathetic. Quite touching. You don't hear many like it, that's for sure ... This letter was written by the father of that ungrateful union shit who gave it to me this morning. Reading the letter ..."

164

Amaldi looked up from his own sheet of paper.

"Yeah, yeah, I've read it," Frese admitted. "You can see right away why he's got it in for his father: jealousy. Pure and simple. The old guy thought more about Ajaccio than about his own son. I mean, one is your own flesh and blood, and the other is some foundling you never saw again. He spun a whole myth round Ajaccio, he beat himself to a pulp with his guilt over the years. You'll have to give it to Ajaccio," said Frese, and seemed to have finished his speech.

"Drum roll, please," thought Amaldi to himself.

"So, the story of Ajaccio?" he asked, in an effort to help move on his deputy's narrative.

He wasn't the slightest bit interested in the matter, but the background noise helped him think. Maybe the block capitals were the initial letters of words that were made up with the lower-case letters.

"The story of Ajaccio," echoed Frese, raising an eyebrow. "The 'This is Your Life' true story of Ajaccio? Okay. Where was he found? Where did the road sweeper find him? Next to a pile of rubbish, right? We know that. But where exactly? In a shoebox. Our man is busy cleaning, it's dawn, he hears a wail. Picture the scene . . . The cleaner thinks to himself, 'How strange, if I didn't believe I was completely thick I would think I'd just heard a baby crying.' He shrugs his shoulders, grips his broom and his fork and sets into the pile of shit in front of him . . . And then he hears the wail again. 'But that's a baby's wail,' he says to himself and not a pram in sight. 'Now where the hell is that coming from,' he probably says to himself, or words to that effect. And then the shoebox. And what's written on the box? A. AJACCIO, LUXURY SHOE MANUFACTURERS. So our man takes the baby to the nuns and they call him Augusto with a capital A and Ajaccio, because the

165

name had saved his life, in a sense. A really touching story, right?"

"Yeah . . ." More initials.

Then an urgent need gripped Amaldi and he shot to his feet and went to throw the window wide open, as if all the air had suddenly gone from the room. Once more he was seized by the need to run, to escape, to wipe out all the pathetic tales the world bloated itself on, as though people needed to feel stronger and stronger emotions, as if they wanted to sink deeper into the quagmire, as if they could play with feelings without getting hurt. "It isn't pathetic, it's disgusting. What's touching about it?" he said furiously. "Those nuns who named a child rejected by its mother and father after an advertisement for luxury shoes were sadistic bitches. Do you realize that Ajaccio was condemned to a kind of mental rickets? They forced him to grow up in a shoe-box. And the letter? You've read it. What does it say?"

"That he would've liked to adopt him but . . ."

"You won't give that letter to Ajaccio." He turned round to look at his deputy and stabbed a finger at him. "You won't give it to him. He's already dying of cancer, all he needs is to become an orphan for the second time. You and the chief can leave the man in peace." He turned his back on Frese again. "Let him die in peace," he murmured.

After a while Frese asked, "Did you go to see him?"

"No."

"Why?"

"Because I wouldn't have known what to say to the man. Because . . . he's so, so . . ."

"Mediocre?"

Amaldi kept looking out the window.

"Mediocrity frightens me too," said Frese in a low voice. "It's worse than cancer for some of us, right?"

166

"Yes . . ."

"Well that's just bullshit. We don't have cancer."

"No . . . No, we don't."

"You should go and see him."

"After we catch this guy."

"If we catch him . . . and if Ajaccio stays alive long enough."

Amaldi looked out of the window. The traffic in the streets was deafening. When he turned around Frese had already gone. On his desk there was no sign of either the letter to Ajaccio or the man's personal file. There was just the copy of the phrase written by the murderer. 'Descend into the bowels of the earth, rectifying you will find the occult stone.' Amaldi felt the message was aimed at him. Had he got wind of a tragedy just to remain on the surface of things? Had the blonde girl to whom he had promised a house full of light died so he might find himself where he was today: rooted to the spot, thirty-seven, alone and untouchable? She had laughed, loved, given herself to a rapist and bled to death for what, so he could filet the flesh out of life? She had died so he could bear her like a vessel in a crusade, or use her like a shield to hide behind?

He sat down and prepared sixteen pieces of paper and wrote one of the block capitals on each piece. Then he tried recomposing the killer's message.

CLONE CUES . . . Didn't mean anything. LONE CARS, SLAIN CURER . . .

He felt a desire to call Giuditta, to tell her about everything. But he wouldn't have known where to start.

He got up, put the photocopy and the pieces of paper in his coat pocket and went out. He had to speak to someone about this.

When he found himself standing in front of the

hospital he realized that he was going to talk about it with Augusto Ajaccio. Absolutely ridiculous, he said to himself as he knocked and entered room 423.

Before him Amaldi saw an old man with strong, stooped shoulders, unsteady legs and knotted hands. Ajaccio's likeness to Amaldi's own father was so striking that for a moment he convinced himself he could even smell his father. As though his nostrils had been duped by his eyes and his eyes by his memory. A streak of sweat that trickled out of his past. The old man, and at fifty-two Ajaccio looked old, gave off the same smell of sweat as his father. As though the two men had sweat in their veins rather than blood, as if they belonged to the same race of people who had been exhausted for ever.

"Come and look," said the cop in pyjamas and invited Amaldi over to the window.

Amaldi joined him and tried to see what Ajaccio was showing him, on the other side of the window.

The huge, disorderly pile of rubbish bags, and of rubbish without bags, made one think of mysterious plagues hidden somewhere beyond the rotten fruit peel, fleshless bones and black, fermenting vegetables. From his hospital room window, Ajaccio had watched the mound grow day by day, had studied it and observed how people had come, at first furtively, guiltily, to throw their rubbish on the heap and then how, with the passing of time, they had simply tossed the bags onto the pile with an air of defiance, of challenge.

"The stench comes all the way up here, you can smell it all the time," Ajaccio said, as though he were carrying on with something he had been saying earlier. He rasped as he spoke. "I feel like the whole city has got sick along with me." He turned to look at Amaldi. "It's terrible, you know. All my senses have expanded,"

168

he said, puffing in Amaldi's face. He took two unsteady steps, grabbed hold of the headboard and guided himself round the bed slowly. His naked feet dragged along the floor; they left the ridged brown tiles with difficulty. "I'm tired," he said, as though he were talking to himself. "I'm always tired and cold." He got in under the bedclothes and closed his eyes.

"Me too," Amaldi felt like telling him.

Then Ajaccio seemed to wake up with a jolt. He looked at his visitor and asked, "Who are you?"

Amaldi took one of the two visitors' chairs and moved it closer to the bed. He reached out and placed a hand on Ajaccio's arm. "My name is Giacomo Amaldi, I'm a chief inspector . . ." And then he didn't know what else to say.

"I'm afraid," said Ajaccio. His eyes glistened with fever and pain. Beyond the ceiling that reflected the light from outside, beyond the curve of the sky, Ajaccio was looking up at those spirits he had thought had no place in his small life but that now poured down to take control of the abandoned ruins, the old towers covered in ivy, the lonely ponds, the clearings they had always loved. He saw them thronged in dark streaks of cloud playing with lightning, and on the brighter clouds warming themselves in the silver rays of the moon or in the red rays of the late-afternoon sun, ready for the final assault that would see them victorious lords of his decaying body. "I'm afraid."

Amaldi squeezed the cop's arm harder. He had just realized that there was nothing to say. That at times it was enough to listen.

"Do you smell incense?" There was a querulous note in Ajaccio's voice.

Amaldi sniffed the air. "No . . ."

"No?"

169

"No."

"Never mind. I just wanted to be sure . . . That's all
. . . I just wanted to be sure. You know, the nurse . . ."
But he didn't finish. His voice trailed away. And with
his voice, an absurd hope. On his neck, the purple
burn mark that Frese had told him about. It really did
look like a tongue.

When Ajaccio began talking again his gaze was even
more distant, so remote that Amaldi found it difficult
to make out what the man was saying because it seemed
as though his words were being sucked into the emptiness of his expression.

"I had a visit from the widow yesterday morning . . .
my landlady, I mean. Well, the lady who rents me a
room, anyway. I don't have an apartment, you know,
just a room overlooking wharf nine. She brought me
some pastries and asked me how they were treating
me, if they were giving me enough to eat, and told me
about the time she had her appendix out in this very
hospital and what they gave her to eat . . . Watery broth
with no salt, and baby food . . . She told me that I was
like a son to her, and even if we had never eaten
together in all these years she had always thought of
me very fondly, day and night, and that I was really
like a son to her." Ajaccio smiled a disjointed smile.
"Then she asked me to pay my rent because I was a
week overdue. She understood my problems but she
has problems of her own and that was why she had
come to the hospital . . . And . . . and then she said to
me, 'What do you think you'll do with the room? Are
you coming back or do you want me to put your things
in a suitcase? I don't mind doing it. You mustn't think
it's a bother . . . Because if you think you won't be
coming back I could make a start on letting your room,
couldn't I?' That's what she said to me. To me, to

someone who is like a son to her. She asked me to vacate my room . . ."

Then Ajaccio seemed to shake himself awake again. He looked Amaldi straight in the eye. He withdrew his arm from under the covers and took Amaldi's hand in his own. Amaldi felt the rough skin of that hand and thought that once upon a time there had been strength in those fingers. Now they were merely clutching his. Now it was Amaldi who held him.

"I need your help, Ajaccio," he said.

The sick man's face brightened. He pulled himself up. He seemed less pale.

"I've noticed something: I'm learning, and I want to learn, everything." Ajaccio spoke excitedly. "I'm interested in everything and I learn really quickly and easily. Do you know what I've got? A glioblastoma. That's a hard word, isn't it? Did you know that tumour means swelling and pride, from the Latin *tumor* . . . and that Saint Augustine uses the expression *tumorusus* to mean 'swollen with pride' . . . and that cancer comes from the Greek word *karkinos*? Do you need all that learning?"

"Yes."

"I read everything, you know. And I understand it all too. Thanks to my disease."

"Thanks?"

"Did I say thanks?"

"Yes."

"Thanks, eh?"

"Yes."

"Well, thanks isn't such a good word," reflected Ajaccio. "But it's the right word." Tears clouded his eyes. "Yes, thanks to my disease. It's incredible. Do you believe me, or do you think I'm crazy?"

"I believe you."

"I think I'm crazy. Hallucinations, changes in personality . . . Dr Civita was very clear on the subject. I might even forget where my dick is and piss on myself while I go round the room looking for it." There was anger in his voice now. "He tells me everything, you know. Every little detail. Like he enjoys making me imagine how I'm going to die." His eyes clouded again. He tilted his nose upwards and breathed in. "Incense," he said. "I wanted to become a priest, you know. First the Lord and then the Force . . . Doesn't make sense, does it? Does it make any sense to you? Does it make any sense that my brain starts understanding things it has never understood in fifty-two years? Does it make any sense that I can smell incense . . .?"

Amaldi felt something intense flare within him. A mixture of terror and pleasure. Just as it must have been terrifying and immensely pleasurable for this stupid man to suddenly discover intelligence. He gripped Ajaccio's hand.

"I need your help to solve a riddle," he said again.

Ajaccio beamed like a baby.

Then there was a knock at the door. A man of about sixty in a white coat, short and stocky, almost completely bald, and with a rather aloof and unfriendly expression came into the room, followed by three young doctors.

"I'm Professor Civita, head of this department," he began. "I'm sorry I haven't been to see you before now but I've been away at a conference and I've only just got back."

Amaldi felt Ajaccio stiffen. He looked at him. The man was gaping, his mouth wide open in silence. His lips, flecked with spittle at the corners, were drained. He shook his head in denial.

"That's not him," he finally managed to say. "It's not

172

him . . . it's not him." He clutched hold of Amaldi's chest, and shook the detective.

Completely unfazed, Professor Civita smiled a little formal, pitying smile at Amaldi and motioned to one of his assistants. Then he rolled up Ajaccio's sleeve.

"I'm not crazy . . ." stammered Ajaccio.

"Keep calm, now," said Civita and jabbed a needle into the muscle of Ajaccio's arm. "You'll feel better in a moment." His voice was calm.

"I'm not crazy . . ." Ajaccio said once more and then let go and fell back onto the pillow, completely winded.

"There, you feel better already, don't you?" asked Professor Civita.

Tilted towards the ceiling, Ajaccio's eyes looked like glass.

XV

"Good evening, Doctor," said the man, stepping out of the rubbish-filled shadows.

The young woman, loaded with shopping bags, turned reluctantly towards the voice. As soon as the man's face was lit by the street lamp she recognized him. She gave a little start, and then an overly wide smile, then tried in an exaggerated fashion not to show just how pleasantly surprised she was to come across him in front of her own building, on a dark and damp and lonely evening, like so many of her other evenings. The man bridged the gap between them with measured, feline steps. As though he were gliding rather than walking. His eyes were bright and intense and fixed on her. He looked as though he had been scorched.

"Well, what brings you to this part of town?" the young doctor asked and her tongue darted instinctively to the side of her mouth.

"Oh, I was just killing time," the man replied, with a note of melancholy in his voice. "I don't really like to go back to that big cold house now that mother isn't there."

The woman instinctively felt sorry for him.

"And you?" he asked her.

"Me? I live here." And she turned her head to the building they were standing in front of.

"Really?"

"Yes."

"What a coincidence."

"Why's that?"

The man looked at her for a long time before replying. "Well, if I had gone past a minute earlier or a minute later I wouldn't have met you."

The doctor looked at the ground.

"Do you believe in destiny or chance?" he went on. "I've noticed that people can be divided into two groups. The people who trust in chance are like rafts tossed against rocks by the current, with no plan. The people who follow their destiny, on the other hand, know how to recognize the signs and give things their proper worth and meaning. They never get tossed about. They drop anchor, they reach their mooring. Destiny does not mean having to be passive, as so many think ... What do you think, Doctor?"

The young woman caught herself wondering if the man in front of her had always spoken with that hypnotic voice.

"I believe in destiny," she replied.

The man smiled at her.

"Isn't it wonderful that two strangers such as ourselves can discuss things so freely? Standing outside on the pavement, on a damp, and rather sad, evening." As he continued speaking, his voice became warmer, his gaze more penetrating. "We don't know anything about each other and yet we've already exchanged such an intimate secret ... It doesn't happen that often, does it?"

"No," she murmured.

"No," he confirmed, his expression serious. "Will you follow my advice?"

The woman, cocked her head to one side, a perplexed expression on her face.

"Will you take good care of your legs tonight?"

The doctor felt her cheeks blaze.

"But here I am wasting your time," said the man, brusquely dispelling the atmosphere. "Those bags look heavy. I'm sorry to have kept you standing here. It was very nice to have met you . . ."

"Yes, it was . . ." She took a deep breathe and then, feeling awkward and stupid, like a teenager, she added. "But maybe it wasn't a coincidence."

For a moment she thought she saw the man stiffen. The paper around the huge parcel he was carrying under his arm crackled. His expression grew harsh.

"Destiny," she hurriedly added.

The man relaxed.

"Destiny . . . indeed. Can I help you with those bags? I could carry them upstairs for you?" and so saying he reached out with his left hand.

It was only then that the doctor noticed he was missing two phalanges of his little finger and that the amputation had probably occurred many years ago. The skin of the stump was yellow and rough. They didn't speak while they went up in the lift. When they reached the fifth floor another resident was on his way out to walk his dog.

"Good evening," he said. The dog wagged its tail enthusiastically.

The doctor returned the greeting. Despite the fact his hands were full with the bulky parcel and the shopping bags, the man leaned down to pet the dog. He didn't speak until he was sure the neighbour couldn't hear his voice.

"I live here," said the woman, feeling very uncomfortable, at the door to her apartment.

"Are you expecting anyone?" the man asked her.

The doctor shook her head.

"I would really like to prepare dinner for you and put a cushion under your feet."

Her heart raced. It had been a while since anyone had been back to her place. She couldn't answer.

"You're right, yes, of course," the man said after a moment. "I'm sorry for putting you in an awkward position . . . I've been stupid and ill-mannered. Please, I want to make it clear that I didn't take your professional kindness for anything more . . ."

"No . . ." Her voice was mangled, unpleasant. "No, it would be nice, thank you, if you don't mind something heated up and a bit of untidiness."

The man smiled without speaking.

"Come in," said the doctor and turned to enter the apartment. Behind her she heard his measured, stealthy steps. "And I'm sorry if I behaved like a teenager before, it's just . . ."

"There's no need to apologize," he interrupted, and set the bags down on the floor. "Don't say any more about it." He put a hand on her shoulder.

She turned round, convinced he was going to kiss her.

"Let me help you off with your coat," the man said, instead.

"Would you like something to drink? Make yourself at home. If you don't mind I'm going to freshen up."

He stared at her with that sensual, blatant, violent look. He dominated her, she thought. And how pleasant it was to yield to him.

The doctor went into the bathroom and washed her hands and rinsed her face. When she felt she had regained control of herself she looked at her reflection in the mirror. Her plain face struck her as being more interesting, her hair less drab. She smiled at herself in the mirror and her coquettishness made her blush. She felt better. She left the bathroom and found him still standing in the middle of her living room.

The man had looked round discreetly. He had already noticed the ugly armchair with the misshapen cushion in front of the television set. The well-made white sofa was in perfect condition. When she reappeared he took her by the hand, which felt fresh and pleasantly damp, and led her to the armchair and made her sit down, all without saying a word. He moved the low coffee table over to the armchair, took a cushion from the sofa, put it on the table, kneeled down at the woman's feet, looked intensely at her and before unlacing her shoes said, "Please, let me do it." Then he raised her feet with great delicacy and brought them to rest on the cushion. He caught the smell of her tights. "The kitchen is through there?"

She nodded feebly. Equally feebly she made to get up. But she allowed the man to stay her with slight pressure from his hand on her feet. Her attention was caught once more by the stump of his little finger. She felt a quiver of excitement at his touch. Her professional experience taught her that the mutilated finger was almost totally without feeling. If she had bitten it he wouldn't have felt any pain. Then she thought of how that ruined digit could give pleasure without experiencing the sensuality of touch. Like some inanimate object.

"I'm not a great cook. I hope you won't mind too much," he said as he got to his feet.

"No," she said flatly, made numb by her own thoughts. By the whole absurd situation. By her readiness to yield. By her recklessness. By the comforting, seductive feeling of having a man in her apartment after such a long time. Uneasy because of the strange hypnotic trance she was willingly falling into. Embarrassed at the thought of how pleasurable it was to feel herself pulled into that vortex, of how easy it was to wed herself to the sensation of vertigo. To lose herself. To let herself be comforted and cradled by the muffled sounds of saucepans and dishes and running water that came from the kitchen, so far away. She closed her eyes.

In the meantime, the man had checked the shopping bags, put a pre-cooked meal in the oven, and out of the bag that he had leaned against his huge parcel he had taken two candles and a little sachet of white powder that he kept hidden in his trousers. Every so often he glanced over at the woman. He could only make out three-quarters of her, and her strong legs resting on the table. She was completely still, relaxed. He didn't say a word to her. The ambient silence spoke more smoothly. It worked with him, and for him. In the midst of this dense silence the man's inner voice announced the next step in the shining path of his grand design, described it minutely, exalted it. As he busied himself in the kitchen, his life unfolded before him. He put all the scattered tiles from the mosaic of his past into place: the past when he still believed in chance and not in destiny. When he was just someone in pain. He remembered when he was a boy, in his room, the only room that was to be his because all the other rooms he used to wander around in had been dismembered and transformed by the builders, architects and his mother, to meet the needs of the orphans. He remembered that he had been in his room when he had heard the gravel scrunch. He had put his face to the window and had leaned the palm of one hand against the cold glass. Then the other palm. Then his forehead, his nose, his lips, and finally he had pushed his chest against the cold glass, hoping the cold would penetrate him and stop him suffering what he was suffering. He hoped the icy touch would anaesthetize his pain, kill it off, help him not see what was plainly before his eyes. The procession of orphans had struck him as being like an invasion of sick crickets. The sadness that had kept him company during the night evaporated instantly at the sight of the orphans and he felt instead that he hated them, without any real reason, without their having committed any sin. And then he remembered his mother's doll, with its lacy undergarments, the soft velvet that puckered at chest level where its maker had modelled a hint of a bust in the plaster. Severe yet violable like his mother after the accident that had paralysed her. And he remembered another day four years earlier when he had started trailing the orphan from his past that had been delivered to him by Clara, the chosen one, the prostitute.

"Thank you," he said, out loud, to his destiny.

"Sorry?"

"Shhh . . ."

He looked over at the woman again. She was quite still. For the past two days he had followed her and observed her. He had unlocked her ordinary existence and measured her solitude. He lit the two candles on the kitchen table, set out each place with great care, so that forks did not overlap knives and no piece of cutlery exceeded the ideal square that was supposed to contain the circumference of the dishes. He served up the food, cleaned up every stain, carefully folded the paper napkins and when he was satisfied with the result he took the sachet from his pocket. He opened it and mixed the white odourless powder into his host's meal. He heaved a long sigh and then announced in solemn tones, "Dinner is served," before going to help the woman get up.

The lights in the kitchen were off. The table and the room flickered in time with the trembling candle flames.

The woman squeezed his hand.

"I found them in a drawer and took the liberty of lighting them," he said. "Shadows sometimes reveal things that the light hides."

"I don't remember having any candles."

"Well, that can happen. Why don't you sit down?"

He poured her something to drink, looked at her and settled down in the chair opposite.

"This has never happened before . . . You must think that I'm . . ." she began, her eyes glittering. "I don't know what to say." She laughed in embarrassment.

The man raised his right hand to interrupt her, then reached across the table and stopped less than an inch from her cheek. With a slow, fluid motion, he followed the line of her face, of her shoulder, her arm, without actually touching her. Almost a caress. When he reached her hand he lightly touched her with the tip of one finger. He brushed against the back of her hand, and described the outline of her fingers.

"What use is talking?" he murmured. "Have we not already said everything we need to say?"

Then he got up and moved his chair closer to the woman's, took her fork, dipped it in the food and brought it up to those lips without make-up.

"Let me do it for you," he said.

She opened her mouth without taking her eyes off his. She bit down and barely managed to swallow once he had extracted the fork from between her teeth.

"Why me?" she asked.

"Because you have touched my mother," he replied.

"Is that all?" she said, disappointed.

"And because I need your legs."

The woman didn't speak until he had finished feeding her. Then he took the napkin and cleaned her lips with a gentleness that she hadn't thought possible and that almost hurt. His face was close to hers, she felt his warm breath on her cheeks. The man dropped the napkin. She gave her lips over to his touch. She closed her eyes.

"Just like a doll," he murmured in her ear.

She opened her eyes again.

"You can kiss me," she said.

"No." He smiled the most delicate smile in the world. "There isn't time."

As though in a dream, the woman watched him stand up, leave the kitchen and get his bag and big parcel, never once taking his eyes from her, with an expression full of love and attention. She felt strangely heavy, dazed. She saw him take tools out of the bag and set them out, calmly and in an orderly way on the kitchen table. She recognized a scalpel and a surgical saw. The first spasm folded her in two. A violent pain in her stomach. She sat up in her chair and tried to breathe but her lungs refused to open. They were on fire. And she was burning with terror. The man began to unwrap the parcel. No, there was no love in that expression, it was just attention. And then the pain stopped. She was anaesthetized. She couldn't even move her eyelids. Paralysed. The oxygen in her lungs was rapidly depleting. He had finished unwrapping the parcel. The woman saw that it contained two wooden legs connected by a metal hinge where the hips would have been. Knees and ankles were jointed. The two wooden feet, which hung inertly, had been painted with little red shoes. Ballet shoes.

Then the woman saw nothing. Her dream became dark and silent for ever.

The man massaged the stump of his little finger. Many people presumed he couldn't feel anything, perhaps because of the stump's appearance. But that was not the case. It was, if anything, his most delicate part. That scar that had never completely healed put the whole world in direct contact with his soul. In the calloused yellow of the last surviving phalange was concentrated all the pain of his existence.

With the stump of his little finger he stroked the contracted face of the doctor who looked after his mother. He ran his finger down her neck, down, down, along the sternum, without touching the breasts, and down, down again to the abdomen. Then he grasped the hem of the dress and lifted it up for a first inspection.

XVI

ARSENIC . . . CONCEAL . . . COERCE . . . ARSON. Giacomo Amaldi made an angry gesture and straightened up in his chair. He was trying to make some sense out of the capital letters the killer had left in his message on the victim's shop wall.

He looked at the sheet where he had noted down a few combinations.

ANUS, SANE, RACE, CLUE, LURE, ROUSE, CRUEL, CURSE, UNCOIL, CANCEL, ALONE. As well as a few nonsense phrases. I CAUSE CANCER, A CURE OR SIN, I SEE CLEANER, LICE ARE NO CLUES, LIES ARE NICE, SORE LONER.

"This is crazy!" he spluttered. "What have you managed to come up with?"

Frese looked up from his piece of paper. He was sweating and red in the face.

"ARSE ON CUE," he said.

"Is that all?"

"Oh, no." His deputy picked up his sheet. "ARSE RECOIL, ARSE ON COUNCIL. How about CONE IN REAR? Here's a good one. Uses up nearly all the letters: I CURL ONE ARSE. I should get double points for that."

"I don't think that was what the killer wanted to tell us. But it does offer us some interesting insights into your personality."

"Think so?"

"Definitely. Obsessive and monomaniacal."

"Because of my interest in backsides."

"Exactly."

184

"Well, for that matter I also found I USE CORE CLEANER."

"That settles it then."

"This is all bullshit, Giacomo. What about the forty other lower-case letters? Maybe they have to be combined too? How can we be sure that it wasn't just a way of throwing us off the trail? Or a coincidence."

"Not a coincidence. Our man doesn't leave anything to chance. The leaves didn't just happen to be there. He put them there. I have no idea what the leaves, the capital letters or the lower-case letters might mean, but it's all organized down to the last detail. It's a riddle. Maybe it's just something for the killer, part of his ritual . . . But it's certainly not a coincidence. And he definitely isn't trying to throw us off the track. He's not worried about us. He's got a plan and he's going to carry it out in every detail, without panicking. He doesn't improvise."

Frese stood up and tucked in his shirt.

"This hot spell was the last thing we needed."

Amaldi threw him a puzzled look.

"The scirocco . . . it makes it a lot hotter," said Frese, by way of explanation. "Can't you smell the stink of rubbish that's filling the streets?"

"Oh, well, yes . . ."

"The forecast said it's going to be like this for a few more days. Let's hope they've got it wrong. Don't you think the smell is absolutely unbearable?"

"I hadn't noticed, to be honest," replied Amaldi. "It's the smell of the old town. It comes up off the streets, from the port, from the blocked sewers, it gets inside the houses . . . You live with the smell of it in your nose if you grow up in the old town. After a while you just get used to it."

"Lucky you."

"Oh, yes, very fortunate."

"I've heard that they want to organize outside squads . . . Contract out the rubbish collection until the strike's over."

"I've talked to the mayor about that," said Amaldi. "He called me in to ask my opinion. It might be unconstitutional . . ."

"Unconstitutional my arse," grunted Frese. "And what did you say to him?"

Amaldi looked at him placidly. "What would you have told him?"

Frese thought for a moment.

"That I would be concerned about public unrest," he replied.

"And I agree. I'll take the smell over urban guerrilla warfare."

"And so we'll be under siege from the bin bags for God knows how long," muttered Frese, shaking his head.

"Something tells me the mayor was none too keen on my opinion."

Frese pictured long nights spent quelling riots, and tense days spent breaking up unauthorized marches and playing bodyguard to blacklegs.

"Are you still wasting your time checking the orphanage file?" Amaldi asked.

"Yes. Why?"

"Well, while I was with the mayor," began Amaldi, looking out of the foggy window on his left and speaking in that detached tone he used when he wanted to say something without saying it, "I did mention the orphanage . . ."

Frese perked up.

"I asked him about the fire."

"And . . .?"

"He shook his head . . . He said, 'Bad business, a tragedy, if memory serves,' and then he sent me on my way . . ."

"*If memory serves?!*"

"Yes, and not one word about the fact that he was the one in charge of the investigation. Now wouldn't you say that was a bit of a strange way to behave?"

"I always thought he was honest," said Frese, who had already understood what Amaldi wasn't saying: Don't give up, Nicola, dig.

"I've always thought he's honest, too."

"But we aren't infallible, are we?"

"No, we make mistakes, we're far from being infallible."

"I think I'll just pay a little visit to Records," said Frese. "I've put Peschiera to work."

"Who?"

"Our chief archivist."

Amaldi nodded.

"By the way, Ajaccio phoned me this morning," added Frese, casually. "Is it true that you asked him to help you?"

"I didn't know what to say to him . . . I just thought that if we kept him busy he might not think so much about what's happening . . ."

"You're a good man," Frese remarked.

"Be careful not to give him anything too important. Most of the time he doesn't know what he's saying. Did you know he scribbled on his own chest and they found him naked and unconscious? He swears he wasn't the one who did it. He smells incense, says he hears voices. When I was there, the head of department, Civita, I think his name was, came in and Ajaccio started shouting that the man wasn't Civita at all, that he was someone else. Poor soul. I feel sorry for him."

"He acted strange when I was there, too. Maybe we shouldn't involve him in this case. I'll get him to help me with the orphanage file, instead. I'm over in Records if you're looking for me," said Frese and left.

Alone, Amaldi picked up a memo he had found that morning on his desk. Giuditta had been looking for him. But not at home. There weren't any messages on the machine. She would soon give up, he thought. And it would be much better for her. A feeling of intense irritation forced him to his feet. He couldn't drag them all out of the old town. It wasn't his job. He didn't ask anything of anyone. He had never asked anything of anyone. What did Giuditta expect? That he'd ask her to move in with him? That he'd drag her out of her gutter of an apartment? Just because they had fluttered their eyelashes at each other a few times? He crumpled the memo and hurled it at the wastebin.

He turned his attention to the murderer. Did he know the antique-dealer? Why had he chosen her? How did two people attract one another? Had he had an affair with her? Had he been betrayed? There was nothing to go on in this case, no evidence of sexual assault, absolutely nothing under the victim's nails. A dead end. The halberd was the murder weapon; the fatal blow had been to the stomach. The blow had been delivered with considerable violence: the blade had been stopped by the spine after having sliced through the body, which fact allowed them to suppose the killer was a man. The limbs had been removed using a scalpel. The man had not used ordinary sutures but twist, or linen yarn, and the knots were not surgeon's knots. The pathologist had added a note at the bottom of the report, to the effect that twist was used by taxidermists. So was the killer a taxidermist, then? They would check it out. There weren't that many left. If he was a professional. And what if it was just some amateur? They would check with suppliers. But who kept proper books these days? There might be a trace if the murderer had asked for an invoice. Amaldi had trouble imagining a serial killer reclaiming expenses on the tools he used to torture and kill his victims. Maybe they could get the names of the people who had that kind of equipment sent to them. They had to try, of course, but Amaldi didn't fool himself. They wouldn't catch their murderer by following logical paths.

His background in psychology made him think that from a clinical point of view they were dealing with a psychotic, a disassociated schizophrenic with a history of violence. But that was just so much waffle, theories. Obvious stuff. The same theories would allow them to consider the antiques store, with its long, narrow shape, as a womb. Everything represented something in psychology. There were no such things as coincidences. He remembered his first lessons very well: the psychologist could not accept chance. He shouldn't concern himself with coincidences, besides which coincidences were there to be explained. "Even those things which apparently seem to have no meaning in and of themselves acquire meaning for those who know how to observe, experience and study the consequences," his teacher always used to declare, and on this occasion the man would most certainly have concluded by saying, "Thus, for us, the shop is, must be, a womb." And from "womb" he would have inevitably worked his way back to "mother". A mother who was loved and hated, almost certainly the object of sexual desire. And maybe even a mother killer, or potential killer. Because people who kill learn to do so in the cradle. Thus, the murderer had killed the antique-dealer in order to kill

189

his mother. Amaldi believed that this was the most likely interpretation a criminal psychologist would give to events, and he was a criminal psychologist. And in killing the mother, he would have killed himself, symbolically. Would have killed the killer he was and knew himself to be. And where did he do this? In a shop that, surprise, surprise, resembled a uterus, which would thus contain him in his unborn state. Psychotics always had a very clear idea of what was good and what was bad. Unconsciously, and in ways which so-called normal people would find incomprehensible, illogical and ruthless, psychotics were actually trying to heal themselves. They plunged into the worst recesses of their beings in order to face the illness that was torturing them. There was something heroic in that. For the police and the public, the key player in the drama was always the psychotic. But for the sick person it was always his own sickness. A sickness that often had anthropomorphic characteristics, was a separate entity, with which the psychotic compared himself, to which he talked and with which he struggled. The sick man had a very intense relationship with his sickness. The sickness had its own voice, unique and recognizable, its own character, impulses and fears. The sickness was, to all intents and purposes, a real person. A sitting tenant. A companion. And thus, because it took up space and got in the way, the sick man confronted it, challenged it, provoked it. To establish who was in charge. They argued over the steering wheel, as it were. That was why the car swerved all over the road. And that was why the psychotic wanted to fight his sickness. To assess the extent of his own control. Even if he was constantly frustrated. And what was self-control, in such cases, if not an effort to affirm one's own existence? "Who exists? Me or the sickness?" the sick man would ask himself. One might even feel sorry for him. Like Ajaccio. But Ajaccio, whose intelligence had suddenly been brought to the surface with the cancer, and who probably asked himself the same question every day, Ajaccio had not killed Viviana Justic. Nor had he amputated her arms, nor stuck fish hooks into her lips nor glued her eyelids nor written messages in Latin using his victim's blood.

The murderer was an educated man. Not particularly young. That was an obvious conclusion: it took time to absorb the kind of cultural learning needed to set out that sort of crime, and it took even longer to assimilate it to the point that it polluted your unconscious. But, thought Amaldi again, that was just so much hot air. All of this served to decipher the "why" after the fact. Like an art critic who could talk for hours on a given painting and explain to the artist why he had painted what was on the canvas. Yet no critic could imagine the artist's next painting.

The only certainty was that the psychotic had probably gone through a whole *seminary of perversion* before reaching that point. That was their only valid, solid starting point. A red line. Amaldi decided to look for other, cruder crimes that might have something in common with the Justic case. But maybe he had it in for animals. Almost all psychotics practised on animals. In which case it would be very difficult to find him.

The shrill ringing of his telephone brought him back to the present.

"There's a Miss Luzzatto asking for you, Inspector," croaked a voice from the receiver.

"I'm not in."

"She said it was important . . ."

So, she wasn't going to give up so quickly after all.

191

"Put her through," he said, irritated.

He would convince her himself to forget about him.

"Giacomo . . ."

"Miss Luzzatto, I really have a lot to do. What is —"

There was silence at the other end of the line. Good. The message was getting through.

"Miss Luzzatto . . .?"

Deep sighs. Maybe she was crying. Well she would cry less later, then.

"He . . . he sent me . . ."

"He who?" Cold, uninterested.

"He . . . he sent me a parcel."

"Who sent you a parcel?"

Giuditta's voice was barely a whisper. She was crying uncontrollably.

". . . In the box . . ."

More tears. She wasn't crying for him.

"What was in the box, Giuditta?" Amaldi's voice softened.

"The kitten."

"What kitten?"

"A few months old . . . Why did he hurt the kitten? What harm had the kitten done to him?"

"Where are you, Giuditta?"

"At home."

"Is anyone with you?"

"No, I'm on my own . . ."

"Wait for me."

"Yes."

"I'll be over straight away."

"Yes . . ."

"Don't be afraid . . . I'm on my way."

Amaldi pulled on his coat and bolted from his office. He collided with Frese in the corridor.

"I was right, look at this," his deputy said excitedly.

192

"No time now," said Amaldi, continuing on his way.

"What's up?" Frese hurried after him, towards the lift.

"A dead cat."

"What?"

"Forget it."

The lift doors began to shudder open. Amaldi squeezed through them.

"Well, when you do have time, read these. They're photocopies, doesn't matter if you lose them," and Frese pushed some sheets of paper at him. "I was right," he said again.

Amaldi grabbed the sheets and shoved them in his pocket while the lift took him to the ground floor. When he left the station he was assaulted by a gust from the sirocco. He kicked a bag of rubbish away from the station entrance, crossed the road and headed into the old town with one thought in his head: he didn't want Giuditta to cry on her own.

XVII

The two cops who had lifted him bodily from the university had not said one word, nor offered him a shred of explanation during the journey. It wasn't regular procedure but Chief Inspector Amaldi had been very clear: the suspect had to reach the station in a state of blind panic. And few things were more frightening than total silence inside a speeding police car that rushed through traffic with its sirens wailing. When they reached the station, the two cops, guns in hands, pushed him out of the back door of the car. They took him up to the third floor and shoved him into a bare room. The table in the middle of the room was bolted to the floor, as were the two solitary chairs. One of the cops motioned at him to sit down and returned his gun to its holster.

"I need . . . I have to go . . . go to the toilet," stammered the fat youth, eyes wide open, sweating profusely.

"Name and surname," said the first cop.

"Max Peschiera."

"Max?" said the cop in disgust and looked at his colleague.

"Max is a queer's name," remarked the other.

"Massimo . . ." said the fat boy.

"Are you queer?"

"No . . ."

"Are you fucking us around?"

"Don't fuck around with us, you queer shit."

"No . . . I . . ."

"Is your name Massimo or Max?"

"Massimo . . ."

"Well why did you say Max? Were you trying to be funny?"

"No. Look, I really need to go to the toilet."

"Massimo what?"

"Massimo Peschiera."

"Peschiera? You sure about that? We're not going to discover that Peschiera isn't your surname like Max isn't your first name?"

"No, my name is Peschiera . . . Massimo Peschiera and I really need —"

"You're just a fat shit and you think you can play the comedian."

"You should go on a diet, Max, instead of fucking us around."

"I'm not fucking you around."

"Fucking? Did he say *fucking?*"

"The fat guy said fucking, I heard him myself."

"Wash your mouth out before you speak to us, Max."

"Please, I really need —"

"So, what's your name, then?"

"Massimo Peschiera!" The fat boy leaned his arms on the table, hid his face and burst into tears.

The cop nearest to him pushed him upright.

"Sit up straight."

The youth's cheeks were streaked with tears. His small eyes were red.

"Please, I really need to go to the toilet." He wiped away a trickle of spittle with the sleeve of his military-style jacket.

The two cops turned their backs on him and left the room without another word. Frese was waiting for them in the corridor.

"He's cooked," one of them said.

"He can stew a bit longer," said Frese. "We'll wait for Amaldi."

"He has to go to the toilet."

"He will."

"He's nearly pissing himself."

"What do you care? Do you do the cleaning around here?" Frese snapped.

"No . . . but . . ."

"Get back inside. Never leave them alone. How many times do I have to tell you? If he hurts himself, you'll be responsible. Got that?"

The officer went back into the interrogation room.

"What's his name?" Frese asked the other man.

"Massimo Peschiera."

"Peschiera? What? Like our Peschiera?"

"Who?"

"The archivist, dickhead! Go over to Records and ask him if he knows this guy." He watched the man move off down the corridor, clearly unsure of where to go. "And don't get lost!" he yelled after him.

Frese stood on tiptoe and peered through the door's spyhole. The lad wasn't more than twenty years old. He had straight, short hair, tiny, scared eyes and rodent's teeth. Fat. You're no maniac, he concluded. Just a womanless wanker, right? Frese knew what it was like to be plain at that age. The same thing had happened to him. But he had never made obscene phone calls. It was a lot easier to go see a few whores. And he had certainly never killed some animal just to get a girl's attention.

"Great plan, lad," he muttered to himself.

He paced the corridor with his hands behind his back, his head lowered, thinking that Amaldi's interest in an incident like that when they had a homicidal madman on the loose was, to say the least, strange. Unless Amaldi had set his sights on the girl. It would be the first time in all the years he had known the inspector. On the only occasion he had seen them together, the way his superior had looked at her had not escaped Frese. Almost imperceptible signs that would have been quite meaningless in an ordinary human being, but for Amaldi they spoke volumes. They would make a great couple, thought Frese, and smiled a little sadly because he knew he could never aspire to having girlfriends who were that pretty. Unless they were for sale on the street. But they didn't count. Amaldi did not have the remotest idea of how lucky he was. That girl could drag him out of whatever pit he was clearly falling into. And if it did happen, Frese would be the first one to be delighted.

"Is it my nephew?" asked a breathless voice.

Frese turned towards the lift. He watched the archivist waddle up the corridor. The man was plump, flat-footed and bow-legged. Straight hair, piggy eyes, big yellow teeth that he couldn't quite conceal behind his lips. The family resemblance was striking.

"No idea," said Frese. "Look for yourself," and invited the man to look through the spyhole.

"Shit!" snorted the archivist. "Excuse me, I . . ." The archivist broke off, red in the face. "Yes, that's Mouldy all right . . . What's he done? Why's he here?"

Frese explained about the obscene phone calls and the foul messages and finished with the dead cat in a box sent with an anonymous letter.

"And Mouldy did all that?"

"We think so. Why do you call him Mouldy?"

"He's my sister's son. She's a widow. She lives off her husband's pension and does a few jobs here and there. I never married so I help her out whenever I can . . .

It's not easy putting a child through school and then university . . . He's a very intelligent boy, detective. But it takes a lot of money. He's all my sister has, and all I've got is my sister so . . ."

"And Mouldy?" Frese reminded him.

"Oh, yes, Mouldy. We call him that because ever since he was a kid he's always latched onto anyone who shows him a bit of consideration. You know the way mould grows?"

"Do you want to talk to him first?" asked Frese.

"Thank you," said the archivist and went into the room.

Frese motioned the policeman out of the room. As he closed the door he saw the fat boy get to his feet and exclaim through his tears, "Uncle!" The archivist stabbed a finger in the boy's face and snarled, "Sit down! I'm going to kill you!"

Then Frese heard no more, and he did not look through the spyhole to see what was happening.

Amaldi was coming out of the lift. His face was gaunt with tiredness.

The day before, when he had been standing in front of the door to Giuditta's building, he had had to admit that the girl meant something to him. It just wasn't like him to behave that way, to lose control. It wasn't like him to abuse his position and arrest a suspect on the flimsy evidence they had. He had stopped in front of the main entrance, out of breath. He had been frightened by what he was feeling. He was terrified at the idea of losing his way. Then he had pressed the buzzer, had heard Giuditta's distorted voice, and his worries had evaporated. How long had it been since he had last looked after someone who was alive? The bolt on the door had sprung back. Hardly had Amaldi set foot in the hallway when he had immediately recalled

198

all the clammy, sticky smells of his childhood, the unhealthy air that drained colour from your skin and crushed your lungs. Instinctively, he had stretched out his arm to push aside cobwebs, like he used to do when he was a kid. Giuditta had been waiting for him at the top of the stairs. She had burst into tears when he reached her. He had hugged her stiffly, resisting the swell of emotion within him. Then he had entered the apartment. In the meantime Giuditta's mother had come home. She was a dull-looking woman, worn down, fatigued more by life's disappointments than by work. She didn't look like Giuditta. And probably hadn't when younger, either, when she too must have had high hopes for herself. Amaldi had seen in her eyes that the woman was condemned to resignation. With the mother in the room, Amaldi had managed to regain the composure and confidence he had felt he would surely lose if he had been alone with Giuditta. He had hastily examined the box with the burned animal. The sight of that mangled little form, blackened and unrecognizable, with the emptied skull and a few carbonized bones that protruded from the mass of flesh had made his stomach turn. He had read the obscene anonymous letter. Whoever had written it certainly wasn't a maniac. His instinct and the years of horror he had faced in his job told him as much. He had understood that he would never have given such a trivial matter so much attention if it hadn't been for Giuditta. This knowledge had made him feel uncomfortable again. Giuditta's mother had shuffled over with two cups of coffee, one for her daughter and one for him. After she had rebuked Giuditta for her behaviour and the way she dressed, the woman had shuffled off back into the kitchen. "It's not your fault," Amaldi had told Giuditta as soon as they were alone again. The girl had looked at him, her eyes full of gratitude. Then Giuditta's father had arrived. He was a good-looking man, with a proud, yet delicate air about him. Amaldi had admired the man's priorities. Someone had obviously told him about what had happened. He had gone straight over to his daughter and had hugged her and whispered words of comfort into her hair and had not let go of her until Giuditta had unlaced herself from his embrace. In all that time the man had not once bothered to look at Amaldi, and only did so afterwards because Giuditta introduced them. He was as tall as Amaldi, slim. Nimble but not nervous. The man's eyes and hair seemed to compensate for the absence of sky and sea in that home. He was dressed shabbily and smelled of wine but he had dignity. He had been the one to close the lid on the box that was still in plain view on the living room table. Something that neither Amaldi nor Giuditta's mother had had the sense to do. Without commenting or drawing attention to himself he had carried it quietly into another room. Amaldi had liked him at once, instinctively. The inspector had taken his leave and the box, as proof. He had promised Giuditta that he would put an end to her misery. On the threshold, Giuditta's father had joined them. He had shaken Amaldi's hand and thanked him for what he was doing for his daughter. There was not a trace of jealousy in his eyes. No misplaced emphasis or servility. As though it was perfectly natural that a chief inspector from the homicide squad should be going out of his way to help his daughter, the priceless treasure that made him so immensely rich and fortunate. "Inspector," he had said and then lowered his voice, "I heard about your request over at the Union, for help in looking for, well, in finding, I mean, that poor woman's arms. I'm sorry they refused." The man hadn't lowered himself, he hadn't volunteered, he hadn't made excuses, or complained about life's injustices. He had simply said he was sorry. Amaldi knew he was sincere and that the affirmation had nothing to do with Giuditta. He had thanked the other man for his solidarity and all the way home he had pictured Giuditta's fearful, pained face. She was prettier when she laughed. The macabre content of the cardboard box under his arm rattled about with every step he took.

That morning he had the box and its contents with him. And he was going to make that little sadist eat every bit.

"It's Peschiera's nephew. The archivist," Frese told him. "He's in there with him now."

Amaldi shook his head and put the box on the floor. Frese looked at it.

"Have you had time to read those photocopies I gave you?" he asked his superior.

"What photocopies? Oh . . ." Amaldi put a hand into his pocket and pulled out some rumpled pages. "No, I forgot about them. What are they?"

"Parts A, B and C of the document from the orphanage fire registered as number six. That means we have five and six now. There is a declaration from the architect who refurbished the villa. He says that Mrs Cascarino commissioned work to turn the villa into an orphanage four months before the fire. He spent a month on the plans and then they started. The woman was in a terrible hurry, according to the architect. He went to the police of his own accord after the fire and made that statement, filed as document 6/A, that is, document number six, part A." Frese waved the folder under Amaldi's nose. "It's followed by 6/B. Interrogation of Mrs Cascarino, who denied everything. Her version was that she had commissioned a boarding school and not an orphanage. A hard woman, reading between the lines. And at the end she added that she had refused the architect's advances and that the man was probably slandering her out of some desire for revenge . . . You believe any of that?"

"The boarding school story works."

"Exactly. That's what I thought. So why go overboard with that ex-lover story?"

"It might have been true."

"Well, okay. But listen to this . . ." Frese picked up another sheet and started to read. "Where are we? Okay. 'That nonentity . . .' Nice beginning, right? 'That nonentity deluded himself that my widowhood and my reduced economic circumstances put him in a position to take advantage of me. I would have squashed him like a worm if I hadn't needed to finish the work in a hurry.' Just a bit haughty, eh?"

"Well, she does come from a noble family . . ."

"But we're not in the Middle Ages. 'Squashed like a worm', she said. She's as hard as nails, is our Mrs Cascarino. She wanted to put the boot in. Winning wasn't enough for her. She wanted to squash him like a worm, that's why she made that statement."

"What next?"

"6/c. Cross-examination of the architect. I'll save you the details but let me tell you they put the poor bugger through the wringer. And they treated her with kid gloves. He caved in in the end. He admitted that maybe he might have made a mistake and that perhaps Mrs Cascarino had indeed said boarding school and not orphanage. He withdrew. But he did insist he had never tried to woo her."

"You're losing your sense of objectivity, Nicola. There's nothing strange in anything you've told me."

202

"As a matter of fact, there are quite a few strange things. To start with, I found the first document in the personal file of Augusto Ajaccio, one of our men, who was one of the orphans who survived the fire and was then a guest at Villa Cascarino. Coincidence? Ajaccio's file was started when he joined the Force, nearly ten years after the fire. How did that document get into his file? It was put there later. But how much later? The file is updated every year. I went through it looking for his insurance cover and I came across the blueprints for the rebuilding. It could have happened to anyone. It is therefore reasonable to presume that those papers were put there recently. Second thing: document six, the one I've just told you about, was in the Farhid file. You remember? That Indian woman who killed her husband and son with an axe and then gassed herself and blew up half her building. Two years ago. The case was filed two years ago. Same question: how did a thirty-five-year-old document get into such a recent file? Answer: someone put it there."

"Why?"

"Okay. The really strange thing is this: you want to do something dirty? Illegal? Fine, for the sake of argument let's say you have a good reason to. Or that you don't, it doesn't matter. The fact is that you want to do something dirty. You disappear the architect's statement from the orphanage file. Why not just destroy it? Why do you shove it into some other file? Sooner or later some git like me is going to come along and discover it and you know, you have got to know, that a thing like that will make me suspicious. Why did someone spend their time moving the documents around and no more? Without destroying them? It's as though, trusting the decision to fate, you wanted to be discovered, sooner or later . . ."

The door to the interrogation room opened. Peschiera the archivist came out, his head lowered. He was rubbing his hand, his expression cloudy. Frese and Amaldi saw that the fat boy was still seated and that he was trying to staunch a nose bleed with a paper tissue. He was crying.

"He's admitted everything," the archivist began, in a doleful voice. "He was the one who made the phone calls and sent the letters . . . He says he likes the girl but that she never even looks at him . . ."

"If you knew how many women never look at me but I still don't —"

Amaldi put a hand on his deputy's arm. Frese shut up.

"I know," said the archivist, still hanging his head. "I know . . . I really let him have it . . . But he's my nephew. I used to hold him in my arms when he was a baby . . . He's my sister's only son . . ." The piggy eyes filled with tears and the big yellow teeth bit the man's lower lip.

"And what about the cat?" asked Amaldi in a neutral tone.

The archivist shook his head and made a grimace that might have been a smile.

"It's not a real cat . . . He says he always sees the girl giving milk to a cat outside the university. So he took a toy cat that I had given him when he was little, he stuck the skull and bones of a rabbit inside along with a few bits of meat and then he set fire to it with petrol. Mouldy's not a bad lad . . . he's just a moron. He's got the real kitten at home. He hasn't done it any harm and he takes good care of it. He just shaved a bit of its fur off for effect, to make the fake remains more credible." The archivist looked up for the first time and turned imploring eyes on Amaldi. "What are you going to do to him?"

Amaldi thought for a moment, looking at the box by his feet through different eyes.

"Well, the girl filed a complaint against persons unknown, even though she suspected your nephew . . . and she was right. The news that the cat is alive and well might help her calm down and maybe even convince her to withdraw her complaint. In which case . . ." He looked at Frese. "What do you think?"

"What about the obscene phone calls and the letters?"

"If his mother ever heard about that it would break her heart," said the archivist. "I told him I would kill him if he every did anything like that again."

"And what did Mouldy have to say?" asked Frese.

"He believed me. I've never hit him before. I've got a heavy hand . . ."

"I was just thinking," began Frese, turning to Amaldi, "about that orphanage business. Peschiera here has so much to do. What if we found someone to give him a hand? All those dusty files . . . tedious hard labour in a shitty place where only cops go . . . And Peschiera could straighten him out if he always had an eye on him. What do you say?"

Amaldi saw the archivist's eyes light up.

"Make sure the chief doesn't hear about this and make sure your nephew doesn't hurt himself, or we'll all be in trouble," he said.

"Thank you, Inspector. And he'll go right round to that girl's home with a bunch of flowers to tell her how sorry he is."

"Well, maybe we can forget about the flowers," said Frese, and Amaldi nodded. "And you'll go with him, in uniform, understand, and you'll let her know beforehand."

"Yes, of course, quite right," said the archivist.

"Oh, and one last thing: take him to see some whores, will you? It's a lot better than nothing at all." Then Frese put his head round the door of the interrogation booth. "Mouldy, get your fat arse out of here."

The fat boy, still holding the paper tissue to his nose, got to his feet and walked past Frese and Amaldi. The chief inspector and his deputy didn't look at him. As the boy walked away with his uncle, they saw that his trousers were wet and smelled the trail of urine he left in his wake.

"Did he not ask to go to the toilet?" Amaldi asked the officer who had watched over him.

"Yes . . . but . . ." the man began.

"You think the cleaning woman is here to work for you?" Frese interrupted. "Now you'll clean up that piss. And throw this box away as well. Let's go," he said to Amaldi and more or less frogmarched him down the corridor. They hadn't reached the lift when they heard the officer kick the wall.

"Why do you always play around with them like that?" asked Amaldi, who had grasped the situation.

"They have to grow up in a hurry. I don't want to find them with a knife in their back just because they dropped their guard with some bugger who looked harmless."

"You know, they ought to make you commissioner," said Amaldi and meant it.

"Piss off," retorted Frese and stumbled.

XVIII

Giacomo Amaldi walked along briskly, his hands in his pockets, looking around him. The chief inspector had a strong feeling that the rubbish-strike situation could degenerate from one moment to the next. The city council had no grasp of the real extent of the problem. Police stations across the city had already received alarming reports. A colleague who Amaldi had met over at headquarters had told him that armed bands were springing up all over the place. They were using rifles, slings and various other objects as offensive weapons to hunt down cats, rats and stray dogs. They had even displayed the animals like trophies or criminals. When Amaldi had asked his colleague if the authorities or the police had an action plan, the man had shaken his head and on his face had appeared the expression that policemen everywhere knew how to interpret immediately. It meant bureaucracy. It meant politics. It meant that no one would make the first move until it was too late. At which point the ensuing chaos would conveniently muddy the responsibilities, not to mention culpability, of certain individuals and as if by magic the rivalries would disappear. The day before Amaldi had read an interview with a psychologist who justified these sadistic acts against animals, saying that the citizens' behaviour was a completely normal reaction. The concept the man was advocating struck Amaldi as completely delirious. The learned doctor maintained that the acts were motivated by a kind of envy of the animals because they were enjoying a situation that was disagreeable for everyone else. Systematic and organized aggression towards animals was thus cathartic and liberating.

It was sixteen days since the beginning of the strike. As he reached his destination, Amaldi calculated that in the residential districts, where buildings were no more than six storeys high and housed twenty families or so, each building would have produced up to 320 bags of waste by that point. If he considered that in a residential street there could be anywhere between fifty and a hundred buildings, then the total amount of waste . . . let's see, 320 . . . the total would be between 16,000 and 32,000 bags. The council tower blocks were ten storeys high and housed at least sixty families, who must have spewed out about 1,000 or 2,000 bags each, for an absolutely staggering number of between 100,000 and 200,000 bags per street. Doing the calculations helped him relax. He had nearly reached the university.

The total number of bags of waste accumulated across the city, he thought, was simply beyond counting.

When a car shredded yet another bag under its wheels, and its contents splattered across the tarmac, Amaldi realized that there was no more room. "Either the people or the rubbish," he concluded. "One of us has to go." And the possibility, given the circumstances, didn't strike him as being so far fetched.

When he reached the university steps, he looked around him. He recognized the man at once, among the mass of students. And not only because of his age, but also because of his austere posture, his elegant coat, the leather briefcase in the left hand, and the air of impatience. Just before greeting him, Amaldi checked his watch.

"Good day, Professor Avildsen," he said. "I'm not late, am I?"

The teacher shook Amaldi's hand without taking off his kid leather gloves and did not reply. Amaldi had already found the man to be unfriendly, when he phoned Avildsen to make an appointment. The professor had been very terse, had explained how terribly busy he was and that he had time for the briefest of meetings on the university steps at the end of his lesson. Amaldi had not insisted on learning why they couldn't meet indoors. He imagined that the lecturer thought a conversation on the move would have come to an end all the sooner.

"Thank you very much for giving up some of your time," said Amaldi, in very civil tones. He had heard that Avildsen was considered quite a luminary in his field and he needed the man's help.

Avildsen's smile was brief and formal.

"Shall we deal with the matter in hand?"

"Of course," replied Amaldi and took from his pocket the photograph of the message the murderer had left on the door of the antiques shop. He didn't mention the fact that the message had been written in the woman's blood. The papers had already made a big deal out of the information. None of the Force's experts knew where the phrase came from. One of them had said that it might be a passage from the Bible. That type of murderer often had religious obsessions.

Professor Avildsen took the photograph. He looked at the image for a long time, turning his head slightly as he did.

"It's the VITRIOL," he said, after a while.

"Excuse me?"

"The initials of the phrase make up the acronym VITRIOL, and that is what scholars call it for the sake of simplicity. It is a well-known formula used by alchemists, which condenses their doctrine. This is Kurt Speligman's version. It is not the most widely accepted. I personally prefer the classical formula, '*Visita interiora terrae rectificando invenies . . . operae lapidem*' and not '*occultum lapidem*'. That is, the stone of the Opus, or Work, rather than the occult stone. This second version is a little more theatrical. But the initials, as you can see, are the same. Do you need me to explain what they mean?"

"That would be helpful, thank you."

"It is an initiatory motto. It encapsulates the law of a process of transformation. The return of a person to the most intimate nucleus of the human being. Is that sufficiently clear?"

"No, not really."

"You do know who the alchemists were?"

"Sort of, but I stop at the business about changing lead into gold."

"Of course. But that's it, really. This motto is the synthesis of alchemical operations at different levels of transformation, both those of material things and those of human beings. In the case of human beings, the symbol obviously has deeper significance. It is a question of rebuilding the self, starting from the various degrees of unknowing, ignorance and prejudice. A reconstruction that is based on the irrefutable awareness of being, through which man may discover the immanent and transformative presence of God . . . in himself. Regardless of which text one uses, the symbolism is always the same. In the most accredited version, '*rectificando*' is usually translated as 'distilling'. But the result remains the same."

Two passing students greeted the professor but Avildsen seemed not to notice.

"Can you tell me anything about the image?"

"It is the alchemical symbol for vitriol. Is that all? Have we finished? As I explained before, I am in somewhat of a hurry."

"One last thing, Professor. I have to ask you to keep this conversation to yourself. We haven't made any of this information public, to help us catch out liars and copycats."

Professor Avildsen showed no sign of being interested in what Amaldi was saying. He continued to level his frosty gaze at the detective.

"If you would be so kind . . .?" he said.

"Yes, of course." Amaldi's voice was calm, controlled. "We found some dry leaves at the scene . . ." Amaldi waved his hand about, as if he had trouble finishing what he wanted to say. "At the scene . . ."

"Of the crime. Yes, do get to the point."

"I was wondering if . . . that meant anything to you?"

"Leaves?"

"Yes, some dry leaves."

"Mr . . . I'm sorry, I've forgotten your name."

"Amaldi. Inspector Amaldi."

"Mr Amaldi, leaves may represent a great many things in symbology. What can I say? In the Far East they are symbols of happiness and prosperity. Does that strike you as relevant? Leaves are a feature of all springtime rites. The 'little man of the leaves' in Russia. Jack-in-the-green in Britain. The Pentecost Fool in Fricktal, Switzerland . . . However, these are all symbols of joy and revelry."

"And nothing else comes to mind?"

"Not off the top of my head," replied the teacher tersely.

"Professor. A woman is dead. Brutally murdered —"

"Don't lecture me," Professor Avildsen interrupted him. "Don't try for one moment to burden me with the responsibility for the outcome of your investigation. That kind of trick won't work with me."

Amaldi tried to fight against the mounting rage that churned his stomach.

"Professor, please . . ."

"In some islands in the East Indies, they believe that it is possible to cure epilepsy by striking the sick person in the face with the leaves of certain trees and then throwing away the leaves. The witch doctors and their patients are convinced that the sickness passes into the leaves and can be thrown away with them. The final thing that comes to mind is a hunting ritual. On the island of Nias the natives hunt wild pigs. They dig pits and cover them. When the hunters pull the pigs out of the traps, they rub them with nines leaves fallen from nearby trees in the hope that nine other pigs will fall into the pits. It is a homeopathic principle; the pigs fall into the traps just as the leaves fall from the trees. How many leaves do you have?"

"Three."

"Nine is a multiple of three, but apart from that I can't see any connection." Professor Avildsen looked at Amaldi with an ironic smile. "Unless your particular hunter will be happy with just three more little pigs, that is."

"One more thing."

"I was under the impression that you had already said your last thing."

"I'm sure you've noticed that in the . . . VITRIOL phrase some of the letters are block capitals? Have you any idea what they might mean?"

"An anagram?"

"Maybe. But we're having trouble cracking it."

212

"I am sorry for you." And without another word Avildsen left.

Amaldi watched the man walk over to his car. A group of laughing students helped him reverse by kicking rubbish bags out of the way. It was only then that Amaldi realized that Avildsen had not given him back the photograph. He had simply dropped it on the ground where he had been standing. Amaldi picked it up and looked round for Giuditta. He caught sight of her several feet away, sitting on a low wall that bordered a flight of steps. She was busy feeding a cat.

"Absolutely charming, right?" asked Giuditta.

"The cat?"

"Professor Avildsen," she said, clearly amused.

"It's nice to see you laugh," said Amaldi, avoiding commenting on the teacher. He was still shaking with rage.

"This is the kitten's mother," said Giuditta, stroking the cat between its ears. "I went to visit the kitten . . . and I met the uncle and mother of . . . Max. The kitten's fur will grow back, he only shaved off a bit . . . I felt sorry for him . . . Max, not the kitten. I'm making an effort to call him by name, because, maybe, that way I'll manage not to hate him. I do feel bad, but I still hate him . . ."

"It's only natural."

"The kitten will be fine at their place . . . Max's mother is a nice woman . . . and lonely. The kitten will keep her company. Max must feel quite lonely too . . ."

"There's still no excuse for what he did."

"Yes, I know . . ." Giuditta took Amaldi by the hand. "Thank you, Giacomo."

Amaldi tensed and then, as he smiled at her, he felt his rage recede.

"Can I walk you home?" he asked.

"I'm off to the hospital. It's my day for volunteer work."

"Well, I can walk some of the way with you."

Giuditta got up and their hands unentwined. The cat watched them, stretching. As they walked, their awkward conversation revolved once more around the rubbish strike. And then they stopped talking. In spite of the roar of the city around them, Amaldi was aware of the silence that enveloped them. Not so much a cloak, as a kind of bell jar. And in the midst of that comforting silence, he reached out and gently took Giuditta's hand. He squeezed it. Giuditta squeezed back, and in silence they carried on walking. By the time the outline of the hospital began to materialize above the roofs of adjacent buildings, they had escaped from the city and from their own thoughts and were huddled together in the cradle of their hands, rocked by fingers that had not once stopped talking.

Suddenly, Amaldi crossed the street and led Giuditta down a steep, slippery side alley into the old town. They turned the corner and found themselves in a kind of dark hollow formed by the overhang of two abutting balconies that against all logic had been built a few inches apart. Amaldi came to a halt. Giuditta looked at the ground, breathed in deeply and then, slowly, yieldingly, offered her lips to Amaldi. He caressed them, gently, smoothing out the little crinkles of her upper lip as he had imagined doing and Giuditta smiled, her eyes half closed. When she closed them completely and, standing on tiptoe, pushed her face closer to his, Amaldi plunged his hand into her hair, brushing against her earlobe, and placed his hand on the back of her neck. He pulled her towards him, and kissed her passionately, roughly, for a long time, forgetting the gentle gestures he had prepared

214

for that moment, forgetting caution and modesty, and abandoning himself to the warm, wet merging of lips, to the almost imperceptible noises of tongues that were exploring each other as their fingers had done earlier. When the kiss ended, neither of them opened their eyes, savouring their ascent from the velvet depths into which they had plunged. Their mouths remained close together, their lips slightly apart, inert, their breathing heavy. The sound of their panting, Amaldi's guttural gasp and Giuditta's soft hiss, echoed round the alleyway until they formed one breath, as though they had been transformed into a single animal. Then they both relaxed and opened their eyes. They smiled at each other in embarrassment, not knowing how to deal with the intimacy that their bodies had already discovered. Their second kiss was gentler, like a bridge created to span the two worlds. When they let go of each other and looked at each other again there was no hint of awkwardness in their eyes. They no longer felt the need to smile. They simply drank in the sight of each other, offering themselves up for inspection. They opened doors that had been closed to almost everyone. And like two blind people their hands touched and stroked and traced the outline of each other's face, caressing lines and contours. They discovered each other's most hidden features, touched what was flesh and blood and not just illusion, giving form to the pleasure of being able to violate what was, by nature, inviolable. Their caresses entwined in a flurry of fingers and fingertips, so much so that Giuditta found herself touching her own face while seeking out Amaldi's hand, and discovered the lines of her face not as she knew them, but as her lover saw them. And Amaldi, when he brushed his lips against Giuditta's, saw himself reflected in her grey eyes, in her dilated pupils. In his mouth he felt the girl's breath, as if it were his own. It filled his lungs and bent his knees, making him tremble. When they kissed again, a languid, leisurely kiss, without urgency but full of desire, their lips slipped, unable to lock together, impeded by fingers exploring teeth, by teeth yearning to bite and nibble, seized by the desire to give flavour to the outlines they had discovered. Their lips grazed cheeks and eyes, which they offered up in turn to the soft touch of the other.

Then Giuditta took Amaldi's hand, and firmly guided it along her neck, her shoulder, down, down, pushing aside her coat, until it touched her soft breast. Her back arched, almost against her will. A swift caress that made her quiver. Amaldi also shuddered, shaken by a painful spasm. He pulled Giuditta to him, almost crushing her, and felt the girl's lungs empty.

"The hospital . . .?" he murmured into her ear.

"Tomorrow," she replied. She looked at him and started kissing him again.

But Amaldi pulled away from her. He looked at the ground and kicked a stone into the alley. Then, suddenly, he took hold of Giuditta's face, a haunted expression in his eyes.

"There's something . . . you have to know."

Giuditta's heart lurched.

"You're married?" she asked.

"Yes . . ."

Giuditta felt her whole body stiffen.

". . . to a dead girl."

In the silence that followed Amaldi went to sit on a step made from smooth, greying stone in front of a door eroded by damp. His head was in his hands, his hair rumpled. After a moment he looked up at Giuditta and held out his arms to her. But it was a slow gesture, as if his shoulders were suddenly burdened by every sack of coffee beans his father had ever unloaded at the port, as if his arms were pinned down under the weight he had been carrying for too many years. Giuditta moved towards him. He took hold of her and sat her on his knees. He buried his face in her hair and began to tell his story.

"You remember back at the greasy spoon you asked me why, and I thought you wanted to know why I did this job?"

Giuditta nodded. Amaldi couldn't see her but felt her head move slowly, up and down.

"That evening I told you it was because it was my work. But that's not all . . ." A brief pause. "It's the second time this week that I find myself telling this story to someone . . . and I'd never told it to anyone before. It isn't nice, Giuditta, and I'm sorry you have to hear it . . ."

Giuditta placed a hand on Amaldi's back and pulled him closer.

Amaldi began talking. Not in the mechanical tones he had used when he had spoken to Frese a few days before, but in a warmer voice. Tears welled up in his eyes before he started speaking, and this time he cried without shuddering jolts. His tears poured down his cheeks with all the gentleness of a bleeding wound. And Amaldi offered no resistance. He told Giuditta about the girl with the golden hair whom he had fallen in love with, and to whom he had promised a house full of light somewhere away from the old town. He told her about their plans; about the girl's mother who worked as a prostitute; of their first, and only time together, down on the rocks, when they were just two awkward kids. He told her about the day he had been wandering around the streets of the old town, his mind

217

full of sex and love, which he had discovered at the same time. He told her about the dark side street that he had turned into, drawn by the crowd that had gathered.

". . . The first thing I saw was an old woman. I brushed past her, back to back, and I heard her praying. A prayer I had often heard the women reciting before, sitting outside in a patch of sunshine, whenever the weather permitted. But the sounds the old woman was making weren't the same muffled, rhythmical sounds the women made when I was a kid, sounds that blended in with the waves of the port lapping against the breakwaters, or the screech of heavy trolleys pushed by strong men with big shoes that wore out as they heaved loads back and forth on the wharfs . . . They were sounds . . . there was fear in that noise. Desperation, horror . . . and that resignation that I hate more than anything else in the world. And I remember seeing a policeman crying, this big, strong cop weeping silently . . . and then the screams of a woman, and people trying to hold her back, telling her not to look . . . and the cop didn't do anything, he just stood there, like he was beaten, lifeless . . . So I pushed through, even though I knew I shouldn't . . . because all these years later I've convinced myself that I knew, that I knew what I was going to find . . ."

Amaldi squeezed his eyes shut and sobbed harder, picturing the crowd that parted around the glistening black of the rubbish bags.

". . . like a sack, a bag. A body like a bag, Giuditta . . . A girl like a bag full of rubbish . . . Just left there, in that alley, just thrown away, her killer just threw her there like a bag of rubbish, a piece of waste tossed aside . . . not her. It wasn't her any more. She had her golden hair and the shoes . . . the shoes I had given her

. . . but it wasn't her any more, Giuditta . . . It wouldn't be her any more . . . just a body like a bag . . ."

He didn't tell her that the gleaming river of blood that was spreading around the body also looked like plastic, nor did he tell her that the girl's eyes were wide open, staring at nothing, looking up at the leaden sky that suffocated the old town. Or that the murderer had sliced her there, where her virginity had been taken a few days before, gently, softly, by a boy her own age, down on the rocks, on a blanket taken secretly from home, after a flight on a bicycle.

"She was sixteen . . . and no one knows who killed her . . . no one knows who threw her into the alley, among the rubbish bags . . ."

Amaldi had always suspected that it had been a client of the girl's mother, that mother who, when it no longer mattered, when it was too late, had stopped working.

"And that's why I do what I do . . . That's why I investigate murders. Because I don't know how to forget. Because I don't know how to give up."

Amaldi lifted his red eyes towards Giuditta's face.

"I had to tell you . . . you had to know, Giuditta . . . Because that's what I am . . . because I don't think I can be anything else. Because I've condemned myself to catching someone . . . because I've condemned myself to hunting through the rubbish . . . I had to tell you . . . because I don't know if I'll ever manage to bury her . . . because I don't know what I have to give you . . ."

Giuditta dried his tears and kissed him. She ran her hand through his hair and straightened his shirt collar.

Just at that moment the door opened behind them and an old woman, dressed in black and wearing thick socks and worn shoes cut off at the toes, appeared on the doorstep. She gave a startled gasp at the sight of them.

"Clear off and find yourselves a bench somewhere, you dirty pair," she said as soon as she had recovered, and waved her bag at them.

Amaldi and Giuditta got up and apologized and hurried away. Giuditta held Amaldi's hand tightly in hers. They walked on in silence for a while.

"When you look at me, do you think of her?" Giuditta asked him suddenly.

Amaldi stopped in his tracks.

"No," he replied.

"Will you show me that alleyway?"

Amaldi stared at her in surprise.

"I'm not afraid."

XIX

The following morning when, on her way out, Giuditta saw a letter in the mail box with just her first name on it, no surname, she hesitated to take it because she thought at once of the obscene letters she had already received. Then she noticed the police crest on the envelope and realized it was from Giacomo Amaldi. She clutched it to her chest and started to tear open the envelope. Then she stopped herself, checked the time, saw that she was late and began walking briskly towards the hospital where she was going to make up for her previous day's absence. She decided to read the letter later, to resist her growing sense of curiosity. She decided she would put the moment off, like in an erotic game, and reach pleasure through suffering.

As she walked up through the narrow streets of the old town towards the wide avenue that led to the hospital, she thought again about what had happened the day before. The intense excitement she had felt in that embrace, the feeling of time stopping, the marvellous sensation of Giacomo's lips, his skin, the touch of his hands. But above all she thought of the murdered girl. Of that alleyway that she had seen dozens and dozens of times before, without ever suspecting that it had been the setting for something so gruesome. The alleyway had suddenly become dangerous and terrifying, as if the spectre of evil had been woken by the mere fact of the story's being told to a new listener. It was as though stories had the power to step outside time and to remain hanging in the present, living things, although they involved dead people. Giuditta caught herself thinking that if the girl hadn't been murdered, she would never have been able to have Amaldi. In a parallel story, Amaldi was happily married. He wouldn't have become involved and changed the course of events. The fat boy would probably have carried on tormenting her until he had got fed up. In that story Amaldi would not have kissed her, or pulled her close to him. Giuditta had felt the presence of that girl in the alleyway, beside Amaldi. She was alive. She wasn't dead. It struck Giuditta that she didn't know what the girl was called. Amaldi had never referred to her by name. If he had spoken her name out loud, thought Giuditta, then the victim would have become real, she would have come back from the past. And maybe then Amaldi would have admitted defeat.

Until that happened, Giuditta told herself as she entered the hospital, she would have to learn to live with that painful ghost. She headed for the room on the ground floor where the nurses changed. And she would have accepted that other presence without complaining because she felt she really could fall in love with Giacomo Amaldi. If she hadn't already, she thought with a smile.

"You're in a good mood today," said an old nun who met her on the first floor corridor, dressed now in her volunteer auxiliary's uniform.

"Hello, Sister," replied Giuditta. She was radiant and her hand clasped Amaldi's letter in her pocket, still unopened. "Shall I do the usual rounds, or is there something urgent?"

The nun thought for a moment, her hands tucked under her habit.

"Ask the charge nurse, she's having the devil's own

time today. Dr Cerusico still hasn't arrived." Then she added, "If you have time, call on Mrs Lete in 144. Our Lord sent her a terrible night. In a foul mood . . . Mrs Lete, that is, not Our Lord." She laughed at her own joke, and agitated her hands under the folds of her robe. "Bowel trouble," she said by way of explanation, and hobbled off on her old legs.

The charge nurse did not share the elderly nun's opinion. Foul moods and diarrhoea could wait. It was more important to empty bedpans and help the patients with their ablutions.

"Our dear sisters still think they're back in the convent where the care of the body is something that happens by accident," puffed the charge nurse, "They can't cope with the idea of a hospital that exists to treat the body rather than the spirit."

Giuditta smiled. It was an old gripe that would doubtless last until the final trumpet. The truth of the matter was that the nuns were excellent nurses and the hospital could certainly not afford to do without their disinterested help. And the charge nurse knew this much better than anyone else. But, as she had once admitted to Giuditta, a good gripe added a bit of zest to life.

"When you do your round would you just gather up in a bag all the bits of paper and other rubbish the patients have left, and bring the whole lot down to the incinerator. As long as the strike lasts we'll have to be really careful about hygiene. We can cope, of course, but we can't be complacent. You know where the incinerator is, don't you?"

"Yes, I went there once."

"Right, well, get busy then, Miss Volunteer." The woman's tone was mocking. "You know volunteers are halfway between nuns and nurses, don't you? Watch out . . . if you become a nun you'll have to cut that long hair of yours . . . and give up a lot of other nice things. You know what I'm talking about, don't you?"

"Yes," replied Giuditta dreamily, feeling Amaldi's kisses on her lips. She touched her mouth.

"Oh, no," exclaimed the charge nurse. "A volunteer in love is worse than a nun."

"And just who would be worse than a nun, then?" asked the old nun who had returned.

"No one, Sister," the charge nurse said quickly, raising her hands to heaven. "No one could be worse than a nun."

"When Our Lord asks me to put in a good word for you, I shall sew my mouth closed and let him send you off to your own personal incinerator," said the nun, pointing at the charge nurse and laughing.

Giuditta left them to it. She knew the duet would carry on for a while.

"Well, that's a fine example of good Christian spirit, Sister," she heard the charge nurse say as she walked away.

"Our Lord treats his brides well, don't forget that I have friends in high places. All I have to do is say a few rosaries and I'll be forgiven. But you . . . you'll be roasted, mark my words."

Giuditta didn't listen to the charge nurse's retort but she was sure that their banter would cheer up the ward for a few more minutes. For the next two hours she worked in the three wards on the ground floor, trundling her rubbish trolley before her. Then she descended into the basement, a part of the hospital where only the staff went. It was radically different from the rest of the building. The walls were painted in a dark colour, the ceilings were much lower, and along the walls ran metal tubes and wiring, covered in years of dust. The corridors were crammed with lockers and bits of furniture, battered and rusty. The rooms had wire grills instead of doors, and numbered padlocks. The dim lighting was provided by long, crackling fluorescent tubes. Many of the tubes were broken and Giuditta walked in and out of the shadows with a sense of unease. She turned right, remembering the route she had taken just once before with one of the nurses, and at the end of the corridor she heard the low grumble of the incinerator room, which joined the squeaking of her trolley wheels. She reached the closed metal door, pulled it open and was assaulted by a wave of damp, hot air. The incinerator was located in a huge dark space that smelled of kerosene and stale air.

"Anybody there?" Giuditta asked timidly.

There was no answer. Just the incinerator rumbling in shadows ripped by the flame flaring from the innards of the machine.

"Anybody there?" she said again, more loudly.

She slipped the rubbish bag out of the trolley and walked down the three steps that led from the little landing into the room proper. The closer she got to the incinerator, dragging the heavy bag along the floor, the more intense the heat became. She was panting by the time she got as far as the heavy cast-iron hatch. She touched the handle to make sure it wouldn't scorch her, and then she tried to turn it.

"Hold it!" shouted a husky voice behind her.

Giuditta turned in fright and saw a huge figure loom out of a dark corner. As the man came towards her he fumbled with the zip on his trousers.

"Coming, coming," said the man. "I was in the toilet, Nurse."

He came level with Giuditta and effortlessly lifted the bag of rubbish with one hand, twirling it over his head and strangling the neck of the bag. Then with a flurry of fingers he tied a knot in the plastic and tossed it a several feet away, into the pile of other bags waiting to be burned.

"New, Nurse?" he asked, drying his brow with a tissue. "Want to get a good tan? Don't you know that if you open that door while the monster is eating you'll get a blast that'll burn you alive. Not to mention that I'm in charge here and if something terrible happens I'm the one who gets fired." He looked at Giuditta's bust, which strained her blouse buttons. "And what a lot of meat there is to roast, too." His laugh rattled with phlegm.

Giuditta crossed her hands over her chest and started to leave. The man's hands were on her, holding her back.

"Excuse me, Nurse," he said. "I can see you're new. The other girls always let me have my little joke. You can get really bored down here all day long, you know?"

"Let go of me," said Giuditta, her voice strident.

"And some of the girls even let me have a . . . closer look? Know what I mean?"

Giuditta pulled herself free of the man's grasp and bolted for the door. Behind her came the man's chesty laugh.

"Joking, gorgeous," he shouted after her. "I like to have a little joke."

Giuditta rushed up the three steps and ran along the corridor. She had gone a few feet when the lights went out. She didn't slow down, and ran headlong into a piece of furniture. The metal boomed in the silence. Something sharp cut through her blouse at rib level and she felt a piercing pain. The man's laugh reverberated in a distant echo. Terrified, Giuditta tried to grope ahead in the dark. Then the lights blinked and flickered into life.

"Have a good day, Nurse," shouted the man after her, in his hideous voice.

Giuditta only stopped running when she had reached the entrance hall on the ground floor. Her heart was pounding and her throat was dry. She rested a hand on her chest and waited until her breathing was under control, then she put a hand in her pocket, looking for a handkerchief, and found Amaldi's letter. She still hadn't read it. She gripped it tightly and decided the time had come to take a break. She looked around her and saw that the charge nurse, head bowed, was coming in her direction. If the woman noticed her, she would probably find some other task for her. Giuditta turned on her heel and went into the toilet. She waited until the charge nurse had gone past and decided the best place to sit and read her letter in peace would be room 112, the room of that poor woman who lay mute and paralysed in her bed. She felt a little guilty as she opened the door.

The room was dark, the shutters closed. There was a feeble light from a lamp on the bedside cabinet. And a chair next to the bed.

"Hello, Mrs Cascarino," said Giuditta, without expecting either an answer or a sign that the woman had heard her.

She went over to the bed, pulled up the covers, stroked the woman's smooth forehead. The old woman's icy gaze betrayed no reaction. A metal stand on the other side of the bed held a drip jar that fed impossibly slowly into a purple vein. Giuditta looked the woman in the face, a harsh face that inspired neither sympathy nor compassion. The mask of a respiratory machine covered the patient's mouth. The transparent plastic was foggy and the ventilator bellows rose and fell rhythmically.

"How do you feel today, Mrs Cascarino?" asked Giuditta. "Do you mind if I keep you company for a while?"

She sat down in the chair beside the bed, raised the light on the bedside cabinet a little and pulled Amaldi's letter out of her pocket. She smiled to herself as she finished tearing open the envelope. Before starting to read she glanced once more at the old woman. Then she unfolded the sheet of paper.

I would like to ask you to give me time, Giuditta, but it would be wrong. I would tie you to a false hope and I don't want to fool you."

Giuditta felt her heart plummet. Her blood froze. Her hands began to tremble as she read the opening lines of what she had thought was a love letter.

I would like to ask you to give me time, Giuditta, but it would be wrong. I would tie you to a false hope and I don't want to fool you. I would like to ask you for time, but I can't, because your time and my time are not measured in the same seconds and minutes. Yours is the time of youth, mine an old man's time. Yes, Giuditta, I feel old, an old man made old by his obsession, an old man who has lived the same moment too many times, as if it were a whole life, too many times to be able to forget it in a hurry. I will forget it, of course, in time, thanks to you. But my time doesn't match yours. Have you ever noticed what a strange contradiction our ways of living time are? Young people, who have all the time in the world, are always running, and old people, like me, who have so little, fritter it away in slowness, incapable of putting the moments that are left to good use. Some people call it wisdom. It's really just exhaustion. Your heart will tell you to accept my proposal that you wait for me, I know, I've seen you, and felt you, and known you enough now to be able to say that. But how long could you wait? Is it right for you to waste your life like some

228

old woman waiting for an old man? I'm tired, Giuditta, and lifeless. Don't wait for me. I've added too many horrors to the first one. How long will it take me? I'm a pig-headed loner. And my ghost is even more stubborn than me. Did you see her in that alley? Did you feel her there? That ghost is alive. She's only now accepting that she has to die. It's taken twenty years to make that decision. How many more years will go by before the decision is put into practice? Let me go, Giuditta. I'll carry you with me always, believe me, and it will be thanks to you if I start living again. But let me go. Don't look for me, and I won't look for you. G.

Giuditta sat holding the letter, spread out before her eyes that began to cloud, blurring the words and making them illegible. Amaldi's voice echoed in her ears. *Don't look for me, and I won't look for you.* She felt her heart stop beating, her breathing froze. She sat still for a long time, as her tears made puddles of Amaldi's words. The old woman lay beside her, immobile. The only living thing in the room seemed to be the respiratory machine. Giuditta felt something had broken inside her. She felt a knife blade raking her insides. She sat still, as still as the old woman. Minutes went by and no one came into the room. She lost track of time, of that time that Amaldi didn't want to give her, as though she wasn't mistress of her own life, as though she couldn't decide for herself. Pain gave way to anger and she snapped into motion, screwing up the letter and hurling it to the floor.

Then she thought she heard a noise behind her. She turned round.

A figure detached itself from the shadows and stood up from the chair that was against the wall, in the corner near the door. The man moved forward and showed his face.

"You?" said Giuditta, shaking herself and standing up.

"Yes. Hello," said the man with that very particular voice that vibrated like metal, and he put his left hand on her elbow, in greeting.

It was only then that Giuditta noticed that the little finger had been amputated. As she looked at the yellowish stump, Giuditta felt a mixture of compassion and repulsion. The deformity took something away from the man's charm, but at the same time made him more human.

"I had wondered during lessons if you were the volunteer who looked after my mother . . ." Professor Avildsen smiled.

"This poor lady is your mother, Professor?" asked Giuditta incredulously, trying to dry her eyes.

"Yes . . . alas . . ." There was something ambiguous, out of place, in the man's voice.

"Your surnames are different . . ."

"Yes, my mother wiped out everything that reminded her of a hated, and awkward, husband. All it took was a court order. Nothing was left of him. As far as the bureaucrats are concerned I am not Avildsen. I keep the name, oh, from force of habit . . ."

"I'm sorry, I didn't know . . ."

"And even though you didn't know I've seen you go out of your way for my mother. It's to your credit."

"Thank you."

"You needn't thank me. Yang Chu, an oriental philosopher, says, 'He who does good deeds, although he is not spurred by desire for fame, will derive fame therefrom nonetheless. Fame in itself has nothing to do with gain, but gain will undoubtedly derive therefrom. Gain in itself has nothing to do with struggle, but in the end he will not be able to avoid it. That is why the nobleman is wary of doing good deeds.'" He stared at Giuditta intently. "And you, are you ready to struggle?"

Giuditta felt herself burn under that gaze. She drew herself in within her blouse.

Then Professor Avildsen took a silk handkerchief from his pocket and with his left hand dried Giuditta's tears. She drank in the feel of the smooth silk and the rough skin of the finger stump as they brushed her cheeks.

"You've been crying," said the man.

Giuditta was embarrassed.

"It's an unpleasant sensation. I too often cry because of pain. I started a long time ago." Avildsen looked at his mother, lying still in her bed. "But not her. Never. She never cried, not once. She's a strong woman. Very strong."

Giuditta moved her face away and Avildsen was left holding his handkerchief. He held it out to Giuditta.

"Blow your nose."

Numb with pain and the sound of Avildsen's voice, Giuditta took the handkerchief and blew her nose.

"You may keep it," said Professor Avildsen.

"Thank you."

Avildsen bent down to pick up Amaldi's letter.

"I'll throw this away . . . I don't want you to suffer any more."

Giuditta would have preferred to take back the letter, to read it again. But she discovered she couldn't speak.

"And anthropology interests you?" asked the man.

"Oh yes. A lot."

"Good . . . I hope your exam will meet the very high standard of your previous papers. You have an excellent average."

231

"How do you know that?"

"I keep an eye on you . . . Giuditta." A slight smile and then he left the room before the girl had a chance to say anything else, leaving her alone in the dark labyrinth of her pain.

The ventilator bellows rose and fell, rhythmically, like a winded accordion that was incapable of producing a tune.

XX

The table Professor Avildsen was leaning over was spattered with thick, sticky bloodstains. The smell that clung to his workshop was unbearable. Contained by the closed windows and intensified by the humidity. His mind on his work, Avildsen reviewed his past with painful nostalgia and reopened a wound that was far from being born. He started to cry, and the tangled threads of his memories and emotions began to unravel. Dark tears of guilt streaked down his cheeks and disappeared into his brown and red beard. Now he knew, as he had always known, what his terrible weakness was. But only now, his grand design in hand, with a present that justified his past, and a luminous future that would redeem him, only now could he look it squarely in the face.

He made two little holes in the upper part of the right leg that he had taken from Dr Cerusico, one on the outside and one on the inside of the thigh. Then he used a scalpel to peel very delicately the epidermis from the dead woman's flesh. He used a vice attached to the wall to immobilize the muscle and the head of the femur that he had exposed. He took a firm grip of the skin and began to pull slowly. An irritating noise echoed round the workshop, the disjointed sound of sticky tape coming away with difficulty. In just a few minutes the epidermis peeled off and turned inside out, like a stocking, but without the slightest laddering. Professor Avildsen picked up his bloody stocking and gave all his attention over to his courtship ritual. He cleaned the skin of any impurity and remaining traces of flesh. He stood the skin upright and smeared it with a salve made of alum, arsenic and soap to soften and preserve the skin. He released the naked leg from the vice and successfully performed the same operation on the left leg. After skinning his prey, as embalmers liked to put it, Avildsen stuffed the skins roughly with tow, to keep them until he was ready to mount them, and left them to dry under powerful infrared lamps. He took a magnifying glass and examined every inch of the epidermis and noticed that the hairs had grown a little longer in the few days since he had acquired the legs. He prepared a solution to strengthen the holes and fix the follicles. Then he wiped them down.

While waiting for the legs to dry, he measured them. Like every self-respecting taxidermist, Avildsen had measured the legs when they were still fresh. He compared the measurements to check that the legs were not shrinking, as had happened with the antique-dealer's arms. He breathed a sigh of relief when he saw that the measurements coincided. Just as he had foreseen, Dr Cerusico, the woman who had nourished his mother's blood, who had touched and examined his mother so often that she had absorbed her, Dr Cerusico had hardier skin than the antique-dealer. Less refined, perhaps. But better suited to what the taxidermist had in mind.

Avildsen looked in annoyance at the arms that had shrunk by four inches, and which were thinner too. He had finished them now. The problems had started during skinning. The epidermis had torn in a number of places and the arms now glistened with glue where he had had to patch them up. The tanning phase had only partially protected them. The skin was so fine that the greatest difficulty had been to smooth out the many folds and puckers that formed during stuffing and final mounting. Avildsen brought one of the antique-dealer's hands to his face and used it stroke his cheek. Hard, but light to the touch, velvety. He felt himself quiver and immediately pulled out of the embrace. His eyes started to water again, and the fingers of his right hand sought out the stump of his little finger, to apply a comforting massage. He lowered the antique-dealer's arm and noted with satisfaction that the joints functioned perfectly: wrist, elbow and shoulder. He continued to massage the stump of his little finger; that small, yellow excrescence that was his whole world. It had showed him the pleasure of suffering.

Professor Avildsen returned to his childhood. As if he were being sucked into a whirlpool, only this time he was not afraid of drowning. He had his grand design. He remembered his mother's doll, so severe yet so violable. And he thought of his mother lying in her hospital bed, perfumed with disinfectant, pure and aseptic, now. Immobile, severe, yet violable, like the doll. 'You're just like her, now,' he thought with a shiver of old fear. The doll that had once occupied his mother's chair when she was absent. Those chubby, fragile fingers, that frizzy blond hair around the puffy oval of its inexpressive face, and the velvet costume under which fluttered miniature lace underwear. And the slippery chalky skin. The cruel doll that had spied on him while he studied or when he was being punished, isolated within his isolation, because he had been wicked, or had thought wicked thoughts. The doll that had betrayed him with its blue, glass eyes. The doll sitting rigid on his desk, splayed legs revealing its lacy undergarments, its lids closed, hiding its eyes, every time it was tilted. The doll's eyelids, those

235

thought thieves, opened and closed, opened and closed, opened and closed.

He pictured again in a flash that first time, when, looking at an art book, studying the picture of a sharp-eyed cherub pinching a woman's nipple and coaxing droplets of milk that splashed onto the World, he had discovered for the first time that the lump of pale, limp flesh between his legs had a life of its own. Unbidden, it began to move, to push against his cotton underpants, forming a bulge in his shorts, straining the buttons. More from wonder than from understanding of what was happening, he freed this stranger, and let it blossom in the open air. It looked a little silly and he felt seized with a strange and new euphoria. His hands were open, unmoving on either side of his pulsing discovery, ready to catch it should it make an attempt at escape. Nothing of the sort happened, however: his member was incapable of flight and was not as self-sufficient as he had supposed. It twitched in the air, like an unsaid prayer, and he felt he should do something but didn't know what yet; it was a sorrowful, seductive prayer, insistent and perhaps just a little bit annoying. It was asking for help but didn't say what was to be done. After minutes spent in ecstatic contemplation his gaze fell on the picture again and he noticed the resemblance between the woman and the doll, the same talc-white skin, and that he looked a lot like the cherub, the same copper highlights in their hair, the same slim, tapering fingers, the same languid expression. And so, through some illogical association, he pinched his slender child's member between two fingers, in the same gesture as the cherub. The mere touch of flesh upon flesh worked a miracle. His eyelids partially closed. He saw two little drops of milk, just like the drops from the woman's breast, land on his fingers. It only lasted an instant. The doll was watching him. He felt dirty, like his fingers. The doll had seen everything. So he pushed it to one side, touching it for the first time in his life. As the doll tipped back, it half closed its eyes. A tiny drop of milk stuck to its velvet costume. He rubbed it energetically in an effort to clean it. He had never touched it before and now he was touching it again and again. He felt something hard under the soft fabric of the doll's clothes. And another hard protuberance on the other side of its chest. He touched again and again and again until he had another erection. First the two sticky fingers, then his whole hand, grasped his penis while he continued to rub the doll's minuscule nipple until they both partially closed their eyes, together. In his heart of hearts he knew that very afternoon that the doll would betray him, that the doll was wicked, that it would have closed its eyes in pleasure while he touched it, but that it would never have been his accomplice. They came again together. The doll got down from the desk and helped him with its tiny plaster hands, with its hard thighs that were soon damp. The velvet began to tear and was soon caked in the milk he left on the little plaster breasts.

Then, as his mother opened the door of the room, the doll pulled back, screaming. It fell to the floor, and the plaster legs shattered revealing the lace knickers that had been so obscenely violated. An eye rolled out of its socket, the immaculate temple, just under the frizzy blond hair, cracked open and an arm was flung upward, pointing at him, accusing him. His mother bent down and hurriedly began picking up the pieces. He saw that the doll didn't bleed where it had been wounded. He noticed that the plaster shell was stuffed with tow. Thousands of tangled threads made up the soul of the doll who betrayed him.

The infrared lamp switched itself off. Professor Avildsen surfaced from his memories. He went over to the two strips of skin. He caressed them. This time the operation had been a complete success. He emptied the tow out of them. Then he took two metal objects from a bench. They were light, with well-oiled joints at the ankles and knees. The tops of the two metal objects were joined by a hinge to replace the hips. Deftly, after filling the skins with fresh, clean tow and then covering the structure with a thin layer of wax, which he had always preferred to plaster, too stiff and brittle for his tastes, he sculpted the muscles. Then, with infinite delicacy, he rolled the skin stockings over the two metal legs. He had to make a small incision at the knees to allow the skin to roll over the thick thighs. Then he did some invisible mending with suture thread. He used twist for thread, thin and resistant. Finally he attached the skin to the layer of wax. He modelled it delicately, as if he were massaging Dr Cerusico's legs. With infinite lightness of touch. With love. With delight. With all the knowing skill of a practised lover.

When he was with his animals, creatures without hearts or innards, he became a child again. His life was stuffed and padded, not in the least bit compromising. An excellent imitation of a life. An embalmed dream. An embalmed memory. Embalmed emotions and feelings. His desires never became dangerous and if he didn't manage to feel happy, at least he achieved a well-padded serenity.

But ever since he had become aware of the grand design which he had carried within him since birth, he had found his own true self. His soul was no longer stuffed and padded, pinioned under a metal skeleton, held together with twist stitches. Now he was free. And as he stroked and stroked the smooth legs of Dr Cerusico and tested the joints and the degree of tension the stripped skin could take, Avildsen thought bitterly of the fact that he had not found someone, years earlier, who loved his work as much as he did, who grasped its every facet and who possessed his own, innate aesthetic sense. If the nun who had sewn up his little finger had only had his passion, then the stump would certainly have looked less wretched today, he would have looked less repugnant. He ran his stump over the stuffed legs and felt a tremor in his groin, warm like a wound, and comforting as a caress. As dangerous as a doll.

After his mother had gathered up all the pieces of the doll, after she had felt how sticky they were, she had turned her gaze upon her son. She had seen it in his eyes, even before noticing his undone trousers, the guilt and the filth. She had made him get up from the chair, had taken him over to the wardrobe, opened the door with the mirror and had made shown the depraved child a pervert's reflection. The child had seen his own reflection, his hands clamped about his penis in an obscene embrace.

The memory made Professor Avildsen feel like retching. He shuddered. He thought of the old brute he had surprised out in the rice fields three Sundays before, when the huge weight of his destiny, which had been gathering all these years, had suddenly begun rolling at incredible speed, as if all those years he had been waiting for a sign, a voice, to shake him awake and prompt him to act.

His mother had shaken him, she had torn his hands away from their embrace, she had done up his trousers and in doing so had touched him through the wet cotton. She had led him to a dark room, where the gardener kept tools for household repairs. She had ransacked the room until she had found what she needed. Steel wire and wooden sticks. Ten wooden sticks, one for each finger of those abominably guilty hands. She had bound the sticks to his fingers using the steel wire, which she had closed tight using pliers so that the metal bit into his skin. Paying no heed to the child's screams. Then, after she had immobilized his hands, she had left the room, switching off the light and locking the door behind her. He had screamed, and begged, battered the door with fingers sprouting wire. Then he had started to cry. To bite the metal.

Professor Avildsen shook himself. He saw it in front of him every day, a few inches from his tear-streaked face, he still saw that closed door, especially at night, in the dark. The barrier his mother had erected between them, for ever, from that moment onwards. After she had buttoned up his trousers. After she had touched him.

In the end the Voices had come to comfort him. And they had not left him since. They had filled up his solitude.

The child had spent the night in that cubbyhole and only the next day had his mother opened the door. The pain in his fingers had already stopped.

The Voices had taught him how to tolerate pain.

But when he had been freed from the steel wire, the little finger on his left hand was infected, and a week later the doctor who came to check on the orphans had amputated it. His mother had explained that it was the result of an accident. Then a nun had sewn up his wound without much care. But the child he was then hadn't felt any pain.

In a fit of rage, Avildsen brandished one of Dr Cerusico's legs above his head, like a weapon. Then he put it down and fell to his knees. He clasped the stump of his finger to his chest, protecting it with his other hand, sheltering it from the world's pain, which continued to invade him through a wound that had never healed. He started butting his forehead against the edge of the bloodied table. But there was no physical torture that he could not bear.

The Voices, which drew him more and more often into their darkness, had taught him how to stand any kind of pain. And transform it into pleasure.

XXI

"But you do remember the petrol smell?" Frese asked.

Augusto Ajaccio was lying in bed. He was thin, his skin was sallow, two heavy, dark bags were gouged under his eyes and his hair was unkempt. His broad chest was almost skeletal. He looked at Frese with a vacant expression.

"Petrol?"

"Yes, I found a report that stated the fire was deliberate."

Peschiera and his nephew Mouldy had uncovered the third and fourth missing documents. Number twelve and number thirteen. Document twelve was the first report from the fire services which already put forward the hypothesis that the fire had been deliberate. Document thirteen was the official confirmation, compiled by an expert, who had set out in some detail the origin of the fire, the fuel used and the path taken by the flames before they engulfed the dilapidated municipal orphanage building. As the fire had been started deliberately in a dwelling that was permanently inhabited, the incident qualified as murder in the first degree.

Frese leaned forward, making the seat creak. He reached out and gently shook Ajaccio. The sick man seemed to return to his senses for a moment.

"The fire . . ." he said.

"Yes, the fire," Frese confirmed.

"The fire . . ." said Ajaccio again with difficulty.

He began to talk about the smoke-filled rooms reeking of the petrol that was probably the origin of the fire, picturing again the grotesque scene of poor children scrambling to gather up their few, wretched belongings; remembering a fat nun who went hurrying around the orphanage looking for the register that contained the children's names, as if it were the only goal of her vocation, as though those boys had nothing but their identity. And he thought that for many years he had blocked out the heart-wrenching sounds of screaming orphans, sounds that were now ringing in his ears.

"Do you know what? I've only just realized something strange ... The youngest kids' crying wasn't any different from usual. The same sound they always made, like when they hurt their knee or were hungry. Do you understand what I mean? As if crying was a foreign language you need to learn the grammar for."

"Tell me about the smell of petrol," Frese interrupted, his senses alert.

"The petrol?" whispered Ajaccio, who was following the trail of abstract reasoning through the altered state he lived in, a world that collided constantly with the sphere of hard facts and practical questions and punctilious interjections. "The petrol . . .?"

"You told me you remembered the smell of petrol. What was petrol doing in the orphanage? What did you do with the petrol?" insisted Frese.

"Petrol? Oh, yes, the petrol . . ." Ajaccio's voice had become so feeble that Frese had to lean closer. "The petrol . . . The smell of the petrol . . ." he repeated in a monotone, his eyes fixed on those distant days when the dressings stuck painfully to his burns and sleeping was almost impossible and all people talked about was

243

the inexplicable smell of petrol. Everybody thought someone had deliberately set fire to the orphanage, although no one could understand why. His past swirled by his widened pupils in a rich kaleidoscope of colours and smells and details that did not strike him as being memories. Rather it was like awakening from a coma. "Petrol," he said again and again. "Everyone remembers the petrol ... the red streaks of petrol bursting into flames ... the explosions ... the petrol ..." But he couldn't say anything else because the images were rushing past too quickly and words could not grasp and translate them. But he clearly remembered arriving at the new orphanage, with the big garden that would soon be theirs. The plants with wide leaves bathed in cool morning dew that the orphans brushed over wounds that were healing and itching. He saw again the stretch of white gravel, which they had covered like a lazy wave of mud, a brown mass dressed in rough jute uniforms; he recalled the paintings on the ceilings of the villa that depicted heroes and beautiful women; he saw the boy who spied on them from the first floor, and then from behind a window. And the colours began to pulsate and swirl and form new pictures and Ajaccio remembered that he had pointed his finger at some place behind the boy and shouted 'It's him! It's him! It's him!' until a nun had slapped him. But he couldn't find a way to say this to Frese who was shaking his arm and calling him back, back to the hospital room where he was going to die. When Ajaccio realized he was being summoned, he resisted. He didn't want to go back.

"Tell me about the petrol, Ajaccio. The petrol. Did you know Mrs Cascarino didn't have a penny to her name? Did you talk about that? What did people say?

Did you know her husband had died in the arms of a whore and that he had frittered away the family fortune? Ajaccio. Ajaccio, are you listening to me?" Frese yelled at him.

The door to the room opened and a nurse appeared.

"It's okay, everything's fine," said Frese, reassuring her. He waited until the woman had closed the door behind her and then shook Ajaccio again. He lowered his voice.

"Ajaccio . . . Ajaccio"

The man turned towards Frese with a drugged smile. They weren't allowed to mention the fire in the new orphanage, he explained. It was against the rules. And punishment was severe, much harsher than for other transgressions. The word petrol was banished from their vocabulary. Then an image of "the lady", as they all called her, swam into view. Clear. Vivid. His eyes wide open now, Ajaccio looked at the woman who had taken them into her home and only at that moment was he struck by the fact that she was wicked, cruel. "Could have killed someone . . ." he said. Somewhere far away he heard Frese ask, "Who? Who?" He managed to bring the detective into focus, for a moment. He felt the man's breath spreading over him. He smiled. "If you had seen how harshly she treated her son . . . Yes, her son, she could have killed him. She always talked about him as if he was some child prodigy, destined for great things . . . and we had no trouble believing her. The boy was special . . . But she could have killed him, yes, I think she could have . . . if he didn't do what he was told . . ."

Frese settled him back onto his pillow and stroked his forehead. It was cold. Very cold. He was about to get up when Ajaccio took him by the hand and held him back.

"I saw him, you know?"

"Who?" asked Frese, without much hope.

Head back on his pillow, Ajaccio looked tired, although his eyes were no longer veiled.

"I was down in the basement," he began, in a calm, clear voice. "I had to get firewood. I was the biggest. The strongest. I caught sight of him for only a moment. Short, very thin, with a face like a rat. He didn't see me. I think he must have heard me and run away. And after that everything burst into flames. They spread rapidly. And then I understood where that petrol smell was coming from. The whole basement was doused in petrol. I ran upstairs but there was the smell of petrol there, too, and flames everywhere. It only took a moment. Chairs, tables, curtains, beds . . . everything caught fire in just a few seconds. But I had seen him . . ."

"Who was it?" Frese was on a knife edge.

". . . and I recognized him."

"Who the hell was it, Ajaccio?" insisted Frese, fearing that the moment of lucidity was going to fizzle out.

"When we arrived at the new orphanage I saw the boy at a window on the first floor. And then I saw him again behind a window that overlooked the courtyard. And behind the boy I saw him, the one I had seen in the basement, bent over a hedge. He was dressed as a gardener and was holding a pair of secateurs . . . short, skinny, with the face of a grinning rat . . . I shouted. I was afraid he might hurt the boy . . . I pointed at him. 'It's him! It's him!' I cried . . . Someone slapped me. They opened the window but he wasn't there any more. He'd gone. There was just the boy. A good-looking kid, with a lost expression . . . petrified. His mother came out and she threw him on the ground,

246

right there on the gravel. Then she made him get up and told him she was going to put him in a dark room and not serve him dinner . . ."

"Get back to the gardener."

". . . But it wasn't him, it wasn't the boy . . . The shadow of death . . ." Ajaccio's gaze wandered off into the distance again. "The man from the fire . . . the shadow of death . . . was standing behind him . . . such a cute kid, and so frightened . . . The shadow of death and flames standing behind . . ."

Frese slapped him.

Ajaccio looked at him. He smiled sadly.

"I never met him again," he said. "That same day I caught sight of a car that was taking people away from the gardener's lodge. But I didn't see him. Maybe he was in the car. Maybe he was already far away. And then I saw the owner a few days later, talking to some people, to a young man and his even younger wife. She hired him as gardener and they went to live in the lodge. The owner said there had never been another gardener . . . She told me so . . ."

"You spoke to her?"

"No, she spoke to me. Mother Superior had told her that I wanted to tell somebody about what I had seen, that I thought the police should know about it . . . So she summoned me to her study and told me . . . she told me . . . I've always been stupid, you know . . . I was stupid . . . She told me I couldn't have seen anyone . . . that the police would have taken me for a fool and that I would have made her and the nuns look really bad . . . that they would have closed the orphanage and me and all the others would have been tossed into some foul, damp place . . . She told me I had dreamed everything . . . and I convinced myself I had dreamed it all . . ." Ajaccio shook his head. "But I didn't dream it . . . and I didn't dream the fake Civita . . . and I didn't write on my own chest . . . I didn't . . . I'm not crazy." He stared at Frese. "I'm not . . ." He stopped, tired, his eyes full of a pain that no longer knew who to hurt. He looked around him, convinced that his voice, if he had managed to start speaking again, would sound hoarse and hopeless. He pursed his lips. He didn't want to hear a dying man's voice echoing inside him. He looked around him, trying to recollect the useless thoughts he had just expressed and that were already splintering against the walls of the room like shards of crystal.

"Okay, calm down now," said Frese. "Calm down. You've been really helpful."

"Really?"

Frese nodded and Ajaccio seemed to relax.

"You've done a great job," he added.

"Really?" the sick man said again.

"Yes, really."

Ajaccio smiled. He looked like a child.

"You know that the chief inspector has another job for you?"

"Chief Inspector Amaldi?"

"Yes, Amaldi."

"He told me about it. I remember . . ."

"Good."

"Amaldi? About the case?"

"Yes." Frese put an envelope on Ajaccio's bed. "It's a sentence in Latin written by the murderer. We've translated it and we know it was used by the alchemists. But that isn't important. Some of the letters are lower case, the others are capitals. We think the capital letters mean something, that the murderer wants to tell us something. But we understand shit all, to be honest. You've got to help us."

Ajaccio took hold of the envelope without opening it, as if it were precious.

"Me?" he said.

"You, Officer Ajaccio."

Making a huge effort, Ajaccio lifted himself up and threw himself at Frese's neck. The two men hugged each other fiercely. Two strong carcasses clutching at each other, reverberating, hollow and afraid.

When the nurse came in, a quarter of an hour later, to remind Frese that visiting time was over, she found them still embracing. While Frese helped him to recline, Ajaccio forgot why he had been clutching the other man like that. There was a vacant, dreamy look in his eyes. As if he were in another world. In one hand he still held the envelope with the riddle left by the antique-dealer's murderer.

Frese went out into the corridor and spoke with the nurse. He wanted to understand what was happening to Ajaccio. He asked her if it was really possible that his tumour could make the man more intelligent. The nurse replied in vague terms, flattered that the detective was asking her opinion and at the same time having no idea what to tell him. Frese realized this and changed the subject.

"Have you ever seen anyone else going into Ajaccio's room? I mean, apart from myself and another detective, quite tall . . ."

"The good-looking one?"

Frese nodded. Well, If Amaldi was the good-looking one, he must be the one who *wasn't* good-looking, then.

"Yes, he's been by two or three times . . . but he's very discreet, isn't he? He went about the place as if he didn't want to be seen . . . You know, looking around . . ."

"Two or three times? You're sure about that?"

"Yes, sure. I've seen him myself, a couple of times. He's a man you'd notice. Tall, well dressed, nicely trimmed beard . . ."

"What beard?"

"Your colleague, doesn't he have a beard?"

Frese grabbed the woman by the shoulders.

"Can you describe him?"

"Well, yes, of course. He's tall . . . at least six feet, thin, broad shoulders. He's got a beard, like I told you . . . Why are you asking?"

"It doesn't matter, carry on. The beard, and then . . .?"

"Short beard, trimmed, well kept, you know, trimmed close on his throat . . . brown hair, medium length, long, narrow eyes. Light-brown eyes, hazel, yes, hazel. A sort of golden sheen to them. A noble nose, quite striking, aquiline, and a full mouth. Red lips, almost like a woman's. A very handsome man, believe me."

"I do, I do believe you."

"It's a pity about that defect of his. But I've always thought that certain imperfections —"

"What defect?" snapped Frese, on the alert for the description of those tiny details that were essential in making an identification.

"I was just getting there," replied the nurse testily. She was rattled because Frese had interrupted her little speech. "As I was saying, certain defects in such a handsome man only make him all the more human, more . . . how can I put it . . .?"

"Accessible?" suggested Frese, raising an eyebrow.

"Yes, that's it, accessible," confirmed the nurse, who hadn't caught Frese's sarcasm.

"Fine. Shall we describe this imperfection in a bit more detail, then?"

"His finger," said the nurse, snorting in annoyance.

"The poor man was missing a finger. His little finger, if you really must know, although I can't see what all this —"

"Which hand?" insisted Frese.

"But who is this man, anyway?"

"Tell me which bloody hand it was before I strangle you!"

The nurse stepped back, unsure if she should take offence and walk away, or cooperate. She knew the man in front of her was a policeman. He was ugly and she hated him, but he was a policeman.

"The left," she said eventually.

"And . . .?"

"And what?" she snapped.

"Completely missing . . . or a bit left over like a pig's tail? Is there enough for him to pick his nose? I don't know. You were the one who saw him."

"I noticed one time when I saw him stroking the door to Mr . . . to Officer Ajaccio's room, before going in. I was over in that storage room." She turned and pointed at a door several feet away. "I heard footsteps and I was worried it might be the staff nurse so I —" She broke off and flushed.

"Listen," said Frese hurriedly. "I don't give a damn if you were in there with some pretty male nurse or if you were having a quick smoke. Just go on."

"I put my head out of the door and I saw him."

"And he was stroking the door?"

"I know it's strange. But he really was stroking the door. Like it was a person, you know? And then he rubbed his little finger, that is, the . . ."

"Stump?"

"Yes, the stump."

"So, there was a bit of it left, then?"

"Yes . . . just the first phalange, I think . . ."

"You think?"

"The first phalange, I'm sure of it."

Frese sighed. He had heard what he had wanted to. But it was strange that Ajaccio had never mentioned these visits. And Frese wanted to know just what stage Ajaccio's disease was at.

"And you haven't seen anyone else?

"Just a woman . . . old. She looked, well, she looked poor."

That would have been the widowed landlady Amaldi had mentioned.

"Thank you very much. And please accept my apologies for my tone."

"Tone? I didn't notice," said the nurse and walked off, her head high.

Frese remained in the corridor for a few moments more, then pressed his ear to the door of Ajaccio's room. He thought he could hear the man talking. He put his head round the door and Ajaccio turned to look at him

"You're here then, are you?" mumbled Ajaccio.

Frese understood at once that Ajaccio was not in his right mind. He had never spoken to Frese in that familiar tone before, and his eyes were closed.

"Yes," he answered and went into the room.

"You're not Professor Civita."

"No," replied Frese, taking his cue from the sick man.

"You're here to deliver the notice, aren't you?"

"Yes . . ."

Ajaccio huddled under his bed covers, clearly frightened. Frese went closer and heard that the man was talking. Just a whisper. He raised the covers and listened. Ajaccio was praying, dejectedly, recommending his soul to God. In one hand he was holding the sheet with the phrase written by the killer, in the other he held a pencil. Frese took them from him gently and examined the page. Under the typed phrase Ajaccio had written his own name and surname, using the same system as the murderer. An apparently random combination of capital and lower case letters. The capital letters he had picked out in his name were U, S, T, J, C, I. Frese imagined those letters might have some link with Ajaccio's memories of the orphanage. Maybe he was trying to spell out something. Justice, maybe he wanted justice for the fire?

The nurse came into the room carrying a tray containing a thermometer, a glass of water, some coloured pills and a syringe nestling on some cotton wool that smelled of alcohol.

"Are you still here? What are you doing?" she asked Frese.

"No, please, no, I don't want to," moaned Ajaccio.

The nurse put the tray down on the bedside cabinet and glared at Frese.

"Will you please leave him alone? Can't you see how much he's suffering?"

"Was it you who found Ajaccio with that writing on his chest?" asked Frese, ignoring the woman's accusation.

"Yes, why?"

"Look at this." He showed her Ajaccio's signature at the bottom of the page. "Was it written like this?"

"Yes . . . first name and surname."

"No, look again, please. Can you see that certain letters are in capitals and others are lower case?"

"Yes, now that you mention it. But I couldn't say now if exactly those letters were capitals or not. I don't remember."

"But it was something like this, right?"

The nurse nodded.

"You are an angel," said Frese. "Take good care of my friend, now."

Then he bolted from the room and headed down the stairs. He had a horrible feeling and he had to tell Amaldi about it.

XXII

"Maybe he was telling the truth," Frese was saying to Amaldi. "Perhaps he didn't write on his own chest . . . You can't tell me that that style of writing was a coincidence."

Amaldi was bent over the page. Just six capital letters to combine. He took a sheet of paper and wrote out the letters. He was struck immediately by the J, and the rest was easy.

"And he said 'notice'?" he exclaimed, looking up at Frese.

The deputy nodded.

Without another word Amaldi showed him the solution to the riddle.

Frese read it.

"J-U-S-T-I-C. Justic! Shit! Viviana Justic, the antique-dealer!"

"Deliver notice about what? Viviana Justic's death? Ajaccio's chest was written on before the woman was killed, right?"

"It couldn't have been Ajaccio."

"No, but he's involved."

The two policemen sat in silence for a few moments. They were searching for connections, for the key that would open the door. Amaldi picked up the phrase left by the killer on the door of the antiques shop.

"So these letters make up a name," he said.

"Maybe," echoed Frese.

"It is a name. But this time it's more difficult to crack."

"If it is some sort of notice, as Ajaccio called it, then I think we'll only know after he's struck again."

Amaldi scowled at Frese, but knew he was right.

"Where do we start?" asked his deputy.

Amaldi didn't answer. His gaze had fallen on a pile of papers and something had drawn his attention. Like an alarm bell ringing. He raised his open hand to Frese, requesting silence. Then he took the sheets of paper and begin skimming them hurriedly, in search of something that had escaped him. He had made the connection, he knew what to do next. He didn't need to work slowly. When he found what he was looking for, he would know it. Five minutes passed and then he stabbed his finger at one of the sheets.

"I knew it."

"What?"

"Another coincidence," Amaldi said, holding the sheet out to Frese. "This is the file on the Rice Fields Massacre report. I had it sent to me because . . . well, you know why. We're in luck and we need to play on our luck. Have you looked at it yet?"

"What?"

"There's a list of things that were found at some distance from the scene of the crime. Have you got it? The murderer's prints were all over those objects. Read it."

"Five traps, different sizes, in metal and wood . . ."

"Forget the descriptions, skip to the list."

"Three jars of resinous glue . . . two bags, one coloured, the other . . . Contents . . . live bait, string, a hat, gloves, two knives, a spool of thread —"

"There, stop there," ordered Amaldi. "Read the note."

256

Frese looked down the page and found the footnote.

"Fuck me! 'Upon examination the spool of thread was identified as twist, a kind of linen yarn generally used by taxidermists.' Fucking hell, is it him?"

"The same kind of thread used on Justic. A rare kind of yarn used only by embalmers and taxidermists. What do you think? Is it him or not?"

Frese scratched his head.

"It's their case."

"No way!" snapped Amaldi.

"It started on their patch."

"And it's going to continue on ours! What happened there was just an accident. He went there to hunt animals, not people. He was seized by some kind of fit. He messed up, did an untidy job. But it opened his eyes for him, made him see his real nature. That girl with the bandaged breast. Torn away and then put back in place. That's what brought him into contact with his dark side. But it was just chance. Now he isn't taking any more chances. He doesn't leave any prints, he follows his ritual, he sets the scene . . . and now we know he even leaves advance notice. Not for us. For his next victim . . ."

The silence descended again.

"Get a few men on the case. Tell them to get a name out of those letters."

"It could be any name."

"I know that! I know. But we have to try." Amaldi thought for a moment. "Tell them to proceed like this: it might just be a surname, like in Viviana Justic's case, but sixteen letters is a lot for a surname. Let's assume he's written first and last names just to keep us guessing. The first thing they do is list all the first names that correspond to those letters. Women's names. I'm beginning to think that he has a problem with women

257

. . . or maybe with one woman. Yes, we have to go for it, women's names. With the remaining letters they have to work out her surname. All the surnames they can come up with. And then they have to go through the directory and see if the first name corresponds to the surname."

"But there could be hundreds of combinations."

"What do you want to do? Give up? Wait until he kills the next one without at least trying to do something about it?"

"No . . . of course not. I'm on it." Frese left the office.

Amaldi heard him bellow in the corridor. Despite Frese's scepticism, he knew his deputy would put every available man to work. Now he had to deal with Ajaccio. How was he connected to the murderer? Amaldi pulled on his coat and headed out of the building, straight for the hospital. It was outside visiting hours, but he would just throw his weight around, if he had to.

Along the way he suddenly realized that the rubbish strike situation was completely out of control. The security forces' forecasts had been alarmingly confirmed in the last few hours. In just twenty days every street, from the most wretched and isolated to the most chic and well travelled, had been invaded by tons of rubbish. No one had paid any heed to the mayor's appeal in the first days of the strike to reduce household consumption and waste. The whole population seemed to have adopted an attitude of defiance towards the authorities. It was as though the accumulation of black, yellow and blue rubbish bags, the piles of cardboard boxes, old chairs and broken fridges were a message that declared, "We'll see if you don't do something about it tomorrow, we'll see!" And the indignant citizens carried on piling rubbish upon rubbish. But not one of them had the foresight to understand that

258

the amount of fetid waste produced by such a large community would eventually send the whole city grinding to a halt and spiralling into chaos. Perhaps the only people really capable of calculating how much waste accumulated in two, three, seven, ten days, were the striking road sweepers and binmen. Of course, they did not criticize the population. "That's just what we want. This way people will finally understand just how important our work is," the binmen said. And even if they had been able to foresee that the city would have filled up with rubbish in a week, no one had been able to work out just how much space the waste would have occupied after twenty days of stalemate. So after those twenty days the whole city had taken to the streets en masse, and stared wide eyed at that malodorous ocean. At the beginning, shopkeepers, for example, had coped as well as they could, clearing away the rubbish in front of their stores, lifting the heavy, sticky, filthy piles of waste themselves and dumping them in side streets, but after a few days they had had to give up. The improvised dumps were full; rubbish bags were shredded under car wheels, distributing waste over the roads and making the stench all the worse; residents had banded together, street by street, building by building, to defend their already devastated territories. The initial wave of carelessness and irresponsibility had been followed by a spirit of provocation. And now the city's population was in a seething fury. Anyone spotted with a rubbish bag in his hand was lucky to get away with encountering hostile glances and harsh, angry words. There had been a number of reports of violent exchanges and serious incidents of intolerance. The youngest, the strongest, who had at first come together to protect their own patch, were now offering their services as mercenaries. The "bin militia", as they were called, patrolled streets or whole blocks. They were armed with chains and sticks. After the first sensationalist headlines in all the papers, quite a few people had realized that there was money to be made both in drawing up a map of the city which featured protected areas so people knew where they could risk venturing without being beaten up, and in creating a genuine vigilante organization. The security forces had been unaware of all of this, or had underestimated the gravity of the problem, until it was too late. It wasn't long before the families that had produced the first mercenaries were forced to pay others to watch over their districts. As the circle tightened and the city became saturated with controlled zones, and free districts became scarcer, human ingenuity, which knew no limits in finding shortcuts without actually resolving the problem, gave a new twist to the Trash Wars, as everybody was calling them. In return for a higher offer, mercenaries would undertake pollution raids into protected territories. The enterprising squad members would get hold of trucks and load them full of rubbish during the day. Then at night they would crash through enemy roadblocks and pump out their putrid munitions onto the battlefield. Why no one, or almost no one, ever bothered to go a few miles further outside the city limits and dump their waste comfortably and peacefully at sea or in the countryside was a mystery. A number of psychologists became popular writing articles and essays on man's intrinsic need to wage war. They got carried away with adventurous descriptions of the soul and the unconscious, seeking out the root causes of rage and frustration. But none of these learned articles gave a convincing explanation for why, when the strike was over, there were over three hundred wounded. At the height of the crisis a journalist trumpeted THE CITY HAS GONE MAD. And there was nothing else to add. The people who were arrested, and those who were interviewed almost all said the same thing, as if they were reading from the same script. They persisted in saying that urban guerrilla warfare was motivated by the citizens' drive for survival. Taking the rubbish outside the city, even burning it, would have been a concession to the administration's ineptitude, tantamount to condoning the council's culpability. What was clear was the fact that, despite the efforts of individuals to fight back with every means at their disposal, including some rather unfair ones, despite having thought up the perverse mechanism of the mercenaries and having themselves sparked off the trash wars, the city's inhabitants were bonded in their collective role as the offended party, and had every intention of staying that way. The Oppressor State, above every other dispute or disagreement, was the true guilty party.

Amaldi quickly retraced his steps and asked for a car. It was not at all wise to wander around the city alone, without an escort. In the wake of the antique-dealer's murder, Amaldi's face had been constantly plastered over newspapers and television screens. An exasperated citizen would be more than capable of venting his frustration on Amaldi and the inspector had no intention of taking that risk. When the car was ready he sat in the front and told the driver to take him to the hospital. When they arrived he advised the man to park in the restricted access area reserved for ambulances, and not to draw attention to himself.

"Do we have to hide ourselves now?" the young constable asked with a hint of pride.

"Don't play the hero," Amaldi admonished him. "I need you to take me back to the station."

As soon as he stepped into the entrance hall Amaldi was stopped by a nurse who reminded him that visiting hours were over.

Amaldi showed her his badge.

"And?" asked the woman, and continued to file her nails.

"Shoot me," retorted Amaldi, losing patience, and headed for the lifts.

The nurse shook her head, put down her nail file and picked up a container of flame red nail polish.

While he was waiting for the lift Amaldi turned and looked towards the corridor that led to the first floor. He recognized her at once, even from behind. Those long legs that emerged from her nurse's smock, the straight hair that lay on her shoulders. He felt a sharp pain and the temptation to turn away, to hide. To run. The letter he had written was an act of love. Of love and cowardice, he had told himself. Love, because he wanted to avoid suffering. Cowardice because he didn't think he had the strength to break away from his ghost, from his obsession. And because he wasn't sure he wanted to start living again.

Giuditta said hello to a nun and went towards a door. Amaldi caught sight of her face for a moment. Her eyes were red from crying, her hair seemed dirty and there was something spent about her whole person, as though the light were avoiding her. Amaldi felt immensely sorry for her as well as a desire to go and comfort her. He took a step forward. But then the lift door opened behind him. He turned and when he looked round again Giuditta was gone. With a heavy heart Amaldi got into the lift and pushed the button for the fourth floor.

"Giuditta," he murmured.

The lift came to a juddering halt. Amaldi stepped through the automatic door and turned right. The long wide corridor was thronged with patients and nurses. Nearly everyone was smoking, breathing in hungrily and constantly checked the butts of their cigarettes. They were concentrated around the ashtrays, above which hung notices explaining that smoking was forbidden. They were thin and sallow. Along the corridor, on the right, windows were set high into the thick wall; on the left, three double doors gave onto the wards. The corridor crossed another smaller, darker passage from which doors opened onto single rooms. Amaldi arrived at number 423 and knocked. He went in without waiting for an answer. Ajaccio's unmade bed was empty.

"Can I help you?" came a voice from behind him.

Amaldi turned.

"I was looking for Officer Ajaccio," he replied.

"It isn't visiting time yet," the nurse said.

"Yes, I know, but it's urgent."

"No visits outside hours."

"Police business," said Amaldi, showing her his badge. "Where is Ajaccio?"

"He's in radiotherapy," the nurse replied, annoyed. "I have to make the room up. If you want to wait it will be at least an hour" She regarded Amaldi defiantly. "No one can go in. Not even the police," she added with a triumphant smile.

Amaldi looked around him. The room had changed a lot since his first visit. Ajaccio had given it a personality. Books were piled on the bed, newspaper clippings were tucked into the frames of two anonymous prints on the wall. There were numbers written in thick pencil on the opposite wall illuminated by the sun that filtered through the venetian blind, forming a kind of rudimentary meridian. The overall impression was of an operations centre. It was not the usual passive and desperate waiting room for death. Frese hadn't told him about this. Amaldi looked enquiringly at the nurse, who was waiting for him with her fists planted firmly on her hips.

"He said you would pay for everything, that you're all one big happy family . . ."

"Did he now?" asked Amaldi, smiling.

"Yes, and he said if we didn't like the idea we could kill him."

Amaldi became grim again. "Yes . . . well."

"He's a good man, kind."

"Yes."

Amaldi turned to leave and noticed the photos on the door. They were all alike, all showing the same subject against the same background, each one marked with the date and time it had been taken.

"I went to buy the camera myself. He wanted an automatic, you know, one of those instant ones that gives you the photo right away."

Amaldi went over to the photos. They had been taken a few hours apart. As though Ajaccio were trying to time the changes that were taking place within him. The disintegration of his own body. He probably compared them, thought Amaldi, and established a kind of chart that meant something only to him. Documenting his advancing death. It was quite macabre. But perhaps understandable.

"For Mr Ajaccio," said the nurse, "hours have suddenly become very important. Hours are like days to him, now."

A way of prolonging life, thought Amaldi, and left without saying goodbye to the nurse.

When he reached the ground floor his eyes wandered over the corridor where he had seen Giuditta, then he lowered his head and went back to his office.

XXIII

Professor Avildsen had informed the vice-chancellor that he would have to leave for a long trip and that the university would have to find someone to replace him for the rest of the semester. He had foreseen the vice-chancellor's indignant bluster, his objections and even his threats. But he had also foreseen the way to obtain the approval of the university's highest authority: a promise to acquire a few collector's items. What he had not imagined was the alacrity with which the vice-chancellor allowed himself to be corrupted. Avildsen had hardly finished explaining his proposal when the man began wagging his tail like a dog that has been offered a juicy bone. They had settled on a fetish used in the fertility rites of an extinct tribe, and on the embalmed hand of a village chief that certain witch doctors used to restore sexual vitality in their patients.

As he left the university Professor Avildsen thought about the uses to which the vice-chancellor would put his trophies. Was he an old man who wanted to satisfy at any cost the lubricious requirements of a young wife? Did he want to have a child? Avildsen smiled, amused. And then he thought of the exhilarating sensation of not needing the university any more. Show over. Now that he was wearing the disguise of Anyman he could come down from the stage and abandon it. He could mingle with the audience, mix with the crowd, pretend to be one of them. His destiny and his design allowed him to do that. He was free from risk. He was one of them. He was one of the orphans.

He drove towards the town centre, his car wheels tearing open the bin bags that covered most of the tarmac. He had one more little job to take care of before dedicating himself body and soul to his grand design. He had to deliver a present.

He parked in an authorized area and continued on foot, without wasting time. He sniffed at the humanity that was pressing in on him. As he walked briskly along he reviewed those last weeks, which had changed him so radically. He had uncovered, in what the journalists theatrically dubbed the Rice Fields Massacre, a sign that had shown him his path.

Back at the villa he had taken shelter in the dormitory that housed his stuffed animals. He had hugged his dog, Homer, with the glass eyes that hadn't worked out properly, had let himself be rocked by the voices of his friends as he had listened to stories that did no harm, trying to regain his balance, to breathe. But the nausea grew. "Who are you?" he had shouted, his hands raised to the blistered ceiling, without knowing if the question was directed at the nausea, or his weakness, or himself. He had stormed over to the workbench. First two, then three, then all of the bloodstains on the ruined surface had attacked him, sticking to his clothes, to his hands, and the more he dodged them, tried to shrug them off, detach himself from that foul embrace, the more ferociously the stains gripped hold of him, like leeches, like the tentacles of some beast. Floundering in panic he had tripped and fallen. "Enough!" he had yelled. "Enough! Tell me who —" but he had been unable to finish his question because his mouth had filled with gastric juices. He had spat out the bile and coughed, convinced he was suffocating.

Then, instead, he had started breathing again. At last, as though he had found peace at the moment when, unconsciously, he had decided to yield, when he had picked himself up, his legs shaking and his eyes still watering, he had understood everything.

It had all started with the girl's breast, that breast he had put back as though he had been following orders. The breast that once back in place had stopped the girl's screams. She had become docile and he had believed he wanted the best for her. He was almost sorry now not to have taken her away with him. He would have looked after her, as he had always looked after his animals. She was pretty, he remembered that much now. For the first few days the scene had come back to him in nightmare bursts, illuminated by some sort of disco strobe. The shapes that came closer, that fell to the ground in slow motion. The disorder. And then, illumination. The girl had come to him in a dream and had shown him the scar under her breast. It had been sewn perfectly, not a drop of blood had fallen. She had thanked him. "You put me back together," she had said. He hadn't understood, at first. What did she mean? And then everything had become clear. The girl had come to him in a dream again and had opened her breast to reveal what was inside: tow wadding. "It doesn't hurt any more," she had told him. Wadding. Tow wadding in her breast where once there had been flesh and blood. The secret was the wadding, the tow stuffing. The answer had been within his grasp for such a long time without his realizing it. Now his mother would be able to rest in peace. She could be proud of her son. He would take care of everything, now that he had the answer to all his questions.

The incident, if he could call it such, had been altogether providential, thought Professor Avildsen, as he turned the corner into a side street. It had mapped out his path; it had illuminated him. It had always been there in front of his nose, and he just hadn't seen it. Hadn't been able to imagine it. For years. Years darkened by paralysing fear. But wasn't that how things went? Things revealed themselves when one least expected it. Was this not what happened to saints when they became enlightened? What were visions if not a hidden door in the heavens, a doorway to one's destiny, a gateway to one's nature that was revealed by chance? That opened, allowing access to a new world, a world that was the right size, the right way up, and not topsy-turvy. A tidy world. It really took so very little to keep things in order. And with that hint of order everything worked perfectly. Everything added up, as the maid might have said, checking the change against the shopping receipts. The account was settled. And it was all so simple. And pleasurable.

He would wipe out the constant reproach he saw in his mother's infallible eyes.

Avildsen abandoned his reflections as he neared his destination. He spent almost two hours hugging the shadows before Clara, the prostitute, pulled down the shutters to satisfy a client. He crept out of his hiding place and shoved an envelope under the metal shutter. Then he returned to the shadows and waited. When he saw that on his way out the client noticed the envelope and picked it up to give it to Clara, Avildsen felt irritated. He didn't like to see other hands touching his gift. It was like a kind of contamination. He glared at the departing man's back, a look full of hate.

"I could take you for what you just did," he said to himself, and the thought seemed to have a calming effect.

Then he turned his attention to Clara. She wore the

same bored expression as always when she opened the envelope. The flaccid look worn by someone who expects nothing from life. She slipped the letter from the envelope and began reading. It was a simple message, concise and to the point. The gift was not in the form but in the content.

Your torturer Augusto Ajaccio is dying. A brain tumour is devouring him and forcing him to suffer what he has made us suffer. The show will run for a few more performances only, in room 423 in the municipal hospital.

Unsigned.

Clara read the message a few more times. There was no trace of boredom in her taut face. She clasped the letter to her chest and squeezed it with both hands.

Professor Avildsen quivered with delight. Four years earlier she had resurrected Ajaccio from the past and delivered the man to him, and now he was making her a present of Ajaccio's death. The promise of freedom.

Avildsen thought back to when he was a child, in his room, the only room that was to be his, because all the other rooms he used to wander around in had been dismembered and transformed by builders, architects and his mother in order to house the orphans. He remembered he had been in that room when he heard the gravel scrunch. He had put his face to the window and had leaned the palm of one hand against the cold glass. Then the other palm. Then his forehead, his nose, his lips, and finally he had pushed his chest against the cold glass, hoping the chill would penetrate him and make him stop suffering what he was suffering. He had hoped the icy touch would anaesthetize his pain, kill it off, and help him not see what was plainly before his eyes. The procession of orphans had struck him as being like an invasion of sick crickets. They had seen each other for the first time then. Halfway along the line there was a boy who might have been sixteen or seventeen years old, and who at that time had struck Avildsen as being extraordinarily big and hairy. The orphan had looked up and caught sight of him on the other side of the dark glass. The boy had stopped in his tracks, a head higher than the others, his arms hanging limply at his sides, his body as shapeless as the jute sack that had been cut out for him to wear. He had remained there, his face expressionless, showing neither surprise nor curiosity, his neck tilted back and his mouth was slightly open, joined by some invisible thread to the window. The other half of the line of orphans went past him, without anyone else bumping into him or looking up. Then the line of orphans had disappeared, and the tall boy, pulled along by the sudden vacuum, his head still turned towards the window and the figure behind the glass, had smoothly rejoined the flow of the convoy, the caravan of children he had not really left because, the professor thought with a stab of pain, he was an integral part of it.

That had been the first time they had seen each other.

And even then, although he had only been a child, he had felt pinioned and stripped by that insistent gaze. When his mother had let the orphans into the garden, he had gone down to spy on them from behind another partially open window. He had listened to their voices, and smelled the odour of their bodies, and he had seen the burns under their shabby clothes. Some were leaning on wooden crutches, others were moaning in pain. Seen up close, many of the wounds were even more striking, not only yellowing and purple,

270

but shiny, as if they were covered in mucus. One child had licked his burn and then spat on it. The tall boy, standing nearby, had laughed at him when he saw this. It was a hollow laugh, from weak lungs, and didn't last. Then someone called out the boy's name and rebuked him. From behind his window, the child who was excluded had memorized the name he heard. Augusto Ajaccio. He hadn't known what he was going to with that name, but he had repeated it over and over again so as not to forget it. While he whispered the orphan's name, as if he were reeling off his rosary, he had become totally absorbed in those wounds. He pictured the scene. The skin that cracked under the flames, the acrid smell of burning flesh, although it was something he had never experienced. He saw the skins of the youngest orphans swell and blister, their welts bursting. He heard the moans and screams of the orphans who trod each other underfoot as they struggled to find a way out through the thick, suffocating blanket of smoke. He had felt an enormous terror grip his small soul, a nameless fear that was not part of the scenes summoned by his imagination. The fear of something that couldn't be thought. Looking at his mother, it had seemed to him that those ravenous flames that he had just imagined were still flaring in the woman's icy eyes. And then he had understood that his mother was right, that he was indeed a wicked boy. Because he thought things that shouldn't be thought.

And it was at that very moment that the tall orphan, Augusto Ajaccio, had raised his hand and pointed at him. 'It's him! It's him! It's him!' he was shouting. What happened after that wasn't important. From that day on, the child had understood that Augusto Ajaccio could see his guilt and hear his thoughts. He knew his secret. The image of Augusto Ajaccio had tortured him from childhood. Cain and Abel. Saint and sinner. Augusto Ajaccio had become his obsession. His greatest fear. He was master of Avildsen's nightmares.

Augusto Ajaccio had read his images of fire. He knew who Avildsen had thought about. The orphan had learned of that thing that shouldn't be thought.

And that was why it wasn't enough for him to die. When the Voices had revealed to Avildsen the grand design he was destined to accomplish, three weeks earlier, they had whispered to him a way of silencing Augusto Ajaccio for ever. He would be the head. The head with the mouth sewn shut.

He looked over at Clara, but didn't see her. She had already gone back into the store where she sold her second-hand goods.

XXIV

The corpse was found at dawn by an angler.

"He was down on that rock with his rod," Frese explained to Amaldi. "He's a pensioner, not a real angler. He said he saw her straight away. Thought she was out sunbathing."

"At dawn?" asked Amaldi.

"An hour later when it started raining and he decided to go home he noticed that the woman, the corpse, wasn't moving . . ."

"How very observant."

"He's old, Giacomo. And he's very upset. He came all the way over here to ask her if she needed anything and found her like this."

Amaldi looked at the corpse again. The woman was stretched out on a deck-chair. Sunglasses, headscarf covering her hair, shirt knotted above her navel. She was wearing shorts. Her spread legs were supported by two rods jammed into the sand. The position was probably meant to be sexual. An invitation to penetration. In fact, the two legs held up that way made Amaldi think of what women must look like during an examination by their gynaecologist. He couldn't see the wooden legs inserted at groin level, but they had already told him that a metal hinge through the victim's abdomen kept the two legs together. The folds of skin, the flesh, tendons and bones had all been cut with great care and then sewn back again.

"Wooden legs, metal joints. I should think they come

from the same mannequin doll he used for the antique-dealer," remarked Frese.

"It looks like it. Let's just check it out in the lab."

"Yes, sure."

"I don't understand why they still haven't worked out where these pieces come from."

"From a doll."

"And the doll? Where does that come from?"

"It isn't easy to find a doll. Even an old one like this. There isn't a single antique-dealer in the whole city who has sold one."

Amaldi walked around the corpse in silence.

"Sunbathing in this position, was she?" he said at last.

"I've already told you, Giacomo, he's old. I'm pissed off too but it's no use taking it out on him. Even if he had phoned us an hour earlier, what difference would it have made? She's been dead at least three or four days."

Amaldi nodded his agreement. The corpse was swollen. The hordes of bacteria and micro-organisms that corrupted and transformed the flesh had been active for some time. Amaldi bent down to examine the sand round the deck-chair.

"Nothing, not a drop of blood. He didn't kill her here," said Frese.

"She's cyanotic. Maybe due to decomposition . . . or poison."

"Yes, the examiner thinks she was poisoned. He'll be able to tell us more after the autopsy."

"Is it the same one as last time?"

"Who?"

"The examiner?"

"Yes."

"That young guy?"

"The same."

"Very encouraging start to his career ... Where he is?"

"He had to leave us for a moment."

"Well, when he's finished throwing up, tell him I want to speak to him. Not now. Tomorrow. After the autopsy."

"Okay."

"Photos, prints, everything taken care of?"

"Yes. But no prints."

"Have them take the body away," said Amaldi, who had glimpsed a group of curious onlookers, armed with binoculars, on the other side of the rocks. "Did you get hold of the owner?"

"He's on his way. During the winter he's a swimming instructor at a municipal pool. But he already told me on the phone that he hasn't set foot here since the end of the summer season."

"And the deck-chair?"

"The killer broke into one of the beach cabins. We found a broken padlock."

"So he knew this place, too. He doesn't like improvising. He must have worked during the night. Try and find out if anyone noticed a car parked here three or four nights ago. Which I doubt."

"I've already sent two men to do the rounds. As soon as we finish here I thought I might pop over to Villa Cascarino, it's not far from here, and maybe I could have a few words with the old woman about the fire ..."

Amaldi didn't answer.

"What are you up to?" he asked aloud. "Same ribbon on the throat? Same pencil marks?" he asked Frese.

"Same velvet, same colour ... same thick pencil marks."

"What are you up to?" Amaldi asked himself again. "You take a pair of arms, then a pair of legs and you substitute them with the limbs from a doll. You use linen twist, which leads us to think you might be a taxidermist. There are strong grounds to suppose you keep the arms and legs . . ."

". . . to make a new doll," concluded Frese.

"Exactly. But there is something that doesn't fit. And maybe he doesn't even know it himself. I have to think about it. But something just doesn't fit."

Frese didn't speak. He knew how important it was not to interrupt an investigator when he was thinking. Words often brought the most hidden sensations to the surface.

"On first examination two things are missing. The leaves and the advance notice. Am I right?" Amaldi went on.

Frese nodded.

"We have to find out who this poor girl is. Maybe he killed her in her own home or in her shop, if she has a shop. The notice and the leaves should be there. What do you think?"

"What do we do about identifying her?"

"How are you getting on with the sixteen letters from the last notice?"

"They're still checking."

"Maybe someone has already reported her missing. For a start let's cross-check the names you've come up with so far against the names of this week's missing persons. There can't be that many. If we're lucky that's where we —" Amaldi stopped speaking and looked at Frese. "I actually said 'lucky', didn't I?"

"We do a shitty job, Giacomo. And this is all the proof we need to remind us."

Amaldi walked off without answering. His feet sank into the sand. Suddenly he sprang round to look at Frese again.

"He didn't leave a single print?" he shouted, to make himself heard.

"No. He cleaned everything." And Frese pointed at a rake that had been left at the foot of the concrete steps leading to the road.

Amaldi moved off again, thinking of the murderer. They had to identify the victim as quickly as possible to establish any links with the antique-dealer. They had to understand how their man chose his victims, in order to predict his moves. Decipher his plan before he finished it. When Amaldi got as far as the rake the monster had used to wipe out his trail he stopped again and looked up. The murderer had climbed down a hundred steps with the corpse over his shoulder, then he had walked about sixty-five feet over the sand, then he had forced the lock on the beach cabin, picked up the deck-chair and set up his scene. Then he had found the rake and cleaned the beach. He must have been exhausted by the end. As it was logical to presume that he had done all this in the middle of the night, in all likelihood the man had used a torch. Was it really possible that no one had noticed?

Amaldi called out to the officer who was acting as his driver and had the man take him back to the city. He needed to think.

Once back in his office he cleared his desk until it was just an empty surface. He imagined that his mind was like the desktop. He caught sight of a stain and cleaned it with a tissue. Giuditta. A thought he couldn't rid himself of. He forced himself to concentrate on the clear surface of his desk. He polished it. When he felt ready he tried to review everything they had in chronological order. First of all, the Rice Fields Massacre. He took the file on that first, chance incident, and placed it on his desk. He rapidly scanned the information it contained. Two men and a woman. The murderer had ferociously brutalized one of the men, the old voyeur. The other had died almost immediately from a shot to his stomach at close range. The murderer had probably not paid any attention to him. He had simply thrust him aside, like a bush that lay across his way. And then the woman. He had smashed her skull in after having put her mutilated breast *back in place*. He had made an incredible number of mistakes on that occasion. Stupid things. His prints were everywhere, especially on the girl's body. Prints from blood-smeared hands. Prints that didn't show up in any archive. Prints from a man with no previous convictions. Which confirmed his hypothesis about the seizure the killer had suffered and about the man's social status. Such a ferocious nature probably had a whole arsenal of protective mechanisms and cultural inhibitions. If the murderer had been some ignorant wretch his sickness would have come to the fore much earlier. And he certainly wouldn't have been equipped to cope with his real nature. Their man had dominated his sickness for years. He had delayed the inevitable. Perhaps he had found a replacement in hunting animals. The gun was loaded with the kind of pellet that was designed to pulverize flesh, not just to kill. But the prints had a peculiarity. According to forensics the little finger of the man's left hand was mutilated. There was just one print to support this, but it was clear enough. Blood made excellent ink, and never lied.

The killer's second mistake was leaving his tools so close to the scene of the triple murder. This showed that he was overwhelmed and not in complete control. Evidence that it was his first time. He had lost his virginity in the rice fields, as it were. The things he had left behind still didn't allow them to trace him, but linen twist was rare and that might be the trail to follow. Forensics had found other prints on the glass jars that matched the ones found on the girl. Prints of almost all the fingers, of both hands. Nine in all. No print for the little finger of the left hand, which confirmed the mutilation beyond doubt. A more thorough investigation had uncovered resinous glue on a log nearby. So, thought Amaldi, this man practised two types of hunting. The first, with his shotgun, was ruthless, killing for its own sake, almost certainly driven by the desire to touch blood. The second was more refined, with the purpose of keeping his prey intact. In all likelihood it was connected with his taxidermy work on animals. But investigations along that line had failed to produce any results, either in the jurisdiction of the Rice Fields Massacre or here in the city. There were few professional taxidermists, most of them were very old and they all had solid alibis. So the killer had to be an amateur. Or, Amaldi deduced, somewhat arbitrarily, a sadist.

He closed the file and pictured the sequence of events. In chronological order came the murder of the antique-dealer. Amaldi picked up the case file and placed in on the polished desk top. Viviana Justic.

"No!" he said aloud. "No . . . Ajaccio first. First he wrote the notice on Ajaccio's chest."

Amaldi took hold of the sheet on which Ajaccio had written down his own name and surname, following the murderer's upper-case pattern of letters. He put it down between the Rice Fields Massacre and the file on the antique-dealer. Then he sat very still and thought. Why Ajaccio? Ajaccio struck a false note. Amaldi made a hasty review of the dying policeman's life: abandoned and discovered among the trash by a road sweeper; road sweeper obsessed; road sweeper's son jealous; Ajaccio handed over to an orphanage; the orphanage burned to the ground; Ajaccio badly burned; Ajaccio saw the person responsible for the fire . . . Credible? Then he saw the same person again at Villa Cascarino, home of the new orphanage. Credible? Ajaccio grew up and joined the priesthood. Then the Force. End of story.

No, thought Amaldi, Ajaccio developed cancer and was hospitalized. He's not a celebrity. He's not news. So whoever wrote the notice for the antique-dealer's death on his chest was either a regular at the hospital and had chosen Ajaccio by chance, or knew the man already and knew what had happened and where to find him. Or perhaps a combination of both: the murderer is a regular at the hospital and knows Ajaccio from before. A chance encounter was very unlikely . . . this murderer does nothing by chance. Even the Rice Fields Massacre, regardless of whether it was unpremeditated, the result of some homicidal fit, has a certain logic to it . . . a certain design . . . He does nothing by chance . . . so . . . he knows Ajaccio from before. He chose him because Ajaccio means something to him . . . So . . . Amaldi stared long and hard at the sheet of paper where Ajaccio had written his own name and surname.

"So," he continued out loud, "chronologically Ajaccio comes before the Rice Fields Massacre!" and Amaldi put the sheet at the beginning of his paper trail.

Ajaccio, the Rice Fields Massacre, Viviana Justic and the unidentified woman from the beach. But even now there was something that didn't fit. Amaldi cleared his desk and polished it again. He started from the beginning. He considered only the two murders that were clearly linked: the antique-dealer and the unidentified woman. Arms and legs. Was he making a human doll? That seemed logical. But if that had been the case, then the murderer could have chosen his victims following some sort of aesthetic criteria. Fine arms and pretty legs. At least according to his personal tastes. That would have made it very difficult for the police to second-guess the murderer's plans and identify the next victim before the murderer did. They had to hope that the two women were somehow linked by something else. Ajaccio? They had to find out if the women had had anything to do with Ajaccio.

Amaldi wrote his first note on a sheet of white paper: "Why Ajaccio? Links with victims?"

But there was still something missing from the overall picture. Amaldi closed his eyes and pictured the two corpses. Arms, legs, the wooden limbs beckoning, inviting, the antique-dealer fixed in an embrace, the woman on the beach in a much more sexual pose. Theatre. Representation. The first one killed with a halberd, the second one probably poisoned. The first killing more elaborate. But perhaps that was due to the fact that the murderer was able to create his set in a safe, risk-free environment. He had taken a great risk when he left his notice, the alchemists' V.I.T.R.I.O.L. that unpleasant Professor Avildsen had told him about. In the second instance the murderer had had to work in a hurry in the open air, where he would be easily spotted, as logically he would have had to use a torch. And perhaps the closer he got to his goal, the more fed up he got with the theatricals. But just what *was* the murderer's goal?

If he wanted to make a doll, which parts did he still need? A torso and a head. Amaldi couldn't think of any other joints. Four parts in all. The two arms counted as one part, as did the two legs, which left the torso and

281

finally the head. Four parts, four crimes. Four crimes, four notices. The first had been left on Ajaccio, the second the shop door of the antique-dealer. The third, when they finally identified the corpse from the beach, would probably be in the place where he had killed her. Would it help them get to the third woman in time? Amaldi was reasonably certain that the murderer only went after women. That type of crime always had sexual roots. It was an act of sex and power.

"Unless your particular hunter will be happy with . . . just three more little pigs," Avildsen had said, hazarding his own interpretation of the murderer's intent in leaving the dry leaves. It seemed solid enough. The first little pig was Viviana Justic. The second, the woman on the beach. The third would be the torso and the fourth the head, though not necessarily in that order. Put like that, the murderer's design seemed much clearer. And it was obvious that the hunter was an educated man. Who might know about the customs of some tribes of savages? An acadecmic? How many other people, apart from Professor Avildsen, would have known that particular fact and been able to use it as the starting point for this scenario.

"Call on Avildsen" was the second note Amaldi jotted on his piece of paper, irked at the idea of having to meet the anthropologist again.

He turned his mind's eye to his mental picture of the two corpses. Arms equals legs, no real difference. Pieces. Organized scene. Symbolism: availability, wantonness, invitation, probably erotic. Sexual organs on display but taken care of, *put back in place*. Deactivated by death. Rendered less dangerous?

And what else? Amaldi asked himself.

And then he saw the velvet ribbon and the thick pencil mark.

That's what wasn't right!

Amaldi felt his pulse quicken in excitement. He knew he was getting closer. But closer to what?

Closer to his way of seeing things, he said to himself.

The murderer had marked out the head, a part of his human doll, on his first victim, but not the legs or torso. Even though he needed those as well. And he hadn't marked out the torso on his second victim, although it was still missing. He had only marked out the head and then hidden the mark under a velvet ribbon. A sexual fabric, seductive. A very feminine material. But why mark out only the head?

Amaldi corrected himself: Close to his way of *feeling* things, of *thinking* them.

Two designs in one, he wrote on his sheet of paper.

The murderer was fulfilling two plans in one. The first was the human doll. Sexual, perhaps oedipal, in motivation. A straightforward background of violence. Repression, and probably a very strong notion of the struggle between Good and Evil. The need for control. To establish once and for all who had the power. But the second plan, nebulous even for the murderer himself, perhaps subconscious, in any case deeply unconscious, the second plan was tied to the head. The head separated from the rest of the body, from the rest of the doll. A head the murderer wanted to prevent from thinking? From hearing messages from his body? His own head?

"Because a head that thinks," Amaldi said aloud, articulating every word, "thinks death."

Without a doubt there was a double message. His own head thought death. But what was worse, someone else's head thought death. And he had to put an end to those thoughts. He had to kill death.

"Eleonora Cerusico!" panted Frese as he burst into

Amaldi's office. "Dr Eleonora Cerusico. On the staff at the city hospital. She hadn't been to work for five days and the administrator had reported her missing. Sixteen letters in her name. They match the notice. You were right. You were absolutely right."

"The same hospital as Ajaccio?"

"Yes."

"Ajaccio is the key."

XXV

Crouched down behind a car, Giacomo Amaldi and Nicola Frese tried to take shelter from the hail of stones and bottles that the rabid crowd was hurling at the security forces. Events had taken a turn for the worse. People had grown tired of the war between rival vigilante groups and between districts and individual roads. They had poured out into the streets en masse, as if at a signal. There had been no announcement, no organized demonstration or protest march, nothing from the usual rabble-rousers. Before it drowned under its own rubbish, the city had simply reared up, like a startled horse, and was now foaming at the bit and bucking wildly.

"If we don't stop them, they'll kill each other." Frese shouted to make himself heard above the roar.

Amaldi craned forward to look at the crowd. Riot police armed with shields and tear gas were trying vainly to disperse the demonstrators.

"Let's go," he said.

Frese followed him, glancing upwards, on the look-out for falling stones.

"Couldn't we just give them three or four binmen and let them hang the buggers?" he said. "You can bet that would calm them down."

They turned down a deserted street and headed towards Dr Eleonora Cerusico's apartment building. Their visit to Ajaccio had been a waste of time. The officer's condition had suddenly got worse. They had found him in a pitiful state. He babbled on about the smell of incense that filled his hospital room, like some kind of sign. When they had understood that they wouldn't be able to get any sense out of him, Amaldi and Frese had left Ajaccio with a heavy heart. Then they had encountered the furious crowd. Now they walked along briskly, looking over their shoulders, hugging the walls. They had almost reached the end of the road when suddenly a tall, thickset man appeared before them, his jacket lapels ripped and his tie pulled to one side. He walked with a stagger but didn't look drunk. It was though his whole body was full of springs that didn't want to uncoil. He was holding a gun. Amaldi and Frese came to an abrupt halt. Only then did the other man see them. He pointed the gun at them, but not aggressively, as though he were pointing at them with his finger, and started walking toward them.

"Well?" he asked, as if he were taking up an interrupted conversation. "Did you not find any? Not even one?"

Frese shook his head, humouring the man. Amaldi stood petrified.

"Not even one?" continued the man, who was now upon them, the hand with the gun straight out before him. The barrel of the gun came to rest against Amaldi's sternum. The man's eyes were red, startled, and the corners of his mouth were dry and drained of colour.

"Why don't you put that thing down?" said Frese.

Amaldi noticed the absence of fear in Frese's voice. He felt his own legs almost give way beneath him when the man stared at the gun stupidly, turning it towards his eyes to get a better look.

"Not even one?" he repeated, lowering the gun.

"Not even one," echoed Frese. "Perhaps we should all go home and get some rest and go hunting later? What do you say?"

There was a sudden glow in the man's eyes. He loomed over Frese, and Amaldi didn't know what to do. Frese reached out and touched the man on the shoulder. He shuddered as if shaken by an electric shock. Frese squeezed harder. The man started, lifted the pistol, waved it about for a moment and opened and closed his mouth without managing to say anything. Then his eyes filled with tears. Frese took the gun from him and he fell to the ground where he moaned a few times.

"It's time to go home," Frese told the man, who, dirty and shapeless like the rubbish bags around him, no longer seemed so big. "Where do you live? Can we take you there?"

The man continued to shake his head from side to side, slower and slower until he stopped, his gaze lost among the rubbish.

"Come on now, up you get," said Frese and almost dragged the man to his feet. "Go home, do you hear?" Frese took hold of the man's face and forced him to look at him. Then he slapped him. "Go home, understand?"

The man nodded.

"Good. Now, do you remember where you live?"

The man nodded again.

"Look at the state you're in," said Frese as he tried to straighten the man's lapels and tie. "I wouldn't like to be in your shoes when your wife gets hold of you."

The man managed a faint smile.

"Off you go now," said Frese and gave him a slap on the back, like you do with donkeys. And just like a donkey the man began to shuffle off towards his stable.

287

They watched him until he had turned the corner, then they set off again. A few minutes went by and neither of them spoke. Amaldi berated himself over and over again that he had been seized by panic and hadn't been able to react. And Frese must have noticed.

"Thanks," said Amaldi after a while.

"Well, if I hadn't done it, you would have," replied his deputy generously.

"No," said Amaldi. "I wouldn't have."

The chief inspector ploughed on, head down, in silence, replaying the scene, seeing the madman's red eyes that had pinned him down and feeling the gun barrel against his chest. And the fear, the awful fear he had felt. He felt the terrible weight of his defeat. He had lost it. It had happened. His great, superior intelligence had been short-circuited. He felt a terrible fury swell up within him, a blind hatred for himself. While they showed their badges to the two officers on duty in the murdered doctor's apartment Amaldi put a hand on his heart, as if he wanted to make sure he still had one. As though he wanted to apologize for having forgotten all about it, for having put it to one side.

"Fucking hell," exclaimed Frese, on the doorstep.

They could already make out the pool of blood on the kitchen floor.

Amaldi lowered his hand and mechanically stepped into his role, concentrating, alert, soaking up every detail. Each time it was as though the crime were a personal matter, between himself and the killer. He regained all his feline grace.

"She knew him. She let him in. She trusted him," he said to Frese.

His deputy nodded and pointed silently at a wall. Amaldi looked in the direction Frese was indicating. There was something written there.

"The notice," said Amaldi.

They went over to the wall and read what was written there:

pure and undefiled religion, before god and the father, is this: to visit the fatherless and widows in their affliction, and to keep oneself untainted by the world. Letter to a servant of God from san <u>Giacomo</u>

"What the fuck is that about?" asked Frese.

Amaldi shook his head.

"It's strange," he said after a while, as though he were talking to himself. "Usually this kind of person tends to simplify the message as they go on. They make it easier to understand. They don't enjoy it if the people hunting them fail to understand how intelligent they are. They want to make you part of their plan. In a way, you lend objectivity, stability . . . You're the real world and they try to be part of that world."

"Just two capital letters," remarked Frese. "L and G. They look thicker to me, like he wrote over them twice. The L would be a capital anyway, at the start of a sentence and the G of God, well . . . It must be a bit strange to see your name in blood."

"It's not my name. It's just a name."

"Fine. But why did he underline it?"

"Let's start at the beginning. L and G, just those two letters. Not a coincidence, or he would have put capitals on the first 'god' and 'father' and probably 'pure' at the start of the piece, as well as 'giacomo'. L and G . . ."

"The initials of the next victim. The shit thinks we've worked out his game and doesn't want to get caught."

"No . . . that doesn't make sense. There must be something else."

"Like what?"

"I don't know . . . Let's think about this . . . The leaves. Look for the dry leaves. He must have left them somewhere. Let's see now . . . Maybe he wants us to go on some sort of treasure hunt." And with that Amaldi pulled on latex gloves and set about examining the kitchen.

Frese followed his lead and examined the living room.

The two men spent the next ten minutes looking through plates, furniture, cushions, in the bedroom, in the bathroom, everywhere, putting everything back in place afterwards.

"Giacomo," Frese called, with a tremor in his voice.

Amaldi, in the bedroom, immediately picked up the note of tension. He went back to the entrance and found Frese holding a crumpled letter and envelope in one hand and two dry leaves in the other. Amaldi recognized the letter at once, before taking it from Frese.

"I read it, I'm sorry," said Frese. "That's why . . . why he underlined your name . . ."

I would like to ask you to give me time, Giuditta . . .

"Inside . . . The leaves were in . . . in the envelope?" stammered Amaldi.

Frese nodded.

Amaldi had to sit down in an armchair. He loosened his shirt collar. He felt as if he were suffocating. Now it really was personal. Just like all those years ago. Just like the first time.

"Who the fuck is the guy, Giacomo?" asked Frese.

But maybe this time he would be able to make a difference. Amaldi leaped to his feet.

"The L is for Luzzatto, and the G stands for Giuditta. I've got to warn her," and he picked up the phone.

He called enquiries and got Giuditta's home phone number. He dialled it, a lump in his throat. Mrs Luzzatto answered and said that Giuditta was at the hospital that day.

"Listen, if Giuditta comes home, I want you to tell her to stay there and not to open the door to anyone. Even someone she knows. It is very important." And without further explanation he hung up.

He called enquiries again and got the hospital's number. All the lines were busy.

"Send a car," he said to Frese, "and then try phoning again. Tell them to make Giuditta wait. I'm going there." Amaldi left without waiting for an answer, and headed towards the hospital.

XXVI

Professor Avildsen looked at his watch in the gloom of his mother's room. There wasn't long to go. The old woman lay in her bed, her head back, looking up at the ceiling. Her eyelids didn't move. A butterfly needle stuck out of her arm, a sight so familiar that it seemed to be part of her, like a wart. From time to time little bubbles formed in the tube that entered her nose. Avildsen looked at her, almost without recognizing her. The old woman's lids were slightly raised and her pupils rolled back, revealing whites like sheets of paper on which no one had yet written.

"Mother," the man murmured in a child's voice.

Mrs Cascarino remained impassable, deaf to her son's lament. Professor Avildsen looked at her again. Her hipbones barely wrinkled the covers, two little mountain ranges between which lay the fertile valley that had generated him. Where was the doll? Where were the punishments? Where were those eyes of ice that always knew, that bored and dug, that denounced him to the world, protecting him from the evil that coiled within him.

"If only you had looked after me . . ." he said.

The bellows on the artificial respiratory machine rose and fell rhythmically.

"Where did we go wrong, Mother?" he asked in an childlike voice that shocked him and broke something inside his heart, as if the sound had been a tear and the tear had had the gift of forcing open a door that had been closed for ever. Carried away by this phantom emotion, he reached for his mother's limp hand. He took it in his own and squeezed. He felt the fragile bones in those fingers that would now allow him to do anything he liked, dead, or almost dead, inside that wrinkled skin, like dice inside a velvet bag. His mother could no longer avoid his caresses.

Avildsen give a little start. He had never looked at things from that point of view before. Yet it had a certain logic. Perhaps his mother was not, as everyone believed, immobile, he thought, grasping desperately at that illusion. Perhaps she was merely pretending to be paralysed in order to allow him to do what she would never have permitted otherwise. All his other thoughts evaporated in an instant and Avildsen felt that he was a child again and knew that the woman was his, now. Abandoned to his caresses, to his love. Just as the doll had once been.

The man's hand brushed the length of the old woman's arm until it reached her shoulder. He pulled back his hand and looked at his mother. No reaction. No change in the rhythm imposed by the respiratory machine. His mother didn't flee. She let him caress her. Her eyes full of disapproval didn't seek him out. Once more he stretched his hand towards her, towards the sharp bones of her pelvis. He felt their hardness under his fingertips. He raised his hand and studied it. It was his hand and he saw it just as it had been before, small, pink, with little shallow lines that crossed the palm. The stump of his little finger had just been amputated and the stitches pulled on skin that had trouble healing. He lifted the covers and let his hand glide between the sheets and his mother. Her hips were even harder now, without the padding provided by the bed clothes. He pushed his fingers forward, towards a softer, more welcoming spot. He looked at the whites of his mother's eyes. She was as blind as his dog Homer. His hand crept slowly towards the fertile valley that had engendered him. Avildsen's eyelids closed.

He saw himself as a child once more. He was looking through the art book. He was locked in his room, segregated because that was how it had to be, because his mother had been the first to spy in his nature the terrible wickedness that possessed him. That wickedness that he carried about like a sickness, always ready to break out and poison him. Like the mark of Cain, God's own thumbprint stamped on his forehead, and his mother had seen it all too clearly. And the book's pages slipped between his fingers, one after the other, glossy, flat, full of colours that he couldn't see. And then she appeared, the doll, Eve, the woman floating in the air who scattered milk over the Earth, white milk, thick droplets that shot from her nipple. And the nipple was pinched tight between his pink fingers, between the pink fingers of the assassin, the son.

Avildsen's hand was on her soft abdomen when it contracted in a spasm. A wave of nausea choked him. He opened his eyes and through a film of tears looked at his mother's eyes, lifeless, as white as the sheet of paper on which he was about to write his last obscenity. His closed fist, under the bed covers, was like an animal. Or some swollen tumour. The professor was petrified, incapable of escaping from his own hand, or of withdrawing it. He gazed upon it in horror, as if it were somehow alien to him, or perhaps in the hope that its very immobility would prove its separateness. He could have stayed there for ever, one step from the chasm, if only his mind's eye hadn't summoned up the painting again. And then he remembered that the woman was holding an apple in one hand, the symbol of original sin, and in the other an arrow, which pointed at the cherub's back.

He pulled his hand out from under the covers in annoyance. The buzzing Voices filled his head. And the Voices told him that the woman was a murderer. That she was going to kill the child. That she would have killed him if only she had been able to. If he hadn't pulled back. He brought his hands to his ears to block out that inner clamour and opened his mouth wide in a silent scream. When he had reconquered the silence he felt tears streaming down his cheeks.

His mother's pupils were fixed on the void. Avildsen brought his finger stump to his mouth and dropped some spittle on it. Then he passed his wet fingertip under his mother's eye, letting the frothy fluid gather at its corner to form a kind of tear.

"You never taught me how to pray, Mother."

The old woman made no reply.

Avildsen looked at his watch.

"I have to go now," he said in a hard voice and stood up.

He didn't turn round to look at his mother as he left the room. He was once again the new man he had been for the past few weeks. Anyman. The man who had a grand design to fulfil. He reached his car, got in behind the wheel, arranged the rear-view mirror to get a good view of the hospital entrance, and waited. She appeared a few minutes later. He let her get a head start and then started the engine. He gave a last glance in the rear-view mirror and caught sight of a familiar figure elbowing his way through the crowd, running.

"Saint Giacomo," he said, smiling, and put the car in gear.

He drove slowly along the road strewn with bags of

rubbish and then accelerated so that he reached the crossing just as Giuditta was about to cross the road. He braked loudly, in an effort to attract her attention. The girl turned round. She saw him, recognized him and smiled.

"Can I give you a lift?" he asked

Giuditta hesitated.

"It isn't prudent to wander around alone today, the city has gone quite mad," Professor Avildsen insisted.

A car horn blared behind them; the driver wanted to pass.

"Please, do get in, before they lynch me."

Giuditta smiled again and made up her mind. Professor Avildsen opened the door and the girl got in beside him, uncovering her fine, long legs. The man didn't bother to look. He already had the legs. And the arms. He needed a torso now.

"Where shall I take you?"

"I was on my way home. I live —"

"I know where you live," the man interrupted, keeping his eyes on the road.

Giuditta stiffened. She felt a jolt of alarm.

"I took the liberty of asking for your address at the hospital," he continued, after a moment. "I have the impression that my mother very much appreciates your company. I can't explain why, it's just a feeling I have . . . you mustn't think I'm being foolish, but I would so like to make her last days as comfortable as possible . . . So I asked them for your address, just in case. I hope you can forgive me."

Giuditta felt guilty because of her own apprehension.

"How is your mother?" she asked.

"She cried today." He looked at her. "She's never done that before."

"I am sorry."

"No, there's no need ... It was a wonderful experience for both of us." They drove on in silence for a few more minutes before Giuditta realized that they weren't heading in the direction of her home.

"I hope you don't mind, Giuditta," said Avildsen, as if reading her thoughts. "I have an errand to do before I take you home. It will only take a moment."

"No, of course not," she replied in embarrassment, and once again felt an unpleasant feeling of alarm.

The man hummed as he drove, and eventually he turned down a dark and empty street near the port. He stopped the car and looked around him. He leaned down and took a clear plastic bag out from under his seat. Giuditta saw that it contained a wet swab. Avildsen opened the bag. The pungent smell immediately filled the car.

"This will only take a moment, Giuditta," said the man, his voice heavy with menace. He clamped the swab over her mouth and nose.

Giuditta struggled and thrashed but after a few seconds her movements became slow and awkward until her body fell back onto the seat. Professor Avildsen pushed back a lock of her hair and straightened her skirt that had been pulled up to reveal her thighs all the way to her groin. He put on her safety belt and started the car.

XXVII

Amaldi was in his office, standing in front of the window that showed him the outside world. The crowd, exasperated by the refuse collectors' strike, were still in the street, yelling and hurling stones. Amaldi's thoughts churned with an old terror that seemed destined to repeat itself. He had reached the hospital too late. Giuditta had not returned home safe and sound. The nurse on duty at the entrance had said goodbye to Giuditta a few moments before Amaldi had reached the hospital. Since then no one had seen or heard from her.

Which meant that the murderer had managed to intercept Giuditta on her way home.

Which meant they had very little time to save her.

Otherwise Giuditta would be found dead and mutilated.

"Let's start all over again," he said to Frese.

Then in a burst of rage he swept everything off his desk, scattering it across the floor. He felt a desperate fury building within him. He picked up the folders on the crimes and opened them.

"We must have missed something."

Frese moved closer to the armchair.

"Where could he have seen Giuditta?" began Amaldi, repeating out loud the question he had already asked himself dozens of times. "At the university or in hospital. Okay, he could have seen her anywhere in town. But we need to narrow the field. University and hospital.

Let's take the hospital. Dr Cerusico worked in that hospital. Giuditta worked . . . works in that hospital, too. Ajaccio is in the same hospital . . . Ask someone to find out if the antique-dealer had anything to do with the hospital before she was killed. She visited someone or went in herself . . ."

Frese got up and left the office for a few moments. Amaldi thought. He thought and looked. And he saw two moments that were connecting, the connection produced by the very act of thinking and seeing. The girl like a bag of rubbish, twenty years before. And now Giuditta. He was exactly in the middle, his whole life suspended between those two moments, hanging in a void that existed for no other reason than to let him observe the chasm that would soon close up again. He was in limbo, he told himself, and had to get out.

"Now or never," he vowed as Frese came back in.

"They're on it," said his deputy.

"Okay. The hospital. Next . . . Dr Cerusico let him into her home, so she knew him. What did the neighbour who saw them say?"

"Nothing much," said Frese, rummaging through the files. "Here we are. Male, maybe had a beard, he didn't get a look at his face . . . He had a large parcel under his arm and was carrying shopping bags."

"The large parcel contained the wooded legs."

"Yeah, probably."

"Still nothing on the doll?"

"No."

"He poisoned her. The examiner said she had been eating when she died. So they were having dinner together. They were friends. Maybe lovers? Did anybody mention anything about this in the hospital?"

"Might as well have been whistling in the wind."

"I wrote that letter to Giuditta shortly after Dr Cerusico was killed. So the murderer had the keys to the apartment. He went back and left the letter, right?"

Frese nodded.

"The letter was crumpled. Giuditta probably threw it away after she read it . . ." Amaldi rubbed his face. "If I hadn't written that letter she might still be alive."

"Bullshit."

"I can't get it out of my head . . ." Amaldi's voice was strained.

"Let's tackle another question," said Frese. "This shit knows you, too. You hadn't signed the letter. Either Giuditta had talked to him about it or he knew who had sent it to her. Both notices mentioned the name Giacomo and the name was underlined. I don't think that leaves any room for doubt."

"No . . ."

"What do we know about this guy? The best description is probably the one from the nurse who looks after Ajaccio. Good looking, tall, distinguished, around forty, beard and that fucking stump of a finger. The same man from the Rice Fields Massacre, that much is obvious. No previous convictions, his prints don't match any criminal on file. No record. He's Mister Nobody. Educated, refined. Think, Giacomo, have you come across anyone like that recently?"

Amaldi shook his head.

"No one comes to mind," he replied. "I would have remembered him just from the finger stump . . . But if he had kept his hand in his pocket I wouldn't have noticed anyway . . . No, no, let's start again. From the beginning. Ajaccio. He served the notice but he didn't kill him. Why Ajaccio?"

"Because the shit prefers women and Ajaccio's a man? Because he had to start somewhere? Because

300

. . . How the fuck do I know why!" exploded Frese, banging his fist down on the desk.

Some of the papers fell from the pile. Lost in thought, Amaldi put hem back in order, mechanically.

"That's not enough," he said after a while. "He didn't choose Ajaccio on a whim. Otherwise a wall would have done just as well for the message. He went to visit him, passed himself off as a doctor, as the head of department no less, and tortured him with a minutely detailed description of his cancer. Ajaccio says he heard a voice mention the word notice . . . Our man again, probably. He chose Ajaccio because Ajaccio is the starting point of his personal history, of his nightmare. Did you tell the guard on duty that the situation could be dangerous? Is he armed?"

"He knows what he's doing. He's disguised as a nurse."

"Is he armed?"

"Yes, Giacomo, of course he's armed. Just relax."

"The last notice mentioned orphans. What did it say again?" Amaldi picked up the photo of the writing on the wall.

pure and undefiled religion, before god and the father, is this: to visit the fatherless and widows in their affliction, and to keep oneself untainted by the world. Letter to a servant of God from san Giacomo

"The fatherless and widows. That might mean something. The first notice was vaguer. The 'depths of the earth' that we have to descend into probably represent his nature. Maybe that's where his sickness is. Or the cure . . . The 'hidden stone'. But he's revealing himself. He's showing us something. He's gone too far, he doesn't want to be anonymous any more. He

301

thinks he's invincible . . . He's challenging us. Visit the fatherless and widows. Ajaccio is fatherless; he might be the orphan in question. The gardener? Ajaccio says he recognized the gardener at Villa Cascarino as the man who set fire to the orphanage, right?"

"Yes . . . But just how credible is Ajaccio? You've seen what state he's in. He smells incense all the time, he babbles on and on, and it looks like he's getting worse."

"This is no time to quibble, Nicola," snapped Amaldi. "It's all we have to go on. Let's just hope it leads somewhere."

"It was thirty-five years ago. The gardener will be an old man by now. He wouldn't have the strength to carry the doctor's body all the way down to the beach, and the nurse described him as being in his forties."

"I'm not saying it was him, but maybe he has a son . . ."

"A gardener's son who writes in Latin and quotes from the letters of St James, and knows about alchemists and the hunting rites of some tribe lost in the arse-end of nowhere?"

"If the gardener did set fire to the orphanage," said Amaldi, breathless, his face burning, as if he had never stopped running, "who do you think was behind it? Don't tell me you think he did it himself? His disappearance from Villa Cascarino was just a coincidence? Do you think the people behind the fire just sent him packing with a polite thank you? No. They either killed him or paid him off handsomely . . ."

"And with the money his son went to university. Is that what you're getting at?" demanded Frese.

"Our killer comes from a background of violence. Something in his past made him the way he is . . . No, no, it didn't make him that way. He was already like that. And this violence, real or imagined, triggered his

302

sickness . . . That's why he's looking for the 'hidden stone' . . . We've got to get that gardener's name." Amaldi ran a hand through his hair. "His personality seems to point to a mother, not a father . . . The signs he leaves all point to an unresolved oedipal complex . . . but, psychology doesn't always get it right." Amaldi was silent for a few moments. "But he talks about the fatherless and widows. Ajaccio is the orphan . . . or maybe the murderer is. But the widow . . ."

"The only widow we have is old Mrs Cascarino, if we go back to the orphanage fire trail . . . or the gardener . . ." said Frese.

"Did you go round there?"

"Yeah, I spoke to her son. Didn't let me in, though. Said he was in the shower. Said he hadn't noticed anything on the beach the night before. Told me his mother was . . . Shit! His mother's in that damn hospital, too. She can't talk. She had a stroke. Or that's what Mr Cascarino told me, the son, I mean." Frese picked up the phone and dialled.

While Frese gave orders that someone should go over to the hospital and check that Mrs Cascarino was indeed a patient there and in what condition she was, Amaldi struggled to avoid superimposing Giuditta's image on his picture of the girl killed in the alley, the girl he had loved and who had been left like a bag of rubbish. He went back to the window. He wanted to take to the streets, run like a madman through the city shouting Giuditta's name at the top of his lungs in the absurd hope she might hear him. But he had to keep his mind on the details, focus on the information they had. If there was but one slim chance of saving her it lay somewhere in the papers scattered over his desk and in his ability to decipher them. He sat down again. He had asked the colleague who was looking into the

Rice Fields Massacre to give him the list of everyone who had come up in the inquiry, as well as the names of the customers of shops that sold twist. Amaldi's men had made the same enquiries in town without any results. Now the names were being rechecked in the light of the new information.

"Where are they checking the list?" he asked Frese.

"Over in Records," his deputy replied.

"Let's go. I'll go mad if I sit here any longer doing nothing."

They left the office and headed down the corridor. Amaldi moved in long strides while Frese took rapid little steps, almost running to keep up with his superior.

"Where are they?" asked Amaldi as soon as they arrived at the door marked Records.

Frese smiled. He knew full well that the chief inspector hardly ever ventured into Records. He always had the files brought to his office. And if he ever did visit the archive, there was usually someone there to take him by the hand and then do the research for him.

"They'll be over in the smoking room," replied Frese, heading off in that direction.

"The *smoking* room?"

"Yeah, that's what they call it. Or the library. It's the only room with a table and chairs . . . You know, the rank and file have to do things differently to you chief inspectors," said Frese, a mischievous look in his eye as he glanced at Amaldi. "They're not allowed to take the files out of Records. So they go into the smoking room, sit down and read to their little hearts' delight. There's a coffee machine and, of course, they can have a cigarette."

Amaldi had no idea how the archives were organized. As he followed Frese, who moved around the place like it was a second home, he discovered an incredible number of communicating rooms, contained one inside another and lined from floor to ceiling with metal shelves packed with thick folders. The windows were all closed or blocked by the shelves. As they went through one of the rooms Frese stopped and indicated the files with a sweeping gesture.

"This is where they keep the orphanage files. We found all the missing folders in here. If they'd just been scattered around the place we'd never have managed."

Amaldi saw any number of folders piled up on the floor.

"We're doing things by elimination," Frese carried on, with the air of a tourist guide. "The fact that all the missing documents were in this room made me think that someone, the person who took them and hid them in the first place, that someone wanted the documents to be found. Sooner or later."

Amaldi was stunned. "But don't we . . . don't we use computers?"

"For the most recent cases, yes. But every case produces paperwork. And that paperwork is filed away neatly in the archive. It's like a back-up copy, you see. We're entering data from older cases, but we'll never get round to putting everything on computer. If the city suddenly became the earthly paradise tomorrow, and all our citizens became saints, it would still take us a hundred years to get through the backlog of our past sins. And this city is not home to that many saints, and it's certainly no earthly paradise. So we'll never get there . . . But I like it here." From the way Frese spoke Amaldi knew he wasn't being sarcastic. "We don't keep documents here. The whole archive *is* the document. Everybody's in here, victims and butchers, good guys and bad guys, cops and robbers." Frese laughed, clearly amused, and started walking again.

Amaldi followed him to a tiny, bare, windowless room lit by the harsh light of a bulb hanging from the middle of the ceiling. Around a long table were sitting four young officers who Amaldi did not recognize, but who sprang to attention when they saw him. He motioned at them to carry on with their work. Then he said hello to the head archivist, Peschiera, and his nephew, the fat youth who had molested Giuditta.

"You remember him, don't you?" asked Frese. "Massimo, known as Max, known as Mouldy."

"Of course," said Amaldi and managed a faint smile before taking Frese to one side and whispering, "What's he doing here?"

"He's turned out to be a bright lad, very quick," replied Frese. "He's really in his element, like he was born here. He's the one who found the last documents from the fire. He's got a real nose for sniffing through paperwork."

"Nicola, this is a murder invest—"

"Listen to me, Giacomo. Most of the cops just fall asleep over these files, they get distracted thinking about tits and getting laid . . . It's bound to happen. These are men of action. Mouldy here puts on his glasses and concentrates on everything he reads and doesn't miss a single comma. He was born to study. He's got a real talent, believe me. Out there he's just a fat wanker. In here, he's destined to become a god. In the time it takes those four over there to check ten names from the hospital and all the related files, Max does fifty on his own. We don't have that many men available, they're all out patrolling the streets because of the strike. We need the fat guy."

Amaldi spread his hands in defeat. He looked at the

306

table and the mountain of files. The list of hospital employees, the names of the patients, the names of people who had bought linen twist and material for taxidermy and the list just in from the place where it had all started with the Rice Fields Massacre, with the names of everyone who had been questioned or who had been added for some reason or other. It was going to mean hours and hours of cross-checking.

But, thought Amaldi, with a shiver, they just didn't have those hours.

"Found anything?" he asked.

The four cops shock their heads. Their eyes were puffy and they all looked as if they wanted to sleep. The head archivist looked at his nephew and nodded at the boy to speak.

"Well, I think, that is, I might . . ." began Massimo, turning red and stammering ". . . have found, found something."

"For fuck's sake, Mouldy, if you've got something spit it out, now," snarled Frese.

The fat youth's face grew even redder, his rat's teeth bit at his lower lip and he swallowed hard and took a deep breath. Amaldi saw him stretch out his hand and clutch at a ball of greasy paper that probably covered a *pannino.*

"I've got a list . . . of shops . . . and of a factory that makes twist . . . here in town that didn't show up in the . . . investigation reports."

"What?" snapped Frese. "How is that possible?"

"Let him speak," said Amaldi. "Go on, Max."

"I extended the search to companies that weren't in business any more, as you suggested, Inspector Amaldi." Max grew bolder as he spoke. "I mean companies that had closed down."

"Get to the point, Mouldy."

"Right, well, I did some research . . . I went back five years. I found six shops and a factory that don't exist any more. I got hold of their accounts and two names came up, two people who bought large quantities of twist. The first date's from three years ago and the second from last year. He bought at closing-down prices . . ."

"The names. Any matches? Hospital employees?" Amaldi was electrified.

"No. No matches with names on the list —"

"The next word better be 'but' or I'll throttle you," Frese interrupted him.

"Okay . . . But . . . the two names are very strange. One is Alake. The other is Abeokuta. Apart from being very strange names, I was suspicious because . . ." Max darted a glance at the four uniformed men.

"Come on, this is no time to be shy," said Frese. "Why were you suspicious?"

"Well, the Alake is the king of Abeokuta . . . I heard that in an anthropology lesson and I, well, I just remembered it." He looked at the four uniformed men again, an expression of embarrassment on his face. "It was a bit of luck, right?"

"I don't understand any of this," said Frese. "Who gives a shit about some king? What are you saying, Max? That monarchs like a good stuffing too?"

"Go on, lad," said Amaldi, going over to Max and putting a hand on his shoulder.

"They're false names, or at least I think they're false, because if there had been just the one it might have been a coincidence, but two different ones together, well it sort of . . ."

"Stank." Amaldi finished it for him.

"Yes, exactly. So I checked the addresses the material had been delivered to . . . lots of stuff, not just the twist. Tanning acids, sterile tow for stuffing, preserving solutions and so on. The two addresses match, I mean, they're the same. The same address for the two names." He held out a sheet of paper.

"We've got him!" exalted Frese, seizing the piece of paper. "Whatever his name is, it's him."

"Look at the address," said Max, handing Frese another note.

"Villa Cascarino!"

"The street number is different," continued Max, paying no heed to Frese's look of disappointment. "According to Land Registry records it corresponds to the gardener's lodge in the villa's grounds."

"The gardener," breathed Amaldi.

"Or his son," added Frese excitedly. "And if he's missing a little finger he's fucked."

"Let's go, now," Amaldi almost shouted, leaving the room.

Frese overtook him and guided him through the labyrinth of rooms towards the exit.

"I want at least two units, experienced men," Amaldi was saying, running now, towards something solid at last, his heart full of hope. "And another two in radio contact."

"And fuck the strike."

They were already in the lift when they heard a breathless voice call after them.

"Wait," shouted Max. "Wait."

Amaldi held the lift doors open.

"You said the killer is missing a little finger?"

"Yes, what about it?" said Frese.

"Professor Avildsen. Professor Avildsen is missing a little finger."

Frese and Amaldi looked at him, failing to grasp the link.

"Alake, Abeokuta . . . I heard those names in one of his lessons."

"Look, Mouldy, you've done a great job, but we'll take over from here. The man we're looking for is —"

"But he's Mrs Cascarino's son!"

XXVIII

Giuditta came round less than an hour after she was kidnapped. Her head was heavy and she felt terribly nauseous. She tried to get up but something was holding her back. She turned her head and saw that her arms were tied down. She opened and closed her numb fingers. She tried raising her head in spite of the pain, and discovered that her legs were also firmly tied to the hard surface she was lying on. Then panic seized her. She tried to scream but the urge to retch contracted her stomach muscles. Her throat filled with acid bile and she spluttered.

"You've dirtied your blouse, Giuditta," remarked Professor Avildsen as he came towards her, a damp cloth in one hand, to clean her mouth. "There's no point in getting agitated. If you start screaming you'll just force me to plug your pretty mouth with rags. And I don't think you want to risk suffocation, do you, now?"

Giuditta was rigid with terror.

"Don't you want to answer your teacher's question, Giuditta? Don't you think that would be the civil thing to do? If you can't speak, just move your head. You really don't want me to fill your mouth with rags and leave you to suffocate in your own vomit, do you?"

Her eyes wide in fear, Giuditta shook her head.

"It must be a horrible way to die. Don't you think?"

Giuditta nodded and started to cry.

Avildsen dipped the stump of his little finger in her tears and then sucked on it.

"I love salt. But I mustn't overdo it. Did you know that salt raises the blood pressure?" Avildsen laughed, amused.

"Please . . ."

"You didn't answer my question. Did you know that salt can raise your blood pressure?"

Giuditta nodded again.

"You're a good student. You might even deserve an extra lesson. I'll think about it. What would you like to learn before you die?"

Giuditta let out a tortured moan. Avildsen stroked her face gently.

"There is something I must do first, however," he said, moving away.

His calm, measured steps echoed round the spacious, foul-smelling room. He went over to a dirty mirror and cleaned it. His reflection smiled back at him confidently, letting him know that the way was clear, that there were no other obstacles in his path. The transformation had begun. The man picked up a pair of scissors and began to trim his beard. Then he rinsed his face and covered it in soap before finishing off the job with a razor. He rubbed his soft white checks. He looked in satisfaction at his own face, so childlike now. The fleshy pink lips, the green eyes, like two glittering scarabs, the fragile, aquiline nose.

"They could take you for a girl," he told his reflection.

He turned back to Giuditta. He looked down upon her and smiling slipped the scissor blade between the girl's skin and her blouse. He started to cut. When he encountered the resistance from her bra he increased the pressure, and when the fabric ripped he gave a little moan of pleasure.

"You might feel the cold a little, Giuditta," he

whispered in her ear and then put the scissors down on the table.

He took hold of a flap of the blouse and moved it aside, revealing half the girl's chest. Giuditta sobbed silently. Her skin was white, as though it had been covered in talc. Her large, soft breast, freed from the restraints of her bra, had blossomed over her torso like a fleshy flower. Her nipple was pink and delicate. Avildsen looked at her in satisfaction. He pinched her skin between thumb and forefinger and pulled it towards him.

"You have such marvellously elastic skin, Giuditta," he complimented her.

He walked away and Giuditta heard him open a cupboard. When he returned he was holding what seemed to her, through her tear-clouded vision, to be a lifeless body.

"You're the first person to see my bride," Avildsen told her. "Do you like her?"

Giuditta turned to look at the thing that he was showing her. The first thing that struck her was the wooden head, with eyelids that opened and closed and the blond wig. At the base of the neck there was a metal joint connecting it to the torso, also wood. From this emerged two large floppy breasts made from flesh-coloured velvet. Avildsen guided a hand of the life-sized doll towards Giuditta's face and stroked her. That contact, both soft and hard, winded her. She suddenly understood who was standing in front of her and whose hand it was.

"Please . . ." she whimpered.

"You should feel honoured, Giuditta." Avildsen brought the doll's hands to his lips and indicated that she should be quiet. "I didn't allow so much to the others. It is a very valuable piece. Eighteenth century.

313

It is so true: there is absolutely nothing new under the sun. It might not be the most suitable topic for a young lady but I must tell you that this doll was used for certain purposes, how shall I put it . . . Well, it was a doll that one could marry. Do you follow my meaning?"

Giuditta remained petrified with horror.

"It's lined with velvet . . . Inside . . . it has a velvet lining. And do you know what the most amusing thing is? Do you know?"

"Please . . ."

"I asked you a question, Giuditta," said the man, no change in the soft, metallic tone of his voice. "Do you know what the most amusing thing is?"

Giuditta shook her head.

"And would you like to know?"

Giuditta nodded.

"Good. Well, then I'll tell you. The most amusing thing of all is that the person who sold it to me is the same lady who gave me these arms." Avildsen waved the antique-dealer's stuffed arms.

Giuditta turned away, terrified. She was half naked and half covered by the torn blouse.

"She called it her baby. She kept on about how 'soft and warm' her baby was, just like her, she said. She was a foul woman, who thought she could drag me down into the mud with her baby. But she didn't succeed. I saved her. Like I saved Dr Cerusico, in the hospital. Did you know her?"

Giuditta's hands closed in a spasm.

"She gave me her strong legs. Look? I've already mounted them."

He made the thing dangle its legs. Giuditta noticed the red ballet pumps on its feet.

"And now I'm going to save you, too, Giuditta, and you'll give me a little present, something that belongs

314

to you, to thank me. Look, read what it says here, just here above this lovely lady's navel."

Avildsen brought the wooden abdomen right up to Giuditta's face.

And Giuditta read her own name, written in pencil. She screamed with all the breath left in her throat. The man put down the doll and punched her viciously on the mouth.

"I don't need your face, Giuditta," he said, in a calm voice. "Which means that you could suffer a lot before you're saved. It's up to you. Do you understand what I'm saying?"

Giuditta nodded; she could taste blood.

"Good. I knew I could count on you."

The man lifted the doll off the floor and laid it down beside Giuditta. The wooden head lolled against the girl's tensed arm.

"You look so pretty close to each other," said Avildsen, in a dreamy voice. "But soon you will be even closer. You'll be . . . *together.*"

Smiling, he stroked her forehead, cleaned her split lip with a handkerchief, and. then, rather lazily, he began to peel away the other half of the blouse.

When he saw her ribs Professor Avildsen grimaced in horror and replaced the flap of material. He closed his eyes and breathed with difficulty. Giuditta saw that he was sweating and trembling.

Avildsen slowly calmed down. He opened his eyes and pulled back the blouse again. Giuditta felt his hands shaking. He undressed her completely and stared in horror at his victim's ribs, turned round and went to a nearby workbench covered in blood. He came back with a magnifying glass and silently examined an area of Giuditta's skin. He shook his head and mumbled words she couldn't understand. Then he pressed his finger down on the spot he was examining. Giuditta felt a stabbing pain and realized that Avildsen was focusing on the wound she had acquired a few days earlier, when she had collided with a piece of metal furniture while running away from the man in the hospital's incinerator room.

"I can't . . ." said Avildsen, as though he were talking to himself. He continued to shake his head. "I can't . . . it's damaged." He glared at Giuditta and snarled, "You're damaged! Now I'll have to wait until it heals. You've ruined everything," he said in a tone of petulant reproach.

Giuditta watched him walk away. She heard a thump, as if something had fallen to the ground. Then nothing for a very long time. Finally, when the daylight filtering through an opaque window faded away, she called out to him.

"Professor. . . . please, Professor."

And then she heard smothered sobs coming from the far corner of her prison.

The sound of a child crying.

XXIX

Everyone knew her as Clara. No one knew her surname. In the few months of innocence that the old town allowed them, the youngest children would probably have said what they thought Clara's surname was, repeating what they often heard the grown-ups say. And if they had known how to write they would have probably have spelled it as "Thewhore".

The mob of demonstrators seemed to have declared a truce for a while. The people who had poured into the streets screaming for the heads of the binmen and city councillors had gone back to their everyday occupations. The original colours of the garish yellow and blue and pink rubbish bags that were scattered over the streets had bled away into the dirt and filth and muddy rain and car exhaust fumes. And the day was no less grey, nor the sky less ferrous. It was as though that lifeless light had appeared with the dawn for no other reason than that was how it was meant to be, not driven by the need to grow and come into being. And for the same reason it would probably continue on through the day unchanging only to disappear, completely depleted, when night fell.

That afternoon Clara did something rare for her. She did not open her two metal shutters, nor did she display herself on her wide, inviting bed. She did not put on garters or garish negligée, nor did she offer her reassuring neckline to the gaze of passers-by. She dressed soberly: a little black bag with a stiff handle and a gold-coloured clasp in the shape of a brass bow, thick, charcoal-grey tights, shoes with no more than a hint of heel, a little black outfit with a jacket that hugged her waist and had fake mother-of-pearl buttons, a skirt with just the slightest of splits at the back, and over everything a black coat that stopped just below the knee, with a velvet collar. As she walked through the slippery, rubbish-strewn streets of the old town, she felt uneasy, just as a virtuous housewife might have felt if she had to behave like a prostitute in Clara's shop. The people who met her took a moment to greet her, partly because they didn't recognize her at first, and partly because they were stunned by what they saw. No one asked her where she was going. Dressed in mourning as she was, they thought better than to force her to tell them a tale of woe.

When she had gone beyond the confines of the old town, Clara blended into the crowd, just another woman out buying groceries or doing a little window shopping. Quite a few men turned to look at her, despite her age and the fact that she was not exactly pretty. But Clara was used to that, and had been since she was a child. The hungry eyes of men were part of her everyday life, like church bells on Sunday, or the siren blasts from ships leaving the port.

Clara had been born in the country. She had grown up in a house that was home to four farming families. She had run away on the day of her sixteenth birthday and had washed up in that low, filthy city by the sea, which had immediately sucked her in. It had taken her only a few days to choose her profession. And in that profession, which over the years had taught her so much, she had found the kind of balance that she had never discovered in her proud life in fresh country air among modest people of sound principles. She

318

learned quickly that customers didn't choose a prostitute for her physical attributes, but because they were sure they knew who the woman was and what she would be able to give them. And Clara always gave her fellow men exactly what they were expecting. It was like a game. She was the actress, and the clients were the writers who had come to check the script. Clara's fortune, as it were, lay in the fact that she made men think of tenderness and warmth. She became the muse of weak and hungry men who were often delicate, fragile, a little tearful at times, who came to her in search of solidarity and attention, but were never dangerous. She didn't know if she would describe herself as happy, because she had never felt pain, she never exposed herself to anything real, but the life she led seemed to satisfy her. She had no sense of the future, so she had simply slipped into adult life without any upheavals.

And then one night Ajaccio arrived.

Ajaccio had defective vision, in a way. He couldn't see what generations of customers had turned into hard fact through having affirmed it so many times. He couldn't understand that Clara did not belong to that category of women who were there to be raped. Clara didn't have that shoddy air that lent itself so well to the disdain of violence. Nor did she possess a candid purity to be broken and profaned. That night, four years ago, Ajaccio had chanced upon Clara and equally by chance, obeying his instinct, he had raped her. It could have been any woman. And perhaps it was because of this defective vision that he so fatefully came into contact, uninvited, and the only person to do so, with Clara's true nature. He never understood what had happened, but Clara knew full well, and every day thereafter she feared and hoped he would come back to rape her.

And that was why Clara was walking across town towards the hospital where she had learned, by way of that strange note, that Ajaccio lay dying. Mourning dress had seemed the most suitable attire in which to visit him. To celebrate the death of violence. Deep down Clara suspected that Ajaccio himself had written her the note.

"Relative?" asked the nurse when Clara reached the cancer ward.

"Yes," she replied, without hesitation.

"It's late."

"Please."

"Room 423," said the nurse, still undecided. "But you'll have to speak with that pol— with that nurse over there."

"Look," said Clara, touching the nurse's arm. "Do you think we might be alone, just him and me, without being disturbed for an hour or so."

The nurse understood at once just what kind of family ties there were between the two and smiled indulgently.

"Wait here," she said.

She spoke hurriedly with the large, well-built man who stood in front of Ajaccio's door. At first the man shook his head, but then he seemed to agree, and motioned Clara to come nearer.

"I'm sorry," said the man in embarrassment, "but I have to . . . search you."

Clara smiled at him, handed over her bag and stretched out her arms. The disguised policeman patted her discreetly, nodded and stepped back a few paces.

"I could lock you in," said the nurse, smiling. "You'll just have to ring the bell when you want to leave."

Clara's look said yes. As she entered the room she

heard a bunch of keys rattle behind her. She closed the door without turning round. Her heart beat a little faster when she heard the lock turn. She was trapped. Imprisoned with her executioner, and exposed to the cold, pitiless fluorescent light that poured down from the ceiling.

"I almost didn't recognize you," said Ajaccio in a whisper from his bed. He tried to sit up, but his arms couldn't take the strain. Under the sheets one of his hands contracted in an involuntary spasm.

Clara said nothing. She went over to the sick man and loomed above him. Then she took off her coat and tossed it onto one of the chairs. She did the same with her bag, which fell onto the floor.

"Why are you here? Who called you? Frese?"

"No."

"Were you feeling sorry for me?"

"No."

"Why then?"

"Maybe I wanted to see you die," said Clara without rancour or cruelty.

"Of course . . ." said Ajaccio in that sliver of a voice that was all he could manage. He was yellow, his skin withered.

"Does it seem so strange, then?" asked the prostitute dressed in mourning.

"No . . ." He coughed.

"Really?"

"Yes."

"Any regrets . . . now?"

"No." And Ajaccio's death's head face seemed to brighten for a moment, a light so dim only someone who had loved him would have noticed it. "Not for me. For you, yes. Now I can see what you've been. If I had any regrets or remorse it wouldn't make any sense." He looked at her from far away. She was beautiful. "I've changed a lot . . . I don't think I could . . ."

"No, you couldn't do it any more," she said, a trace of harshness in her voice, a fading quiver of the revenge she had thought she was planning.

Ajaccio felt his eyes cloud over.

Clara pulled the sheets back from Ajaccio's body. Then she sat on the edge of the bed and began to unbutton his pyjama jacket. When she had opened it she turned him over, roughly, first on one side then on the other in order to pull the sleeves from his arms. She left him like that for a moment, on one side, and studied the wide, dark-red burn mark that wrapped its way round his back. She brushed her nails over it, without scratching him, without caressing. She followed its contours, as if she were measuring it, until she reached the knot that gathered round the man's neck, and then she turned him over on his back. Then she undid the two buttons of his pyjama bottoms, which were stained yellow, and pulled them down over his bony ankles. She tossed them beside her black coat with its velvet collar. She let her eyes wander over that naked, old, sick and totally defenceless body. He would never be able to rape her again, even if he had wanted to with all the muscles and hormones that he had left. His legs were very thin. His knees, in contrast, seemed enormous. The skeleton alone held that pile of loose skin together. Clara bent down and leaned her head on Ajaccio's stomach. She heard it gurgle. She looked at a lock of her red hair draped over his swollen, smelly penis. She kissed the penis. No reaction. She turned round. Ajaccio didn't look at her, and he had an indecipherable expression in his eyes that embraced both past and future in a single gaze.

"Do you think you can manage it?" she asked and as

322

she got up she took off her tights and knickers and pulled her skirt up over her soft backside.

Ajaccio neither spoke nor moved his eyes.

"You know," she said as she straddled him and began to rub against him, "a while back a university professor came to talk to me . . . an interview, he called it . . . and asked a lot of personal questions. But he was paying me and he seemed safe enough so I accepted. He was a good-looking man, with a beard . . . a bit strange, really, I never completely trusted him . . . I thought he was like me, but that was just stupid. So, anyway, this professor —" Clara looked between her legs. "You really can't get it up, can you? Don't worry, just listen. This professor kept telling me that if I did the job I do it was because I needed to exercise control over sex. I've always thought that being a whore was just a handy enough way to make a living, and I told him so, but he kept on saying it was all about control, that I wanted control. And to convince me he always used the same example . . . He said it was just an example, something he had made up . . . but he described this imaginary man who kept me under his thumb . . . that's what he said, under his thumb. And there seemed to be pain in his voice when he said it. Pain and anger . . . almost like it had something to do with him . . . That's when I thought we were alike. And as I refused to accept what he was saying he carried on describing this man . . . He told me what he looked like, how he moved, how he talked, everything. And you know what? This man sounded a lot like you, really a lot. I almost convinced myself that he knew you . . . But that wasn't possible . . . And then he told me that this man was a priest, a man of the cloth . . ."

Ajaccio gave a start.

"Oh, something's moving then?" asked Clara and

323

continued rubbing against him. "Well, then this professor just disappeared, but I thought a lot about it . . . Not about him, about what he said about control. And maybe he wasn't totally wrong. It can be very exciting to be in control. I don't mean sex, I mean being in control of a situation, of a person. Hasn't it been like that for you, all these years?"

Ajaccio looked at her. She smiled and opened her tight-fitting black jacket and revealed a generous portion of her breast. Ajaccio tried to stretch out his hand but another spasm held him back. His fingers closed. Clara took his hand in hers and massaged his fingers, opened them out and laid his hand on her breast. She moved his hand on her breast and moved her breast as well, swaying back and forth. Then she let go. The fingers clawed into the upper edge of her bra, and remained there, inert.

"Now it's as if our roles are reversed," said Clara. "You can't put up any resistance . . ."

"No . . ."

"No, you can't . . ." She sighed and looked between her legs again, legs that were so strong and vital compared to his skeletal limbs. She raised herself a little on her knees and saw the large pink and worn lips of her vagina that hung down, pendulous between her thighs, like a rooster's comb, and the sparse hair covering them. She took hold of Ajaccio's flaccid penis and, pushing the foreskin back with her index finger, managed to bring off a pathetic penetration. She pushed down on him again and felt a warm glow kindling deep in her belly.

While she rocked and pushed she thought about the day she had run away from her home in the country, on her birthday, the day of her father's funeral. The room was in half-light, the shutters firmly closed on the windows. Outside the air was cold and damp. Her father was laid out on his bed. A candle stump was burning on a bedside table to the right of the bed. No one else was in the room, apart from her father and her. She was sitting on a seat that creaked with every little movement and the old straw prickled her backside. The man, who was still young and strong, lay on the bed with his hands crossed on his naked chest. His ribs showed through his broad, hairy torso, empty now. He was wearing just a pair of woollen longjohns from which protruded his dirty feet, covered in earth, the nails black. There was a badly wrapped parcel beside the bed, the rough string held together with a small grey lead weight. The girl knew what was in the parcel. A long, full dress, cream in colour and printed with fleur-de-lis and lilies that he had seen at some fair. Her father would have given it to her to open on her birthday, so that his "beautiful girl would be even more beautiful", he had said. And now he was lying there, still, his hands folded over his chest, arms that could have stopped a bull and held it by the ring in its nose. Now all he had on was a pair of woollen longjohns and the little mound that pushed against the fabric, there where his legs forked. Clara didn't recall clearly what happened then. Outside the dark room she could hear her mother's subdued crying and the voice of her mother's sister comforting her, and the voices of men she didn't recognize, but suddenly she realized she had begun to sweat. She was there, alone with her father, who was almost naked, in that dark room. She felt dirty and afraid and kept on sweating. She ran to the wardrobe with the mirror, took her father's good suit and his white shirt and the narrow black tie and his socks and the pointed shoes with the iron heel caps, and she dressed him, hysterically, crazed with panic.

325

When they came into the room, her mother and the others, they found her standing, chastely, near the open window. The dead man was on the bed, dressed in his best, ready for his coffin.

She fled while they buried him.

"No," Clara said to Ajaccio. "You can't . . . you can't . . . you can't," and she opened her mouth, just a little, demurely. Her breathing stopped for one brief moment. Her eyelids flickered closed, but she didn't fall into dark abandon. Just a shadow of sexual pleasure, a virginal flavour, almost, pure and timid. Quite unlike the heat that poured out from between her legs spread astride Ajaccio and seeped through the man's rough dark pubic hair.

She bowed her head down to the hand that was clamped to her bra. She detached it. She laid it beside the withered body. Buttoned up her jacket slowly. She got up, pulled on her knickers and tights, and pulled down her skirt.

"Cold?" she asked the sick man.

He shook his head.

She pulled up the covers but didn't dress him. She turned to the chair, picked up her black coat with the velvet collar and draped it over her shoulders. She reached down for her little black bag. She patted it a few times, trying to brush away a stubborn stripe of white dust.

Ajaccio watched her from behind, her body thickened now, buttocks straining against the seams and zip of her skirt, her thighs pushing against the fabric of her tights.

I should thank you, he thought, but I haven't got the strength any more. All my words are dying with me.

Clara tried to open the door and remembered that she was locked inside that disinfected coffin.

"Can you ring the bell?" she asked him without turning round.

"Yes . . ."

Moments as long as your life, thought Clara. She had only just discovered that she knew how to love, that love wasn't what they said in the books, it was something altogether more overwhelming and at the same time silent, that everyone got the love they looked for and, maybe, the love they deserved. And sometimes you got a love that you shouldn't have been able to have.

When the blonde nurse opened the door she read the terrible pain in her eyes. Clara's arms were crossed over her chest, like a corpse, and the little black bag with the brass clasp dangled stupidly from her elbow. Clara seemed to be clutching at her own hands, and her hands were clutching at her body. Hands that pressed down on and staunched a wound. The nurse instinctively lowered her gaze to the brown-tiled floor.

As she walked past the nurse Clara muttered something. And then she slowly vanished.

Ajaccio knew he would never see her again.

"What did she say?" he asked the nurse.

"I think she said something like, 'Can't we have anything more?' Could that be it?"

"No," said Ajaccio, answering Clara's question, and feeling all the more cruelly how life was abandoning him.

"Oh well, I must have misunderstood then," snorted the nurse and closed the door.

XXX

Just in front of the police station a group of about twenty citizens armed with rocks and metal bars had surrounded the two patrol cars that Amaldi had requested. On his way out of the gate Amaldi pulled up abruptly at the sight of them. The frantic crowd suddenly fell silent and concentrated all its attention on the new arrival.

"If you all clear off now we'll pretend none of this has happened and no one will get into trouble." Frese was yelling into a megaphone he had snatched from the hands of a clueless cop. "The demonstration is over. Why don't you all go home now?"

At that very moment street lamps came on all over the city. The artificial light that poured down upon the demonstrators streaked their faces with shadows, bringing into relief wrinkles and expressions that the soft, deceiving glow of saffron dusk had blurred. Stones and crowbars glinted in the alley and the small crowd seemed to come to life again. The demonstrators surged forward in unison, the menacing crash of a crazed river bursting its restraining banks.

Amaldi was trapped in his nightmare. He saw the two moments that contained the essence of his life collide. The girl like a bag of rubbish. The beginning. And Giuditta. The end. He knew that the few miles that separated him from Villa Cascarino would show him whether he had lost Giuditta as he had lost the girl from his childhood. And if had lost her then he would have lost himself as well. He would have failed and he would have no life left to live for. He would go on in some kind of anguished trance. If he managed to go on at all.

He was on hold, he thought once more. And it was time to make the break. To drag himself out of the quagmire.

He bolted forward, seized by some uncontrollable impulse. He lifted the flap of Frese's jacket, pulled from his deputy's waistband the gun he had taken from the madman who had stopped them in the alley that morning, and fired a shot into the air. Then another. And a third.

"Get in the cars," Amaldi ordered the stunned cops, some of whom had thrown themselves to the ground.

The roar of car engines spilled into the alley in front of the police station and ascended into the brooding sky. The crowd scattered rapidly. Frese got in beside Amaldi in silence. He gazed in astonished admiration at his superior.

"Siren on, and step on it," Amaldi ordered the driver.

The officer in the passenger seat beside the driver turned round and looked open-mouthed at the chief inspector.

"Keep your eyes on the road and your mouth shut," Frese growled at him. "And don't piss me off."

No one spoke as the car pushed through the bags of rubbish that covered the streets. As they pulled away from the suburbs, fewer and fewer street lamps lined the route, until darkness was complete.

Only noise seemed to exist in the darkness. The air itself felt thicker, denser, amplifying every little sound, and the feeling of unease within the car grew steadily more palpable.

"We'll make it," Frese said at length.

Amaldi looked at him with a wan smile on his lips.

"Yes," he replied.

He shifted his gaze towards the window and let it wander over the vast, menacing void of the sea below them, without really recognizing it.

". . . And I went to him for help," he said, his voice incredulous, thinking out loud. "He had gloves on. I didn't see the finger stump . . ."

"It's not your fault," Frese interrupted him.

"Unless your hunter will be happy with just three other pigs . . ."

"What?" asked Frese.

"He was the hunter. He knew damn well what those dry leaves meant. And how many victims he needed. He just played with me." Amaldi covered his eyes, trying to banish the picture of those slain, mutilated women. "And he called them pigs. That's all they are to him, pigs . . ."

"We'll get him . . . and we'll save Giuditta."

"Maybe he saw me that day with her. Maybe I was the one who brought her to his attention . . . made him chose her . . ."

"No, Giacomo. You said so yourself. He had it all planned out beforehand. You're just a coincidence."

"Coincidence . . ." mumbled Amaldi, thinking that it was no coincidence that twenty years ago he had fallen in love with a girl who was killed by a maniac and that now history was repeating itself. He was at a turning point. It was now or never.

"Turn off the siren," he ordered the driver.

The officer did so and the patrol car behind them followed suit.

"Tell the two back-up units to do the same thing."

The driver radioed the order.

"Do you want a service revolver?" Frese asked him as

they drove through the villa's unhinged main gate, seeing that his superior was still clutching the gun he had used to disperse the crowd of demonstrators. Only then did Amaldi seem to realize he was holding it. He relaxed his grip and the gun slipped from his fingers onto the seat. His deputy picked it up and stowed it away in a pouch behind the driver's seat.

"Okay, this is it," said Frese, lightly patting the two cops on the back. "Keep your eyes open."

The house was steeped in darkness. It loomed over the eight men as they warily got out of the cars, their feet crunching on the gravel. One of the officers touched Frese on the arm and pointed upwards, towards a window on the second floor.

A dim light could be seen through the shutters.

Frese pointed the light out to Amaldi, who whispered, "Where are the other two units?"

"They'll have reached the gate by now," replied Frese.

Amaldi nodded and motioned to two of the men to take up positions at the back of the house, and to maintain radio contact. Then he and the others headed for the door. They held their breath as they went up the four porphyry steps. Amaldi pushed lightly against the door with one hand and with the other he turned the handle. He turned to the others and shook his head. Locked. One of the officers ran to the car, opened the boot and returned with a heavy, metal battering ram. Amaldi moved to one side and another officer fell in beside the man who was holding the battering ram.

They looked at Amaldi, waiting for the word.

"Once inside, you go left, you go right," Frese told the two men who were going to ram the door. "You two, up the stairs with us. This is a hostage situation.

Shoot if necessary. I don't give a fuck about that shit. We want the girl alive. Got it."

The four men nodded. The pair whose hands were free began arming the guns.

"You sure you don't want one, too, Giacomo?" Frese asked his superior.

Amaldi lifted his hand to refuse the gun and at the same time give the signal to ram the door. There was something unnatural about the still night air. Amaldi dropped his hand and the battering ram crashed against the door. The wood around the lock splintered and yielded. The six men threw themselves into the hallway, turning on their torches. Amaldi ran to the stairs, followed by two officers, guns in hand. Frese followed a few steps behind.

As he pounded up the stairs Amaldi's mind was blank. His whole body was tense with effort. The short distance that separated him from Giuditta seemed endless. His nostrils filled with the acrid stench of rotten meat as he reached the first floor. He stopped breathing.

"Upstairs," he yelled and began running again.

He shouldered open the door to the room from where the dim light was coming. He threw himself to the ground while the other two knelt down, guns trained.

A movement to their right made them turn.

Partially picked out by light from the torches, a shape was leaning towards them. One of the men fired. The shape rolled to the ground.

"Hold your fire!" shouted Amaldi, picking himself up.

The torches swept round like crazed eyes and revealed a chilling sight. They were in a huge room, at least thirty-two feet wide and sixty-five long. At the far end of the room a lamp shone feebly onto a blood-spattered table.

"Hold your fire," Amaldi repeated, waiting for his eyes to get used to the gloom.

The two policemen were open mouthed, limp from shock. There were thirty-five single beds, side by side, each one covered by a mouldering mattress. Each bed was the resting place for at least one stuffed animal, its glass eyes drinking in the torch-light and glittering as if it were still alive. The shot that had been fired had hit a dog. Under the beam of his torch Amaldi saw that smoking wadding tumbled out of the gaping hole left by the impact. The grey fur had been scorched by the pellet. The animal's legs were rigid, its lips curled back in a growl that revealed its canine teeth, and the expression in its dull eyes was vacant.

Frese's voice came from the stairwell. "Found anything?"

"Nothing," replied the cops on the ground floor.

Amaldi collapsed onto one of the beds.

A weasel, stuffed by Avildsen in the act of biting into a chicken, bounced, lost its balance and toppled over without letting go of its prey.

Amaldi grabbed it and hurled it at the wall.

On impact, one of the coloured glass beads that served as eyes popped out of its socket and rolled through the silence and across the floor. As it rolled it produced a strange, mournful sound, then gradually came to a halt, like a clockwork toy that had unwound.

Amaldi stood up, went over to a window and opened it wide. He leaned both hands heavily on the window sill and looked out into the gathering night. In the distance he could make out the weak, feverish flicker of the city's lights.

"Where are you?" he yelled, with all the desperation his throat contained.

The only answer he got was the useless croaking of police radios down in the forecourt.

XXXI

"Last lesson," announced Professor Avildsen. His tears had evaporated, leaving his eyes dry, as though he had never cried. Lifting up the scalpel to check the blade, for a moment he did not recognize his reflection in the shiny metal. Then his upturned counterpart flashed him a smile as sharp as the instrument that called him into being. Avildsen put down his tool and went back to his lesson. With a thick pencil he marked out the line on his prey's skin along which he was going to slice.

"Do you hear the Voices, too?" he whispered into his immobile victim's ear. "Everybody hears them. All of us. And do you know why the Voices talk to us? Because they cannot do without us. Because the Voices can't tell their stories on their own. What would a voice be without its instruments? What would a voice be without lungs? Breathless . . . What would a voice be if lips and teeth and tongue didn't modulate it? A pointless lament that would rise up only to invoke silence. And what would a voice full of notes and with strong lungs be if no one bothered to lend it an ear? An encyclopedia published millions of years before man decided to walk upright. An absurdity . . ." And he stroked his victim's face, a face marked by suffering, sighing and staring into his victim's eyes, sucking in the lingering remnants of a pain that would soon be extinguished, losing all the twitching desperation of live flesh. "But have you ever heard of a beast of burden that revolts against his master's mistreatment? Man is such a beast. If only he rebelled against the Voices he could overturn the world and leave the Voices to their void . . . to their impotence. Turn them into failed phantoms. 'Death, lie thou there, by a dead man interred.' Can you picture it? Thwart our sirens . . . who infect our ears, shipwreck us upon the rocks. The Voices that carry with them the Pride that makes us stand on two legs and straighten our backs. And the Pride that becomes Conscience. And Conscience that opens wide the doors of illusion to the Power to command nature. And Power that buys the services of the whore with two heads, Desire and Senses . . ." And the accumulation of his desires and frustrated senses, of that upturned mountain that it invoked, black and mud-clad, that hurtled downwards, dragging him with it, showing him in the deepest depths of the chasm the overturned summit that towered over a different world, in which the bottom was the top, all the waste and refuse of his appetites muffled his voice, the base voice of some prophet of evil. "The Voices that, just when you think you are astride the celestial canopy, for the mere pleasure they derive from a stupid laugh, make you wake up at the bottom of the deepest hole your imagination is capable of conceiving."

Professor Avildsen pulled back the sheet that covered his victim, all the better to savour that painful impotence. Staring fixedly at his prey, and racked by his swelling excitement, it seemed to Avildsen that he could have drunk in that pain. Fed upon it. And he knew that such an intense sight would have satisfied him, slaked his thirst, even if not for ever.

"We handed the world over to the Voices," he began again, his own voice a suffocated gurgle, "so long ago, when we committed the first sin, when the first man was born . . . who, in order to be born, had to renounce his mother . . . the widow . . . To be born, man had to display her naked, just as she was. To be born, man had to plunder the very thing that had given him life . . ." A theatrical tear. "And for what?" He laughed. "To become . . . the first orphan."

Avildsen crouched down, huddled, on the ground, at the foot of the bed to which his prey was anchored. He took hold of the scalpel and sliced into his palm, watching the blood bubble slowly from the wound, immersed in his own thoughts on death. Then he stood up and with a loving gesture stroked his victim's cheeks until they were smeared with a glistening, vibrant red.

"Pain is the last link in this chain. The last gift from the Voices. A pain so pure . . . that it is the very essence of our lives. That crystal pain, suspended between the drive to life and death, is our only reason for being, our condemnation . . . our secret . . . You do understand this, don't you?"

The victim didn't answer.

"Pain is not a sickness. Nor is it the fear produced by sickness. Pain is something much nobler. The mourning garb we wear for our next death. The struggle of the soul . . . is the soul's own justification. Suffering is the Voices' most sublime creation, the deepest summit, the upturned mountain. That is what man thinks . . . and that is why he has never banished the Voices. By means of the pain to which man has condemned himself he seeks to expiate his guilt . . . at having betrayed his mother, at having renounced her . . . at having thought things that should not be thought. The cause of suffering is sin . . . but whose sin is it?" Avildsen waved the scalpel about, caught up in the maze of his own madness. "Eve committed the sin . . . the Original Sin. A sin that exists in us today. Habitual,

337

hereditary. Inherited from our mother. The mother . . . strips the son because of a guilt that is not really his. She strips him of all his grace and wounds and mutilates his very nature." Enraged, moaning, he cut into his calloused, yellow finger stump with the scalpel. "The ideally pure is, in fact, impure. Corrupted by his very birth as the son. In so far as the son is a manifestation of the mother, his destiny is sealed, he is condemned from the outset, born with a stain, with a defect: he has inherited the trait of corruption. And from the corruption of the flesh and from the sins and sicknesses and actions new life will rise to be corrupted in turn, in a never-ending cycle. Spirits and demons that possess and tyrannize man, who hinder his path towards the Golden Age of poets, the Earthly Paradise. . . ."

Drained and panting, Avildsen stopped talking. He sucked avidly on his bleeding finger. When he began speaking again, his voice was no more than a low whisper.

"For some men, however, the Voices reserve a luminous destiny . . . showing them the path to killing Pain, to setting the world right. The Voices breathe the answers into the hearts of these men. The Voices teach these men how to erase the Original Sin . . . give them the chance to turn back. To the beginning. Without having to renounce the mother . . . the widow. The Voices show these men how to purify the mother . . . to transform the mother into what she should have been from the start. *Everything is . . . as it should be.* To those chosen few, the Voices dictate the rules of the world. They give them a mother and a bride worthy of them . . ." Avildsen's face shone with languid pleasure, as he lost himself in the delirious future he was constructing. The human doll he was going to marry.

The noises outside did not disturb him. He knew he was nearing his goal. No one would stop him. The design was about to be fulfilled.

"The New . . . Perfect Mother," he breathed into his victim's ear. "Immaculate . . . indulgent . . . accessible."

He ran his finger along the pencil mark that traced the outline of the incision he was about to make.

"The Voices," he said with a note of finality, "whispered the answers to me. That is why I will always prefer answers to questions. And I don't mean the extraordinary answers to absolute questions. No, I also prefer the comforting warmth of a mediocre answer to the exalting dizziness of the most vertiginous question. I prefer geometry to chaos. And this is what the Voices do for the chosen. They establish order and provide explanations. They dictate the answers. Not all of them miraculous. But all of them, without fail, achieve their aim. They annul every question. They silence them . . ." Avildsen knelt down and opened his arms wide, as though he were offering his breast to the tempest. "They silence the elements. Can you hear? Listen . . . The wind ceases to blow . . . the earth no longer trembles . . . the ocean becalms its fury . . . the devouring flames no longer burn . . ." The professor collapsed to the floor, as if he had really fought his good fight. "Can you hear? Listen. The silence. Listen . . . Is it not a marvellous thing this silence? Is it not our salvation?"

The moments stretched out as the professor remained on the floor, his eyes lost in his hallucination.

"The Voices told me that just as it is possible to transfer a bundle of wood from one's own shoulders to someone else's, so it is possible to shift the grave weight of one's own pain and disappointments to the heart of another person." He looked up. He rose to his feet with difficulty, and leaned towards his victim, to make sure the other knew just whose heart Avildsen was talking about. He articulated every word. "Is . . . it . . . possible . . . to transfer . . . one's . . . burden . . . of . . . suffering . . . to someone . . . else's . . . shoulders?"

He grasped the scalpel and plunged the blade down into his prey's flesh.

"We shall soon know," he said, his head bent low over his work, ready to slake his thirst on the blood that would come spurting out of the artery he was about to open.

XXXII

"Stop here," Amaldi suddenly barked at the driver, breaking the sombre silence that choked the air inside the car.

The car pulled up in front of the entrance canopy of the city hospital.

"Put as many men on it as you can," Amaldi told Frese, opening the car door. "We've got to find out where he's hiding . . . Where he's keeping . . . Giuditta." The look he darted at Frese was full of worry. "You know we've run out of time."

Frese nodded. He had already radioed the order to arrest Avildsen. It was late but the manhunt had started. A simple notary's deed had muddied the investigation, hindering logical connections. Two surnames. The same person. It was all so simple, now. Avildsen had no chance of escaping. But they had to find him before he killed his prey.

"I'll have one last go with Ajaccio," added Amaldi as he got out of the car. "You never know. He might have one of those lucid moments, remember something and . . ." He left the phrase hanging in the air.

Just like his hopes.

Frese pulled the car door shut and touched the driver on the shoulder. The car sped off into the night.

On the other side of the road a vagrant was rummaging through the rubbish looking for some treasure or other. When the man caught sight of Amaldi he hunched over and shuffled away in fear.

Amaldi stared up at the grey bulk of the hospital. The main entrance was closed, in darkness. The only lights came from the nearby entrance to Accident and Emergency.

"You can't go up to the wards . . . don't you know what time it is?" asked a nurse when she saw him marching towards the door that led into the main hospital building.

"Be quiet!" snapped Amaldi and flashed his badge at her.

As he crossed the deserted main atrium, Amaldi glanced down the corridor where he had last glimpsed Giuditta, dressed in her volunteer auxiliary's uniform. He saw her eyes red from crying, and that heartbreaking look as though her whole being had been snuffed out, as though she were avoiding the light. Amaldi was racked once more by his own pain and thought again that if only he had heeded his instinct and run to comfort her then everything would be different now. Then he pictured his desolate home, with its bare bulbs swaying from the ceiling, the unopened boxes. He was seized by the overwhelming desire to furnish it. For Giuditta. He felt he could have brought it to life for her. And that unwelcome thought forced open another wound because it made everything so much more real and human.

When the lift stopped at the fourth floor Amaldi realized that he didn't expect anything at all from Ajaccio. He was merely responding to the need to find somewhere to hide so he could think. As he leaned his hand on the door to room 423 he admitted to himself that perhaps, really, he needed to escape from the emotional phone calls from Giuditta's parents, because he wouldn't have known what to say to them, how to comfort them.

342

He pushed down on the door handle, feeling more tired and emptied than he ever had before in his life, and went quietly into Ajaccio's room, expecting to find the man asleep.

A nun was bent over the sick man. She was whispering incomprehensible words.

Amaldi stood still, glad to have a reason to set aside his own thoughts.

The nun seemed not to notice the intrusion. The rhythmical warmth of her murmuring filled the room.

Amaldi felt himself drawn into that lullaby, as if the nun's melody were soothing his tense nerves. The sound rippled over him in fluid, hypnotic waves, as if the woman were telling a story rather than saying a prayer. He couldn't make out the words, but he let himself sink into the comforting litany. The muscles in his legs, his abdomen, his shoulders began to relax, as if some absented-minded puppet-master had lessened his grip on the strings holding up his marionette. He noticed that he had moderated his breathing so as not to interfere with the nun's low, rhythmic song, her nursery-rhyme rosary. He slipped into an opiate daze, where childhood sensations, reflecting reality, distracted him from the present. Old and familiar faces, guided by the nun's lullaby, began to superimpose themselves on the terrible images of the past few weeks.

Then the nun froze. The sound she made registered, not exactly as a change in emphasis, but more as an imperceptible jolt. Or a dip. A swerve. But barely audible. It translated into a rigidity about the shoulders rather than a change in her voice. Just for a moment. Maybe even less.

Amaldi did not perceive it as something concrete, as something he could have described. He had the vague and unpleasant sensation that there had been a mistake in the ritual he was watching. Or an imperfection. A flaw.

Somewhere in a corner of his mind, which was struggling to pull itself out of the fog that had engulfed him, a warning voice was telling him that he hadn't noticed any officer on guard duty. The comforting images were holding him back, slowing down his thought processes as he began to realize that the nun was too tall and thickset. He moved, his legs responding to instinct more than volition. The words he intended to say to the nun caught in his throat. One step. Two. His eyes struggled to focus on the scene. Something stopped him from looking round, as though he already knew.

In a corner of the room, next to the wide-open door, the lifeless body of the officer disguised as a nurse. A rip in his shirt. A red stain on the fabric.

The lullaby suddenly became a menacing grumble. Too tall and thickset, Amaldi thought again as he moved forward, with no plan, ready for anything except that wounded look, the eyes full of enraged agony, that the nun now turned on him.

"He doesn't have any blood for me . . ." the nun told him, and it seemed that the whole edifice was crumbling down.

He wasn't prepared to recognize the nun, to read that childish disappointment on the man's face. He caught sight of the scalpel. He edged back slowly, hoping the dead cop still had a gun on him.

"He doesn't have any blood for me . . ." and this time it was the man who spoke.

Amaldi recognized him at once, even without the beard. He seemed younger. Like a child. Or a girl. Their eyes met. Amaldi's squinting, as if blinded by the surprise. Avildsen's widening in rage at the unexpected irruption.

"He doesn't have any blood for me," he said again, gripping the scalpel, his knuckles white against the metal, allowing the intruder no possibility of escape.

"Professor Avildsen, try to calm down," began Amaldi, trying to keep his voice steady, realizing that he would never reach the other cop's gun in time to fire. "Give yourself up . . . It's over . . . It's over . . ."

"No . . . no . . . no . . ." repeated the killer, his eyes ablaze with desperation, barely shaking his head. "No . . . no . . . no . . ."

Amaldi's whole body was tense, ready to dodge the other man's attack. Suddenly he was no longer afraid, no longer in a rush. He had the man in front of him. After years and years of nightmares, the man was in front of him. The phantom that had killed all the women in the world was standing in front of him. The end of the story. One way or another. A profound feeling of peace spread through Amaldi's soul.

"It's over . . ." he said again, this time to himself.

As if he had sensed that suspension of time, Avildsen stopped shaking his head and his eyes glinted with a new light. He lowered the weapon he held in his right hand and with his left he pointed at the body of Ajaccio.

Amaldi saw the finger stump. It dripped blood onto the sheet.

"Why Ajaccio?" he asked.

Smiling sadly, Professor Avildsen caressed the face of the orphan he had obsessed over his whole life.

"He's dead . . ." he said simply.

Amaldi kept still. He hoped the professor would remain distracted so that he could grab the gun from the dead cop.

"He's dead . . ." repeated the killer.

"It's over . . . Put down the scalpel and raise your hands," said Amaldi.

Avildsen's eyes hardened. His jaw tightened.

"He's dead!" he yelled, taking a step towards Amaldi, brandishing his weapon. "Can't you understand that?"

Amaldi prepared himself for the assault. But Avildsen had calmed down. As though he had withdrawn into his own inscrutable world.

"He was already dead . . ." he said in a distant voice, shaking his head again, stepping back and laying his left hand on Ajaccio's cold forehead. "He was already dead . . ." Avildsen brushed against the slit he had cut into Ajaccio's neck.

Amaldi saw a thick, flaccid flap of skin. Almost white. Quite dry.

"He has no blood . . ." Avildsen was saying in his child's voice. "Dead . . . he was already dead when . . ." He shook his head, his eyes brimming with tears. "He was already dead when . . . he was supposed to give me his head. It was mine . . . his head was mine." He glared at Amaldi again. He took hold of a flap of the cut skin and pulled at it. "He hasn't got any blood for me." Then he turned his gaze on Ajaccio. "You see?" he said, in a light voice, as though he were looking for solidarity of agreement.

Amaldi sprang forward, his hand reaching for the scalpel.

Avildsen caught the movement from the corner of his eye and lashed out at the air. The blade sliced through Amaldi's coat and sank into his shoulder. Amaldi felt the stab and pain burned along his arm. He missed his step and shot headlong past Avildsen who had stepped aside after landing his blow. The detective fell sprawling over Ajaccio. The smell of the gaping flesh and the disinfectant assailed his nostrils. He could see the thick pencil line traced out on the dead man's neck. On the other side of the bed, on the floor, he saw a wooden head, its eyelids half closed, wearing a blond wig. Instinctively Amaldi lifted his leg as he tried to turn round and regain his balance. Avildsen's second blow split his boxer shorts and skewered his calf. Amaldi yelled in pain. Grinding his teeth, the professor turned the blade in the wound and pushed up. Amaldi felt the metal against his bone. He thought he would faint. For a moment he went blind. Then he felt the scalpel at his throat.

It is finished, he thought, astounded at his own lucidity and at the inner pace that pervaded him. He understood that he had reached the end of his journey and that soon all his nightmares would bleed out of him with his own blood. He knew then that he had finally given up.

Avildsen looked him in the eyes for a long time, without recognizing him.

"So you're dead too?" he asked Amaldi in a child's voice, imperceptibly relieving the pressure of the blade on the detective's neck.

That was enough for Amaldi. His desire to live won through. He kneed Avildsen in the stomach and pushed with all his might. As he got up he dodged the swiping blow the professor was quick to deliver, grabbed the other man by the shoulders and forced him onto the bed. The scalpel stuck into Ajaccio's corpse with a dull, damp sound.

Amaldi threw himself on the body of the dead cop and fumbled at the man's belt. He heard the assassin growl behind him. He grabbed hold of the gun butt and hoped that it was loaded and that the safety was off. He fired blindly, before he had a chance to turn round.

A flare. An explosion.

A smothered groan.

Then, off in the distance, the sound of agitated voices drawing nearer.

As his vision clouded, Amaldi saw the nun drop the scalpel and cup his hands over his stomach, where the black habit was torn.

Avildsen staggered towards him, opened his hands to show Amaldi the blood, his face frozen in amazement.

"Blood . . ." he said, falling to his knees.

Amaldi was on the verge of passing out. He saw the nun pick up the gun. He didn't react. He felt like he was floating in a dream as dark and dense as the blood that flowed thickly from his shoulder and leg and neck. The warm barrel pressed into his forehead.

"Where . . . is . . . she?" he managed to say. "Where is Giuditta?"

Then he saw the nun bend down, like a dog. In his eyes the incredulous expression of an animal fatally wounded. A puerile smile puckered the professor's lips.

"Mother . . ." said Avildsen, pushing back the hood of his habit.

Amaldi saw that he had shaved his head. The skin had been cut in a number of places by the razor.

"Mother," he said again, in a feeble, imploring voice, like a child resigned to receiving no answers. "Can you smell the perfume . . . the incense?"

Amaldi pushed his head against the gun barrel, with all his remaining strength.

"Where's Giuditta? Tell me or shoot me . . ."

"Mother . . . Mother . . . the incense. This is what incense smells like, isn't it, Mother? Mother?"

"Shoot! Shoot!" screamed Amaldi as his vision fogged over completely and he was sucked down into churning darkness, at the bottom of which he could make out Giuditta, who smiled up at him serene and welcoming.

The voices outside the room were so far away.

"You never taught me how to pray . . . Mother . . ."

Amaldi heard the shot.

And then nothing.

XXXIII

The first face he recognized as he came round was Frese's.

"Giacomo . . . Giacomo . . . can you hear me?"

Amaldi struggled to focus. Then he felt the nurses' hands on him as they tried to lift him up. He tried to speak but his voice was bogged down in his throat. He stretched out his hand and motioned at the nurses to stop. He blinked and tried to remember. There was the body of a nun beside him, head exploded by a bullet. He grabbed at Frese, his eyes burning with the question he couldn't give voice to.

"You want to hear about Giuditta?" said his deputy, reading his mind. "That's why I'm here. I was coming to tell you that there's a chance . . ."

Amaldi managed a weak smile and felt a jolt of energy course through him, as if he were stirring from a nightmare.

"Let's . . . go," he managed to stammer as he tried to get up, tears of relief threatening to cloud his vision again. "Don't . . . try . . . stop . . . me. I . . . got . . . to . . . come . . ."

Frese glanced at the doctor who was examining Amaldi's wounds. The man shook his head.

"You sure you can do it?" Frese asked his superior. "You're in a real mess."

"Help me," replied Amaldi and tried to stand up.

Frese bore Amaldi's weight and motioned at the doctor to be silent.

"They have to dress your wounds, okay?" he told Amaldi.

"Not . . . necessary . . ."

"Of course it's bloody necessary. You're bleeding like a pig at the butcher's. You'll ruin my car if I let you go near it in that condition."

Amaldi gave a flicker of a smile.

"Stretcher," said the doctor tersely, "and take him downstairs."

In the brief journey down the corridor Amaldi heard the nurses' swift steps, remote and booming, as if they were the only noises in the whole hospital, remote and booming. The lights hanging down from the ceiling flooded over him and then receded only to wash over him again as he advanced on his stretcher. Three times. Three waves. Three cones of light for three zones of darkness. The doctor continued to bandage the torn calf, trying to staunch the haemorrhage, and a nurse was treating the wound on his shoulder and neck.

Amaldi abandoned himself to the medical team's care, incapable of talking. Over and over he replayed the scene in which the nun stabbed him and then pointed a gun at his forehead.

The doors to the service lift clanged shut with a noise that reminded him of the gunshot. He wasn't dead. And there was hope for Giuditta, Frese had said so. He turned and his eyes sought out his deputy. Frese looked tense, drawn. Amaldi fought against the desire to surrender. He could no longer feel his wounded calf, but the pain throbbed above his knee and along his thigh, winding him. His shoulder burned and stank of disinfectant.

Then the lift came to a halt, the doors opened and the stretcher floated through a throng of curious onlookers, hospital staff, patients in pyjamas and their visitors, who all threatened to burst through the cordon established by the few cops available. Amaldi closed his eyes. Outside, the cold air lashed at him and seemed to revive him.

"Can you manage?" Frese asked, handing him his coat.

Amaldi nodded and began to get up, very slowly. Two officers helped him into his coat and as far as the car. They closed the door and Frese got in beside him.

"Where?" husked Amaldi, as soon as the car started.

"At the port," replied Frese. "Mouldy did it again. For a tub of lard he is an absolute phenomenon. He found the last missing document: the last will and testament of the widow Avildsen née Cascarino. Document number thirteen. Leaves everything to the city, especially the villa, which was to be turned into a centre specializing in the treatment of children's burns. Can you believe it? Children's burns, for fuck's sake. Sounds like a very bad joke. First she roasts them and then she wants to treat them . . ."

"Where?"

"In the list of properties there is a place that has been in the family since the days when the Cascarinos were sea merchants. A warehouse down at the port. We have good reason to believe Giuditta is there." Frese looked at his superior. "She's there, Giacomo. She's got to be there . . ."

Amaldi didn't mange to smile. He was quite sure she was there. The question was whether she would still be alive. The probability was zero, he told himself. Otherwise why would Avildsen have gone on to his next victim? The fact that he had tried to decapitate Ajaccio showed that the head was the missing part. The last part. He must have got his torso already.

352

A doleful silence fell upon the occupants of the police car as it roared through the rubbish-ravaged streets, sirens wailing. Amaldi looked out of the window and sighed deeply. Pain flared in his shoulder.

"It's not a will," Frese was saying, in an effort to break the mounting tension, "it's a confession. From Mrs Cascarino and . . . the witness who countersigned the document."

Amaldi looked at him.

"The detective in charge of the investigation into the orphanage fire. Our current mayor." Frese whispered in his ear, to make sure the two cops in the front seats didn't hear him.

Amaldi was incapable of formulating the next question. He was too weak. He twitched his hand.

"I don't know what to say, Giacomo," Frese carried on in a whisper. "He countersigned the clause in which Mrs Cascarino accepted that this testament was the only valid one, and waived all possibility of drawing up another one. And the date it was signed corresponds with the date they closed the case. Do we need anything else to draw our conclusions?"

Amaldi shook his head.

"Why?"

"No idea. The guy was a chief inspector, he was certainly no cretin. He knew damn well that his signature amounted to a confession," replied Frese.

"Why?"

"I think that to answer that question we'll have to go and ask him."

Amaldi placed a hand on Frese's thigh.

"Your case . . . all . . . the credit . . . yours."

"Yeah . . . well, maybe. I could have done without all this crap, though."

Amaldi nodded and looked at the road again. They

were heading down to the port. A few hundred yards more and he would know if his life would be measured by another girl lying like a bag of rubbish.

Frese picked up Amaldi's anguish.

"You've got to be strong, Giacomo. At least you got him . . ."

"No, I didn't . . . get . . . him," replied Amaldi, thinking of the nun sprawled on the hospital room floor. He looked at Frese. "Ajaccio . . . already dead. That saved me . . . and Ajaccio."

Frese nodded. He was thinking of the cop who had been killed. Nothing had saved him.

Now it was his turn to ask, "Why?"

Amaldi shrugged. There would be a lot of questions that would get no answer.

The car pulled up. The siren stopped wailing. The headlights picked out the glistening rubbish bags scattered around an empty square. As he opened the car door, Amaldi caught himself thinking that his nightmare had been born twenty years earlier among the rubbish bags, and that was how it was going to finish. One way or another. And Ajaccio. His life had begun abandoned among the trash and had ended just the same way.

"It's that one over there," said Frese, pointing at a rusting metal shutter. "Wait here."

"No," said Amaldi, grabbing at Frese's arm. "I've got to do it."

He pulled himself out of the car, unheeding of the pain. Helped by Frese, and favouring his wounded leg, he hobbled to the shutter.

"Giuditta!" he yelled, hammering on the metal sheet while two officers forced the lock in order to lift up the shutter. "Giuditta!" he screamed again, galvanized, unable to control himself. "Giuditta!" he cried for the

354

third time, with all the meagre mental and physical strength he had left. The time had come to learn if his world was about to fall apart. And he couldn't put it off any longer.

The metal shutter buckled ominously and screeched up on its runners.

"Giuditta!" He threw himself into the opening.

Light tumbled sluggishly through a filthy skylight onto the wide, empty space before them. In the middle, like an altar, there was a workbench. Giuditta absolutely still, looked as if she had been crucified, her outstretched arms tied down by two leather straps; her legs fixed by a length of rough hemp. Her unkempt hair was spread wildly over the metal surface. She was almost completely naked. Another body lay beside her. Or the remains of a body. Two human arms. Two legs. A wooden torso. Headless.

Amaldi pushed forward desperately. He saw her blood-smeared face. He had almost reached the bench when Giuditta turned towards him.

Amaldi's heart lurched. He threw himself upon her. He stroked her face, murmured nonsense in her ear. He freed her arms from the leather straps, untied the hemp cord around her legs and covered her with his own bloodied coat. Giuditta was deathly pale, dehydrated and almost unconscious.

"Ambulance!" Amaldi screamed hysterically, turning to Frese.

"It's coming," replied Frese, twitching his head in the direction of the approaching siren.

Amaldi hugged Giuditta to him, pulled her up, kissed her cheeks, softly stroked her broken lip.

Giuditta's gaze was far away. Then, slowly, she seemed to come round. Her eyes met Amaldi's. She didn't understand what he was saying but saw he was covered in blood. She touched the wound on his neck. Amaldi cleaned the blood from her lip. They were rediscovering each other through their broken flesh.

Giuditta opened her dry mouth.

"Don't speak," said Amaldi, smiling.

Their tears diluted the blood, making it less vivid, less real.

The two officers helped Giuditta reach the exit and Frese offered his arm to Amaldi. As Giuditta walked ahead and Amaldi tried to catch up with her, she glanced over her shoulder, seeking him out. They were both laughing now.

As they were putting her in the ambulance, Giuditta caught sight of Max Peschiera, and stiffened. He grimaced in concern.

"He's the one . . . who saved . . . you," whispered Amaldi as he sat down beside her.

Giuditta fell back onto the ambulance bunk. She felt a needle prick her skin and something warm and vaguely irritating invaded her. Then, as they strapped an oxygen mask onto her face, she felt incredibly tired. Her lungs filled with oxygen and her head began to spin. She twitched her hand and Amaldi immediately took it in his, squeezing it, caressing it. Giuditta looked at him and thought that she loved him.

"Forgive me," he seemed to be saying. But it didn't matter. Nothing mattered any more.

Giuditta lifted the oxygen mask from her face.

"Stay with me," she managed to say.

Amaldi nodded gently, and closed his eyes.

"Have you given up?"

Amaldi leaned over her, his expression serious, and brushed her lips with a kiss. Then he put replaced the oxygen mask and put an index finger to his own lips, to quiet her.

356

Giuditta closed her eyes and let the monotonous wail of the sirens lull her.

Amaldi continued to squeeze her hand.

XXXIV

The refuse collector clambered into his lorry and turned the key in the ignition, hoping the battery had not gone flat. The engine chugged into life on the second attempt, and belched a thick black cloud of exhaust fumes onto the tarmac.

The driver leaned out of the lorry window and shouted in excitement, "She's started."

He nodded to his partner, who climbed on board. The driver put the lorry in gear before the other man had time to close the door and the huge vehicle shuddered forward.

"They're in a hurry," Frese remarked to Max Peschiera and manoeuvred their car in behind the convoy of refuse-collection lorries that was pulling away from the depot in the suburbs.

A few hundred yards later the lorries headed off in different directions, each one with a police escort. On the first day back, the first day of the city's return to normality, the authorities had decided it would be better to maintain security. The violent incidents of the past few days had left their mark. The whole community had been traumatized by the month-long strike and the population still harboured hostile feelings towards the binmen. The police feared for their safety.

Frese was convinced that it would be a day for celebration. Yawning, he followed lorry 135/57 as dawn light began to tinge the deserted streets.

The man behind the wheel of the dustcart drove

along quickly, and caressed the wrinkled, faded leather of the seats, the stubborn gear stick that had made him swear so often, the slippery pedals. It had been exactly one month since he had last got into that lumbering old lorry. He had never thought it possible that he could miss the rickety behemoth, but that morning he had to admit that he had done.

"Know who that is, Mouldy?" Frese asked the fat youth beside him, with a malicious smile.

Max Peschiera shook his head. He was tired and hungry and would gladly have stayed at home in bed, but this escort duty was part of his re-education, it seemed. His uncle had insisted that he join Frese.

"That's Big Tits' father, Mouldy," explained Frese. "You hear me? That's Giuditta's father."

Max felt his blood freeze and his face burn at the same time.

Frese burst out laughing and slapped his thick thigh.

The binman glanced at the police car in his rear-view mirror. He had asked to be assigned to duty in the old town. He wanted to start in his own neighbour-hood, among his friends and acquaintances. He wanted the kids in the port to be the first to play in clean streets. He rolled down his window and gestured to the car behind him.

In reply Frese turned on the police lamp and gave a quick blast on the siren.

"You did a really good job, Mouldy," said Frese as they headed down to the old town. "Damn good job."

Max smiled.

"I'm just sorry that you won't be mentioned in the official encomia," Frese continued. "You really deserve it."

"Thanks."

"Fuck the thanks, it's true."

"Well, thanks anyway."

Frese turned and looked at him.

"You know . . . I probably shouldn't tell you this, but . . ." He jabbed a finger in Max's face. "If one word of what I'm going to tell you gets past those big teeth I'll make you eat them, got that?"

Max nodded.

"Good . . . I went to see the mayor . . ."

Max was all ears.

"I let him know, in private, so to speak, what we had uncovered on the city orphanage fire case. I told him about the will . . ."

"And . . .?"

"And what the hell do you expect someone to say when you nail them with that kind of proof? Exactly what you would expect, right?"

"Well, I suppose so . . ."

"Well, he didn't."

"He denied it?"

"He hugged me."

"In what sense?"

"He hugged me. What sense is it supposed to have? Don't piss me off, Mouldy. Haven't you ever hugged anyone?"

"No . . . I mean, yes . . . I mean . . ."

"He was relieved." And Frese told the story of how the then senior police officer had become convinced in the space of a few days that the arson and Mrs Cascarino were closely linked. He had referred the fact to his superior who had then taken the matter to the mayor. "Politics, Mouldy, politics," said Frese, shaking his head. "They put pressure on him to cover everything up." And Frese explained to Max, who was gaping at him, that the city fathers, although more than certain they were dealing with a killer, were a little

360

short of money at the time and entered into a pact with Mrs Cascarino. "They blackmailed her. 'We won't put you in prison and you will undertake to hand over every penny you earn and absolutely everything you possess to the City . . . and to children like the ones you roasted.' Stinks to high heaven, doesn't it?"

Max was speechless.

"By the way, from a strictly legal point of view, the will would have been null and void if this story had ever come out. That mad son of hers could have had it overturned . . . so could any of the murdering old woman's surviving relatives, no matter how distant . . ."

"And then . . .?"

"And then, and then . . . Well, politics rears its ugly head again." And, heavy-hearted, Frese bowed his own head. "The mayor still had the will. He had kept it from the day it had been signed. From the day the case was closed. One day he was over at the station and he asked to visit the archive. He got your uncle to give him the file on the fire. He started out working in Records, too, so he knew what he was doing . . . He scattered the papers around the place. He had heard about Ajaccio . . . You know how it is, remorse, guilt. Over the years he had followed every one of the orphans who survived the fire. Felt he owed them something. He was the one who got Ajaccio into the Force, put a word in the right places . . . Mind you, Ajaccio never knew that, poor bugger." Frese was distracted for a moment by images of the mayor's waxen, vanquished face, and Ajaccio's, yellow and sunken, disfigured by the scalpel. "He told me that when he had learned Ajaccio was sick with cancer he took it as a sign from destiny . . . He's a busy fucker this destiny, isn't he? The bigger the bastard, the more they blame things on destiny . . . Anyway, the mayor was feeling guilty, he knew we would go looking through Ajaccio's file and he set out the trail for us, to make sure we found him . . . He's an old man who wants to pay his dues, clear his conscience. He won't say who was behind the pressure to hush things up, but it doesn't take much to work it out. The mayor at the time was finishing his term and supported the then chief's bid for office, so our friend went from humble investigator to commissioner. Then later on it was his turn to play mayor. Simple, really."

"And now it's your turn to run for office?" asked Max.

"Well, I suppose if we did go ahead with this business I might get myself a very modest promotion."

"And would you accept?"

"I didn't say we were going on."

Max goggled at him.

"They've screwed me, Max," snorted Frese. "The mayor wants to pay his dues and clear his conscience, thirty-five years later. You know what would happen? The mayor and Mrs Cascarino would be both prosecuted and condemned but neither would go to prison, for different reasons . . . Mrs Cascarino is practically dead, anyway . . . Some bugger would object to the will, some stupid judge would find in their favour, and the burns centre would never be built. They screwed me, Mouldy, I told you. If I open my mouth, nothing happens, as usual. If I keep my mouth shut, well, then, at least . . ." His voice trailed away.

"So no official encomia for you, either, Detective?" said Max after a while.

"Well, that's life for you."

Max remained in silence, thinking for a few minutes. When he spoke they had almost reached the port, in the heart of the old town.

362

"Is that why my uncle wanted me to come with you this morning? For this lesson?"

"Maybe."

"Uncle Max remembered the mayor?"

"Your uncle isn't a moron. Of course he remembered. And he can put two and two together."

"So he knows all about this story, then?"

"A good cop doesn't need to know, Max. All we need is to imagine. It takes very little to make us happy."

Max said nothing. He watched the dustcart slow down before turning into a narrow street that led to the huge clearing that formed the port's loading area. The worn surface was patched here and there with grey and black daubs of tarmac. A crane stabbed into the sky, looming over them like a metallic sentry. As soon as they had learned about the end of the strike, the inhabitants of the old town had spent the previous day, Sunday, gathering up rubbish, and carrying it to the loading area, halfway between their homes and the sea, where the dustcarts would have easy access. The accumulated waste had built up into a mountain. A majestic mountain. A kind of temple to filth. Apart from the crane and the container ships at their moorings, Max saw the sea. The stagnant sludge of the harbour and the free, foaming sea beyond, framed between the breakwaters and the horizon. On the other side of the loading area, where houses began sprouting one on top of the other, a mob of spectators was waiting.

The crowd came to life when people caught sight of the arriving lorry.

"Let's hope they behave themselves," said Frese.

As the dustcart cleared the slope into the loading area it slowed down, chugged, belched smoke, and shuddered.

363

"They're waiting for us," said Giuditta's father, grinning, and greeted the assembled crowd with two loud blasts of his horn.

The crowd started applauding.

Frese relaxed his white-knuckled grip on the steering wheel. In a sudden rush of euphoria he turned on the spotlight.

But the crowd had eyes only for the refuse lorry.

Giuditta's father stopped his vehicle, got down from the cabin and pulled on a lever that opened the double upper hatch. Then he waved at the man sitting up in the cabin of the crane, a distant point above their heads. The neck of the metallic creature rumbled into action, swung round over the huge pile of rubbish and opened its mouth. It closed its metallic maw down on the living flesh of the mountain of waste, and jerked up again, full, scraps of its meal falling to the ground as it swung round to regurgitate the bolus into the stomach of the lorry, which began chomping and churning. Giuditta's father then went over to the crowd and began shaking hands. Then he raised his head to look up at the grey bulk far above the coloured houses.

Frese was about to get out of the car when he noticed the man's gaze and looked up in the same direction.

The hospital, he thought. Giuditta and Amaldi must be enjoying the show from one of the windows up there.

Max also studied the brooding outline of the hospital that pushed against the sky, touched by the pale light of a new day.

"I've discovered something else ... about the orphanage fire documents," he said.

Frese froze, the door half open, one foot already out of the car.

"Well, it's not really a discovery, just something strange, that's all."

Frese swivelled round suddenly, and slapped Max on the side. There was a dull squelch and the sound of paper rustling.

"What the hell have you got in your pocket?"

"A *pannino*," Max murmered confusedly.

"You really are a fat shit, aren't you, Mouldy?" said Frese, shaking his head. "Well? What have you discovered? Don't keep us in suspense."

"Well, I . . . Okay, let's say we give a letter of the alphabet to each numbered document. For example, document number five was missing. So that's the letter E. Thirteen is letter M, one is A, six is F and twelve is L. Okay? Well, if we put the letters together they spell FLAME . . . That's all . . ."

Frese gazed at Max in astonishment.

"Do you think the mayor did it on purpose?"

Frese thought about it.

"No," he said after a moment. "I suppose if we asked him he would probably go on about bloody destiny again."

"And what do you think?"

"I think it's just coincidence," replied Frese, getting out of the car. He turned round to look at Max. "You know, Mouldy, you're not just a fat shit. You're a very smart fat shit. And I like you. Come on, let's go press the flesh." And with that he headed towards the dustcart.

Max checked that Frese hadn't completely destroyed his snack, then, feeling very awkward, followed the detective.

"We'll need to make at least twenty trips," Giuditta's father was telling Frese. "At least twenty. But I would do a thousand to make this city clean."

His colleague nodded, without enthusiasm.

"It was like a mudslide," Giuditta's father began again. "It's horrible what we're capable of doing. It's a crime . . ." The man stumbled over the word that had become all too commonplace during the last few days, and cast another glance up towards the hospital.

"She needs to rest now. And forget," said Frese, guessing what the man was thinking. "But she's okay. She's safe."

The man nodded, a lump in his throat.

"Yeah, my little girl's safe," he repeated, as if he needed to hear the words for himself. Then he saw Max. He recognized the lad and stepped towards him.

Max stepped back, hunching over.

"Two weeks ago, I wouldn't have thought twice about killing you," Giuditta's father told him. "But they explained everything to me. I know my daughter's alive thanks to you, too." He pulled off his dirt-encrusted glove and held out his hand to Max.

The youth raised a hand to his face, instinctively.

"Thank you," the man said solemnly.

Frese laughed. Max timidly took hold of the bin-man's hand. His face was burning. He felt as if everyone was looking at him.

"Now that Giuditta is officially engaged to a senior police officer," Frese told Max, jabbing a finger at him, "the next time you decide to play the stupid wanker they'll castrate you, deport you and condemn you to hard labour for the rest of your days."

Giuditta's father burst out laughing, and Frese joined him, pleased at his own joke. Max was bright red with embarrassment.

"If you don't laugh as well, I'll kick you round the square in front of everyone," threatened Frese.

Max managed a wan, worried smile.

Frese and Giuditta's father laughed all the louder and slapped each other on the back.

The crane operator sounded his horn to attract the binmen's attention. Giuditta's father went over to examine a gauge.

"Two more loads," he told the operator by radio. Then he turned to Frese. "The strike was like a kind of disease for the city," he remarked, contemplating the dwindling mountain of rubbish.

"No. It was a fight in a good cause. From now on people are going to remember who we are," said the other binman proudly.

"You think so?" wondered Frese. He wasn't so sure. No one would remember that wretched month for very long. People lived in the present. That's the way life was. Nothing else mattered very much. People would soon forget even the monstrous Avildsen and the horror he wreaked. And maybe even Amaldi and Giuditta would forget too. Together.

The sky suddenly darkened. A violent thunderclap drowned out the noise of the crane and the dustcart and a moment later it started to rain. But it wasn't the slow, persistent rain of autumn. It was more like a violent spring storm; a youthful tempest that sprinted down upon the crowd, who laughed aloud, delighted, without knowing why, without cursing the sudden downpour, standing still under the rain with arms raised to the sky. And just as suddenly as it had arrived, the storm blew over in less than five minutes.

Soaked to the skin, Frese looked first out to the dark sea, which brightened as the storm clouds raced away. And then he looked at the city. The horizon parted, washed with the clear light of advancing morning, and revealed, beyond the houses that no longer looked so gloomy, that now glittered with

367

orange, yellow, mustard and red, the mountains that enclosed the gulf, their summits glinting like blossoming gems. It was as though the grey walls of the theatre had collapsed, though Frese, and all the tired, stale air could finally disperse. The evil, the stench, had become diluted in a world that was suddenly wider. The mixture was no longer saturated. The mild breeze, redolent of salt and the sea, if you had a good sense of smell, carried away all the memories and scattered them over the countryside. And with the memories the breeze carried away that indifferent sickness, which waited patiently for another chance, who knew where, who knew when. Waiting for an eddy in the air, a vortex, to concentrate it, to saturate the solution, be it with good or evil, just like that, without any real reason.

"Look, more of them are arriving," Frese said to Max, pointing at two other dustcarts that had just turned the corner.

All around the edge of the mountain of rubbish people continued to rejoice. The children laughed and shoved each other playfully. A woman with red hair and soft curves stepped away from the mound and walked towards the dustcart. She carried a blue bin bag and was dressed in mourning.

"May I?" she asked, nodding at the lorry.

Frese devoured her with his eyes. The woman smiled a melancholy smile.

"What's your name, pretty lady?" Frese asked her.

"Clara."

"Can I help you, Clara?"

"No, I'll take care of it myself." So saying she tossed the bag over the edge of the lorry's filthy maw then turned on her heel and swayed away through the applauding crowd.

368

"God, what a beautiful city we have," exclaimed Frese without taking his eyes for a moment off the wide backside of Clara Thewhore. Ajaccio's widow.

THE RUSSIAN PASSENGER

Günter Ohnemus

"A recommended summer thriller. High-octane odyssey across the new Europe and eventually the United States. All the makings of a new genre – the Russian mafia road movie."
The Times

"Much to enjoy in this sharp pacy *roman noir*. Packs an emotional punch rare in a thriller." *Independent*

At fifty the good Buddhist takes to the road, leaving all his belongings behind. His sole possession is a begging bowl. That's fine. That's how it should be. The problem was, there were four million dollars in my begging bowl and the mafia were after me. It was their money. They wanted it back, and they also wanted the girl, the woman who was with me: Sonia Kovalevskaya.

So begins the story of Harry Willemer, a taxi driver and his passenger, an ex-KGB agent and wife of a Russian Mafioso. In an atmosphere of intense paranoia *The Russian Passenger* follows their flight from the hit-men sent to recover the cash. This is not only a multifaceted thriller about murder, big money and love, but also a powerful evocation of the cruel history that binds Russia and Germany.

Günter Ohnemus, born in 1946, lives in Munich and writes novels, essays and translations. He has written three collections of short stories and a best-seller for teenagers. This is his first novel to be translated into English.

"A road adventure that reads like a movie, ... an alternately dark and sunny journey of redemption, with German cabbie and Russian passenger earnestly trying to resolve their nationalist prejudices and absolve their collective guilt – in colorful settings of course."
New York Times

£9.99/$14.95
Crime paperback original, ISBN 1–904738–02–8
www.bitterlemonpress.com

THE SNOWMAN

Jörg Fauser

"A gritty and slyly funny story. About the life of the underdog, the petty criminal, the fixer, the prostitute and the junkie. With a healthy dose of wit." *Cath Staincliffe, author of the* Sal Kilkenny *series*

"German author Jörg Fauser was the Kafka of crime writing." *Independent*

Blum's found five pounds of top-quality Peruvian cocaine in a suitcase. His adventure started in Malta, where he was trying to sell porn magazines, the latest in a string of dodgy deals that never seem to come off. A left-luggage ticket from the Munich train station leads him to the cocaine. Now his problems begin in earnest. Pursued by the police and drug traffickers, the luckless Blum falls prey to the frenzied paranoia of the cocaine addict and dealer. His desperate and clumsy search for a buyer takes him from Munich to Frankfurt, and finally to Ostend. This is a fast-paced thriller written with acerbic humour, a hardboiled evocation of drug-fuelled existence and a penetrating observation of those at the edge of German society.

"Jörg Fauser was a fascinating train wreck: a fiercely intelligent literary critic who also wrote the occasional nudie-magazine filler; a junkie who got clean in his thirties only to become an alcoholic; a tragic figure who died mysteriously at 43 in a 1987 Autobahn accident. Oh, and along the way he managed to crank out one of the most indelible crime novels in Greman history. Fauser writes with a gimlet eye and a black, acerbic (so, German) wit, creating an unflinchingly brilliant tale of a perspective – the outsider among outsiders – he knew all too well." *Ruminator*

£8.99/$13.95
Crime paperback original, ISBN 1–904738–05–2
www.bitterlemonpress.com

IN MATTO'S REALM

Friedrich Glauser

"Glauser's second novel involving the dour Sergeant Studer,
a Swiss Maigret albeit with a strong sense of the absurd.
Studer investigates the death of an asylum director following
the escape of a child murderer. A despairing plot about the
reality of madness and life, leavened at regular intervals with
strong doses of bittersweet irony. The idiosyncratic
investigation and its laconic detective have not aged one iota.
Who said the past never changes." *Guardian*

"Glauser was among the best European crime writers of the
inter-war years. This dark mystery set in a lunatic asylum
follows a labyrinthine plot where the edges between reality
and fantasy are blurred. The detail, place and sinister
characters are so intelligently sculpted that the sense of
foreboding is palpable." *Glasgow Herald*

A child murderer escapes from an insane asylum in Bern.
The stakes get higher when Sergeant Studer discovers the
director's body, neck broken, in the boiler room of the mad-
house. The intuitive Studer is drawn into the workings of an
institution that darkly mirrors the world outside. Even he
cannot escape the pull of the no-man's-land between reason
and madness where Matto, the spirit of insanity, reigns.

Translated into four languages, *In Matto's Realm* was originally published in 1936. This European crime classic, now
available for the first time in English, is the second in the
Sergeant Studer series from Bitter Lemon Press.

Friedrich Glauser was born in Vienna in 1896. Often
referred to as the Swiss Simenon, he died, aged forty-two, a
few days before he was due to be married. Diagnosed a
schizophrenic, addicted to morphine and opium, he spent
the greater part of his life in psychiatric wards, insane
asylums and, when he was arrested for forgery, in prison.
His Sergeant Studer novels have ensured his place as a cult
figure in Europe.

"*In Matto's Realm*, written in 1936 when psychoanalysis
was a novelty to the layman and forensic science barely
recognized, makes gripping reading as Studer questions both
staff and patients and tries to make sense of the inscrutable
Deputy Director's behaviour." *Sunday Telegraph*

£8.99/$13.95
Crime paperback original, ISBN 1–904738–06–0
www.bitterlemonpress.com

BLACK ICE

Hans Werner Kettenbach

"A beautifully translated thriller, not a drop of blood on its pages. The nastiness takes place off-stage which makes it all the more threatening." *BBC 2 "Culture"*

"A natural story teller who, just like Patricia Highsmith, is interested in teasing out the catastrophes that result from the banal coincidences of daily life." *Weltwoche*

Erika, an attractive local heiress, is married to Wallmann, a man with expensive tastes. When she falls to her death near their lakeside villa, the police conclude it was a tragic accident. Scholten, a long-time employee of Erika's, isn't so sure. He knows a thing or two about the true state of her marriage and suspects an almost perfect crime. Scholten's maverick investigation into the odd, inexplicable details of the death scene soon buys him a ticket for a most dangerous ride.

This beautifully crafted thriller set in a European world of small-town hypocrisy was made into a film in 1998. It is written by an essayist, scriptwriter and best-selling novelist whose work is now available in English for the first time.

"*Black Ice* isn't just a class crime novel. It is one of the most beautifully told stories of our years, in which humorous *noir* dialogue and poetry flourish side by side." *Stern*

£8.99/$13.95
Crime paperback original, ISBN 1–904738–08–7
www.bitterlemonpress.com

ANGELINA'S CHILDREN

Alice Ferney

"A wonderful portrait of a woman both imperial and bruised, a greying ravaged mother-wolf that still controls all those around her. A novel of rhythm and grace, a beautiful voyage with the gypsies." *Le Monde*

"Few gypsies want to be seen as poor, although many are. Such was the case with old Angelina's sons, who possessed nothing other than their caravan and their gypsy blood. But it was young blood that coursed through their veins, a dark and vital flow that attracted women and fathered numberless children. And, like their mother, who had known the era of horses and caravans, they spat upon the very thought that they might be pitied."

So begins the story of a matriarch and her tribe, ostracized by society and exiled to the outskirts of the city. Esther, a young librarian from the town, comes to the camp to introduce the children to books and stories. She gradually gains their confidence and accompanies them, as observer and participant, through an eventful and tragic year.

Alice Ferney's distinctive style powerfully involves the reader in the family's disasters, its comic moments and its battles against an uncomprehending, hostile world; in the love lives of the five boys, the bravery of the children, and, eventually, in Angelina's final gesture of defiance.

"A beautifully feminine and fertile book . . . Ferney's prose at its most powerful." *Le Figaro*

WINNER OF THE LITERARY PRIZE
CULTURE ET BIBLIOTHEQUES POUR TOUS

£8.99/$13.95
Crime paperback original, ISBN 1–904738–10–9
www.bitterlemonpress.com